**Praise for *New York Times* bestselling author
Diana Palmer**

"You just can't do better than a Diana Palmer story
to make your heart lighter and smile brighter."
—*Fresh Fiction* on *Wyoming Rugged*

"Diana Palmer is an amazing storyteller, and her
long-time fans will enjoy *Wyoming Winter* with
satisfaction!"
—*RT Book Reviews*

"Diana Palmer is a mesmerizing storyteller who
captures the essence of what a romance should be."
—*Affaire de Coeur*

**Praise for *New York Times* bestselling author
Brenda Jackson**

"Jackson's trademark ability to weave multiple
characters and side stories together makes shocking
truths all the more exciting."
—*Publishers Weekly*

"Brenda Jackson is the queen of newly discovered
love… If there's one thing Jackson knows how to do,
it's how to pluck those heartstrings and stir up some
seriously saucy drama."
—*BookPage*

A prolific author of more than one hundred books, **Diana Palmer** got her start as a newspaper reporter. A *New York Times* bestselling author and voted one of the top ten romance writers in America, she has a gift for telling the most sensual tales with charm and humor. Diana lives with her family in Cornelia, Georgia. Visit her website at dianapalmer.com.

Brenda Jackson is a *New York Times* bestselling author of more than one hundred romance titles. Brenda lives in Jacksonville, Florida, and divides her time between family, writing and traveling. Email Brenda at authorbrendajackson@gmail.com or visit her on her website at brendajackson.net. She invites you to like her author page at Facebook.com/brendajacksonauthor.

New York Times Bestselling Author

DIANA PALMER

TEXAS PROUD

Recycling programs
for this product may
not exist in your area.

**HARLEQUIN®
BESTSELLING
AUTHOR
COLLECTION**

ISBN-13: 978-1-335-49840-3

Texas Proud
First published in 2020. This edition published in 2023.
Copyright © 2020 by Diana Palmer

Irresistible Forces
First published in 2008. This edition published in 2023.
Copyright © 2008 by Brenda Streater Jackson

For questions and comments about the quality of this book,
please contact us at CustomerService@Harlequin.com.

Harlequin Enterprises ULC
22 Adelaide St. West, 41st Floor
Toronto, Ontario M5H 4E3, Canada
www.Harlequin.com

Printed in U.S.A.

CONTENTS

TEXAS PROUD   7
Diana Palmer

IRRESISTIBLE FORCES   269
Brenda Jackson

Also by Diana Palmer

Long, Tall Texans

Fearless
Heartless
Dangerous
Merciless
Courageous
Protector
Invincible
Untamed
Defender
Undaunted

The Wyoming Men

Wyoming Tough
Wyoming Fierce
Wyoming Bold
Wyoming Strong
Wyoming Rugged
Wyoming Brave
Wyoming Winter
Wyoming Legend
Wyoming Heart
Wyoming True
Wyoming Homecoming

Visit her Author Profile page at Harlequin.com,
or dianapalmer.com, for more titles!

TEXAS PROUD

Diana Palmer

In loving memory of Glenda Dalton Boling
(1945–2019) of Homer, Georgia.

You were my cousin, my friend,
my favorite bookseller, my hostess
for over twenty years of book signings with
my friend Jan Walker. You left a hole in the world
with your passing, Glenda. And all of us
who loved you will miss you, as long as we live.

Chapter 1

Her name was Bernadette Epperson, but everybody she knew in Jacobsville, Texas, called her Bernie. She was Blake Kemp's new paralegal, and she shared the office with Olivia Richards, who was also a paralegal. They had replaced former employees, one who'd married and moved away, the other who'd gone to work in San Antonio for the DA there.

They were an interesting contrast: Olivia, the tall, willowy brunette, and Bernie, the slender blonde with long, thick platinum blond hair. They'd known each other since grammar school and they were friends. It made for a relaxed, happy office atmosphere.

Ordinarily, one paralegal would have been adequate for the Jacobs County district attorney's office. But the DA, Blake Kemp, had hired Olivia to also work as a part-time paralegal. That was because Olivia covered for her friend at the office when Bernie had flares of rheumatoid arthritis. It was one of the more painful forms of arthritis, and when she had attacks it meant walking with a cane and taking more anti-inflammatories, along with the dangerous drugs she took to help keep the disease from worsening. It also meant no social life to speak of. Bernie would have liked having a fellow of her own, but single men knew about her and nobody seemed willing to take on Bernie, along with a progressive disease that could one day make her disabled.

There were new treatments, of course. Some of them involved weekly shots that halted the progression of the disease. But those shots were incredibly expensive, and even with a reduced price offered by kindly charitable foundations, they were still out of her price range. So it was methotrexate and prednisone and folic acid. And trying not to brood about the whole thing.

She was on her way to her room at Mrs. Brown's boardinghouse. It was raining, and the rain was cold. It was October and cool. Not the best time to forget her raincoat, but she'd been in a hurry and late for work, so it was still hanging in her closet at home. Ah, well, she thought philosophically, at least she had a nice thick sweater over her thin blouse. She laughed hysterically to herself. The sweater was a sponge. She felt water rolling down over her flat stomach under her clothes.

She laughed so hard that she didn't see a raised portion of the sidewalk. It caught her toe and she tripped. She fell into the road just as a big black limousine came along. Her cane went flying and she hit the pavement on her belly. She was fortunate enough to catch herself on her forearms, but the impact winded her. Luckily for her, the driver saw her in time to stop from running over her. It was dark and only the streetlights showed, blurry light through the curtains of rain.

A man got out. She saw his shoes. Big feet. Expensive shoes, like some of the visiting district attorneys who showed up to talk to her boss. Slacks that were made of wool. She could tell, because she used wool to knit with.

"You okay?" a deep, velvety voice asked.

"Yes," she panted. "Just…winded."

She rolled over and sat up.

A tall man, built like a wrestler, with broad shoulders and a leonine head, squatted down, staring at her with deep-set brown eyes in an olive complexion. His jet-black hair was threaded with just a little silver, and it was thick and wavy around his head. A lock of it fell onto his forehead as he bent over her. He had high cheekbones and the sort of mouth that was seen in action movies with he-men. He was gorgeous. She couldn't help staring. She couldn't remember ever having a man send her speechless just by looking at her.

"Nice timing," he mused. "Saw the limo coming, did we? And jumped right out in front of it, too."

She was too shaken to think of a comeback, although she should have. She checked her palms. They were a little scraped but not bleeding.

"I tripped."

"Did you really?"

That damned sarcastic, mocking smile made her very angry. "Could you find my cane, please?" she asked.

"Cane?"

She heard his voice change. She hated that note in it. "It went flying when I hit the raised part of the sidewalk. It's over that way." She indicated the sidewalk.

"On the other side, probably. It's red enamel. With dragons on it."

"With dragons. Mmm-hmm."

A car door opened. Another man came around the front of the car. He was older than Bernie but younger than the man squatting down next to her. He was wearing a suit.

"What's that about dragons?" the man asked, faintly amused.

"Her cane. That way, she says." He pointed.

The other man made a sound in his throat.

"Look anyway," the big man told him.

"All right, I'm going." There was a pause while Bernie sat in the road getting wetter by the minute.

"Well, I'll be…!"

The other man came back, holding the cane. He was scowling. "Where the devil did you get something like that?" he asked as he handed it down to her.

"Internet," she said. The pain was getting worse. Much worse. She needed a heavy dose of anti-inflammatories, and a bed and a heating pad.

She swallowed hard. "Please don't…stare when I get up. There's only one way I can do it, and it's embarrassing." She got on all fours and pushed herself up with difficulty, holding on to the cane for support. She lifted her head to the rain and got her breath back. "Thanks for not running over me," she said heavily.

The big man had stood up when she did. He was scowling. "What's the matter with you? Sprain?"

She looked up. It was a long way. "Rheumatoid arthritis."

"Arthritis? At your age?" the man asked, surprised.

She drew herself up angrily. "Rheumatoid," she emphasized. "It's systemic. An autoimmune disease. Only one percent of people in the world have it, although it's the most common autoimmune disease. Now if you don't mind, I have to get home before I drown."

"We'll drive you," the big man offered belatedly.

"Frankly, I'd rather drown, thanks." She turned, very slowly, and managed to get going without too much visible effort. But walking was laborious, and she was gritting her teeth before she'd gotten five steps.

"Oh, hell."

She heard the soft curse before she felt herself suddenly picked up like a sack of potatoes and carried back toward the limousine.

The other man was holding the door open.

"You put me down!" she grumbled, trying to struggle. She winced, because movement hurt.

"When I get you home," he said. "Where's home?"

He put her into the limousine and climbed in beside her. The other man closed the door and got in behind the wheel.

"I'll get the seat wet," she protested.

"It's leather. It will clean. Where's home?"

She drew in a breath. She was in so much pain that she couldn't even protest anymore. "Mrs. Brown's boardinghouse. Two blocks down and to the right. It's a big Victorian house with a white fence around it and a room-to-rent sign," she added.

The driver nodded, started the engine and took off.

The big man was still watching her. She was clutching the cane with a little hand that had gone white from the pressure she was using.

He studied her, his eyes on the thick plait of platinum blond hair down her back. Her clothes were plastered to her. Nice body, a little small-breasted and long legs. She had green eyes. Very pale green. Pretty bow mouth. Wide-spaced eyes under thick black eyelashes. Not beautiful. But attractive.

"Who are you?" he asked belatedly.

"My name is Bernadette," she said.

"Sweet," he mused. "There was a song about Saint Bernadette," he recalled.

She flushed. "My mother loved it. That's why she gave me the name."

"I'm Michael. Michael Fiore, but most people call me Mikey." He watched her face, but there was no recognition. She didn't know the name. Surprising. He'd been a resident of Jacobsville a few years back, when his cousin, Paul Fiore of the San Antonio FBI office, was investigating a case that involved Sari Grayling, who later became Paul's wife. Sari and her sister, Meredith, had been targeted by a hit man, courtesy of a man whose mother was killed by the Graylings' late father. Mikey had made some friends here.

"Nice to meet you," she managed. She grimaced.

"Hurts pretty bad, huh?" he asked, his dark eyes narrowing. He looked up. Santelli was pulling into a parking spot just in front of a Victorian house with a room-to-rent sign. "Is this it?" he asked.

She looked up through the window. She nodded. "Thanks so much…"

"Stay put," he said.

He went out the other door that Santi was holding open for him, around the car and opened her door. He reached in and picked her up, cane and purse and all.

"Come knock on the door for me, Santi," he told his companion.

Bernie tried to protest, but the big man kept walking. He smelled of cigar smoke and expensive cologne, and the feel of his big arms around her made her feel odd. Trembly. Nervous. Very nervous. She had one arm around his broad shoulders to hold on, her hand spread beside his neck. He was warm and comforting. It had been a long time since she'd been held by anyone, and it had never felt like this.

Santi knocked on the door.

Bernie could have told him that he could just walk in, but he wasn't from here, so he didn't know.

Plump Mrs. Brown opened the door, still wearing her apron because she offered supper to her roomers. She stopped dead, with her mouth open, as she saw Bernie being carried by a stranger.

"I fell," Bernie explained. "He was kind enough to stop and bring me home..."

"Oh, dear, should you go see Dr. Coltrain?" she said worriedly.

"I'm fine, really, just a little bruised dignity to speak of," she assured the landlady. "You can put me down," she said to Mikey.

"Where's her room?" Mikey asked politely. He smiled at the older woman, and she flushed and laughed nervously.

"It's right down here. She can't climb the stairs, so she has a room near the front..."

She led the way. He put Bernie down in a chair beside her bed.

"You need a hot bath, dear, and some coffee," Mrs. Brown fussed.

There was a bathroom between Bernie's room and the empty room next door.

"Can you manage?" the big man asked gently.

She nodded. "I'm okay. Really. Thanks."

He shrugged broad shoulders. He frowned. "You shouldn't be walking so far."

"Tell her, tell her," Mrs. Brown fretted. "She walks four blocks to and from work every single day!"

"Dr. Coltrain says exercise is good for me," she retorted.

"Exercise. Not torture," Mrs. Brown muttered.

The big man was thinking. "We'll see you again," he said quietly.

She nodded. "Thanks."

He cocked his head. His eyes narrowed. "First impressions aren't always accurate."

Her eyebrows arched. "Gosh, was that an apology?"

He scowled. "I don't apologize. Ever."

"That didn't hurt, that didn't hurt, that didn't hurt," she mimicked a comedian who'd said that very thing in a movie. She grinned. Probably he didn't have a clue what she was talking about.

He threw back his head and roared. *"Police Academy,"* he said, naming the movie.

Her jaw fell.

"Yeah. That guy was me, at his age," he confessed. "Take a bath. And don't fall in."

She made a face at him.

His dark eyes twinkled. "See you, kid."

He walked out before she could correct the impression.

He stopped at the front door. "That room to let," he asked Mrs. Brown. "Is it still available?"

"Why, yes," she said, flushing again. She laughed.

"You'd be very welcome. We have three ladies living here, but…"

"I'm easy to please," he said. "And I won't be any trouble. I hate hotels."

She smiled. "So do I. My husband was in rodeo. We spent years on the road. I got so sick of room keys…"

He laughed. "That's me. Okay. If you don't mind, I'll have my stuff here later today."

"I don't mind at all."

"How much in advance?" he asked, producing his wallet.

She told him. He handed her several bills.

"I don't rob banks, if that's what you're thinking," he said with a wry smile. "I'm a businessman. I live in New Jersey, and I own a hotel in Vegas. Which is why I hate staying in them."

"Oh! You have business here, then?"

He nodded solemnly. "Business," he agreed. "I'll be around for a while."

"It will be nice to have the room rented," she confessed. "It's been vacant for a long time. My last tenant got married."

"I'll see you later, then." He hesitated, looking back toward the room where he'd left Bernadette. "She'll be okay, you think?"

"Yes. She might look fragile, but Bernie's tough. She's had to be."

"Bernie?" His eyes widened.

She laughed. "That's what we call her. We've known Bernadette all her life."

"Small towns." He smiled. "I grew up in one, myself. Far from here." He pulled out a business card and handed it to her. "The lower number is my cell phone.

If she needs anything tonight, you call me, okay? I can come and drive her to the hospital if she needs to be seen."

Mrs. Brown was surprised at that concern from a stranger. "You have a kind heart."

He shrugged. "Not always. See you."

He went out, motioning for Santi to follow him. They got in the limo and drove off. Mrs. Brown watched it go with real interest. She wondered who the outsider was.

Mikey was all too aware of the driver's irritation. "They told me to keep an eye on you all the time," he told Mikey.

"Yeah, well, I'm not sharing a room with you, no matter what the hell they told you. Besides," he added, settling back into his seat, "Cash Grier's got one of his men shadowing me with a sniper kit."

"It's a small town," Santi began.

"A small town with half the retired mercs in America," Mikey cut in. "And my cousin lives right down the road. Remember him? Senior FBI agent Paul Fiore? Lives in Jacobsville, works out of San Antonio, worth millions?"

"Oh. Him. Right."

"Besides, I know the sniper Grier's got watching me." He chuckled. "He doesn't miss. Ever. And they snagged *The Avengers* to watch when the sniper's asleep."

"The Avengers?" Santi roared. "That's a comic book!"

"Rogers and Barton. They're called the Avengers because Captain America's name in the series is Rogers, and Hawkeye's is Barton. Get it?"

"Yeah."

"I know how bad Mario Cotillo wants me, Santi," Mikey said quietly. "I'm the only thing standing between Tony Garza and a murder-one conviction, because I know Tony didn't do it and I can prove it. Tony's in hiding, too, in an even safer place than me."

"Where?" Santi asked.

Mikey laughed coarsely. "Sure, like I'm going to tell you."

Santi stiffened. "I'm no snitch," he said, offended.

"Anybody can hack a cell phone or the elaborate two-way radio we got in this car, and listen to us when we talk," Mikey said with visible impatience. "Use your brain, okay?"

"I do!"

"Well, you must be keeping it in a safe place when you're not using it," Mikey muttered under his breath, but not so that Santi could hear him. The guy was good muscle and a capable driver. It wouldn't do to upset him too much. Not now, anyway.

Mikey leaned back with a long sigh and thought of the woman he'd met tonight. He was sorry he'd misjudged her, but plenty of women had thrown themselves into his path. He was extremely wealthy. He had money in Swiss banks that the feds couldn't touch. And while he'd been accused of a few crimes, including murder, he'd never even been indicted. His record was pretty clean. Well, for a guy in his profession. He was a crime boss back in Jersey, where Tony Garza was the big boss. Tony owned half the rackets around Newark. But Tony had some major new competition, an outsider who saw himself as the next Capone. He'd targeted Tony at once, planned to take him down on a fake murder charge with the help of a friend who worked in the federal attorney's office. It had backfired. Tony also had friends there. So did Mikey. But Mikey had been with Tony in a bar when the murder had taken place and by chance, Mikey had a photo of himself and Tony with a date stamp on his cell phone. He'd sent copies to Paulie and Cash Grier and a friend down in the Bahamas. Before the feds could jump Tony, who might have been dealt with handily and at once before it even came to trial, Mikey and Tony had both skipped town.

The next obvious play by Cotillo would be to put out contracts on Mikey and Tony. Mikey smiled. He knew most of the heavy hitters in the business. So did Tony. It wouldn't work, but Cotillo didn't know that. Yet. Meanwhile, Mikey and Tony were playing a waiting game. Both had feds on the job protecting them. Mikey wasn't telling Santi that, however. He didn't trust anybody really, except his cousin Paul. The fewer people who knew, the safer he was going to be.

Not that life held such attractions for him these days. He had all the money he'd ever need. He had a fearsome reputation, which gave him plenty of protection back home in New Jersey. But he was alone. He was a lonely man. He'd asked a woman to share his life only once, and she'd laughed. He was good in bed and he bought her pretty things, but she wasn't going to get married to a known gangster. She had her reputation to think of. After all, she was a debutante, from one of the most prominent families in Maryland. Marry a hood? Ha! Fat chance.

It had broken his heart. Even now, years and years after it happened, it was a sore spot. He was more than his reputation. He was fair and honest, and he never hurt anybody without a damned good reason. Mostly, he went after people who hurt people he cared about.

Well, there was also the odd job for Tony when he was younger. But those days were mostly behind him. He could still handle a sniper kit when he needed to. It was just that he didn't have the same need for notoriety that had once ruled his life.

Nobody needed him. Funny, the main reason he'd enjoyed the debutante was that she'd pretended to be helpless and clingy. He'd enjoyed that. Since his grandmother's death, there had been nobody who cared about him except Paul, and nobody who needed him at all. Briefly, he'd helped his cousin protect a young woman from Jacobsville, Merrie Grayling, before she married the Wyoming rancher. But that had been sort of an accessory thing. He'd liked her very much, yet as a sort of adoptive baby sister, nothing romantic. It had been nice, helping Paulie with that little chore, especially since he knew the contract killer who'd been assigned to get Merrie. He had known how to get the hit called off—actually, by getting Merrie, an artist of great talent, to do a portrait of Tony. The contract killer had ended badly, but that happened sometimes. Most sane people didn't go against Tony, who'd told the guy to call off the hit.

But all that had been three years ago. Life moved on. Now here was Mikey, in hiding from a newcomer in Jersey, trying to protect his friend Tony.

He thought again about the young woman who'd fallen in front of the limo. He felt bad that he'd misjudged her. She was pretty. What had she called herself—Bernadette? He smiled. He'd been to France, to the grotto where Saint Bernadette had dug into a mudhole, found a clear spring and seen the apparition she referred to as the Immaculate Conception, and he'd seen Bernadette in her coffin. She looked no older than when she'd died, a century and more ago, a beautiful young woman. He wondered if her namesake even knew who Saint Bernadette was. He wondered why she'd been given that name.

So many questions. Well, he was going to be staying in the same rooming house, so he'd probably get the chance to talk to her, to ask her about her family. She was nice. She didn't like pity, although she had a devastating medical condition, and she had a temper. He smiled, remembering that thick plait of blond hair down her back. He loved long hair. It must be hard to keep, for someone with her limitations.

His little Greek grandmother had been arthritic. He recalled her gnarled hands and the times when she hadn't been able to get out of bed. Mikey had carried her from room to room when she had special company, or outside when she wanted to sit in the sun. He couldn't remember what sort of arthritis she'd had, but it was in the family bible, along with plenty of other family information. He kept the bible in a safe-deposit box back in Jersey, along with precious photographs of people long dead. There had been one of the debutante. But he'd burned that one.

The car was eating up the miles to San Antonio, where Mikey had left his luggage in a hotel under an assumed name. He'd send Santi in to pick it up and pay the bill, just in case, while he waited outside in the parking lot. You couldn't be too careful. He needed to send a text to Paulie, as well, but that could wait until he was back in Jacobsville. He should ask Paulie about hackers and what they could find out, and how. He still wasn't up on modern methods of surveillance.

He leaned back against the seat with a long sigh. Bernadette. He smiled to himself.

Bernadette took a hot bath, and it did help ease some of the discomfort. Mrs. Brown had been kind enough to add a handhold on the side of the tub so that Bernadette would find it easier to get in and out of the tub. She took showers, however, not baths. It was so much quicker to stand up. Besides, the bathroom was used by all the boarders on the ground floor, although there had been just Bernadette for several weeks, and poor Mrs. Brown had enough to do without having to scrub the tub all the time. She did have a daily woman who came in to help with the heavy chores. But Bernadette was fastidious and it bothered her, the idea of baths when at least one of the former boarders had been male and liked lots of musk-smelling bath oil. For women, especially, baths in a less than spotlessly clean tub could lead to infections. Bernie had enough to worry about without those. So, she took showers.

She dressed in her pajama bottoms and one of the soft, thick T-shirts that she wore with it.

There was a tap at the door and Mrs. Brown came in with a cup of tea in a beautiful ceramic cup on its delicate saucer. "Chamomile tea," she said with a smile. "It will help you sleep, sweetheart."

"You're spoiling me," Bernadette complained softly. "You have enough to do without adding me to your burdens."

"You're no burden," Mrs. Brown said gently. "You keep your room spotless, you never mess anything up,

and I have yet to have to pick up after you anywhere."
She sighed. "I wish we could say the same for the two
nice women on the second floor, and don't you dare tell
them I said that!"

Bernadette laughed. "I won't. You know I don't gossip."

"Of course you don't." She put the cup and saucer
on the bedside table. "What a nice man who brought
you home," she added with a speculative glance that
Bernadette missed. "He's renting a room here, too!"

Bernadette caught her breath. "He is?" she stammered, and flushed a little.

Mrs. Brown chuckled. "He is. The one on the other
side of the bathroom, but that won't be a problem. I'll
make sure he knows to knock first when he needs to
use it."

"Okay, then." She sipped tea and smiled with her eyes
closed. "This is so good!"

"I put honey in it, instead of sugar, and just a hint
of cinnamon."

Bernadette looked up at the older woman. "You know,
he thought I'd fallen in front of his car on purpose."

"You fell? You didn't tell me!"

She sipped her tea. "The sidewalk was slippery and
my toe hit a brick that was just a little out of place. I
went flying into the street. Lucky for me that his driver
had good brakes." She frowned. "It was a limousine."

"I noticed," Mrs. Brown said with a wry smile. "He
was wearing a very expensive suit, as well. I think I
recognized him. He looks like Paul Fiore's cousin."

"I heard about that," Bernadette said, "when I was
working as a receptionist for a group of attorneys, before I got my paralegal certification from night school
and Mr. Kemp hired me. I never saw him, but people

talked about him. He was helping protect Merrie Grayling, wasn't he?"

"That was the gossip. Goodness, imagine having contract killers stalking two local girls in the same family!" She shook her head. "I had it from the Grayling girls' housekeeper, Mandy Swilling. She said the girls' father had killed a local woman for selling him out to the feds on racketeering charges, and the woman's son put out contracts on both Grayling's daughters, to get even. He thought their father loved them so much that it would really hurt him." She sighed. "Well, the man was dead by then, and the woman's son was charged with conspiracy to commit murder. They say he'll be in prison for a long time, even though he did try to help them find the killers."

"Good enough for him," Bernie said. "Murder is a nasty business."

"That's another thing. They say that Mr. Fiore's cousin Mikey is mixed up with organized crime."

"His cousin?"

"The man who carried you inside the house tonight," Mrs. Brown replied.

Bernie sat with the cup suspended in one hand. "Oh. Him." She laughed. She hadn't really been paying attention.

"Him." She laughed. "But I don't believe it. He's so nice. He was really concerned about you."

"Not when I first fell, he wasn't," Bernie said, wrinkling her nose. "He thought I did it on purpose to get his attention." She hesitated. "Well, you know, he is drop-dead gorgeous. When I first saw him, I could hardly even get my breath," she confessed. "It was like being hit in the stomach. I've never seen a real live man who looked like that. He could be in movies." She flushed. "Well, he's good-looking, I mean."

"I suppose some women do find excuses to attract men like that," Mrs. Brown said in his defense.

"I suppose. He changed his mind when he saw the cane, though." Her face grew sad. "When I was in high school, there was this really nice boy. I thought he was going to ask me to the senior prom. I was so excited. One of my girlfriends said he was talking about me to someone else, although she didn't hear what he said." She looked down into the now-empty cup. "Then another friend told me the truth. He said that I wasn't bad to look at, but he didn't want to take a disabled girl to a dance." She smiled sadly, aware of Mrs. Brown's angry expression. "After that, I sort of gave up on dating."

"There must have been nicer boys," she replied.

"Oh, there were. But there were prettier girls who didn't walk with canes." She put down the cup and saucer. "I didn't need the cane all the time, of course. But when I had flares, I'd just fall if I made a misstep." She shook her head. "No man is going to want a woman who may end up an invalid one day. So I go to work and save all I can, and hope that by the time I need to give up and apply for disability, I'll have enough to tide me over until I can get it." She made a face. "Gosh, wouldn't it be nice not to have health issues?"

"It would. And I'm sorry that you do. But, Bernie, a man who loves you won't care if you have them." She added, "Any more than you'd care if he had them."

Bernie smiled. "You're a nice woman. I'm so lucky to live here. And thank you for the tea."

"You're very welcome. You get some sleep. Tomorrow's Saturday, so you can sleep in for a change."

"A nice change." She grimaced. "But I don't want you to wait breakfast for me...!"

"I'll put it on a plate in the fridge and you can heat it up in the microwave," said Mrs. Brown. "So stop worrying about things."

Bernie laughed. "Okay. Thanks again."

"You're very welcome." She hesitated at the door. 'What a very good thing that we don't have many young women living here, except you."

"Why?"

"Well, that nice man who brought you in is really good-looking, and we don't want a line forming at his door, now do we?" she teased.

Bernie blushed, but Mrs. Brown had closed the door before she saw it.

Chapter 2

Mikey waited for Santi in a parking spot near the front door of the San Antonio hotel. He hoped it wouldn't take too long. The streets were busy, even at this time of night, and some of the people milling around were wearing gang colors and had multiple tats. He knew about the Los Serpientes gang. Although they were technically based in Houston, they had a presence here in San Antonio. Paulie had told him about them. They looked out for children and old people. Amazing. Kind of like the Yakuza in Japan.

Japan was a great place to visit. Mikey had gone there for several weeks after his tour of duty in the Middle East. He'd needed to wind down and get over some of the things he'd seen and done there. He'd been with a group of military overseas that included two men from here, Rogers and Barton, who'd been protecting the

Grayling girls from contract killers. He hadn't served directly with them, but Cag Hart and the local DA, Blake Kemp, had been overseas at the same time. From Afghanistan to Iraq, he'd carried a rifle and served his country. The memories weren't good, but he had others he lived with. He just added the more recent ones to them.

He'd been surprised to find his company commander involved with Merrie Grayling. The Wyoming rancher, Ren Colter, had been the company commander of his sniper unit overseas. In fact, the Grayling girls' protectors, Rogers and Barton, had also been part of his group. What a homecoming that had been. Not a really great one, because Mikey had gotten in trouble scrounging materials for a brothel. But his commanding officer had gotten him out of trouble with Ren, because Mikey had the greatest luck in the world at poker. He never lost. It was one reason he was so rich. Of course, he couldn't get into casinos anymore. He didn't cheat. He didn't have to. But that luck had gotten him barred all over the world, even in Monte Carlo. He chuckled. It was sort of a mark of honor, being barred from those places. So he didn't mind that much. He had all the money he'd ever need until he died an old man, so who cared?

The car trunk opened suddenly. Mikey's hand had gone automatically under his jacket to the .45 he'd put there before Santi went into the hotel. He kept it in a secure compartment under the seat, custom-made. He hadn't needed it in Jacobsville, but this was unknown territory, and it was dangerous not to go heeled. He had a concealed carry permit, but for Jersey, not here. He supposed he'd have to go see the sheriff in Jacobs County and get one for Texas. That would be Hayes

Carson. He knew the sheriff from three years ago. They got on.

Santi opened the door and got in behind the wheel. "All the bags are in the trunk, chief," he told his boss. "We need to stop anywhere else before we head south?"

"Not unless you're hungry."

"I could eat."

"Well, there's a nice restaurant in a better part of town. Let's go looking." He glanced out through the tinted windows at a young man who was giving the limo a real hard look. "I'm not overjoyed with the clientele hereabouts."

"Me, neither."

"So, let's go. We'll drive around and see if we can find someplace Italian. I think Paulie said a new place had just opened recently. Carlo's. Put it in the computer."

Santi fed it into the onboard GPS. "Got it, chief. Only three blocks away."

"Okay! Head out."

They were well into their plates of spaghetti when Mikey noticed a couple of customers in suits giving them a cursory inspection.

"Feds," Mikey said under his breath. "At the second table over. Don't look," he added.

"Know them?"

"Nope," Mikey said.

"FBI, you think?"

Mikey chuckled. "If they were, Paulie would have mentioned that I had a tail here in the city."

"Then who?"

"If I were guessing, US Marshals," he replied. "The big dark one looks vaguely familiar, but I can't quite place him. He was working with Paulie during the time I spent in Jacobsville three years ago."

"Marshals?" Santi asked, and he shifted restlessly.

"Relax. They aren't planning to toss our butts in jail. There's this thing called due process," Mikey said imperturbably. "We'll have fewer worries down in Jacobs County. Jacobsville is so small that any stranger sticks out. Besides, we've got shadows of our own."

"Good ones?"

"You bet," Mikey replied with a smug grin. "So eat your supper and I'll move into my new temporary home."

"I don't like being down the road in a motel," Santi muttered. "Even with all the other guys watching your back."

"Well, I'm not sharing the room," Mikey said flatly. "It's barely big enough for me and all my stuff, without trying to fit you into it. No room for another bed, anyway."

"I guess you got a point."

"Of course I do. Besides, it's not like I'm going to get hit until they track me down here."

"The limo is going to attract attention," Santi said worriedly.

"Yeah, well, no more attention than the gossip will, but there's not a place in the world I'd be safer. Strangers stick out here. Remember, I told you about Cash Grier's wife being tracked here by a contract killer, and what happened to him?"

Santi chuckled. "Yeah. Grier's wife hit him so hard with an iron skillet that he ran to the cops for protection."

"Exactly. Nobody messes with Tippy Grier. What a knockout. A movie star, and she's married to the police chief and has two kids. I never thought Grier could settle down in a small town. He didn't seem the sort."

"That's what everybody says." Santi paused. "I feel bad about that poor girl we almost hit," he added, surprisingly, because he wasn't sentimental. "She was nice, and we thought she was trying to play us."

"We come by our suspicious natures honestly," Mikey reminded him. "But, yeah, she was nice. Needs looking after," he said quietly. "Not that she seems the kind of woman who'd let anybody look after her."

"I noticed that."

Mikey glanced at his watch. "We'd better go." He signaled to a waiter for the check.

Bernadette was reading in bed. The pain was pretty bad, a combination of the rain and the fall. She needed something to take her mind off it, so she pulled out her cell phone, on which she kept dozens of books. Many were romance novels. She realized that her condition would keep most men away, and it was nice to daydream about having a kind man sweep her off her feet.

She couldn't stop thinking about the big dark-haired man who'd done that earlier in the evening. He was kin to Paul Fiore, who was married to Sari Grayling. Bernie worked with Sari in the local DA's office. She wondered if she could get away with asking her anything about the man, who'd been very kind to her after mistaking her for some kind of con woman.

She shouldn't be thinking about him. A man that handsome probably had women hanging on to his ankles everywhere he walked. He was apparently rich, as well. There was another woman in her office, the receptionist, Jessie Tennison, a gorgeous brunette in her late twenties, who was crazy about men and openly solicited any rich one who came into the office. Mr. Kemp, the DA, had already called her down about it once. A second offense would cost her the job, he'd added. Her position didn't include sexual harassment of clients.

What a new world it was, Bernie mused, when a woman could be accused of what was often seen as a man's offense. But, then, her coworker was very pretty. She was just ambitious. She had a failed marriage behind her. Gossip was that her ex-husband had been wealthy but had a gambling habit and lost it all on one draw of a card. Nobody knew, because the woman didn't talk about herself. Well, not to the women in the office.

A sudden commotion caught her attention. There was movement in the hall. Some bumping and a familiar deep male voice. Her heart jumped. That was the man who'd brought her home earlier. She knew his voice already. It was hard to miss, with that definite New Jersey accent. She knew about that because of Paul Fiore. He had one just like it.

There was more noise, then a door closing. More footsteps. Voices. The front door opening and closing, and then a car driving away.

Mrs. Brown knocked at Bernie's door and then slipped in, closing it behind her. "Sorry about the noise. Mr. Fiore's just moving in," she added with an affectionate smile.

Bernie tried not to show the delight she felt. "Is he going to stay long? Did he say?"

"Not really," she said. "His driver is staying at a motel down the road." She laughed. "Mr. Fiore said no way was he sharing that room with another man, especially not one as big as his driver."

Bernie laughed softly. "I guess not."

"So you'll need to knock before you go into the bathroom, like I mentioned earlier," Mrs. Brown continued. "Just in case. I told Mr. Fiore again that he'd need to do the same thing, since you're sharing." She looked worried. Bernie was flushed. "I'm so sorry. If I had a room with a bathroom free, I'd—"

"Those are upstairs," Bernie interrupted gently, "and we both know that I have a problem with stairs." She sighed and shook her head. "The rain and the walk and the fall pretty much did me in today. You were right. I should have gotten a cab. It isn't that expensive, and I don't spend much of what I make, except on books." That was true. Her rent included all utilities and even the cable that gave her television access—not that she watched much TV.

"I know that walking is supposed to be good for you," the older woman replied. "But not when you're having a flare." She drew in a breath. "Bernie, if you wrote the company that makes that injectable medicine, they might…"

"I already did," Bernie said softly. "They offered me a discount, but even so, it's almost a thousand dollars a month. There's no way I could afford that, discount or not. Besides," she said philosophically, "it might not work for me. Sometimes it doesn't. It's a gamble."

"I guess so." Mrs. Brown looked sad. "Maybe someday they'll find a cure."

"Maybe they will."

"Well, I'll let you get back to your book," she teased, because she knew about the late-night reading habit. "Need anything from the kitchen before I turn out the lights?"

"Not a thing. I have my water right here." She indicated two bottles of water that she kept by her bedside.

"You could have some ice in a glass to go with it."

Bernie shook her head. "It would just melt. But thank you, Mrs. Brown. You're so good to me."

The older woman beamed. "I'm happy to have you here. You're the only resident I've ever had who never complained about anything. You'll spoil me."

"That's *my* line," Bernie teased, and she laughed. It made her look pretty.

"Sleep well."

"You, too."

Mrs. Brown went out and closed the door.

Bernie thought about that injectable medicine. Her rheumatologist in San Antonio had told her about it, encouraged her to try to get it. At Bernie's age, it might retard the progress of the disease, a disease that could lead to all sorts of complications, the worst of which was deformity in the hands and feet. Not only that, but RA was systemic. It could cause a lot of issues in other parts of the body, as well.

Chance, Bernie thought, would be a fine thing. She'd have to be very well-to-do in order to afford something so expensive as those shots. Well, meanwhile she had her other meds, and they worked well enough most of the time. It wasn't every day that she fell in a cold rain almost in front of somebody's fancy limousine. She smiled to herself and went back to her book.

Breakfast the next morning would have been interesting, Bernie thought to herself as she ate hers from a tray her kindly landlady had provided. But she couldn't get up. A weather system had moved in, dropping even more rain, and Bernie's poor body was still trying to cope with yesterday's fall. What a good thing it was Saturday. She'd have had a time getting to work.

Just as she finished the last drop of her coffee, there was a perfunctory knock and the man who'd rescued her walked in.

She pulled the sheet up over her breasts. The gown covered her nicely, but she'd never had a man in her bedroom in her life, except for her late father and her doctor. She flushed.

Mikey grinned from ear to ear. He loved that reaction. The women in his life were brassy and easy and unshockable. Here was a violet under a staircase, undiscovered, who blushed because a man saw her in her nightgown.

"Mrs. Brown said you might like a second cup of coffee," he said gently, approaching the bed with a cup and saucer.

"Oh, I, yes, I…thank you." She couldn't even talk normally. She was furious with herself, especially when her hands shook a little as she took the cup and saucer from him. He lifted the empty one from the tray, so she'd have someplace to put the new one.

He cocked his head and looked at her, fascinated. Her long blond hair was in a braid, a little frizzled from being slept on. She was wearing a cotton gown, and he could see the straps with their eyelet trim. It reminded him of his grandmother, who'd never liked artificial fabric.

"You aren't feeling so good today, are you?" he asked. "Need me to run you over to the doctor?"

The flush grew. "Oh. Thank you. No, I'm…well, it's sort of normal. When it rains, it hurts more. And I fell." She bit her lip because he looked so guilty. "It wasn't your fault, or your driver's," she added quickly. "I'm clumsy. My toe hit a brick on the sidewalk that was just a little raised and it caused me to lose my balance. That's why I use the cane on bad days. I'm clumsy even on flat surfaces…"

"My grandmother had arthritis," he said softly. "Her little hands and feet were gnarled like tree roots." He wasn't watching, so he didn't notice the discomfort in Bernie's face—her poor feet weren't very pretty, either. "I used to carry her in and out of the house when she had bad spells. She loved to sit in the sun." His dark eyes were sad. "She weighed barely eighty pounds, but she was like a little pit bull. Even the big guys were afraid of her."

"The big guys?" she asked, lost in his soft eyes.

He shrugged. "In the family," he said.

She frowned. She didn't understand.

"You really are a little violet under a stair," he mused to himself. "The family is what insiders call the mob," he explained. "The big guys are the dons, the men who run things. I'm from New Jersey. Most of my family was involved in organized crime. Well, except Paulie," he added with a chuckle. "He was always the odd guy out."

She smiled. "He's married to Sari Grayling, who works in our office."

He nodded. "Sweet woman. Her sister is one hel— heck of an artist," he said, amending the word he'd meant to use.

"She truly is. They had her do a portrait of our local college president, who was retiring. It looked just like him."

He chuckled. "The one she painted three years ago saved her life. Her father whacked a woman whose son hired contract men to go after Grayling's daughters. Merrie painted the big don from back home, and he called off the hit." He didn't add how Tony Garza had called it off.

"We heard about all that. I wasn't working for the district attorney's office at the time. I was working for a local attorney who moved his practice to San Antonio. But we all knew," she added. "Everybody talked about it. He actually gave her away at her wedding, didn't he?"

He nodded. "Tony's wife died young. He never had kids, never remarried." He grinned. "He tells everybody he's Merrie's dad. Gets a reaction, let me tell you, especially when he mentions that her brother-in-law is a fed."

She sipped coffee, fascinated by him.

It was mutual. He smiled very slowly, his heart doing odd things in his chest. It had been many years since he'd felt such tenderness for anything female, except his grandmother.

"Do you have family?" he asked suddenly.

Her face clouded. "Not anymore," she said softly, without elaborating.

"Me, neither," he replied. "Except for Paulie. We're first cousins."

"Mr. Fiore's nice," she said.

He nodded. He was thinking about Tony, in hiding and waiting for developments that would save him from life in prison. Mikey had the proof that could save him. But he had to stay alive long enough to present it. Here, in Jacobsville, was his best bet. He'd agreed, knowing how many ex-mercs and ex-military lived here.

But as he stared at this sweet, kind young woman, he thought about the danger he might be putting her in. Even in a foolproof situation, there could be snags.

After all, the contract killer who'd been after Merrie actually got onto Ren Colter's property in Wyoming and had her bedroom staked out before she came back to her sister and brother-in-law.

Bernie cocked her head. "Something's worrying you."

He started. "How do you know?"

She drew in a slow breath and averted her eyes. "People think I'm strange."

He moved a step closer to the bed. "How so?"

She shifted restlessly. "I…well, I sort of know things about people." She flushed.

He nodded. "Like Merrie. She has that sort of perception. She painted a picture of me that nailed me to a T, and she'd never even met me."

She looked up. "Oh. Then you're not…intimidated by strange things."

He chuckled. "Nothing intimidates me, kid," he teased.

She smiled.

"So. You think something's worrying me." One brown eye narrowed. "What, exactly?"

She drew in a long breath and stared into his eyes. "Somebody wants to keep you from telling something you know," she said after a minute, and saw the shock hit his face.

"Damn."

"And it worries you that somebody might hurt anybody around you."

"Need to get a crystal ball and a kerchief and set up shop," he teased gently. "You're absolutely on the money. But that's between you and me, okay? The fewer people who know things, the fewer can talk about them."

She nodded. "I don't talk about things I know, as a rule. I work for the DA's office. Gossip isn't encouraged."

He chuckled. "I guess not."

Her coffee was now stone-cold, but she sipped it, for something to do.

He stared at her with conflicting emotions. She was unique, he thought. He'd never met anybody in his life like her.

She stared back. Her heart was almost smothering her with its wild beat. She was grateful that she had the covers pulled up, so he couldn't see her gown fluttering with her heartbeat.

There was another quick knock and Mrs. Brown came in. "Finished, dear?" she asked as she went to pick up the tray. "You can just set that on here, Mr. Fiore," she told Mikey with a smile. "I'll..."

He put it on the tray and then took the tray from her. "You're too delicate to be lifting heavy weights," he said with a grin. "I'll carry it for you."

"Oh, Mr. Fiore," she laughed, and blushed like a girl. "If you need anything, you just call me, Bernie, ok?"

"I will. Thanks. Both of you," she added.

Mrs. Brown smiled. As Mikey went through the door, he turned and winked at her.

That wink kept her heart fluttering all day, and it kept her awake most of the night.

She was able to go to the table for breakfast the next morning, even if she moved with a little difficulty. Her medicines worked slowly, but at least they did work. She had prednisone to take with the worst attacks, and it helped tremendously.

"You look better today," Mrs. Brown said. "Going to church?"

"Yes," she replied with a smile. "I'm hitching a ride with the Farwalkers."

Mikey frowned. "The Farwalkers? Wait a minute. Farwalker. Carson Farwalker. He's one of the doctors here. I remember."

Bernie laughed. "Yes. He's married to Carlie Blair. Her dad is pastor of the local Methodist church. I don't have a car, so they come by to get me most Sundays for services. Sometimes it's just Carlie and their little boy, Jacob, if Carson's on call."

He didn't mention that he knew that pastor, Jake Blair. He also knew things about the man's past that he wasn't sharing.

"My whole family was Catholic," he said. "Well, not Paulie. But then, he always went his own way."

"The Ruiz family here is Catholic," she said. "He's a Texas Ranger. His wife is a nurse. She works in San Antonio, too, so they commute. They're very nice people."

"I never met Ruiz, but I heard about him. Ranch the size of a small state, they say."

Bernie grinned. "Yes. It is rather large, but they aren't social people, if you get my meaning."

"Goodness, no," Miss Pirkle, one of the tenants said with a smile. "Your cousin and his family are like that, too, Mr. Fiore," she added, her thin face animated as she spoke. "Down-to-earth. Good people."

"Thanks," he said.

"We have a lot of moneyed families in Jacobsville and Comanche Wells," old Mrs. Bartwell interjected with a smile. "Most of them earned their wealth the hard way, especially the Ballengers. They started out with nothing. Now Calhoun is a United States senator and Justin runs their huge feed lot here."

"That's a real rags-to-riches story," Miss Pirkle agreed. "Their sons are nice, too. Imagine, two brothers, three children apiece, and not a girl in the bunch," she added on a laugh.

"I wouldn't mind a little girl," Mikey said, surprising himself. He didn't dare look at Bernie, who'd inspired the comment. He could almost picture her in a little frilly dress at the age of five or six. She would have been a pretty child. He hadn't thought about children in a long time, not since his ex-fiancée had noted that she wasn't marrying some famous criminal. It had broken Mikey's heart. Women were treacherous.

"Children are sweet," Bernie said softly as she finished her bacon and eggs. "The Griers come into our office a lot with their daughter, Tris, and their son, Marcus. I love seeing their children."

"The police chief," Mikey said, nodding. He chuckled. "Not your average small-town cop."

"Not at all," Bernie agreed, tongue-in-cheek.

"That's true," Miss Pirkle said. "He was a Texas Ranger!"

Bernie caught Mikey's eyes and held them. He got the message. Their elderly breakfast companion didn't know about the chief's past. Just as well to keep it quiet.

"Are you from here, too?" Mikey asked Miss Pirkle.

"No. I'm from Houston," she replied, her blue eyes smiling. "I came here with my mother about two years ago, just before I lost her." She took a breath and forced a smile. "I loved the town so much that I decided I'd just stay. I don't really have anybody back in Houston now."

"I'm not from here, either," Mrs. Bartwell said. "I'm a northern transplant. New York State."

"Thought I recognized that accent," Mikey teased.

Mrs. Bartwell chuckled. "I have a great-niece who lives in Chicago with her grandmother. Old money. Very old. They have ancestors who died in the French Revolution."

"My goodness!" Miss Pirkle exclaimed, all ears.

"My sister and I haven't spoken in twenty years," she added. "We had a minor disagreement that led to a terrible fight. My husband died of cancer and we had no children. My great-niece's mother was from Jacobsville. She was a Jacobs, in fact."

"Impressive," Bernie said with a grin. "Was she kin to Big John?"

"Yes, distantly."

"Big John?" Mikey asked curiously.

"Big John Jacobs," Bernie replied, because she knew the history by heart. "He was a sharecropper back in Georgia before the Union Army burned down his farm and killed most of his family, thinking they were slave owners. They weren't. They were poor, like the black family he saved from real slave owners. One of the Union officers was going to have him shot, but the black family got between him and the Army man and made him listen to the truth. They saved his life. He came here just after the Civil War with them. He didn't even have a proper house, so he and their families lived in one big shack together. He hired on some Comanche men and a good many cowboys from Mexico and started ranching with Texas longhorns. He made people uncomfortable because he wasn't a racist in a time when many people were. He married an heiress, convinced her father to build a railroad spur to the ranch, near present Jacobsville, so that he could ship his cattle north. Made a fortune at it."

"What a story," Mikey chuckled.

"And all true," Miss Pirkle said. "There's a statue of Big John on the town square. One of his direct descendants is married to Justin Ballenger, who owns one of the biggest feed lots in Texas."

"All this talk of great men makes me weak in the knees," Mikey teased.

"Do you have illustrious ancestors, Mr. Fiore?" Mrs. Brown asked with a mischievous grin.

"Nah," he said. "If I do, I don't know about it. My grandmother was the only illustrious person I ever knew."

"Was she famous?" Mrs. Bartwell asked.

"Well, she was famous back in Jersey," he mused. "Got mad at a don and chased him around the room with a salami."

There were confused looks.

"Mafia folks," he explained.

"Oh! Like in *The Sopranos*, that used to be on television!" Miss Pirkle said. "I never missed an episode!"

"Sort of like that," he said. "More like Marlon Brando in *The Godfather*," he said, chuckling. "Afterwards, he sent her a big present every Christmas and even came to her funeral. She was fierce."

"Was she Italian?" Mrs. Brown asked.

He laughed. "She was Greek. Everybody else in my whole family was Italian except for her. She was a tiny little thing, but ferocious. I was terrified of her when I was a kid. So was Paulie. Our folks didn't have much time for us," he added, not explaining why, "so she pretty much raised us."

"I never knew either of my grandmothers," Bernie said as she sipped coffee.

Mikey was studying her closely. "Where were your grandparents from?" he asked.

She closed up like a flower. She forced a smile. "I'm not really sure," she lied. "My father and mother were from Jacobsville, though, and we lived here from the time I was old enough to remember things. I have to get ready for church. It was delicious, Mrs. Brown," she added.

"Thank you, dear," Mrs. Brown said, and grimaced a little. She knew about Bernie's past. Not many other local people did. She could almost feel Bernie's anguish. Not Mr. Fiore's fault for bringing it up. He didn't know. "Want a second cup of coffee to take with you while you dress?"

"If I drink two, I can fly around the room and land on the curtain rods," Bernie teased. "I'm hyper enough as it is. But thanks."

She glanced at Mikey, puzzled by the look on his face. She smiled at the others and went back to her room.

Jake Blair was a conundrum, Bernie thought as she walked in line out the front door to shake hands with him after the very nice sermon. He seemed to be very conventional, just like a minister was expected to be. But he drove a red Shelby Cobra Mustang with a souped-up engine, and there were whispers about his past. The same sort of whispers that followed Jacobsville's police chief, Cash Grier, wherever he went.

Bernie gripped her dragon cane tightly and glanced at the toddler in Dr. Carson Farwalker's arms as he and Carlie walked beside her.

"Imagine you two with a child." Bernie sighed as she went from one face to the other.

Carlie grinned. "Imagine us married!" she corrected with a loving look at her husband, which was returned. "They were taking bets at the police station the day we got married about when he'd do a flit."

"They're having a long wait, don't you think?" Carson chuckled.

"Very long," she agreed. "Imagine, we used to fight each other in World of Warcraft on battlegrounds and we never knew it. Not until my life was in danger and Dad had you watching me."

"I watched you a lot more than he told me to," Carson teased.

She laughed.

They'd moved up to Jake by now and he was giving them an amused grin. "There's my boy!" he said softly, and held his arms out for Jacob, who was named after him."

"Gimpa." The little boy laughed and hugged the tall man.

Jake hugged him close. "If anybody had told me ten years ago that I'd go all mushy over a grandchild, I guess I'd have laughed."

"If anybody had told me ten years ago that I'd be practicing medicine in a small Texas town, I'd have fainted," Carson chuckled.

"I like having family," Jake said, and smiled at his daughter and son-in-law. "I never belonged anyplace in my life until now."

"Me, neither," Bernie said softly.

Jake looked at her kindly, and she knew that he'd heard the rumors. She just smiled. He was her minister, after all. Someday maybe she'd be able to talk about it. Mrs. Brown knew, but she was a clam. Not a lot of other people had any idea about Bernie's background because she'd lived for a few years, with her parents, in Floresville before coming back here with her father just before he died. She didn't like to think about those days. Not at all.

Jake looked behind his family at the few remaining, obviously impatient worshippers and handed his grandson back to Carson. "Ah, well, I'll see you all at the house later. I'm holding up progress," he added, and looked behind Carson at a man who actually flushed.

"Not a problem, Preacher," the man said. "It's just that the line's already forming for lunch at Barbara's Café…"

"Say no more," Jake chuckled. "Actually, I'm heading there myself. I can burn water."

"You can cook," Carlie chided.

"Only when I want to. And I don't want to," he confided with a grin. He kissed her cheek and shook hands with Carson. "I'll see you all for supper. You bringing it?"

"Of course," Carlie replied with a grin. "We know you can't boil water!"

He just laughed.

Bernie walked into the boardinghouse a little tired, but happy from the few hours of socializing with friends.

She wasn't looking where she was going, her mind still on the Farwalkers' little boy, whom she had sat beside in the back seat and cooed at all the way home. She ran right into Mikey and almost fell.

Chapter 3

Mikey just stared at her, smiling faintly as he caught her by both shoulders and spared her a fall. She did look pretty, with her long, platinum blond hair loose around her shoulders, wearing a pink dress in some soft material that displayed her nice figure without making it look indecent. He thought of all the women he'd known who paraded around in dresses cut up to the thigh and slashed to the waist in front. He compared them with Bernie, and found that he greatly preferred her to those glitzy women in his past.

"Thanks," she said, a husky note in her voice as she looked up at him with fascinated pale green eyes. It was a long way. He was husky for his height, and his head was leonine, broad, with a straight nose and chiseled lips and a square chin. He looked like a movie star. She'd never even seen a man so handsome.

"Deep thoughts?" he asked softly.

She caught her breath. "Sorry. I was just thinking how handsome you are." She flushed. "Oh, gosh," she groaned as that slipped out.

"It's okay," he teased. "I'm used to ladies swooning over me. No problem."

That broke the ice and she laughed.

He loved the way she looked when she laughed. Her whole face became radiant. Color bloomed on her cheeks. Her green eyes sparkled. Amazing, that a woman with her disability could laugh at all. But, then, his little grandmother had been the same. She never complained. She just accepted her lot in life and got on with living.

"You never complain, do you?" he asked suddenly.

"Well...not really," she stammered. "There's this saying that the boss has on the wall at work, a quote from Saint Francis of Assisi..."

"'God grant me the serenity to accept the things I cannot change; courage to change the things I can; and wisdom to know the difference,'" he quoted.

She smiled. "You know it."

He shrugged. "My grandmother dragged me to mass every single Sunday until I was old enough to refuse to go. She had a plaque with that quote on it. I learned it by heart."

"It's nice."

"I guess."

He let her go belatedly. "You okay?"

"I'm fine. I wasn't paying attention to where I was going. Sorry I ran into you."

"Feel free to do it whenever you like," he said, and

his dark eyes twinkled. "You fall down, kid, I'll pick you up every time."

She flushed. "Thanks. I'd do the same for you, if I could." She eyed his height. Her head came up to just past his shoulder. He probably weighed twice what she did, and the expensive suit he was wearing didn't disguise the muscular body under it. "I don't imagine I could pick you up, though."

He laughed. "Don't sweat it. I'll see you later."

She nodded.

He went around her and out the door, just as she heard a car pull up at the curb. His driver, no doubt. She wondered where he was going on a Sunday. But, then, that was really not her business.

It was the next morning before Bernie saw Mikey again, at the breakfast table. He was quiet and he looked very somber. He felt somber. Somebody had tracked Tony to the Bahamas and Marcus Carrera had called in some markers to keep him safe. Tony had used one of his throwaway phones to call Mikey—on the number Mikey had sent through a confederate.

Carrera, he recalled, was not a man to mess with. Once a big boss up north, the man had done a complete flip and gone legit. He was worth millions. He'd married a small-town Texas girl some years ago and they had two sons. The wife was actually from Jacobsville, a girl who used to do clothing repairs at the local dry cleaner's. Her father was as rich as Tony. Her mother had pretended to be her sister, but the truth came out when Carrera was threatened and his future wife saved him. Mikey knew Carrera's in-laws, but distantly. At least Tony was safe. But if they'd tracked him down, they probably had a good idea where Mikey was. It wouldn't take much work to discover that Mikey had been down here in Jacobsville three years ago to help out his cousin Paulie. That being said, however, it was still the safest place he could be. He had as much protection as he needed, from both sides of the law.

He looked around at the women at the table. His eyes lingered on Bernadette. He didn't want to put her in the line of fire. This had been a bad idea, getting a room at a boardinghouse. Or had it?

"Deep thoughts, Mr. Fiore?" Mrs. Brown teased. "You're very quiet."

He laughed self-consciously when he felt eyes on him. "Yeah. I was thinking about a friend of mine who's been in some trouble recently."

"We've all been there," Miss Pirkle said warmly. "I guess friends become like family after a time, don't they? We worry about them just as we would about kinfolk."

"And that's a fact," he agreed.

"My best friend drowned in a neighbor's swimming pool, when my family lived briefly in Floresville," Bernie commented.

"Did you see it?" Mikey asked.

She looked down at her plate. Her whole face clenched. "Yes. I didn't get to her in time."

"Listen, kid, sometimes things just happen. Like they're meant to happen. I'm not a religious man, but I believe life has a plan. Every life."

Bernie looked up at him. Her face relaxed a little. She drew in a long breath. "Yes. I think that, too." She smiled.

He smiled back.

The smiles lasted just a second too long to be casual. Mrs. Brown broke the silence by putting her cup noisily in the saucer without glancing at her boarders. It amused her, the streetwise Northerner and the shy Texas girl, finding each other fascinating. Mrs. Brown's husband had died years ago, leaving her with a big house outside town and a fistful of bills she couldn't pay. Opening her home to lodgers had made the difference. With her increased income, she was able to buy this house in town and turn it into a new boardinghouse. The sale of the first house had financed the purchase and remodeling of this one. The new location had been perfect for her boarders who worked in Jacobsville. She found that she had a natural aptitude for dealing with people, and it kept her bills paid and left her comfortably situated financially. But romance had been missing from her life. Now she was watching it unfold, with delight.

Mikey glanced at his wrist, at the very expensive thin gold watch he wore. "I have to run. I'm meeting Paulie up in San Antonio, but I'll be home in time for dinner," he told Mrs. Brown. He got up and leaned toward her. "What are we having?"

"Lasagna," she said with a grin. "And yes, I do know how to make it. Mandy Swilling taught me."

"You angel!" he said, and chuckled. "I'll definitely be back on time. See you all later."

They all called goodbyes. Bernie flushed when he turned at the doorway and glanced back at her with dark, soft eyes and a smile.

She felt good enough to walk the four blocks to work and she hardly needed the cane. Her life had taken a turn. She was happy for the first time in recent memory. Just the thought of Mikey Fiore made her tingle all over and glow inside.

That was noticed by the people she worked with, especially the new girl, Jessie Tennison. Jessie was older than Bernadette's twenty-four years. She had to be at least twenty-seven. She'd been married and was now divorced, with no children. She had a roving eye for rich men. It had already gotten her in trouble with their boss, Mr. Kemp, the district attorney. That hadn't seemed to stop her. She wore very revealing clothing—she'd been called down about that, too—and she wasn't friendly to the women in the office.

Bernie put down her purse, folded her cane and took off her jacket before she sat down.

"I don't see why you work," Jessie said offhandedly, looking down her long nose at Bernie with a cold blue-eyed stare. "I'd just get on government relief and stay home."

"I don't need handouts. I work for my living," Bernie said. She smiled at the tall brunette, but not with any warmth.

Jessie shrugged. "Suit yourself. I'm going over to the courthouse on my break to talk to my friend Billie," she added, slipping into a long coat.

Bernie almost bit her tongue off to keep from mentioning that their breaks were only ten minutes long and it would take Jessie that long just to walk to the courthouse. The district attorney's office had been in the courthouse, but this year they'd moved to a new county building where they had more room. The increased space had delighted the office staff, which had grown considerably. Their new office was closer to Mrs.

Brown's boardinghouse and Barbara's Café, but farther from the courthouse.

She didn't say it, but her coworker Olivia did. "Who's in the courthouse today, Jessie?" she asked with a blank expression. "Some really rich upper-class man who might need a companion…?"

"You…!" Jessie began just as Mr. Kemp's office door opened. She smiled at him, all sweetness. "I'm going to the courthouse on my break to see my friend Billie for just a minute, Mr. Kemp. Is that all right with you?" she added with a cold glance at her coworker.

"If it's absolutely necessary," he replied tersely. He wasn't pleased with his new employee. In fact, he was beginning to think he'd made a big mistake. A glowing recommendation from a San Antonio attorney had gotten Jessie the job, mainly because there were no other applicants. Competent receptionists with several years' experience weren't thick on the ground around Jacobsville.

"It really is," she said, and looked as if it wasn't the whole truth. "I have a friend in the hospital in San Antonio. Billie's been to see him," she added quickly.

"Okay. Try not to take too long." He paused and looked at her for a long time. "You get a ten-minute break. Not an hour."

"Oh, yes, sir." She was all sugary sweetness as she walked out the door in a cloud of cloying perfume.

Bernie's coworker fanned the air with a file folder, making a face.

Not five minutes later, assistant DA Glory Ramirez walked in the door and made a face. "Who's been filming a perfume commercial in here?" she asked.

"Somebody who's mad at me, probably," Sari Fiore,

their second assistant DA, laughed as she came in behind Glory. "Perfume gives me a migraine."

"I'll turn the air conditioner on long enough to suck it out of the building," Mr. Kemp volunteered.

"Ask her to wash it all off. I dare you," Sari said to the boss.

He laughed and went back into his office. The phone rang. Sari picked it up, nodded, spoke into the receiver and pressed a button. It was for Mr. Kemp. She hung up.

"Where's Jessie?" Sari asked curtly. "The phone is her job, not ours."

"There's some rich guy at the courthouse," Olivia told her. "She had a call from her friend Billie, who works as a temporary assistant in the Clerk of Court's office. I guess that was what it was about, although she said she was going to ask about a sick friend."

"She can't do that on the phone?" Sari asked, aghast.

"Well, she can't see the rich guy over the phone," Olivia said demurely and with a wicked smile.

"Jessie's a pill," Glory added. "I wonder how she ever got past the boss to hire on here. She's definitely not like any legal receptionist I've ever known."

"She's big-city, not small-town," Sari said. "She's got an accent like that lawyer from Manhattan who was down here last month."

"I noticed," Glory replied. "How are you feeling, Bernie?"

Bernie flushed and grinned. "I'm doing fine."

"Oh?" Sari teased. "We heard about your new boarder at Mrs. Brown's."

Bernie went scarlet.

"That was mean," Glory told Sari.

"Sorry," Sari said, but she was still grinning. "Isn't

Mikey a doll?" she added. "He could pose for commercials."

"I noticed," Bernie said. "He's very good-looking."

"We heard about the fall. You okay?"

Bernie gasped. "Does he tell you guys everything?"

"Well, not everything. Just when he feels guilty about something." She smiled gently. "He felt really bad that he'd misjudged you. But it's not surprising. He's had women jump in front of his car before."

"My goodness!" Bernie exclaimed, fascinated.

"He is very rich," Glory pointed out. "And some women are less than scrupulous."

"Very true," Bernie said. "But I'm not."

"He noticed," Sari replied, tongue in cheek. "He said you remind him of his grandmother."

Bernie's eyes widened to saucers, and she looked absolutely horrified.

"No!" Sari said quickly. "He didn't mean he thought you were old. He said you had the same kind heart and the same sharp tongue she did. He was tickled when you compared him to that guy in the *Police Academy* movie." Her blue eyes sparkled as she looked at Bernie. "Paul said he really was like that guy, too."

Bernie laughed. "He's a lot of fun around the boardinghouse. He makes our two older ladies very flustered. Mrs. Brown, too."

"He's a dish. But he's not really a ladies' man, despite the appearance," Sari added. "In fact, he doesn't like most women. He had a hard experience some years back. I guess it affected him."

"We've all had hard experiences," Glory remarked. She shook her head. "If anybody had ever told me I'd marry Rodrigo…!"

"If anybody had ever told me that I'd finally marry Paul…" Sari countered, and they both laughed.

Both women had had a hard path to the altar, with some painful experiences along the way. Now they were happy. Glory and Rodrigo had a son, but Paul and Sari hadn't started a family. Despite being filthy rich, they were both career oriented. Paul was FBI at the San Antonio office and Sari was an assistant DA here in Jacobs County. Children were definitely in their future, Sari often said, but not just at the moment.

Bernie would have loved a child. It would have been difficult for her with her physical issues, but that wouldn't deter her if she ever found a man who loved her enough to marry her. She thought briefly of Mikey and her heart fluttered, but she knew she wasn't beautiful or cultured enough to appeal to a man so sophisticated. And if he'd reached his present age, which had to be somewhere in his thirties, unmarried, he was unlikely to be thinking of marrying anybody in the future. What a depressing thought, she realized, and how silly of her to be thinking of it in the first place. He was only here temporarily. He belonged up north.

She sat very still, aware of conversation around her and not hearing it. Mikey belonged up north. But he was in Jacobsville for no apparent reason, and he'd taken a room at a boardinghouse, which meant he was staying for a while. Why?

She knew he was worried about the people around him in the boardinghouse. Had he made somebody really mad, and they were after him? Was he in Jacobsville because he was safe here? She'd heard just a snippet of gossip from Mrs. Brown, that Mr. Fiore was being watched by one of Eb Scott's men. Nobody knew why. But Eb's men were mercenaries, experienced in combat. Bernie hoped that Mikey wasn't being hunted.

What an odd word to think of, she mused as she pulled up the computer program she used in her work. Hunted. She'd guessed that Mikey was worried about somebody else. Her heart jumped. Was it a woman, perhaps? No. Sari said he was sour on women. A man? Somebody from his past with a grudge? He knew a lot about organized crime. Maybe it was somebody he'd come across in his job, because Mrs. Brown said he told her he owned a hotel in Las Vegas. He must, she thought, be very rich indeed if he owned property in that expensive place.

She was well into research on a new case precedent for the boss when Jessie breezed back in, wafting her expense perfume everywhere.

Sari glared at her. "Jessie, I've told you that heavy perfume brings on migraines. I'd hate to have to speak to Mr. Kemp about it."

"Oh, I'm sorry!" Jessie said at once, feigning surprise. "I won't wear so much from now on."

"Thanks." Sari gave her a look she didn't see and went back to work.

"Well, was he there, your rich mark?" Olivia drawled.

Jessie glared at her. "I don't have a rich mark."

"Some wealthy gentleman?" Olivia probed further.

Jessie took off her coat and sat down at her desk. "I don't know. He was riding in a black limousine. He's from New Jersey."

Bernie's heart dropped to her feet. She only knew one rich man in Jacobsville who rode around in a black limousine. It had to be Mikey. Jessie was beautiful and sophisticated, probably the sort of woman Mikey would really go for. Jessie was an oddity in Jacobsville, where most women weren't streetwise. The older woman probably charmed him.

While she was thinking, Jessie's cold eyes stabbed into her face. "He said he's living at Mrs. Brown's boardinghouse. That's where you live, isn't it, Bernadette?"

"Yes," Bernie said shortly.

Jessie laughed, her scrutiny almost insulting. "Well, you won't be any sort of competition, will you? I mean, no sane man is going to want to take on a woman who can't stand up without a cane—"

"That's enough," Mr. Kemp said shortly from his open office door, and he looked even more formidable than usual. "You get one more warning, Jessie, then you're on your way back to San Antonio. You do not disparage coworkers. Ever."

Jessie actually flushed. She hadn't realized the boss could hear her. She'd have to be a lot more careful. There weren't any other jobs available in Jacobsville right now, and she couldn't afford to lose this one.

"I'm very sorry, Mr. Kemp," she began.

"Bernie's the one who's owed an apology."

"Yes, sir." Jessie turned to Bernie. "I'm sorry. That was wrong of me."

"Okay," Bernie said, but she didn't really look at the other woman.

Mr. Kemp hesitated for just a minute before he went back into his office.

"Careless, Jessie," Olivia said in a biting undertone. "Better make sure the boss isn't listening when you start making rude comments about one of us."

Jessie looked as if she might explode. The phone rang and saved her from making her situation any worse.

* * *

At lunchtime, Olivia and Bernie went to Barbara's Café to eat. Glory and Sari went home, where Glory had a babysitter and she could visit with her son while she ate. Sari had lunch with Mandy Swilling, the Grayling housekeeper. Jessie was stuck in the office until the others returned, thanks to Mr. Kemp who insisted that somebody had to answer the phone while he was out of the office. Jessie was almost smoking when the other women went out the door.

"Jessie's a pain," Olivia said curtly.

Bernie's pale green eyes sparkled as she dug into her chef's salad. "You really made her mad."

"Well, nobody else says anything," the other woman defended herself. Her voice softened. "Least of all you, Bernie. You're the sweetest woman I've ever known, except for my late grandmother. You could find one kind thing to say about the devil," she teased.

Bernie laughed softly. "I guess so."

"At least Sari finally said something about the heavy perfume. I know it gives her fits. She's prone to migraines from just the stress of her job. Jessie doesn't care what she does or says unless the boss loses his temper." She frowned. "What's she doing down here?" she added with a frown. "I mean, she worked in San Antonio, where salaries are a lot higher. She doesn't know anybody in Jacobsville."

"The boss said she wanted a slower pace," Bernie replied.

"Sure. Like she has any stress. Unless answering the phone gives you ulcers," Olivia said drily. "Or bend-ing over the desk to show as much cleavage as possible when a wealthy client comes in."

"Oh, shame on you!" Bernie said, laughing.

"I know. I'm bad. But Jessie's worse. She met your fellow boardinghouse occupant, too," Olivia added with a pointed glance at Bernie's flushed face. "She'll be after him soon. Nobody here rides around in a limo except Paul's cousin Mikey. Sari used to, but she mostly just drives now that all the threats to her and her sister are gone."

"He's here for a reason, too," Bernie said.

"A guess, or that intuition that makes most people nervous?" Olivia teased.

Bernie laughed. "Maybe a bit of both."

"Or maybe not." Olivia glanced up and then down again. "Any idea about what he might be doing today?"

Bernie's heart jumped and she felt it flutter. Incredible, that she knew absolutely where he was, without even looking. "He's coming in the door."

She hadn't looked up. She did now, and there he was, in a dark suit with a patterned blue tie, looking around until he spotted Bernie. He grinned as he went to the counter and placed his order, paying for it before he joined Olivia and Bernie at their table.

"Room for one more?" he asked with a grin at both women. "I don't really know anybody else in here, and I'm shy."

"Oh, sure you are," Olivia said with a wry smile. She wiped her mouth. "I have to get back before Jessie turns purple and says we're starving her. You stay and finish your salad, Bernie," she added as she stood up. "You have a half hour before you have to come back."

"Jessie. That the underdressed brunette who works in your office?" he asked.

They nodded.

"Don't tell her I'm here, okay?" he asked Olivia. He shook his head. "I know how deer feel in hunting season."

They both laughed.

"I won't. I promise," Olivia said. She winked at Bernie and went to carry her tray back.

Mikey looked at Bernie slowly, taking in the blond braid and the nice gray suit she was wearing with a pink camisole. "You look pretty," he said softly.

She flushed and laughed self-consciously. "Thanks."

"You're a breath of spring compared to the women I know," he added quietly, watching her. "Brassy, overbearing women don't do a thing for me these days. I guess I'm jaded."

She smiled shyly. "You're very handsome and you're wealthy. I guess women do chase you. Even movie stars and rich women."

He pursed his lips. "They used to. It's the other stuff that puts them off."

Her thin eyebrows lifted. "The other stuff?" she asked.

He shrugged. "My connections."

She still wasn't getting it. While she tried to, Barbara brought his steak and salad and black coffee, and put it down in front of him.

"I hope it's done right," she told Mikey. "My cook tends to get meat a little overdone. One of our customers actually carried his back into the kitchen and proceeded to show him how to cook it properly."

"Jon Blackhawk," Bernie guessed.

"How did you know?" Barbara asked.

"He's the only gourmet chef I know, and he's Paul's boss at the FBI office in San Antonio. They were both down here recently on a case. And nobody eats any-where else in Jacobsville except here," she teased.

Barbara chuckled. "Exactly. It didn't come to blows, but it was close. My temporary cook's from New Jersey," she added.

Mikey's ears perked up. He glanced at Barbara.

She made a face. "His people are heavily federal, if you get my meaning. His brother works for the US Mar-shals Service in San Antonio, and he's a former police-man where he came from. He's retired."

"Oh." Mikey relaxed, just a little.

"I was going to add… Goodness, excuse me," she said, suddenly flustered as she went back to the counter.

Bernie's eyes followed her, and she grinned to her-self as she watched a husky man in a police uniform smile at Barbara as she went to wait on him.

"Okay, what's that little smirk all about?" Mikey teased.

"That guy at the counter. That's Fred Baldwin. He worked as a policeman here for a while, then at a local ranch. Now he's back on the police force. He's sweet on Barbara and vice versa."

Mikey glanced in that direction and laughed softly. "I can see what you mean."

"Her son's a lieutenant of detectives with San Antonio PD," Bernie added.

He nodded. "I met him, last time I was here. Nice guy."

"Her daughter-in-law's father is the head of the CIA," she added.

"I heard that, too. Her son's dad is a head of state, down in South America."

"He does have some interesting connections," Bernie agreed.

* * *

Mikey finished his steak. "What's there to do around here at night?" he asked.

She pursed her lips. "Well, people go to concerts at the local high school on the weekends sometimes. Other people drive in the Line."

"What the hell...heck's the Line?" he amended.

"A bunch of people drive around in a line. Teenagers, married people, even old people sometimes. They have a leader, and they go all around the county, one after the other, sometimes even up to San Antonio and back."

He shook his head. "The things I miss, living in a city." His dark eyes met hers. "How about movies?"

"Jack Morris and his son just opened a drive-in theater outside town," she said. "He even built a snack bar with restrooms. He says he's bringing back the 1950s all by himself. It's pretty successful, too."

"What's playing right now?"

She named the movie, an action one about commandoes.

He smiled. "You like movies like that?" he asked.

"Well, yes," she confessed.

He chuckled. "I thought you had an adventurous nature. Mrs. Brown told me about those books you read in bed. She said you have some on outfits like the British SAS and the French Foreign Legion."

She blushed. "My goodness!"

"So, how about a movie Friday night?" he asked. "I'll have Santi rent a smaller car, one that won't get so much attention from the populace."

Her heart skipped a beat and ran wild. "You want to take me out, on a date?"

"Of course I do," he said softly.

She thought she might faint. "But I… I have all sorts of health issues…"

"Bernadette, you have a kind heart," he said quietly, his dark eyes soft on her face. "None of the other stuff matters. Least of all an illness you can't help." He grinned. "I won't ask you to go mountain climbing with me. I promise."

She laughed. "That's a deal, then."

He shook his head. "Why would you think you're untouchable?"

"A local boy told me that when I was in high school. He said he didn't want to get mixed up with a handicapped girl."

"Idiot," he muttered.

She smiled at him. "Thanks."

"How long ago?"

She blinked, "How long ago was it?"

He shifted. "Clumsy way to put it. How old are you?" he added. His dark eyes twinkled. "Past the age of consent?" he probed.

She closed up and looked uncomfortable.

He put a big, warm hand over hers on the table. "I don't proposition women I haven't even dated yet," he said softly. "And you aren't the sort of girl who'd ever get such a proposition from me. Honest."

She caught her breath. He was so unexpected. "I'm twenty-four. Almost twenty-five."

He was shocked and looked it. "You don't look your age, kid."

She beamed. "Thanks."

He laughed and curled his fingers around hers, enjoying the sensations that ran through him. Judging by the flush, she was feeling something similar.

"Careful," she said under her breath as more people came in the front door.

"Careful, why? Somebody with a gun looking our way?" he asked, and not entirely facetiously.

"Gossip."

He scowled. "What?"

"Gossip," she repeated. "If people see you standing close together or holding hands, they start talking about you, especially if you're local and unmarried. You'll get talked about."

"Like I care," he teased.

She felt as if she could float. "Really?"

His teeth were perfect and very white. She noticed, because he didn't seem to smile much. "I don't mind gossip. Do you?"

She hesitated. But, really, nobody here was likely to gossip about her to him, at least. Not many people knew about her parents or, especially, her grandparents. "No," she said after a minute. "I don't mind, either."

"Just as well. I have no plans to stop holding hands with you," he said. "It feels nice."

"It feels very nice," she said.

He had Santi drive her back to her office. He even got out, helped her from the car and walked her to the door.

"That woman in the courthouse said she works here. That right?" he asked.

She made a face and nodded.

"Then I won't come in. Phew," he added. "She could start a perfume shop on what she was wearing."

"She could in there, too," she said.

He laughed. "Well, I'll see you back at Mrs. Brown's

later. If it starts raining, you call me and I'll come pick you up."

She looked hesitant.

"Oh. Right." He pulled out his wallet, extracted a business card and handed it to her. "Cell phone. At the bottom. You can call me or you can text me. Texting is better. I hate talking on the damned phone."

She laughed. "So do I."

"Okay, then. See you later, kid."

"See you."

He got back in the car. She went into her office and closed the door behind her.

Jessie was watching. Her face was livid. She'd tried to cadge a ride back to the office in that nice limo and been refused. It made her furious that little miss sunshine there had managed it. And she was late back to work, to boot!

Chapter 4

Bernie didn't have to look to feel Jessie's fury, but she sat down at her desk without even glancing toward the front desk. Apparently Jessie wasn't going to push her luck by attacking Bernie, though. She settled down at her desk and busied herself typing up letters for the boss while she answered the phone.

It wasn't hard to avoid her at quitting time. Jessie was always the first one out the door, just in case the phone rang and somebody had to answer it. She was never on time in the mornings, either, something resented by all her coworkers.

"Phew," Bernie said with heartfelt thanks when Jessie was out of sight. "I thought my number was up when we got back from lunch."

"Jessie won't quit," Olivia said quietly. "She's got that nice rich visitor in her sights and she'll do anything to get his attention. You watch out," she added.

Bernie sighed. "I guess she'll really hit the ceiling when she finds out I'm going to a movie with him."

"Movie?" Sari asked, all ears.

"When?" Glory asked.

She laughed. "Friday night. He's taking me to the drive-in."

"Ooh," Sari mused. "Heavy stuff."

Bernie blushed. "He's so good-looking. Honestly, I feel dowdy compared to Jessie."

"He didn't like Jessie, though, did he?" Olivia reminded her. "He told me not to mention he was having lunch with us when I went back to the office. He wasn't impressed by her. In fact," she added with a chuckle, "he said he knew how deer felt during hunting season."

"Wouldn't that get her goat?" Sari teased. "I wasn't kidding about Mikey," she added to Bernie. "He really isn't a ladies' man."

"He could be in movies," Bernie said.

"Yes, he could," Glory agreed. "I wonder." She glanced at Sari. "Didn't anybody ever try to get him to audition for a movie?"

"In fact, Paul says he was pursued by a Hollywood agent who saw him in Newark. He just smiled and walked away. He's shy, although that never comes across. He puts on a good act," Sari added.

"He's good with people," Bernie told them as they went out and locked the door, Mr. Kemp having gone home from a day in court already. "The ladies at the boardinghouse think he's just awesome."

"And what a lucky thing that Mrs. Brown only had one vacancy," Sari said. "Or Jessie would be over there like a flash."

"I still can't figure what she's doing down here,"

Glory said. "She's a bad fit for our office, and she doesn't mix with anybody in town except her friend Billie at the county clerk's office." She frowned. "In fact, Billie hasn't been here long, either, and she's a city girl from back east somewhere. They're both of them out of step with local people."

"Do they room together?" Bernie asked.

"Yes, at some motel out of town. That's got to be expensive, too, since none of our local hotels serve meals."

"Which one do they stay at?" Glory asked.

"The one where all the movie stars live when they're in town filming," Sari told her. "The one with whirlpool baths and feather pillows and mini bars."

"Ouch," Glory laughed. "That's the most expensive place in town. Jessie doesn't make enough here to afford such luxury."

"Well, she and Billie share," Sari said. "I guess they share meal expenses, too. Jessie would never manage it alone."

"Don't mention your upcoming date in the office," Glory cautioned Bernie.

"I might not need to," Bernie said, waving Olivia goodbye as she drove off in her car. "We were sort of holding hands in Barbara's Café," she confessed.

Sari whistled.

Bernie looked at her curiously.

"And Mikey knows about small towns, too," she mused. "Apparently he doesn't mind people knowing that he likes you."

Bernie flushed. "Really? You think he does?"

"Paul does," Sari said. "And he knows Mikey a lot better than the rest of us do."

"Wow," Bernie said softly.

"There's my ride. My boys," Glory gushed, waving to Rodrigo at the wheel of their car and their little boy in the back seat. "See you tomorrow!"

"Have a good night," Bernie called. Glory waved as she got into the car and fastened her seat belt. Rodrigo waved at the women on his way past.

"There's just one thing," Sari said gently, turning to Bernie when they were alone. "Mikey's down here for a reason, and it's a dangerous one. I can't talk about it. But you should know that there's a risk in going around with him."

"I do know," Bernie replied. "I don't care."

"So it's like that already." Sari smiled. "I'd feel the same way if Paul was like Mikey. You know that Mikey's past isn't spotless?" she added a little worriedly.

"You mean, about his hotel business?"

Sari didn't know what to say. She felt uncomfortable telling tales. Well, better to let sleeping dogs lie. "It was a long time ago," she lied, smiling. "He'll tell you himself when he's ready."

"I don't care about his past," Bernie said softly, and she smiled. "I've never been so happy in my whole life."

"Judging by how much he smiles lately, neither has Mikey," Sari laughed. "Paul said he was the most somber man you've ever seen until lately. They grew up together."

Bernie nodded. "Their grandmother raised them. Mikey loved her."

"Yes, he did. Paul and Mikey had a rough childhood. Their grandmother was all they had. Well, and each other, although neither of them would admit it."

"They seem to get along well, from what Mikey says."

"They do now. It wasn't always that way." She glanced

toward the curb. Paul was sitting at the wheel of their Jaguar. He waved. "Well, I'll go home. Can we drop you off?" she added.

Bernie laughed. "I'm doing really good today, and Dr. Coltrain says I need the exercise when I can get it. But thanks."

"No problem. Anytime. See you tomorrow."

Bernie waved them off and walked the four blocks to Mrs. Brown's boardinghouse. She felt as if her feet didn't even touch the sidewalk. Life was sweet.

She got through the rest of the week relatively unscathed by Jessie, although she received a lot of irritated looks when a couple of local people coming into the office mentioned that Bernie had been seen holding hands with Mikey at Barbara's Café. But apparently Jessie still thought Bernie was no competition for her. She did mention, loudly, that she was going to spend more time at Barbara's herself.

"And good luck to her," Sari laughed when Jessie left ahead of them all, as usual, at the end of the day. "Mikey's been in San Antonio for the past two days."

Bernie smiled with obvious relief. She hadn't seen him since their lunch at the café. He'd been out of town apparently. She'd wondered if he was leaving town. She'd hoped he'd say goodbye first, but his absence at the boardinghouse had worried her. Mrs. Brown only said that he had business to take care of, but she hadn't said how long it might take him to conduct it. Bernie figured it was something to do with the hotel he owned. It must take a lot of work to coordinate something so big, and he must have a lot of employees who had to be looked after as well.

"You didn't know," Sari guessed when she noted Bernie's expression.

"Well, no. He just told Mrs. Brown that he had business to take care of. We didn't know where he was."

"He and Paul have something going on together," Sari said, without mentioning what, although she knew. It was top-secret stuff, nothing she could tell even her worried coworker about.

"I hoped he wouldn't leave town without saying goodbye," Bernie replied.

"Are you kidding? He's taking you to a movie, remember?" Sari teased. "How could he leave town?"

Bernie laughed. "I guess he wouldn't, at that." She was beaming. "You know, I've only ever been on a few dates in my life." She hesitated and looked at Sari worriedly. "Mikey's sophisticated, you know? And I'm just a small-town girl with old-fashioned ideas about stuff."

"So was Della Carrera before she married Marcus here in town," she reminded the other woman. "Nobody's more sophisticated than Marcus Carrera."

Bernie smiled. "I guess not." She frowned. "Mr. Carrera was big in the mob, wasn't he?" she added absently.

"He was. He went legitimate, though. He was actually working with the FBI to shut down a crooked crime figure who planned to open a casino near Marcus's."

"I heard something about that." Bernie shook her head. "I don't understand how people ever get involved with organized crime. It seems a shameful way to earn a living."

"That it is," Sari said, but became reserved. Bernie didn't know about Mikey and she didn't feel comfortable blowing his cover. "Well, I'm off. See you tomorrow!"

"Have a good night."

"You, too."

Bernie watched them drive away and started back to Mrs. Brown's. She could hardly contain her excitement about the coming date with Mikey.

Mikey, meanwhile, had been in conference with Paul, Jon Blackhawk and a US Marshal in San Antonio, while the three of them hashed out what they knew and what they didn't know about Cotillo. Mikey had stayed at a safe house with the marshal while they discussed the case and what they were going to do about the threat.

"I don't want the women in my boardinghouse hurt," Mikey said during one long session. "Just being around me could put them in danger."

"They won't be," Paul replied. "You've got more protection than you realize."

"Yeah, well, Merrie Colter had plenty of protection, too, and she ended up in the hospital when that contract man was after her," Mikey pointed out.

"No plan is foolproof," Jon Blackhawk, assistant SAC at the San Antonio FBI office agreed. "But we've got most of our bases covered. And, frankly, no place is going to be perfectly safe. If you leave your boardinghouse, the women who live there could still be in danger if the contract man decides they might know where you were."

Mikey felt sick to his stomach, although nothing showed in that poker face. "I suppose that's true," he said heavily.

"I've never lost a person I was protecting yet," US Marshal McLeod interjected. He was tall and husky like

Mikey, but he had pale gray eyes in a face like stone and a .357 Magnum in a leather holster at his waist.

"You and that damned cannon," Paul muttered. "Why don't you move into the twenty-first century, McLeod, and sport a piece that didn't come out of the eighties?"

"It's a fine gun," McLeod said quietly. "It belonged to my father. He was killed in the line of duty, working for our local sheriff's office back home."

"Sorry," Paul said sheepishly.

McLeod shrugged. "No problem."

"I hope you got earplugs when you have to shoot that thing," Mikey mused.

"I got some, but if I take time to put them in, I'll be wearing them on the other side of the dirt."

Mikey chuckled. "Good point."

"Where's your piece?" Paul asked suspiciously.

"My piece?" Mikey opened his suit coat. "I don't carry a gun, Paulie. You know that."

"I know that you'd better get a Texas permit for that big .45 you keep in your car, before Cash Grier knows you don't have one," Paul said with a smirk.

Mikey sighed. "I was just thinking about that the other day. So. Where's Cotillo?"

There was a round of sighs. "Well, he was in Newark," McLeod said. "I checked with our office there, but he's out of sight now. Nobody knows where he went. We have people checking," he added. "One of our guys has a Confidential Informant who's close to him. We'll find him."

"It's his contract killer we need to find," Paul interrupted. "If he offs Mikey, we have no case, and Tony Garza will go down like a sack of beans for murder one."

"Speaking just for myself, I'd prefer to live a few more years," Mikey mused.

"Especially since you have a hot date tomorrow night, I hear?" Paul said with an unholy grin.

Mikey embarrassed himself by flushing. The tint was noticeable even with his olive complexion.

"Hot date?" Jon asked.

Mikey cleared his throat. "She's a nice girl. Works as a paralegal for the district attorney's office in Jacobsville."

"Bernie," Paul said.

There were curious looks.

"Bernadette," Mikey muttered. "It's short for Bernadette."

"Pretty name," Jon said.

"She's a sweetheart," Paul told them. "Takes a real load off the district attorney, and the other women who work in the office love her, especially my wife." He glanced at Mikey. "Which begs the question, why don't you ever bring her over to the house to eat? You know Mandy wouldn't mind cooking extra."

Mikey shifted his feet. "It's early days yet. I just asked her to a movie."

"A drive-in, at that," Paul mentioned with a grin.

"You've got a drive-in theater in Jacobsville?" Jon exclaimed. "They went out in the fifties, didn't they?"

"In the sixties, mostly, but we've got a local guy who's trying to bring them back. He even built a small café on the premises with restrooms and pizza. So far, he's a raging success."

"My dad talked about going to drive-ins," McLeod mused. "He said it was the only place he could kiss my mother without half-a-dozen people watching. Big family," he added.

"I can't place that accent, McLeod," Paul said. "You sound Southern, but it's not really a Texas accent."

"North Carolina," McLeod said. "My people go back five generations there in the mountains. The first were Highlanders from Argyll in Scotland."

"Mine came from Greece and Italy," Paul said. "Well, mine and Mikey's," he added with a glance at his cousin.

"Mine met the boat yours came over on," Jon said with a straight face. He was part Lakota Sioux.

There was a round of laughter.

"I have some Cherokee blood in my family," McLeod volunteered. "My great-grandmother was Bird Clan. But we're mostly Scots."

"Can you play the pipes?" Jon asked curiously.

McLeod shrugged. "Enough to make the neighbors uncomfortable, anyway."

"I had a set of trap drums," Paul recalled wistfully. "We had some really loud, obnoxious neighbors upstairs when I lived in Newark, long before I moved here." He didn't add that at the time he'd had a wife and child who were killed by operatives of a man he put in prison. "I was terrible at playing, but it sure shut the upstairs neighbor up."

"You bad boy," Mikey teased.

"A man has to have a few weapons," he said drolly.

"Back to Cotillo," McLeod said. "We have someone watching you from our service down in Jacobsville. You don't need to know who, but we're on the job. I offered, but they shut me up immediately."

"They did? Why?" Mikey asked.

"They say my restaurant allowance is abused."

They all looked at him. He was substantial, but streamlined just the same.

A corner of his mouth pulled down. "They say I eat

too much. Hey, I'm a big guy. It takes a lot of food. Besides, I hear some of the best food in Texas is at that café in Jacobsville."

"It is," Paul agreed. "Everybody eats there."

"So would I, if they'd let me. The boss said we needed somebody who liked salads and tofu."

Now they all really stared at him.

He glowered back. "She's a vegan," he said with spirit. "She gets upset if anybody mentions a steak."

"Tyranny," Paul teased.

"Anarchy," Mikey seconded.

"She should move back east, where she'll have plenty of company," Jon agreed. "I'm not giving up steaks, and I don't care if the SAC is a vegan or not."

"That's what I told her," McLeod replied. His black eyes sparkled. "Shut her up for ten minutes at least. But that's when she assigned me to him," he indicated Mikey. "She thinks it's a mean assignment." He chuckled. "I didn't try to change her mind."

"Good thing," Jon said. "I know your boss. She has a mean streak."

"She mustered out of the Army as a major," McLeod replied. "Honestly, I think she believes she's still in it."

"They make good agency heads," Jon said.

McLeod nodded. "But I'm still not eating tofu."

They all laughed.

"What about Cotillo?" Mikey asked after a minute.

"Why does that name sound so familiar?" Paul wondered. Then his face cleared. "Of course. It's that town across the border, you know, the one where an unnamed person that we all know offed the drug lord El Ladron and his buddies in a convoy." The unnamed person was Carson Farwalker, now a doctor in Jacobsville, who'd thrown several hand grenades under El Ladron's limo and was never charged.

"There's a cactus called ocotillo," Jon Blackhawk mused, "but that little town over the border was actually settled by an Italian family back in the late 1800s."

"Interesting," Mikey remarked. He sighed. "But the man is more worrisome than the town right now."

Faces became somber.

"When our CI finds out anything, I'll pass it on," McLeod said. "Meanwhile, he's got somebody watching Carrera down in the Bahamas." He indicated Jon.

Jon nodded. "Our field office has him under surveillance. And Carrera has some protection of his own, for himself and Tony Garza. You know, just because Carrera went straight doesn't mean he doesn't still have some pretty formidable ties to his old comrades. We understand he has two of them staying in the house with Della, his wife, and his two little boys."

"Two of the best," Mikey agreed. "I know them from the old days."

"Mikey," Paul said with real affection, "you never left the 'old days.'"

"Well," Mikey said with a sigh, "we are what we are, right, Paulie?"

"Right."

Bernie didn't really know how to dress for a drive-in movie, so she settled for pull-on navy blue slacks topped with a blue-checked button-up shirt and a long blue vest that came midthigh. She thought about putting her hair up in some complicated hairdo, but she left it long and soft around her shoulders. She'd toyed with having it cut. It was hard for a woman with disabilities to keep it clean and brushed, but she couldn't bear the thought of giving up the length. She had all sorts of pretty ribbons and ties to put her hair up with when she went to work. Even jeweled hairpins for special occasions. Not that there had been many of those, ever.

She glanced in the mirror and smiled at the excited, almost pretty girl in the mirror. She was going on a real date, with a man who made movie stars look ugly, and he liked her. She almost glowed.

There was a hard tap on the door. She got her coat and purse and opened the door. Mikey was wearing slacks and a designer shirt under a nice jacket. His shirt was blue, like hers.

He grinned at her. "Well, we seem to match."

"I noticed," she teased.

He gave her a thorough appraisal and felt his heart jump as he locked eyes with her. She was unique in his experience of women, which was extensive. She was so different from the aggressive, sensual women he'd liked in his youth. His tastes had changed over the years. Right now, Bernie was the sweetest thing in his life. He hoped he wasn't putting her in danger by being close to her.

"You ready to go?" he asked. "We must both be insane. A drive-in movie and it's just a week until Halloween! It's cold, even for south Texas!"

"I love drive-ins," she said softly. "And I don't care if it snows."

He chuckled. "Me, neither, kid." He took her hand in his and felt her catch her breath. He felt just the same. "Come on. I've got something a little less noticeable than the limo to go in."

A little less noticeable, she thought with surprise

when she saw what he was driving. It was a luxury convertible, very pretty and probably very fast.

"Oh, my," she said.

"It goes like a bomb," he said, as he helped her inside the late-model Mercedes convertible. It was a deep
blue color. The interior was leather, with wood trim on
the steering wheel and the dash. She sank into luxury
as she fastened her seat belt.

"Oh, my," she said again as he touched a control
and her seat heated up and began to massage her back.
"This is heavenly!" She closed her eyes and smiled.
"Just heavenly!"

He chuckled. "I'm glad you like it. I go first-class,
kid. Always have, even when I was young and full of
pepper." He didn't like remembering exactly how he'd
gone first-class. She made him feel guilty about the
things he'd done in his pursuit of wealth. She didn't
seem to covet wealth at all.

"I've never ridden in a car that had heated seats," she
said excitedly. "And even a massage! It's just amazing!"

He smiled. He hadn't considered how uptown the
car was to someone who probably rode around mostly
in cabs that barely had heaters and air-conditioning.
"Don't you drive?" he asked.

She felt the words all the way to her feet and averted
her eyes so that he couldn't see the sadness in them.
She couldn't have afforded a car. "I used to," she said
softly. "Not anymore."

"You should go back to it," he replied as he pulled the
car out into the street and accelerated. "I love to drive."

"This car must go very fast."

"It does. I'd demonstrate," he teased, "but you'd have
to come bail me out of jail."

She laughed, the old fear and guilt subsiding. "I would, you know," she said softly. "Even if I had to sell everything I own."

He flushed.

"I mean, I'd find someone who could…" she began, all flustered because of what she'd blurted out. She was horribly embarrassed.

His big hand reached out for her small one and tangled with it. "Stop that," he chided gently. "You shouldn't feel guilty for enjoying somebody's company. Especially not mine." His hand contracted around hers. "I'm used to women who want what I've got," he added coldly.

"What you've got?" His fingers tangling gently with hers had her confused and shaky inside.

"Money, kid," he replied. "I've got enough in foreign banks to see me well into old age, even if I spend myself blind."

"Oh." Her hand stiffened in his.

He glanced at her and chuckled. "Now you think I suspect that you're only going out with me because I'm rich. Not you," he added in a deep, husky tone. "You're not the sort of woman who prefers things to people. I knew that right off. Proud as Lucifer, when you fell in front of the car and I made sarcastic remarks about how you'd fallen." He sighed sadly. "Worst mistake of my life, thinking you were like that. Believe me, I felt about two inches high when Santi found that cane you used."

She bit her lower lip. "I'm clumsy, sometimes," she said. "I fall over nothing when I'm having flares. I wish I was healthy," she added miserably.

"My little grandmother would sit and cry sometimes when the pain got really bad," he recalled quietly. "I'd fill a hot water bottle for her and read her stories in Greek to take her mind off it."

"You can speak Greek?" she asked.

"Greek, Italian, a little Spanish," he replied.

"I learned to read Greek characters," she said. "They're the Coptic alphabet, like Russian."

"Nice," he said, glancing at her with a smile. "Yes, they are. Hard for some people to learn, too."

"I love languages. I really only speak English and Spanish."

"Spanish?"

"Well, we deal with a lot of bilingual people, but some of the older people who come from countries south of ours don't understand English as well as their children. I can translate for them."

"Brainy," he teased.

"Not really. I had to study hard to learn the language, just like I had to study hard to learn to be a paralegal. I went to night school at our local community college," she added.

"I imagine that was hard," he said. "Working and going to school at the same time."

"It was," she confessed. "I wanted to learn the job, but I missed class sometimes. There was a nice woman who was studying it at the same time—Olivia, who works in our office—and she took notes so that I could catch up on what I missed. The professor was very understanding."

"You're a sweet kid," Mikey said softly. "I can imagine that most people bend rules for you."

She laughed. "Thanks." She glanced at him as they drove a little out of town to the wooded area that housed the new drive-in. "Did you go to school? I mean, after high school?"

"I got a couple of years of college when I was in the Army," he said. "Never graduated. I was too flighty to buckle down and do the work."

"What did you study?"

He chuckled. "Criminal justice. It seemed like a good idea at the time. I mean, considering what I did for a living."

She just stared at him, curious.

He felt his cheeks heat. He glanced at her. She didn't understand. "Didn't Sari talk about me at work?" he said.

"Just that you and her husband are first cousins and that you're close," she replied, and her eyes were innocent.

She wasn't putting on an act. She really didn't know what he'd been, what he still was. He hesitated to tell her. He loved the way she looked at him as if he had some quality that she'd never found in anyone else. She looked at him with affection, with respect. He couldn't remember another woman who'd cared about the man instead of the bank account. It made him humble.

He drew in a breath. "Well, Paulie and I are close," he agreed. His hand tightened around hers. "I meant, didn't you know about the trouble Isabel and Merrie had three years ago, when they were being stalked by a cleaner?"

"Oh, that," she said, nodding. "There was a lot of gossip about it," she added. "I don't remember much of what I heard, just that a man who was big in organized crime back east called off the hit man. She painted him." She laughed. "They said he walked her down the aisle when she married Paul. I didn't know her then, except I knew the family and that they were well-to-do. I never moved in those circles. I'm just ordinary."

"Honey, ordinary is the last thing you are," he said

huskily as he pulled onto the dirt road that led to a drive-in with a huge white screen and a graveled lot with speakers on poles every few feet. "And we're here!"

He paid for their tickets and drove them through to a nice parking spot right in front of the screen. He looked at the ticket. "We've got a ten-minute wait," he said.

"What are we going to see?" she asked. "I didn't pay attention to the marquee."

He chuckled as he cut off the engine and turned to her. "You didn't notice?" he teased, black eyes sparkling as they met her pale ones.

"Not really," she confessed. "I was excited just to be going out with you." She flushed. "There are some very pretty single girls around Jacobsville, including Jessie, who works with us."

His fingers tangled softly with hers, caressing, arousing. "Jessie doesn't do a thing for me," he told her. "She's like the women I used to date back east. Brassy and out for everything they can get from a man."

"I guess so. We're not really like that here," she added. "Money is nice, but I have all I need. I'm not frivolous. My biggest expense is the drugstore. And the doctor," she said sadly.

"It doesn't matter," he said solemnly. "You're not of less value as a woman because you have a disability."

"Most local men thought I was," she replied. "I won't get better unless they come out with a miracle drug," she said. "There are shots I could take, but they're really expensive and there's no guarantee that they'd work. There's also infusion, where they shoot drugs into you with an IV and they last several weeks." She lowered her eyes to the big hand holding hers. It was strong and beautiful, as men's hands went. Long fingered, with perfectly manicured nails.

"I read about those shots," he replied. "Just before my grandmother died, I was researching new drugs that might help her. The pain got so damned bad that they had to give her opiates to cope with it." He made a face. "Then the government steps in and says that everybody's going to get addicted, so now you get an over-the-counter drug for pain even if you've got cancer," he added angrily. "Like that's going to help get illegal narcotics off the street! Hell, you can buy drugs, guns, anything you want in the back alley of any town in America, even small towns."

"You can?" she asked curiously.

"Of course you can. Even in prison."

"Wow."

He chuckled. "Kid, you really aren't worldly."

"I guess not," she said with a good-natured smile. "I don't have much of a social life. Well, I do have Twitter and Facebook, but I don't post very often. Mostly, I read what other people write. My goodness, I must be sheltered, because some of the things people post I wouldn't even tell to my best friend!"

"What sort of things?" he teased.

"I'm not saying," she replied.

He made a face. "That didn't hurt, that didn't hurt, that didn't hurt..." And he laughed, softly and with so much mischief that she burst out laughing, too.

He looked around. "Not so many people just yet. So." He caught a handful of her long, beautiful platinum hair and tugged her face under his. "Don't panic," he whispered as he bent his head. "This is just a test. I'm practicing mouth-to-mouth resuscitation, in case I ever have to save you...!"

Chapter 5

Bernie held her breath as she watched his firm, chiseled lips hover over hers. She could taste the coffee on his mouth, feel his breath as his face came closer, so that his dark eyes filled the world.

She clutched at his jacket, more overcome with emotion than she could have dreamed even a few weeks ago.

"I love your hair, Bernadette," he whispered as his hand contracted in it and his mouth slowly covered hers for the first time.

She gasped under the soft pressure, but she wasn't trying to get away. He gazed down at her. Her eyes were closed, her eyebrows drawn together. She looked as if she'd die if he didn't kiss her.

Which was exactly how he felt, himself. He settled his mouth over hers, gently because he could sense her attraction and her fear. It was hard to give control to another person. But it was a lesson she would have to learn. He was glad that she was learning it with him.

He guided her arms up around his neck as his lips became slowly more insistent, giving her time to absorb the newness of it, giving her time to let go of her restraint. It melted out of her as he drew her closer across the console, his lips opening now, pressing hers gently apart.

She heard his breath sigh out against her cheek, felt his arms enfolding her, protecting her. She moaned as the feeling became almost overpowering and her arms tightened around his neck.

"That's it, baby," he whispered. "Just like that. Don't hold back. I'll go slow, I promise."

And he did. He didn't force her or do anything to make her uncomfortable. His mouth slid finally against her cheek to rest at her ear. His heart was doing the hula in his chest. He could feel hers doing the same thing.

It was odd, to be chaste with her. Most women in his past would have been tearing his clothes off at this point, but Bernie was gentle and inexperienced. He could feel the need in her because he felt it, as well. It was new to want to protect and cherish someone. He felt as if he could fly.

"You taste like sugar candy," he whispered at her ear.

Her arms tightened and she laughed softly. She didn't know what to say.

His big hand smoothed the length of her hair. "I'm glad you left it down tonight," he murmured. "Just for me?"

"Just for you." Her voice sounded husky. She felt swollen all over. It was a delicious sensation, like going down on a roller coaster.

His face nuzzled hers. "I never expected something

like this," he said in a deep, lazy tone. "I was going to stay in this little town for a while and bide my time, maybe find a poker game to get into or something. And here's this beautiful little violet, right in my boarding-house."

"Me?" she stammered.

His hand slid under her hair. "You, Bernadette." His cheek slid against hers and his mouth covered hers again, but harder this time, hungrier.

She couldn't resist him. She didn't have the sophistication to even pretend that she didn't like what he was doing. Her fingers tangled in his thick, cool, wavy hair. She loved what he was doing to her. She couldn't hide it.

And he loved that about her. He loved that she felt the same attraction he did, and that she was innocent, untouched, vulnerable. She needed someone to take care of her. He needed someone to take care of. Since his grandmother's death, there had been nobody in his life to fill that need. Bernie's disability didn't put him off in the slightest. It made him feel protective.

Which made him slow down. He was taking things too far, too fast. He drew back very slowly, his dark eyes intent on her face, her eyes half-closed, her pretty mouth swollen, her body warm and soft in his arms. She radiated tenderness.

"It's been a long time since I felt like this," he whispered at her lips, brushing them with his own. "And even then, it wasn't so sweet."

She smiled against his mouth. "I've never felt anything like this," she confessed softly. "Not with anybody." She grimaced. "Not that there's ever been anybody, except a boy who kissed me at a party when I was sixteen." She sighed. "That was just before he said he liked me a lot but he didn't want to get involved with a crippled girl."

"You aren't crippled," he said shortly. "You have as brave a spirit as anybody I ever knew. You're strong and capable. You're a woman with a disability, not a disability that's female. If that makes sense."

"You mean, I have a disability but it doesn't define who I am," she translated.

He smiled. "Yeah. It's like that." He searched her pale green eyes. "I don't mind it. I told you about my grandmother, that she had it, too. Somebody who minds it isn't interested in you the right way. He's looking for somebody more…casual."

She knew what he meant. Her fingers went up to his face and traced it while she studied him with fascination. "I never knew anybody like you," she whispered.

"I never knew anybody like you," he replied, and he was serious. "I can't imagine how I missed seeing you when I was here before, three years ago."

"I heard about you back then. I was working for a firm of attorneys. But people just said you were helping your brother-in-law with some case," she added.

That might be a good thing. He wasn't sure how she'd feel if she knew the truth about him, about exactly why and how he'd helped the Grayling girls.

"You don't know much about me," he said after a minute.

"That's okay. You don't know much about me, either," she replied.

He grinned. "Don't tell me. You're a spy and you have a trench coat in your closet back in the boardinghouse."

"Don't you dare tell a soul," she chided. "They'd send people to sack me up and take me away."

"I'd never do that," he said softly, and he smiled. "Not in a million years."

In the back of his mind, he was hearing a song recorded by Meatloaf about doing anything for love. He sang softly, a little off-key.

She caught her breath. "It's one of my favorite songs," she confessed. "Did you see the video?"

"I did. I watch it on YouTube sometimes." He laughed. "It's one of my favorites, too. What other sort of music do you like?"

Just as she started to answer, there was a gentle rap on the window.

Startled, Mikey let go of Bernie and put her gently back into her own seat before he powered down the window.

Cash Grier was standing there with a very knowing smile on his face, in his uniform.

"I have not been speeding in your town, and I never even jaywalked," Mikey began. "Besides that, we are outside the city limits."

Cash chuckled. "That's not why I'm here."

Mikey just waited.

Cash grimaced. "We've had a development," he said. "Nothing major. But Paul wants to talk to you, at the house."

"We just got here," Mikey said, visibly disturbed. "Can't it wait?"

"Sorry. No, it can't. Paul said to bring Bernie with you," he added with a smile in her direction.

"Oh." Mikey brightened. He turned to her. "Okay with you?"

She grinned. "Okay with me."

"We'll catch the movie another time," Mikey promised. He turned back to Cash. "You headed that way, too?"

Cash nodded. "You'll have two other cars following behind you, as well."

"Following us?" Bernie asked, concerned.

Cash and Mikey exchanged a long look. Mikey shook his head, just a jerk, but Cash understood at once that he wasn't to tell Bernie anything. "It's something to do with a case Paul's working on," Cash told Bernie with an easy smile. "No worries."

"Okay," she said, and smiled shyly.

"We'll be right along." Mikey took the speaker off the window and put it on its stand, powering the window up afterward. "Sorry about this," he told Bernie.

"You're related to an FBI agent," she said. "And I don't mind. Really."

He caught her hand in his as he turned onto the road. "You're easy to be with," he said softly. "You don't complain, you don't fuss. Even when you probably should."

She laughed. "I love being with you. Anywhere at all."

"That's how I feel." He curled her fingers into his and drove the rest of the way to Paul's house in silence. He was worried, and couldn't let it show. It must be something big if Paulie wanted to interrupt a date. His cousin wasn't the sort to interfere unless it was warranted. Which led Mikey to worry about exactly what the new development was.

His first thought was that they'd found Tony in some sort of horrible condition. They knew that Cotillo had a contract out on him, and that he could probably figure out that Tony was in the Bahamas since he and Marcus Carrera were close. He hoped Tony was still alive, even though it put Mikey in more danger.

He glanced at Bernadette and felt his heart clench. He was already attached to her. He couldn't bear the thought of letting her get hurt because of him. And she still didn't know anything about him, really, or the danger he was in. He was putting her in danger. If someone came looking for him, they'd go after the weakest link. An hour in any restaurant or bar around, and they'd know that Mikey was dating this cute little paralegal who worked for the DA. Bernadette could be used against him. In fact, so could Mrs. Brown and her other residents. Mikey had a weakness for motherly women, and people knew about it.

"You're worried," she said softly from beside him.

His head turned. His shocked expression said it all.

"You hide things very well," she continued. "You really do have a poker face. But it's inside you. I can feel it."

He let out a long breath and his fingers contracted. "You see deep, just like Paulie's sister-in-law."

"Merrie was always like that, even in school."

"You've lived here a long time, haven't you?"

"Well, off and on, yes. I was born here, but when I was little, my parents moved to Floresville. My dad worked on a cattle ranch there as a foreman." Her face closed up. "Dad and I moved back here when I was about ten years old."

He was reading between the lines. Something had happened in Floresville that still caused her pain after all that time. He wondered what it was. But he wasn't going to ask. Not yet. They had time.

"I lived all my life in Newark," he said.

"Yes, you told me. You said you own a hotel in Las

Vegas," she added, fascinated. "It must be a lot of responsibility, taking care of something so big," she added.

He chuckled. "You have no idea. I didn't know what I was getting into. I had some spare cash and I thought it would be fun to own something big and elegant. It's not what it's cracked up to be. The labor problems alone are enough to send me to the nearest bar."

"I guess a lot of people work for you."

They did, but not in the hotel business. He employed a number of men who worked just a little outside the law on various projects for him. He wasn't about to go into that with her. He thought about the life he'd lived, the things he'd done to get rich. It had seemed so important at the time, as if nothing was more important than having things, having expensive things, having money. He'd come out of the armed forces with a lot of contacts and even more ideas, and he'd put them into practice in the years since then. Now, when he thought of Bernadette and what a straight arrow she was, he felt uncomfortable. What would she think of him when she knew what he was, what he'd been, what he'd done? Already, the thought of losing her trust was painful.

"You have to stop worrying about things you can't change," she said, reminding him of a conversation they'd had some time ago about that.

He chuckled. "That's the thing, kid. There's a lot of stuff I *can* change. I just don't know how to go about it without getting thrown in the slammer."

She laughed because she thought it was a joke.

He smiled. It wasn't a joke at all. He had men who could take on a contract killer with great success, but it would put him in bad stead with the FBI and the US Marshals Service, which was helping protect him. His hands were tied. He couldn't put Paulie on the firing line by acting on his own. Besides, if he helped put Cotillo away, it put him in a great bargaining position with Uncle Sam. He might need a favor one day. It was to his advantage not to use his usual methods of dealing with threats.

"If you get arrested, I can bake a nail file in a cake and come to see you," she said with a wicked little grin.

He sighed. "Honey, they don't have iron bars on the outside of cells anymore. They're all inside and all the doors lock along the way. You'd never get out that way."

She frowned. She'd never been in a real jail, but he seemed to know a lot about them. She reasoned that he'd probably been with his cousin to see somebody in jail on a case or something. It didn't worry her.

He glanced at her and smiled. She really didn't see the bad part of him. It was amazing—that she had such insight but didn't see wickedness in his actions. Probably she didn't look for it. Apparently, her own life had been a sheltered one.

The big house at Graylings was ablaze with lights when Mikey pulled up into the driveway. There were two black sedans and a black SUV. The sedans had government license plates.

"Feds," Mikey said with a sigh as he helped Bernie out of the car.

She glanced at the backs of the cars parked side by side. She smiled. "Government plates. I guess they think people won't know as long as they don't have flashing lights on top," she teased.

He chuckled. "Good one." He caught her hand in his as they walked up to the front door. He drew in a breath. "Listen, kid," he said as they reached it, "there are things going on that I can't tell you about."

"I don't mind," she said, and looked up at him with perfect trust. In fact, she was in so far over her head that she wouldn't have minded if he robbed banks for a living.

He smiled slowly. "You're almost too good to be true," he chuckled. "Don't you have any wicked, terrible things in your past?"

The door opened, but not before he saw the expression that washed across her face, quickly hidden when Sari Fiore opened the door and grinned at them, holding hands.

"Sorry to have to break up your date," she told Bernie, "but we didn't have a choice. You can keep me company while the men talk. Mandy's gone to bed with a headache, so I'm alone. Well, almost alone," she amended when three men walked into the hall.

"Hey, Mikey," Paul Fiore greeted his cousin.

"Hey, Paulie."

"You know McLeod already," he said to Mikey, indicating a big, dark man, "and this is Senior FBI Agent Jarrod Murdock from our San Antonio office."

"I heard about you," Mikey mused as he looked at tall, blond Murdock, an imposing man who never seemed to smile. "Didn't they threaten to dress up like a ninja and throw you in the back of a pickup if you made coffee again...?" he teased.

Murdock made a face. "Not my fault I can't make good coffee," he scoffed. "I wasn't raised to be a woman."

The two women present gave him a wide-eyed, shocked look.

He cleared his throat. "Well, men aren't built right to

make coffee," he amended. "Our hands are too big." He added that last bit tongue in cheek. And he wasn't smiling, but his pale blue eyes were twinkling just the same.

"That's the only comment that saved you from a picket line outside your office," Sari said in a mock threatening tone.

"God forbid!" Murdock said. "They'd fire me for sure."

"Not really," Paul commented. "You're too good a shot. You and Rick Marquez's wife hold the record for the most perfect scores in the city in a single year."

"She missed one shot last month," Murdock replied. He grinned. "Morning sickness. So I hold the record right now."

"She's pregnant?" Sari asked. "Oh, that's so nice! I hope it's a boy this time."

"They already have two girls," Bernie told Mikey with a smile.

"I like little girls," Mikey said. "Little boys, too. Kids are sweet."

"Not all of them," Agent McLeod said coldly with glittering silver eyes.

"Oh, that's right," Paul commented. "That family you were looking after had a kid who stayed in juvie hall most of his life. What was that he painted your car with?"

McLeod eyes narrowed. "Skull and crossbones."

"And you couldn't touch him, because he was in protective custody."

"Oh, I wouldn't say that," McLeod replied. "I had a long talk with his probation officer. He's getting visits at school, at home, at his part-time job…"

"You vicious man," Sari chuckled.

"Maybe the skull and crossbones was more accurate than we know," Murdock commented.

"Watch it," McLeod said, "or I'll buy myself a ninja suit and a pickup truck."

They all burst out laughing.

"Well, come on into the study," Paul said to the men. He glanced at Sari.

"Bernie and I will be in the kitchen, discussing world politics," Sari replied.

Bernie looked up at Mikey with soft, pretty green eyes. "See you later."

He smiled slowly. "You will." He brought her fingers to his mouth and brushed them with it before he followed the men into the study.

Bernie had to be prompted to follow Sari into the kitchen. She was spellbound.

"If anybody had told me that Mikey would fall all over himself for a small-town Texas girl, I'd have fainted," Sari teased. "Honestly, you're all he talks about when he and Paul get together!"

Bernie flushed. "He's all I talk about at the boardinghouse. I've never met anybody like him. He's so… sophisticated and charming and sweet."

"Sweet?" Sari's eyes were popping.

Bernie laughed. "Well, he is."

"I suppose people bring out different qualities in other people," Sari said philosophically as she made coffee. "I owe Mikey a lot. So does my sister. He helped keep us alive."

"I heard that you were threatened, because of your father," Bernie said quietly. "Not the particulars, of course, just that Mikey helped your husband with the investigation."

"Mikey put us in touch with a gentleman who saved Merrie's life," Sari said, without going into any detail. "She was almost killed."

"I did hear about that. Some crazy man ran into her with a pickup truck, and then died in jail."

Sari nodded. She waited until the coffee perked and poured two cups of it. She put them on the table. She knew from the office that Bernie took hers black, just as Sari did.

Sari sat down across from her. "We lived through hard times," she recalled. "Our father was a madman. There were times when I thought he was going to kill us himself."

Bernie stared into her own coffee. "My grandfather had an unpredictable temper," she said. "You never knew which way he was going to jump. One time he'd laugh at something you said, and the next… Well, Mama and I had to be very careful what we said to him. So did my father."

"Your grandparents lived in Floresville, didn't they?" Sari asked gently.

Bernie's face clenched. She met the other woman's concerned blue eyes. "You know, don't you?" she asked.

Sari nodded. "From a former sheriff who moved here and had dealings with our office. But you know I don't gossip."

Bernie smiled. "Yes, I do." She put both hands around the coffee cup, feeling its warmth. "My grandfather wasn't a bad man. He just had an uncontrollable temper. But he could be dangerous. And he was, one time too many." She grimaced. "We lived out of town on a ranch, but gossip travels among country folk. After it happened, Dad lost his job and wasn't given references, so we came back to Jacobsville. I was only ten. Dad and I were targeted once by one of the victim's relatives."

"I've been through the wars myself, you know. But I don't blame people for what their relatives do," she added firmly.

"Neither do I. But there was some gossip even here. Fortunately, there wasn't so much that Dad couldn't find work. He went to Duke Wright and got a job. He never got like Granddaddy. I used to think if only somebody had forced my grandfather to see a doctor and get on medication. If only we'd realized that he had mental health issues," she said huskily.

"*If.* There's a horrible word. *If only.*"

"Yes." Bernie nodded. She looked up. "You won't tell Mikey? I mean, I'll tell him eventually, but it's early days yet and—"

"Mikey has secrets, too," Sari interrupted. "He won't hold anything against you. He's more worried about what you'll think of him. He's…had some problems in his past."

Bernie cocked her head. "Can you tell me about them?"

"I think he should tell you," Sari replied. "I don't like to carry tales. He's not a bad man," she added firmly. "Everybody has shameful secrets. Some get told, some never do, some we carry inside us forever like festering wounds."

Bernie nodded. "That's like mine. Festering wounds. They blamed all of us, you see, not just my dad. They blamed Mama and me, as well."

"Bernie, you were just a kid. How could anyone have blamed you?"

"They said Mama made him mad in the first place," she explained. She closed her eyes. "I was just ten years old, I didn't have anything to do with it. Neither did Dad. But people died, and I live with the guilt."

"You shouldn't have to," Sari said curtly. "There was no possible way you could have stopped it."

"Losing my grandmother and my mother was the worst of it, especially for Dad," Bernie confessed softly.

She put a hand over Bernie's. "You can't live in the past. I'm having a hard time with that myself. My father killed a woman. He more than likely killed my own mother. I have to live with that, and so does Merrie. We have our own guilt, although I don't know what we could have done to stop it. We were terrified of our father, and he was so rich that nobody around here would go against him. He made threats and people did what he wanted them to." She sighed. "It was like a nightmare, especially when he was arrested. He tried to make me marry a foreign prince so that he'd have money for his defense attorney," she recalled bitterly. "He came at me with the belt and I screamed for help. He died with the belt in his hand. I thought I'd killed him."

"You'd never hurt a fly," Bernie returned gently. "Neither would Merrie. Your father was an evil man. That doesn't mean you'd ever be like him. You couldn't be."

Sari smiled. "Thanks. I mean it. Thanks very much."

"I guess we're all products of our childhoods," she commented. She searched Sari's blue eyes in their frame of red-gold hair. "What was Mikey's like, do you know? He said he grew up in Newark, and his grandmother raised him and your husband."

Sari smiled. "She did. She was Greek, very small and very loving, even though she was strict with them."

"What about their parents?"

"The less said the better," Sari said coolly. "I'm frankly amazed that they both turned out as well as they did."

Bernie sighed. "I know how that feels, except it was my grandfather, not my parents."

Sari nodded. She smiled. "I hope you're prepared for Monday. When Jessie finds out about the hot date, she's going to be a handful. Glory and I will run interference for you. And it isn't as if Mikey even likes her."

Bernie sighed. "That's a good thing. She's really beautiful."

"She is. But as our police chief likes to say, so are some snakes."

They both laughed.

In the office, things were less amusing. One of Cotillo's henchmen had actually managed to get inside Marcus Carrera's Bow Tie Casino in the Bahamas while Tony Garza was in his private study there. Only quick thinking by Carrera's bodyguard, Mr. Smith, who sensed something out of the ordinary, had saved the day. The henchman was arrested and held for trial.

"They found the henchman dead in his cell the next day, of course," Paul told his cousin.

"Of course." Mikey stuck his hands in his pockets. "It's a good bet that Cotillo knows where I am, as well. I've got no place else to go in the world where I'd have protection like this," he added.

"True enough," McLeod said. His gray eyes narrowed. "Once you testify, we have plans for you."

"They'd better be plans for two people, because I'm not leaving here without Bernadette."

The words came as a pleasant shock to his cousin, who'd only known Mikey to get serious about a woman once in his life, and that had ended badly.

McLeod chuckled. "We can arrange that."

"Okay, then."

"But we're going to have to up the protection," Paul said. "Eb Scott wanted to lend us the Avengers," he added, referring to Rogers and Barton, two of Scott's top men, "but they're on a top-secret mission overseas. He sent us Chet Billings instead. And we've got Agent Murdock here assigned to you as well."

"So long as he doesn't try to make coffee for me, we're square," Mikey said with a glance at the tall FBI agent.

Murdock just laughed.

"What about Carrera?" Mikey asked. "Is his family going to be under threat, as well?"

"He hired on some old friends," Paul said. "Several old friends, from back home."

Mikey knew what he meant, without explanation. "If I were Cotillo, I'd fold my tent and go back to Jersey."

"Not a chance," Paul said quietly. "He thinks he has what it takes to put Tony Garza down and take over his whole operation."

"Sounds to me like a man with a huge narcissistic complex," Murdock murmured.

"Or a man on a raging drug high," McLeod inserted.

"Maybe both," Paul replied. "People are getting involved in this who don't even have ties to Tony's business. They just don't like the idea of an untried, arrogant newcomer trucking into their territory and trying to set everybody aside who's been in the business for generations."

"I know several low-level bosses who hate Cotillo's

guts and would love to move on him, There's even a rumor that one of the bigger New York families wants him out," Mikey said. "But Tony's the only one with the power to put him away. If Cotillo hadn't tried to frame him on that murder one charge, Cotillo would be running south as fast as his fat little legs would carry him."

"We've got the video you made," Paul told Mikey. "It's even got the time stamp."

"Sure," Mikey replied with a wry smile. "But the defense could swear that it was photoshopped, that I lied to save my friend."

"Not if you testify," McLeod replied. "You're the best insurance we've got that Cotillo can't bring his murderous operation into Jersey. Listen, nobody thinks you and Tony sing with the angels, okay?" he added. "But there are levels of criminals. Cotillo is a cutthroat with no conscience, who's only in it for the money. He'll kill anybody who gets in his way. Tony has more class than that. And you," he said to Mikey, "never hurt a person unless they hurt somebody you cared about."

Mikey flushed. "Cut it out," he muttered. "You'll ruin my image."

Paul chuckled. "He's right, though," he told his cousin. "Merrie said that after she'd painted you."

"Hell of a painting," Mikey replied. "And she didn't even know me."

"What painting?" McLeod asked.

"Wait a sec." Paul pulled out his cell phone and turned to the photo app. He thumbed through it and showed it to McLeod. It was the painting Merrie had done of Mikey, which Paul had photographed before he sent it to his cousin.

"Damn," McLeod said, looking from the portrait to Mikey. "And she didn't know what you did for a living?"

Mikey shook his head. "She painted that from some snapshots Paul had. Well, from a couple of digital images, from his cell phone, like that one. I was amazed. She did Tony, too. Some artist!"

"Some artist, indeed." McLeod agreed.

"Back to the problem at hand," Paul said when he put down the phone. "We need to double security. And you need to find another way to hang out with Bernie. A safer way than a drive-in theater in the country."

Mikey muttered under his breath. "What, like having tea in her bedroom in the boardinghouse? That'll help her rep."

"You can bring her here," Paul said. "We have the best security in town."

"You mean it?" Mikey asked.

"You bet," Paul told him. "You can watch movies together in the sunroom." He pursed his lips. "Where Cash Grier isn't likely to tap on the window."

"Which brings to mind a question," Mikey said. "Why was Grier looking for me at a movie theater out of town? Not his jurisdiction, is it?"

Chapter 6

"Cash was home and Sheriff Carson wasn't answering his phone," Paul said, "to make a long story short. Our police chief volunteered. His kids were protesting bedtime, so he pretty much walked off and left Tippy and Rory with it," he added, naming Cash's wife and young brother-in-law.

"In which case, he might want to spend the night at a friend's house," Mikey chuckled, "if what I've heard about his missus is true. Did she really use an iron skillet on that guy who came in her back door with a .45?"

"Absolutely she did," Paul confirmed. "She's still a celebrity for that, not to mention being a former model and movie star."

"And gorgeous," Agent Murdock said with a sigh. "Even two kids haven't changed that."

Paul chuckled. "Tell me about it. Not that I did bad

myself in the wife department. My Sari would give all the movie stars a run for their money."

"She's a doll," Mikey agreed. He sighed. "Well, what are you guys doing about Cotillo while he's plotting to have me and Tony killed?"

"We think he has somebody locally," Paul said, suddenly somber. "We don't know who. There are several people who just started working in Jacobsville recently, some of them with pronounced northern accents, like mine and yours."

Mikey grimaced. "I think I met one of them. She works with Isabel in the DA's office. A woman named Jessie." He shook his head. "Apparently she likes rich men and she's predatory. She actually got my cell phone number and called to ask me out."

"I'll bet that went over well," Paul replied tongue in cheek, because he knew his cousin inside out. Mikey didn't like aggressive women.

"It didn't go over at all," Mikey replied. "I told her the number was private and I wasn't interested. Then I hung up and blocked her number."

"I never attract women who want to date me." Murdock sighed. "I guess you have to be handsome."

"There's nothing wrong with you, Murdock, except the way you make coffee," Paul said. "And I did save you from that visiting attorney who mentioned how the ficus plant needed fertilizer."

"Yes, he was looking right at me when he said it," Murdock said and sighed. "Not my fault. Nobody else in the office will even try it."

"I would, but I'm never at my desk long enough."

"I live on the damned telephone," Murdock said heavily. "I get picked every time the boss needs information that he has to get from people out of town. I spend most of the day tracking down contacts."

"You should apply for the SWAT team," Paul suggested. "You'd do well."

"I'd get somebody killed is what I'd do," Murdock returned. "I don't think fast enough for a job like that. I guess, all in all, information gathering is important work and I'm pretty good at finding people."

"He used to be a skip tracer for a detective in Houston," Paul told Mikey. "He was good."

"I still am," Murdock said with a grin. "I tracked down an escaped murderer just a few days ago by calling his mother and telling her I was an old Army buddy. She told me exactly where he was. Sweet lady. I felt really guilty."

"People break the law, they do time," Paul said. "That's the rules."

"Rules are for lesser mortals," Mikey said with a hollow laugh. "I never followed any in my life."

"Until now," Paul said, with twinkling black eyes. "Rules are what's keeping you alive."

"Well, that and Bernie, I guess," Mikey said, and a faint ruddy color ran along his high cheekbones. "We went to the drive-in earlier. We were having a great time until Grier tapped on the window."

"What movie did you see?" Agent Murdock asked.

Mikey cleared his throat. "It was some sort of action movie, I think. The title escapes me."

"I'll bet it does," Paul said under his breath. "Isabel told me that Bernie poured coffee over ice when she went to get a cup, and then she toppled a bookcase, all in the same day. And she's not clumsy."

Mikey's eyes twinkled. "Well, well."

"She's a sweet woman," Paul said. "Sari's protective of her. That woman, Jessie, who works in the office, gives her a hard time."

"DA needs to take care of business and fire her," Mikey muttered.

"He's given her fair warning that she'll lose her job if she causes any more trouble," Paul replied. He put his hands in his pockets. "Back to the matter at hand, though. I phoned Marcus Carrera and asked him how things were going. He says Tony's getting restless. He doesn't like hiding from some cheap hood who wants to take over his territory. He's fuming that he didn't anticipate trouble from that quarter when the guy first moved in with his goons."

"If he comes back, he could die over here," Mikey said. "He knows that Cotillo will have people watching and waiting."

Paul nodded. "That's what I told Carrera. He said he'll talk some sense into Tony and make sure he stays put, no matter what it takes. He's got some old friends from his gangster days helping out. And he hired a group of mercs, one of whom used to live here—that Drake guy whose sister married the veterinarian, Bentley Rydel. Kell Drake, that was his name."

"That's some formidable backup," Mikey conceded. "I hope he won't have to stay there too long. But what about Cotillo?"

"We've got plans for him," Paul said. "I have friends in Jersey, too. They're doing some scouting for me. The agency turned one of our best field agents onto the case, and he's digging into Cotillo's background. With any luck, he'll find something we can use for leverage while we wait for Tony's trial to come up."

"Tony fled the country," Mikey said sadly. "That's going to go against him. Flight from prosecution."

"He didn't fly, he was flown—by us," Paul said with a grin. "So that's not a charge he'll be facing."

Mikey sighed. "His past isn't lily-white. Neither is mine. So far, Cotillo hasn't ever been charged with a crime, for all we know."

"That's right," Paul returned. "For all we know. That's why we're digging. There's a federal prosecutor also on the case, and using his own investigators to look at Cotillo and his associates. Eventually, somebody's going to talk."

"So long as they don't talk about me and Tony and what's in our pasts," Mikey said with a resigned breath. "I've been a bad man, Paulie. I hope it doesn't come back to bite me."

"Not that bad, and you don't have a single conviction," Paul told him.

"No," Mikey conceded with a sad smile. "But that doesn't mean I haven't deserved one."

Paul put a lean hand on Mikey's broad shoulder. "We go one day at a time and leave tomorrow to itself. Right?"

Mikey smiled. "Okay. Right. Well," he added, "I'd better take Bernie home. So much for the movies."

"We have movies on DVD and pay-per-view," Paul reminded him with a grin. "You can watch them together right here, where it's safe. And the door has a lock," he added with amused eyes when Mikey blushed.

Mikey told Bernie about it when he took her back to the boardinghouse, reluctantly. "I'm sorry we had to break it up tonight," he said gently. "But Paulie says we can watch pay-per-view at his place, whenever we want."

"I'd like that," she whispered as he drew her close.

"Me, too, baby." He kissed her hungrily and then put her gently away. "I'm going back over to the house for a while. But we'll make a new movie date later, okay?"

She beamed. "Okay!"

Later, over supper at the house, Mikey drank a second cup of black coffee. He was unusually quiet.

"What's biting you?" Paul asked.

He shrugged. "I was thinking about Cotillo and his stooges. You know, I never stopped having Santi drive me in the limo. I've been pretty visible here…"

"Disguises don't work with people like Cotillo," Paul replied. "Besides, this is one of the safest places in the world when somebody's hunting you. It saved Sari and Merrie."

"It did," Sari added to the conversation. "It will save you, too, and Tony, I hope. Merrie's very fond of him, you know."

Mikey smiled. "Baby Doll's fond of everybody. It's just the way she is."

"That's true."

"Why are you so morose?" Paul asked his cousin.

"I worry about taking Bernie out now that I know I'm being watched by Cotillo's hoods," he said, pushing his coffee cup around.

"We told you that you could bring her over here any time you like," Sari reminded him with a smile. "She's so sweet. I love working with her."

Mikey seemed to perk up a little. "You really meant that? You wouldn't mind?"

"Not at all," Sari replied. "There are plenty of places to walk within sight of the house. We have calves she can pet and cats in the barn, and there's also the sunroom." She cleared her throat and didn't dare look at Paul, because some momentous things had happened there before the two of them married.

Mikey chuckled. "Okay, then," he said. "Thanks."

"No problem," Paul told him, his dark eyes twinkling. "So. How about Saturday?"

"Saturday sounds fine," Mikey replied. "You guys are terrific."

"Thanks," Sari said.

"You're terrific, too, Mandy," Mikey added when the housekeeper came from the kitchen with a cake pan.

Mandy grinned. "Nice of you to say that, and I baked you a chocolate cake, too!"

Mikey hesitated, looked guilty. His face drew up. He didn't want to tell her.

"Mandy, he won't say, but he gets terrible migraine headaches," Paul told her gently. "Chocolate is one of his triggers."

"Oh, my goodness, I'm so sorry!" Mandy began.

"You're a sweetheart, and it's the thought that counts," Mikey told her with a smile. "I love chocolate. I just can't eat it."

"Well, I'll make you a nice vanilla pound cake tomorrow. How's that?" she teased.

"That, I'll eat, and thank you."

"It's no trouble at all. You helped keep my girls safe. I'll never forget you for it, not as long as I live."

Mikey flushed a little. "They're sweet girls, both of them." He glanced at Sari. "Sweet women," he amended.

Sari waved away the apology. "I don't get offended

at every single word people come up with. Besides," she added with twinkling blue eyes, "I got called a whole new word in court by a man I was prosecuting for assault. The judge turned him every which way but loose."

Mikey chuckled. "Good for the judge."

"She's a great judge," Paul agreed. "I had to get a search warrant from her several years ago. We had a long talk about Sari's mother. The judge was friends with her."

"My mother was sweet, kind of like Bernie," Sari said. "She loved to plant flowers and grow things."

"My grandmother did, too," Paul said.

"Yeah, she always had an herb garden, and she grew tomatoes out in the backyard," Mikey added. "It was hard, losing her. She was the only real family Paulie and I ever had. Our parents weren't around much."

"Which was just as well," Paul said grimly.

Mikey nodded.

"Well, I've got some research to do," Sari said, rising. She bent to kiss Paul. "Don't eat my part of that cake," she warned. "I'll be back for it later."

"Would I do that?" Paul said with mock defensiveness.

"Of course you would," she replied. She chuckled as she left the room.

"Damn, you got lucky," Mikey said after she'd gone.

"I did. Maybe you got lucky, too," Paul said. "Everybody who knows Bernie loves her." He grimaced. "Shame what happened to her," he added.

"Yeah, the arthritis is pretty bad," Mikey agreed.

Paul frowned and had started to speak when his phone went off. He looked at the number and groaned, but he answered it. "Fiore," he said.

He listened, glanced at Mikey, grimaced again. "I

see. Yeah, I'll make sure he knows. We'll double up down here. No worries. I wouldn't want to risk Carrera getting mad at me, either, but these guys aren't playing with a full deck, if you know what I mean. Sure. Okay. Thanks."

"Trouble?" Mikey asked.

Paul nodded. "Somebody made an attempt on Tony, a new one. He's in custody and they're hoping he'll sing like a bird when they extradite him back here."

"A break, maybe."

"Maybe. If they don't suicide him, like they did the other one."

"Yeah." Mikey drew in a breath. "You know, my life was going along so well up until now. I've got the hotel. I've got all the money I'll ever need. I was really thinking about a home and a family. I guess I lost sight of what I've been, what I've done." He looked up at Paul. "Maybe the universe is set up so that you get back what you give out, every time, in double measure. I don't mind for me. I just don't want to put her in the crosshairs. She's the sweetest woman I've ever met."

Paul didn't need prompting to know that his cousin was talking about Bernadette. There was a look on Mikey's face that his cousin hadn't seen in many years. "We've got all our bases covered," he told Mikey. "You have to remember, outsiders stand out here. There's already gossip about that woman Jessie in Isabel's office, and even Barbara's new cook at the café. Outsiders draw attention."

"Did you check out Jessie and the cook?" Mikey asked.

Paul gave him a sardonic glance. "What do you think?"

"Sorry."

"No worries. But we dug pretty deep. I think we'd have found anything obvious, like an arrest record. Well, unless the guy's working for one of the letter agencies," he added, referring to the federal intelligence and justice community.

"True."

"You going to bring Bernie over Saturday?" Paul asked.

Mikey chuckled. "What do you think?" he said, throwing his cousin's own words back at him, and they both laughed.

Bernie couldn't sleep. It had been raining all day and the pain was pretty bad. She had pain relievers, massive doses of ibuprofen for when all else failed, but she didn't like it. The medicine messed her stomach up, even when she took it with food. Besides that, there was a limited amount of time that she could take it. It was so powerful that it could cause major problems with the liver and kidneys if people used it for a long period of time without a break. She was afraid of that.

But this was one time when she had to have some relief. She could barely hold back the tears.

She got out of bed painfully and pulled on her white chenille robe. She was going to have to go and get a bottle of water out of the fridge. Mrs. Brown, bless her heart, kept it for her tenants, who were always welcome to anything to drink or any bedtime snacks they could find in her spotless kitchen.

Bernie walked very slowly into the kitchen and almost collided with Mikey, in burgundy silk pajama bottoms with a matching robe. His broad, hair-roughened chest was bare, with the robe open. He looked handsome and sensuous. Bernie's heart jumped wildly at just the sight of him.

Mikey smiled. He could see all that in her face. She was totally without artifice, he thought. An honest woman, who never hid what she felt.

"You look pretty with your hair down, honey," he said gently.

She did. Her long platinum hair waved around her shoulders and down almost to her waist in back. With her cheeks faintly flushed and her pale green eyes twinkling despite the pain, she was a dish.

She laughed self-consciously. "I was just thinking how gorgeous *you* look," she confided with a bigger flush.

"What do you need?" he asked. He was holding a paper plate with crackers and sliced cheese on it, along with some slices of fresh pear.

"Just a bottle of water from the fridge and something to eat. I have to take one of the big pills. Pain's pretty bad," she said reluctantly.

"Here. Sit down. I'll get you some cheese and crackers."

"I can do that…"

"Don't fuss, honey," he said gently. He pulled out a chair and waited until she sat down. Then he fetched the water and sliced a little more cheese and put some more crackers on his paper plate. He sat down, too.

"The pears are nice," he said.

"I like fresh fruit," she said shyly.

They munched cheese in a pleasant silence. She washed it all down with her bottle of water, wincing every time she shifted in the chair.

"I'm sorry you had to have a disease that makes you hurt all the time," he told her quietly.

"Life happens," she said. "I learned to live with it a long time ago."

He frowned. "You aren't that old."

"I'm twenty-four," she reminded him. "But I've had it since I was about nine."

"Nine years old!" he exclaimed.

"Some children are born with it," she replied. "Arthritis isn't just a disease of old people. There's a little boy, five, who goes to the same rheumatologist I do. He's got osteoarthritis and he has to take doses of ibuprofen just like I do."

Mikey winced. "What a hell of a life."

She nodded. "At least I've had it long enough to know how to cope with bad days and flares. It's much harder for a child."

"I can only imagine."

"Why are you up so late?" she wondered.

He moved crackers around on the plate, next to his opened soft drink. "You mentioned that I was worried about putting people in danger by living here," he said, recalling her uncanny perception.

She nodded. "You're in some kind of trouble, aren't you, and your cousin's trying to help."

"That's about the size of it." He leaned back with his soft drink in his hand. He looked gorgeous with his black, wavy hair tousled and his robe open.

He chuckled at her expression. "Your eyes tell me everything you're thinking, Bernie," he said softly. "You can't imagine how flattered I am by it."

"Really?" she asked, surprised.

He stared at her quietly. "I'm a bad man," he said after a minute, and he scowled. "Getting mixed up with me is unwise."

She just looked at him and sighed. "I never had much sense."

It took a minute for that to register. He burst out laughing. "Oh. Is that it?"

She grinned. "That's it."

"Then, what the hell. I've got all sorts of people looking out for me. That means they'll be looking out for you and everybody in the boardinghouse, too."

"Okay," she said, smiling.

He cocked his head. "Do you like chocolate cake?" he asked suddenly.

Her eyebrows arched. "Well, yes. It's my favorite."

"Mandy made me one and I couldn't eat it," he said with a grimace. "I get migraine headaches, real bad ones. Chocolate's a trigger."

"My dad used to get them," she replied. She frowned. "Isn't anything aged a trigger? I mean, like cheese?"

He looked at her and then at the plate of cheese and let out a breath. "Well, damn. I never thought about it. Every time I eat cheese I get a headache, and I never connected it!"

"Dad's neurologist said everybody's got more than one trigger, but sometimes they don't recognize them. He couldn't drink red wine or eat any dark fruit or cheese. And he loved cheese."

"How about chocolate?"

She laughed. "He never liked sweets, so it wasn't a problem."

"Do you get headaches?"

She shook her head. "I had one bad one when I was about thirteen. Never since."

"Lucky you," he told her.

"I guess so."

"Paulie says I can bring you over to the house to visit on Saturday, if you want."

Her heart skipped and ran away. "He did? Really?"

"So did Sari. There are kittens in the barn and horses to pet. I think there's a dog somewhere, too."

"Ooh, temptation," she cooed, and grinned at him.

He laughed. "I thought the kittens might do it."

She cocked her head and her eyes adored him. "The kittens would be a bonus. Spending time with you is the real draw."

He caught his breath. Amazing, the effect she had on him. He felt as if he could walk on air.

"It's like that with me, too, kid," he said softly. "I like being with you."

She felt exhilaration flow through her. "The cane doesn't put you off?"

He shrugged. "I'll get one, too. We'll look like a matched set."

Tears stung her eyes. She'd never dreamed that a man, especially a gorgeous, worldly man like this, would ever find her attractive and not be put off by her condition.

"Aw, now, don't do that," he said softly. He got up, lifted her into his arms and sat back down with her across his lap. "Don't cry. Everything's going to be all right. Honest."

She put her arms around his neck and snuggled close. "You think so?" she asked tearfully.

"Yes, I do." He rubbed her back, feeling protective.

The sound of a door opening broke the spell. But he wouldn't let Bernie up even when Mrs. Brown came into the kitchen.

"Oh, dear," she said, taking in Bernie's tears and Mikey comforting her. "Pain got you up, didn't it?"

"Yes. I came to get a bottle of water so I could take one of those horrible pills, but I have to eat something first. I hope you don't mind…"

"Bosh," Mrs. Brown said. "That's why I keep snacky foods and soft drinks in the fridge."

"The cheese is really good," Mikey said.

"It's hoop cheese," Mrs. Brown told him with a grin. "I get them to order me a wheel of it at the grocery store and I slice it and bag it up. I like it, too. I got peckish so I thought I'd get myself a snack. Is it bad, Bernie?" she added.

Bernie nodded. "I'm sorry if I woke you."

"I don't sleep much," Mrs. Brown said quietly. "You didn't bother me at all."

Bernie got off Mikey's lap reluctantly. "Thanks for the comfort," she said, wiping her eyes. "I don't feel sorry for myself, but the pain is pretty bad."

"Go to bed, honey. Don't forget your water," he told her. "Saturday, if you're better, we'll go see the kittens in Paulie's barn. Okay?"

Bernie's eyes lit up. "Okay."

"Want me to carry you down the hall?" he offered.

"Thanks," she said, a little self-conscious at Mrs. Brown's amused expression. "But I'm good. I hold on to the wall when I get wobbly. Good night," she added to both of them.

"Try to sleep, sweetheart," Mrs. Brown said. "If you need me, you call, okay?"

"I will. Thanks." She glanced at Mikey, flushed, smiled and went out the door.

"She's got grit," Mikey told the landlady.

"Yes, she really has," Mrs. Brown replied. "We all

try to look out for her, as much as she'll let us. She's very independent."

"I noticed," he chuckled.

"You're eating cheese," she said worriedly. "Didn't you tell us that you got migraine headaches?"

"Well, yes…"

"Cheese is a trigger," she said. "Like red wine and chocolate."

He made a face. "I can't eat chocolate at all, but I never thought of cheese bringing on a headache." He laughed. "You know, I used to get headaches all the time and never knew why. It was always after I'd been out with a colleague of mine. He loved cheese, so he always had a platter of it with his dinner, wherever we ate. I nibbled on it and then almost died in the night when the pain came."

"Do you get the aura?" Mrs. Brown asked.

He grimaced. "Yeah. Flashy lights or blind in one eye until the pain hits."

"Do you have something to take for it?" she persisted.

"Just over-the-counter stuff."

"You should see a doctor and get something stronger," she told him. "They even have a drug that can prevent them, if you don't have drug allergies."

"They do?" he asked, and was really interested.

"They do." She laughed. "It's why I don't have them much anymore," she confessed. "Cheese is one of my biggest triggers. But I haven't had a migraine since back in the winter," she added.

"Maybe I should do that," he said. "They get worse as I get older."

"You're not old, Mr. Fiore," she teased.

He shrugged. "Thirty-seven," he confessed. "Really too old for Bernie…"

"Nonsense. I was fifteen years younger than my late husband, and we had a wonderful life together."

His eyebrows arched. "Did people talk about you?"

She nodded. She smiled. "We didn't care. It was nobody's business but ours." She sighed. "I'm so glad you and Bernie are friends. She's never had much in the way of companionship. She's so alone."

"Yeah, me, too," he confided. "After my grandmother died, all I had left was Paulie. He's a great guy."

"So I hear."

He got up. "Well, I'll go off to bed and hope the cheese doesn't do me in. But it was worth it," he added with a chuckle as he put his empty plate in the trash can. "Best cheese I've had in a long time."

"I'm glad you like it. And if you get the preventative, you can eat all you like of it," she laughed.

"I guess so. Sleep well."

"You, too."

But he didn't sleep well. He woke two hours later with a headache that almost brought him to tears. He walked into the bathroom, half-blind, and almost collided with Bernie, who was wetting a washcloth in the sink.

"My goodness, what's wrong?" she asked, because he was deathly pale.

"Migraine," he said roughly. "Any Excedrin in there?" he asked, indicating the medicine cabinet. "I can't find mine. I think I put it in here…"

She opened the cabinet and looked. "Yes, there is."

"Shake me out a tablet, will you, honey?"

"Oh, yes." She did and handed it to him. "You need this more than I do," she said, indicating the wet washcloth. "Come on. I'll help you back to bed."

"You should go," he said, swallowing hard.

"Why?"

"I get sick..." Before he could say anything else, he managed to make it to the commode and lost his supper, the cheese, the crackers, the soft drink and just about everything else.

When the nausea passed, he found Bernie on her knees beside him with the wet cloth, wiping his face. She flushed the toilet.

"Better now?" she asked.

He swallowed and drew in a breath. "Yeah. I think so. Honey, you shouldn't..." he began.

"You looked after me when I was having a flare," she reminded him. "Tit for tat."

He managed a smile. "Okay."

"Come on. I'll help you back to bed."

He let her lead him back into his bedroom and help him under the covers. She put the washcloth over his eyes.

"I'll go get you something to take the tablet with. Want water or a soft drink?"

"Ginger ale, if there's any in the fridge," he said weakly, loving the comfort of her touch, the compassion in her voice. All his life, women had wanted him for his wealth, his power. This woman only wanted him. It was a revelation.

"I'll be right back."

"You shouldn't be walking," he said.

"It's just to the kitchen, and I took the big pill. It's helping. I'll be right back."

* * *

Mrs. Brown was just getting ready for breakfast in the kitchen. She turned as Bernie came in.

"Do you want some coffee, sweetheart?" the land-lady asked.

"I'd love some, but Mikey has a migraine. I found his migraine medicine, but he wants ginger ale to take it with."

"There's one bottle left that's cold," the older woman said. "I'll get some more and put them in there. Is he all right?"

"He lost his supper," Bernie said. "He's really sick. I'm going to sit with him for a few minutes."

"If you need me, just call. We can get one of the Col-train doctors to come over here and give him a shot if he needs them to. Those headaches are horrible. I used to have them before I got on the preventative."

"He should see a doctor," she said as she got the gin-ger ale out of the fridge.

"You make him do that," Mrs. Brown said.

Bernie flushed and laugh. "As if I could."

"Bernie," Mrs. Brown said gently, "can't you see that the man is absolutely crazy about you?"

Chapter 7

Bernie stared at Mrs. Brown as if she'd sprouted grass in her hair. "He what?"

"He absolutely adores you," the older woman replied, smiling. "Everybody noticed, not just me."

Bernie flushed. "Well," she said, stumped for a response.

"You just go take care of your fellow," Mrs. Brown said. "I'll get breakfast ready. If he can eat anything, I'll make him whatever he likes."

"I'll tell him," Bernie replied. "Thanks."

"You come and eat whenever you like. I'll make you up a plate that you can reheat, okay?"

"Okay!"

Bernie went back to Mikey's room and closed the door. She sat down on the edge of the bed. "Still got the tablet?" she asked, because she'd handed it to him earlier.

"I got it."

"Here. It's open." She'd already taken the top off the bottle before she handed it to him. He swallowed down the tablet and handed her back the bottle. "Thanks, honey."

"No problem." She put his drink on the side table. "Will it stay down?" she worried. "Mrs. Brown said we can call one of our local doctors and they'll come give you a shot if you need it."

He swallowed. "Maybe the pill will work."

"Does it usually?"

He smiled. "No. It helps just a little. Nothing stops it."

She smoothed back his cool, wavy black hair. "You just let me know what you need. I'll get it."

His eyes adored her. "There was never a woman in my whole life who'd have taken care of me the way you just did. Well, except for my grandmother."

"I'm sure there were plenty who wanted to," she teased.

"Maybe a couple. But I'm funny about women. Most of them are jaded and glitzy," he added, his eyes cold with memory.

"Maybe you've been looking in the wrong places for them," she said, tongue in cheek.

His black eyes twinkled at her. "Think so?"

"It's a possibility."

He lay back and closed his eyes, wincing. "Of all the things to get from cheese," he groaned. "It's my favorite food."

"You can find a new favorite one. Maybe squash," she teased. "Or okra."

"Stop! You're killing me!"

She laughed. Most of the men she worked around hated both vegetables with a passion.

"Frozen yogurt, then."

"That sounds nice."

They were quiet for a few minutes, but it was obvious that even when the tablet had time to work, it wasn't doing much.

"Pill helping at all?"

He put his hand over his eyes. "Not so much." He closed his eyes and winced. "It's just over-the-counter stuff."

"Let me call a doctor. Please."

He drew in a breath. "Okay," he said finally.

"Be right back."

She phoned Lou and Copper Coltrain's office. The nurse said she'd ask Lou to come right out. Lou was short for Louise, she was blond and sweet and she knew exactly what to do for Mikey.

"You should see a neurologist," she told him after she'd given him an injection for the pain. First, of course, she'd examined him, asked what he'd already taken for the headache and inquired about any drug allergies. He had none. "But in the meantime, I'll write you a prescription for the preventative and something for the headaches that works when you get one." She turned to Bernie. "I'll give these to you, Bernie. You get them filled today."

"I will," Bernie said, smiling at the physician. "Thanks for coming."

"You're most welcome. If you have any more issues, Mr. Fiore, you call the office, okay?"

"Yes, ma'am," he said complacently. He smiled up at her through dark-rimmed eyes. "Thanks, Doc."

"You're welcome."

"I didn't think doctors made house calls anymore," he said.

"Jacobsville's not like most small towns," she laughed. "We do what's needed." She glanced at Bernie. "I thought you might be dying, from Bernie's description. She was very upset."

He opened both eyes and stared at Bernie. "She was?" he asked softly, and smiled at her.

She flushed even more. He laughed. Lou hid a smile, said her goodbyes and left.

"Can I get you anything else?" Bernie asked.

"No, but you can give the prescriptions to Santi. I'll text him." He pulled out his cell phone and made a face. "Damn, I can't see it," he murmured.

"Just a sec." She took the phone from him, pulled up messaging and looked at Mikey. "What do you want to tell him?"

"Ask him to come over right away."

She typed it in. The response was immediate. "On my way," it read.

"He'll think I'm dying or that Cotillo got me," he chuckled.

She frowned. "Who's Cotillo?"

"A bad man. Even worse than me," he said in a husky tone. His eyes tried to focus on her face. "There's a lot you don't know about me, kid."

"Well, there's a lot you don't know about me, too," she said.

His big hand searched for hers and held it tight. "We'll learn about each other. It takes time. Right?"

She smiled. It sounded like a future. She felt herself glowing inside. "It takes time," she agreed.

He took a deep breath and closed his eyes. "I'm going to try to sleep. Santi has plenty of cash for the prescriptions."

"Okay." She got up. "If you need anything, you just call, okay?"

He smiled without opening his eyes. "Okay. Thanks, honey."

"You're very welcome."

She went out of the room, the soft words lingering, touching, making her feel valued.

There was a knock at the front door. She went to answer it. Santi was standing there.

"What's wrong with the boss?" he asked at once.

"Migraine," she said. "We had to call the doctor."

"It's a doctor you know, right?" he asked, and his broad face looked troubled.

"Oh, yes, Dr. Louise Coltrain. She came out and gave him these prescriptions. He asked you to get them filled for him at the drugstore."

He took them from her and nodded. "I'll get right on it." He grimaced. "I don't like being away from him at night, even with all those other guys watching out for him. Listen, you hear any strange noises or if anybody tries to get in the house, you text me. Got your cell phone with you?"

"Yes." She pulled it out and handed it to him.

He pulled up the contact screen and put information into it. He handed it back. "That's my cell phone number. The boss isn't twitchy, so he might pass over something that could be dangerous."

"I'll call you if anything happens here," she promised. "Thanks," she added softly.

He smiled. "You're a nice kid. I'm sorry we were rough on you when you fell in front of the car. It's just that women have tried that before in the boss's old neighborhood."

"Really?" she asked, and she was honestly surprised.

He nodded. "He's loaded, you know? Plenty of women would do anything for money."

She smiled. "I've known one or two of those myself. I like having enough to pay the bills and eat out once in a while. That's about all. Money doesn't make people happy. Very often, it does just the opposite."

"Yes, it does." He held up the prescriptions. "I'll get these filled and bring them back to you. The boss, you're sure he's okay?"

"Why don't you look in and see, before you go?" she asked, leading him down the hall. "He's had a rough night."

"I used to nurse him through these headaches," Santi said. "They're a nightmare."

"I can see that."

She knocked briefly and opened the door. Mikey turned his head, wincing at the pain. He managed a smile.

"Hey, Santi. Had to make sure I hadn't croaked, right?" he teased.

Santi chuckled. "Something like that. You okay?"

"Getting better by the minute."

"Okay. I'll go get your meds and be right back."

"Bernie," Mikey called, when she started to go out, too. She went back in and paused by the bed. "You haven't even had breakfast, have you?" he asked.

"Well, not just yet…"

"Go eat something."

"Okay. Mrs. Brown said you can have anything you want to eat when you feel like food."

He smiled drowsily. "She's a doll. So are you. I'm not hungry yet. I think I'll just sleep for a while. Eat something."

"I will."

"Hey," he called softly when she was at the door.

She turned, her eyebrows arching.

"When I get better, suppose we take in another movie? Paulie says they've got all the latest movies on pay-per-view and DVD. And a door that locks," he added with a wicked smile.

She laughed, flushing as she remembered the last movie they'd gone to but not seen. The memory of his mouth on hers was poignant. "I'd like that," she said.

"Me, too."

"Get some rest. I'll check on you in a few minutes."

He sighed. "Sweet girl. Don't ever change."

"I'll do my best."

She went out and closed the door.

Paul came over to see about his cousin, alerted by Santi after the bodyguard had dropped off Mikey's prescriptions.

"You look rough," Paul said, sitting by his cousin's bedside. "I remember what a misery those headaches are."

"Misery is right. I lost everything I'd eaten. Bernie was right in the bathroom with me, mopping me up," he added. "What a hell of a woman. I never knew anybody like her."

"She's unique," Paul agreed. "Amazing how she keeps going. Her disability never seems to get her down."

"She has good days and bad ones."

"Don't they have shots for that condition now?"

"Yeah, they do," Mikey said. "I overheard her land-lady saying what a shame it was that they were so ex-pensive. Bernie can't afford them." His face tautened. "I can, but she'd never let me do it for her. She's proud."

"She is."

"Mikey, how well do you know Santi?" Paul asked.

Mikey's eyebrows rose. "As well as I know you," he said. "Honor's his big thing. He'd never sell me out be-cause it would seem dishonorable to him. He takes his job seriously. Why do you ask?" he added.

"Just some gossip. They say Cotillo's got somebody close to you."

"It's got to be Mrs. Brown, then," Mikey said with twinkling dark eyes. "Right? I mean, she's the obvious choice. Friendly, sweet, just the sort to set you up for a hit."

Paul chuckled. "Okay. I see what you mean. Just the same, we're checking out everybody who lives here. Just in case."

"That's not a bad idea. You still got Billings some-where with a sniper kit?"

Paul nodded. "I don't think he ever sleeps. He seems to get by on catnaps, but we have an alternate in place anyway."

Mikey drew in a breath and laughed huskily. "These damned headaches. I didn't know there was a way to prevent them. Doc prescribed something, along with a prescription to take when the pain gets bad." He gri-maced. "I hate drugs, you know? But this is a sort of pain that makes you want to hit your head with a ham-mer just to make it stop throbbing."

"Grandmama used to get them," Paul recalled. "They were bad."

"So are mine. Imagine a woman who doesn't run for the hills when a man's losing the contents of his stomach," he said. "Bernie didn't leave me for a minute, not until after the doctor came."

"I hear you did pretty much the same for her the day you met, when she fell in front of the car."

"Yeah," Mikey's mouth pulled down. "I thought it was a trick. You know how women used to come on to me. One even pretended to fall down a flight of stairs. I didn't know Bernie from an apple. I assumed she liked the looks of the limo and wanted a ride. Bad call." He drew in a breath. "She asked us to look for her cane, and we didn't believe her. Santi found it. I felt like a dog."

"Your past isn't full of guileless women," Paul said with a grin. "Understandable mistake."

"I guess." He put a hand to his head. "At least the throbbing has stopped. That doctor's pretty good. Nice looking woman. She married to the redheaded doctor?"

"Copper Coltrain," Paul agreed. "There was a mismatch. She worked with him for almost a year, and he hated her guts for something her father did years ago. It wasn't until she started to leave the practice that he got his ducks in a row. It was a rocky romance."

Mikey just sighed. "Mine's not rocky at all," he said. "You know, I never thought about having a family before. Little girls are sweet."

"Yeah." Paul didn't say any more. He and his former wife had a little girl. His wife and the child were gunned down by one of Paul's enemies, in revenge for his arrest and conviction. It was a sad memory.

"Sorry," Mikey said, wincing. "I forgot."

"I try to," Paul said. "I mean, I'm happier than I ever dreamed I could be, with Sari. But there are times when I think of my little girl…" He broke off.

"We all have bad memories, Paulie," Mikey said. "Mine aren't as bad as yours. I'm sorry for what happened to you. But the guy paid for it," he added coldly.

Paul glanced at him. "Yeah, one of the marshals in Jersey said he thought you might have had something to do with that."

Mikey just pursed his lips. "Who, me? I go out of my way to be nice to people."

"Yeah, but you know people who don't."

Mikey chuckled. "Lots of them."

"Have you told her?" he asked, his head jerking toward the door.

Mikey knew who he meant. He leaned back against the pillows. "I don't know how. At first, I didn't think there was a reason I needed to tell her. Now, I'm scared of what she'll think of me."

"She's a sweet woman."

"Sweet, and innocent. She doesn't see wickedness. She always looks for the best in people. Even in me. I'm not what she thinks I am. But how do I tell her what my life has been like? How do I do that, and keep her?"

"You underestimate how she feels about you, Mikey," Paul said. "You don't love or hate people for their actions mostly. You care about them because of what they are, deep inside. Bernie knows you aren't as bad as you think you are."

"I hope you're right. It hasn't been a long time, but if I lose her, it will be like having an arm torn off, you know?"

"I do know. That's how I feel about Sari."

"She's a winner."

He smiled. "I agree. Hey, if you're not better Saturday, you can bring Bernie over for lunch Sunday, you'll be welcome. You can take her walking around the property, maybe even catch that movie you went to see at the drive-in. It wasn't a new one, because it's on pay-per-view now."

"That sounds nice," Mikey replied. "I hope this stupid headache goes away before then," he added. "They usually last two or three days."

"I remember. You take your meds. Maybe they'll cut this one short."

"I hope so. Thanks for the cousinly visit," he added. "Anything more from Carrera?"

Paul shook his head. "He's got Tony in a safe place, he says, and not to worry."

"I'm in a safer place," Mikey chuckled. "Little bitty town in the middle of nowhere, with half the retired mercs in the country. Lucky me."

Paul grinned. "I'll second that. Ask Bernie over Sunday."

"I will. Thanks."

"No problem. See you later."

"Yeah."

Bernie was delighted with the invitation. It did take Mikey a few days to get over the headache, but he was fine Sunday afternoon. "Are you sure they don't mind?" she asked.

"They wouldn't invite you if they minded, honey," he told her as they sped toward Paul and Sari's house. "You warm enough?"

"I'm fine," she said, huddling down in her warm berber coat. "It's chilly tonight."

"Imagine that, chilly in south Texas," he teased. "Now if you want to see chilly, you have to come to Jersey. We know about cold weather."

"I guess you get a lot of snow."

"We used to get more, when Paulie and I were kids. We had some great snowball battles in the neighborhood. These older boys would lie in wait for us and pelt us with frozen snowballs every chance they got. So Paulie and I got some ice cubes and put them inside our snowballs. Ouch! The bullies ran for their lives."

She laughed. "I'll bet they did."

"Our grandmother was so fierce that they were more afraid of her than even the big boss in the neighborhood," he recalled with a smile. "I told you about her hitting him with a salami. Chased him all the way out the front door with it, and his people didn't dare laugh. It taught him a whole new respect for women."

She laughed softly. "I wish I could have met your grandmother."

"Me, too, honey. She'd have loved you." His hand reached for hers and held it tight. "She had no time for modern women with modern ideas."

She sighed. "Me, neither. I'm a throwback to another generation, I guess. My dad pretty much raised me after we came back here." Her heart felt like lead in her chest. She hated remembering why they'd come to Jacobsville.

"What's wrong?" he asked, sensitive to her mood.

She grimaced. "Things I can't talk about. Bad things."

"Honey, I could write you a book on bad things," he commented. He drew in a breath. "One of these days we have to have a long talk about my past, and it isn't going to be nice."

"It won't matter," she said quietly. "The person you were isn't the man you are today."

"That's not as true as I wish it was," he replied.

"I can't believe you'd do anything terrible."

But he had. Really terrible things. They hadn't bothered him much until now. This sweet, kind woman beside him didn't have any idea about what sort of evil lived in his real world, the world she'd never seen.

"Listen, you read books?" he asked.

"Oh, yes. It's how I get through bad nights, when the pain overpowers the medicines I take for it."

"There's this book—I'll give you the title. It's about a man who paints houses."

"A painter?" she asked.

His fingers contracted. "It's a different sort of painting. If you read the book, you'll begin to get some idea of the sort of world I live in." His face tautened. "It's a hard life. Dog eat dog, and I mean that literally. The man I work for is hiding out from a man even worse than he is. What I know, what I've seen, can clear him. The feds just have to keep me alive long enough until the trial comes up." He turned and glanced at her. "It's a business. Like regular business, in a way. It's just that somebody wants what you have and thinks up ways to get it, most of them illegal and deadly."

She frowned. "I don't understand."

"How could you? Raised in a tiny little town, surrounded by law-abiding citizens, most of whom love you." His face hardened. "In my whole damned life, my grandmother was the only person who really loved me."

Her heart almost stopped. She loved him. And she'd

only just realized it. She was faintly disconcerted by a revelation that should have occurred to her much sooner. "There's your cousin Paul," she said after a minute.

"Yeah, Paulie. We're fond of each other. He'd do anything he could to help me. In fact, he already is. But that's not the same way I felt about my grandmother."

"I don't remember mine very well," she said tightly.

He glanced at her. "Bad memories?"

She swallowed. "They don't get much worse."

His fingers linked into hers. "Can you tell me about it?"

She hesitated. He was insinuating that his life had been a little outside the law. Perhaps he might understand better than most men what it had been like for her, for her family.

"I want to," she said. "Can it wait until later?"

He laughed. "It can wait." He was flattered that she wanted to trust him with something that was obviously a secret, something she kept hidden. It was an indication of feelings she was beginning to have for him. He was beginning to have the same sort for her. If she had something traumatic in her past, it might help her relate to his own life.

Then he stopped and considered what he'd be letting her in for, after the trial, when he went back to Jersey, back to the old life. He'd pledged his loyalty, his life, to the crime family he belonged to. Betraying that code, that omertà, would get him killed. Not that he had any plans to turn his people in to the feds. In fact, even Tony was working with the feds right now, to ward off the takeover by Cotillo. But that was a temporary truce. Nobody in Tony's employ was going to rat out anybody to the feds, least of all Mikey. That would get you killed quick.

On the other hand, if he wanted a life with the sweet woman at his side, and he was beginning to, how could he drag her into the shadows with him?

It would be her choice in the end. But she was sheltered and disabled. Not that his people would be bad to her, oh, no. Even the women would welcome her like a relative. His underlings would treat her like royalty. So it wouldn't be bad from that standpoint. But the rackets Tony and Mikey were mixed up in were illegal. They specialized in online gambling, in numbers running, in casinos in Vegas. One of Mikey's properties was a casino, in fact. He'd told Bernie that it was a hotel. It was a hotel, but it wasn't in Jersey. It was in Las Vegas, and big-name entertainers came regularly to appear there. He ran it like a legal business, but he did do things off the books that could land him in jail. Bernie was such a gentle, trusting soul. She liked the country, the outdoors, little animals. Mikey liked bright lights and casinos. It was going to be a difficult adjustment, if she was even willing to make it.

"You're brooding," she accused, watching the expressions cross his handsome face.

He laughed self-consciously. "I'm brooding." He turned his head for a minute and caught her eyes. "Sorry. I have things on my mind." He made a face. "Paulie said they've got somebody close to me."

"They?"

"The guy who's after Tony and me," he explained. He chuckled. "I told him it was probably Mrs. Brown. You can tell she's just the kind of person who would set a man up," he added with a grin.

She burst out laughing. "Oh, that's wicked."

"I'm a wicked man, honey," he said, and he wasn't kidding.

She frowned. "He doesn't have any idea who it is?" she added.

"Not yet. He's checking people out."

"I'd check out that Jessie person in my office," she muttered. "She's one of the most horrible people I've ever known. She's always cutting at the other women in the office. Poor Glory has high blood pressure. It can be dangerous, you know, and she has a small child. Jessie makes all sorts of unpleasant remarks to her about the medicines she takes, even about the way she dresses."

"Your boss should get that woman out of the office," he commented.

"He'd like to, but he's the DA. He has to have a legitimate reason to let her go or she could take him to court. He'd like her to leave, too. She messes up appointments all the time, another reason Glory's so stressed."

His fingers stroked hers. "We all have our crosses, don't we, kid?"

She nodded. "Nobody gets through life without a few traumas." She sighed. "It's really sad, you know. She's so beautiful. How can a person who looks like that be such a pain to be around?"

"You never know what sort of background people come from," he said simply. "A lot of times, kids turn out bad because of the way they were raised. You know, I only saw my dad a few times in my whole life. My mother died of a heart attack when she was just in her twenties, not too long after she had me. Her mother, my grandmother, took me in. Paulie's mom bit the dust about the same time, so he ended up with our grandmother, too." He grimaced. "Paulie's dad was even worse than mine. He took some licks when the old man was home. Fortunately, it wasn't often."

"Did your fathers work in some sort of away job, like construction?" she asked innocently.

"They worked for the big bosses. They went where they were told, and did what they were told." He smiled sadly. "That's the life, kid. You pledge to obey and you do it. There's a code of honor. We call it omertà. It means you pledge your loyalty to a don and you never forget it. You sell out your colleagues, you meet with a quick and sad end."

Her heart jumped. "But you're going to testify against a man who's a, what did you call him, a don?"

His fingers contracted comfortingly around hers. "That's a different thing," he said. "This guy Cotillo is trying to muscle in on territory that doesn't belong to him. The other families are as much against him as Tony's is."

She frowned. "Tony's your family? Is he a relation?"

He chuckled. "Tony's a character," he said. "No, we're not related, but we'd die for each other. So in that sense, yeah, I guess you could say he's family. The feds are protecting him. Me, too. What we know can put Cotillo away for a very long time. The families are working toward that end, even making a temporary truce with the feds to keep them from prying too closely into our business."

She blinked. "You talk about federal people as if they're the enemy," she said. "But your cousin works for a federal agency."

"It's just a figure of speech, honey," he said, backtracking. "We're all grateful for their help. Nobody wants a guy like Cotillo in charge in Jersey. He's a weasel. First chance he got, he'd start lining up other families for elimination. They know that. So the feds are sort of the lesser of the two evils."

"I see."

"You don't, but you will," he promised. He sighed. "I just hope it isn't all going to be too much for you, Bernie. You've lived a sheltered life."

"Actually, I haven't. Not so much."

"Oh?"

"Well, I haven't lived in a commune or had lovers, or anything like that. But I'm anything but sheltered. I'll tell you," she added. "I promise."

He smiled. "I'll tell you, too."

"That's a deal."

Chapter 8

They were heading down the long driveway to Graylings when his fingers contracted around hers. "No secrets from now on," he said. "I'll tell you about my life today and you can tell me about yours."

"It might matter…" she said worriedly.

"It won't." He sounded very positive. "Nothing you tell me will change anything." One side of his sensuous mouth pulled down. "On the other hand, what I have to tell you, well, that may change a lot of things," he added heavily, and he was regretting things in his past that might drive her out of his life. It was a terrible thought. She was already part of him.

"Whatever sort of trouble you're in, I'll stand by you," she said.

He wanted to pull her over into his lap and kiss the breath out of her for saying that, but he had to restrain himself. His fingers worked sensuously into hers, caressing them. "I never thought I'd get mixed up with a girl from a little town in Texas," he said, chuckling. "I feel just like Carrera must have."

"Carrera?" she asked. "Oh, yes, Delia's husband." She smiled. "Delia had a bad time of it. Her mother turned out to be a woman she'd always thought of as her sister, and her father turned out to be her mother's husband. She saved Mr. Carrera's life in the Bahamas, but she lost her baby. She came home and she was so miserable. It hurt me to see her when I had to go to the dry cleaner's." She sighed. "But then Mr. Carrera showed up with some sort of quilt he'd made for her, and the next thing we knew, they were getting married."

"Yeah, he quilts," he said with a soft laugh. "The guy looks like a wise guy. He's big and rough and he intimidates most people. The quilting habit gave him a lot of heat until he started throwing punches. Now nobody laughs at it. He wins international competitions with his designs, too."

She nodded. "They have one of his quilts in our library, on permanent display. It's a Bow Tie quilt. They say he has one just like it in a casino he owns. Gosh, imagine owning a casino! Those are the richest, flashiest places on earth!"

He hadn't told her that his hotel in Vegas was also a casino. "You ever been in one?" he asked.

"When I was small, my parents took me to the Bahamas on a cruise one year, on summer vacation. I wasn't allowed inside, but they drove me by one over on Paradise Island. It was fascinating to me, even as a child."

His fingers contracted. "Suppose I told you that the

hotel I own is actually a casino," he said slowly, "and it's in Las Vegas?"

Her eyes widened. "You own a casino in Las Vegas?" she exclaimed. "Wow!"

He laughed, surprised at her easy acceptance. "I run it legit, too," he added. "No fixes, no hidden switches, no cheating. Drives the feds nuts, because they can't find anything to pin on me there."

"The feds?" she asked.

He drew in a breath. "I told you, I'm a bad man." He felt guilty about it, dirty. His fingers caressed hers as they neared Graylings, the huge mansion where his cousin lived with the heir to the Grayling racehorse stables.

Her fingers curled trustingly around his. "And I told you that the past doesn't matter," she said stubbornly. Her heart was running wild. "Not at all. I don't care how bad you've been."

His own heart stopped and then ran away. His teeth clenched. "I don't even think you're real, Bernie," he whispered. "I think I dreamed you."

She flushed and smiled. "Thanks."

He glanced in the rearview mirror. "What I'd give for just five minutes alone with you right now," he said tautly. "Fat chance," he added as he noticed the sedan tailing casually behind them.

She felt all aglow inside. She wanted that, too. Maybe they could find a quiet place to be alone, even for just a few minutes. She wanted to kiss him until her mouth hurt.

He pulled into the long driveway and up to the house, which was all aglow with light. It was a huge two-story mansion with exquisite woodwork and a long, wide porch. The front door opened as Mikey helped her out of the car, retaining her hand in his as they approached the house.

"Paisano," Paul greeted him in Italian.

"Salve! Come stai?" Mikey replied, and let go of Bernie's hand long enough to hug his cousin.

"Sto bene, grazie, e tu?" Paul replied.

"Va bene," Mikey responded with a grin. *"Cosi, cosi. Non mi posso lamentare."*

"Benissimo!"

"English, English," Sari Fiore chided. "Bernie doesn't understand Italian," she laughed.

"Just greetings, honey," Mikey told her, and brought her hand to his lips. "I'll teach you some nice Italian words the minute we get some time together."

She grinned. "Okay."

"Come on in," Paul added as two feds got out of the sedan that had trailed Mikey's car. "McLeod, do you and Agent Murdock want coffee?"

"I'd love some," McLeod said, and glanced at Murdock. "As long as that guy doesn't offer to make it," he added firmly.

Murdock, a good-natured man, just chuckled. "I get stuck with making it at our office. People pour it in the ficus tree."

"Yeah, the poor damned thing shivers all the time," Paul commented on the way to the kitchen. "I think it's on the verge of a nervous breakdown. Hey, Mandy, can you make us a pot of coffee?" he called to the woman working to clean up the kitchen counters.

"Of course I can!" she exclaimed, and grinned. "Hey, Mikey! Hello, Bernie. Nice to see you both."

"Nice to see you, too, Mandy," Mikey replied, and

kissed her cheek. "I miss your cooking. Not that Mrs. Johnson isn't good."

"I know she is," Mandy replied. She gave Mikey and Bernie a secret smile when she saw them holding hands.

Mikey noticed, but he didn't let go, even when they sat down together at the long kitchen table with Paul and the two feds.

"Okay," Mikey said. "What's up? You guys tailed us the whole way here," he added to McLeod.

"Cotillo sent one of his boys down here after you," McLeod replied quietly, watching Mikey's face harden. "We caught him at the courthouse yesterday."

Mikey blinked. "How?"

"We have facial identification software," McLeod said simply. "I used it. He's got wants and warrants outstanding in Jersey. Our guys took him into custody and they're delivering him right back to the authorities there."

US Marshals, that was, Mikey knew without being told. He let out a breath. "I guess I'd better be more careful about taking Bernie out to public places."

Her fingers, unseen, contracted around his.

"Not at all," Agent Murdock said. "As long as they're pretty public. Drive-ins aren't a good idea. Too much opportunity for covert work."

Mikey sighed. "I guess so. Damn."

"It's okay," Bernie said. "We can sit in Mrs. Johnson's parlor anytime we like, and talk or watch television," she reminded him.

He smiled at her. "You're a rare girl, Bernie."

She flushed and laughed. "Not so much."

Mikey glanced at the government agents. "So why was he at the courthouse?" he asked.

"We think he was looking for a contact there. But he came after quitting time, so we didn't have the opportunity to find out. When we questioned him," McLeod added, "he said he was looking for San Antonio and got lost. He was just looking for directions."

"Oh, that sounds very sincere," Mikey said sardonically.

"Yeah, considering that he flew into the San Antonio airport," Paul added drily.

"Here's coffee," Mandy said. "And how about some nice pound cake? I made a chocolate one!"

Mikey made a face. "Gosh, I'd love that, but I'm just getting over a really bad migraine. Chocolate's one of my triggers," he reminded her.

"I'm sorry," Mandy said. She patted him on the shoulder. "But I've got a nice cherry pie?" she teased.

He chuckled. "I'll take that. Thanks. You know, she nursed me through the headache, sickness and all," he added, looking at Bernie with evident affection. "She never left me, and even called a doctor out to the boardinghouse to treat me. She's quite a girl."

Bernie's face flamed because everybody was looking at her.

"Yes, she is," Sari said, smiling. "At work, she's always the first one there and the last one to leave, and she never minds staying over if we need her." She made a face. "It's not the same with that new woman the boss hired. Jessie. She's constantly late and she makes clients uncomfortable. She made a real play for one of the wealthy married local ranchers, and the boss gave her warning." She sighed. "I wish she'd do something he could fire her for. Nobody likes her."

"She's an odd fit for a small town," Bernie said. "She's overly sophisticated."

"We have a few overly sophisticated people, like the police chief's wife, but she's nice," Mandy broke in, putting a platter of sliced pound cake, saucers and utensils on the table, along with a saucer containing a slice of cherry pie for Mikey.

"This looks delicious. Thanks, honey," he told the housekeeper and grinned at her.

"You're welcome. Go ahead, people, dig in. We don't stand on ceremony here."

"No, we don't," Sari said, smiling warmly at her husband.

"Oh, that's good coffee," Paul said with a long sigh. "I just hate trying to drink it at work," he added with a pointed glare at Murdock.

Murdock made a face. "Not my fault. My mother always drank tea. She never taught me how to make coffee and I never drink it."

"No wonder it tastes so bad," Paul teased.

Murdock sighed. "There have been threats, you know," he said complacently. "In fact, ASAC Jon Blackhawk's brother, McKuen Kilraven, was openly talking about men in ninja suits and a pickup truck and a big sack."

"You'd never fit in a sack, Murdock," Paul chuckled. "Besides, Kilraven's too occupied with their new daughter to do any such thing. That's two kids now. He and Winnie are over the moon."

"She still working 911 dispatch down here?" Murdock asked.

Paul shook his head. "She's got her hands full with two preschoolers. Kilraven's still with the company, but he's mostly administrative these days. No more hanging out of helicopters by one leg wrapped in camo netting while he fires at enemy agents."

"You're kidding!" Bernie gasped.

"Oh, no, I'm not," Paul chuckled. "The man was a maniac when he was after a perp. He's calmed down somewhat since he married, but he's still good at what he does."

"He was a patrolman here, working for Chief Grier as cover on a covert federal assignment, for a while," Bernie said as she nibbled cake and sipped coffee. She laughed. "There was gossip that Chief Grier wanted to put him in a barrel, drive him to the border and send him down the Rio Grande. They did butt heads a few times over procedure."

"The chief butts heads pretty good," Paul assured her. "He's lowered the crime rate with a vengeance since he's been in charge of our local police."

"Nobody thought he'd stay here when he first came," Bernie said. "He was really tough. Then they made a movie here with the Georgia Firefly, Tippy Moore, and before any of us realized it, he was married to her."

"She's a knockout," Paul said. He slid his hand over his wife's. "I'm partial to redheads, you know," he added, grinning as he studied Sari's red, red hair pinned up over big blue eyes.

She grinned back. "Thanks, sweetheart."

"So what do we do about Cotillo and the trial and Tony Garza?" Mikey asked as he finished his pie and his coffee.

"First things first," Paul said. "We've got tails on Cotillo and his men, with interagency cooperation. Cotillo's killed a lot of people trying to forge new alliances and take over territory. He's made enemies."

"The killings are going to get him in trouble," Mikey said. "The big guys don't like that. It invites the feds in. They want problems solved with dialog, not automatic weapons."

"Well, they do kill people who rat them out," Paul replied solemnly.

Mikey nodded. "Omertà," he agreed. "Loyalty is life itself in the outfit. The number-one sin is selling out your people to the feds. Nobody likes a rat. They get put down and sometimes their whole families do as well, as a warning." He ground his teeth together when he saw his cousin's face. That had happened to Paul. His first family had been gunned down when Paul locked up one of the minor bosses and shut down a lucrative illegal operation. The man had gotten even in the worst possible way.

"I'm sorry," Mikey told his cousin. "Truly sorry. I should never have brought that up."

Paul's face relaxed. "It was a long time ago. Still stings," he said, and his eyes were filled with horrible memories.

"Just the same, I'm sorry."

Paul smiled. "We're family. Don't sweat it."

Mikey sighed. "You're the only family I've got. Well, except for Tony's family." He glanced at the feds. "I hope you guys understand that I'm only cooperating because Tony's being falsely accused. I'm not selling out my people. Not for anything."

"We know that, Mikey," Paul said quietly. "Nobody's asking you to rat out your colleagues."

Mikey sipped coffee, not looking at them. "I took

a blood oath," he said very quietly. "I made a solemn promise. I swore to it, like you'd make a vow in church. I won't break it. Not if they lock me up forever."

"We only lock up people when we can prove they've broken the law," Paul assured him. He leaned closer. "So make sure we can't prove anything on you," he chuckled.

Mikey laughed. "I don't do that stuff anymore. I have a legit casino and I run it like a legit business."

"I know that," Paul replied. "You're not as bad as you make out, Mikey. You saved Merrie's life," he added, referring to Sari's younger sister. Both women had been targeted by an enemy of their late father, victims of professional hit men. Mikey's input had helped save both of them. "In fact, you helped save Sari's, as well."

"I just made a few calls," Mikey replied.

"Well, those few calls helped us catch all the perps," Paul replied.

Mikey grinned. "I like Baby Doll," he said, referring to Merrie. "How's she doing?"

"She and Ren are expecting again," Sari said with a wide grin. "She's over the moon."

"She still painting?" Mikey asked.

"Oh, yes. She never gives that hobby up," Sari told him.

He glanced at Bernie with real hunger. "I'd love her to do a portrait of Bernie for me," he said.

"You know she'd be happy to!" Sari said. She glanced at Bernie, who was flushed and beaming. "Bernie, do you have a few photos of yourself that we could send her?"

Bernie grimaced. "Well, no, not a lot. I don't have anybody to take pictures of me…"

While she was speaking, Mikey took out his expensive cell phone and snapped photos of her from all angles. He showed them to her in his photo app.

"You're really good at this," she said, surprised as she looked at herself in the pictures. She looked happy, mysterious, almost pretty. She laughed. "These don't even really look like me!"

"They do. You don't laugh a lot," he replied. His face tightened. "I love it when you laugh, Bernie," he added. "You're beautiful when you're happy."

She felt her heart almost bursting. He thought she was beautiful. He wanted a painting of her. She could have floated up to the ceiling, she was so lighthearted.

"Thanks," she whispered.

He wrinkled his nose at her and grinned. "We'll have to wait until that movie we were watching comes out on pay-per-view and we can watch it together."

"I don't have pay-per-view," she said morosely.

"We do," Sari said, and grinned. "You can watch it in the library. In fact, we already have it. The drive-in is showing it, but it's not a first-run movie. Wouldn't you like to see the rest of it?"

Mikey pursed his lips. "Would I! It's a great movie."

"It is, but I'd need tissues," Bernie confessed. "One reviewer said it would twist your heart open."

"You can have tissues and more coffee," Sari said. "Mandy, can you do refills and find a box of tissues for Bernie?"

"You bet!" Mandy said, and went to get both.

The government agents left shortly after. Mikey took Bernie into the luxurious study with its plush couch and chairs and the expensive media center, with a fifty-five-inch television screen.

"Wow," Bernie said as Mikey closed the door behind them. "This is awesome."

"They've refurnished it since old man Grayling died," he told her as he went to turn on the television and set up the movie. "In fact, they've redone the whole house. It has some bad memories for Sari and her sister."

"I remember hearing about how badly their father treated them," Bernie said. "He must have been a horrible father."

"From what I hear, he was." He grimaced. "Mine was pretty bad, too."

"My dad was a sweet, kind man," Bernie said sadly. "He died much too young. He lived through a lot of trauma. I think it affects people, you know? Affects their health."

"Maybe so."

He turned on the movie and brought the controller back as he dropped down onto the plush couch beside Bernie. He put the controller on the coffee table and turned to Bernie.

"Gee, look, we're all alone," he said with a grin, "and there are no cars around us."

"Isn't that fascinating?" she laughed.

"Oh, you bet." He pulled her onto his lap, letting her head fall back on his shoulder. "And I have some really interesting ideas about what we could do while the movie runs."

Her arms looped around his neck and her eyes riveted to his wide, sensuous, chiseled mouth. "You do?" she whispered.

He drew her close and bent his head, smiling. "Oh, yes. Very, very interesting."

As he spoke, his mouth slowly covered hers. She

sighed and sank against his big, muscular body, letting him take her weight while he kissed her.

"I could get used to this," he whispered.

She smiled under his lips. "Me, too."

He nibbled her upper lip and traced under it with just the tip of his tongue, loving the way she reacted to him. She wasn't coy or reticent. She met him halfway. If those long, soulful sighs were any indication, she loved what he was doing to her.

He shifted her and his fingers ran gently up and down her rib cage, setting fires, making her hungry. His mouth grew slowly insistent. She twisted against him, hungry and burning with new needs.

His big hand slid under the sweater she was wearing and teased around her breast while he kissed her slowly.

She moaned and twisted up toward that maddening hand whose touch was making her wild for more.

He smiled against her soft lips because he knew that. His thumb slowly trespassed under the lacy cotton cup and against her firm breast. She gasped under his mouth, but she didn't try to stop him. He loved that. His mouth opened on hers, deepening the kiss, diverting her while his hand went to the hooks that held the bra in place and snapped them open. His hand, warm and strong, moved slowly back around, teasing just under her breast. He could hear her breathing change, feel the need in her grow, as it grew in him.

"Oh, baby," he murmured as his mouth grew hard on hers and his big hand tenderly swallowed her breast up whole, his palm rubbing gently at the hard little nub he found.

She caught her breath and moaned.

"This is sweet," he ground out. "Oh, God, it's sweet like sugar candy…"

He moved, turning her so that she was lying under him, full length, on the plush couch. He was on his side, his elbow taking his weight as his hand moved the bra out of his way so that he could touch her more easily.

Her body arched, helpless, as she reacted to the intimate tracing of his hand. She couldn't even pretend not to want it. She was aching, throbbing with hungers she'd never felt in her life. A faint whimper escaped the mouth that his was devouring.

"Yes," he whispered huskily. "It's not enough, is it? Try not to cry out," he added as he slid the sweater and bra up under her chin. "They might hear us…"

What he was saying didn't make sense until his mouth lowered, and she felt it cover and consume her whole breast, taking it slowly into the moist, warm darkness, his tongue sliding over the nipple and making her throb from head to toe.

She had to stifle a cry. She sobbed under the expert touch of his mouth, shivering, arching as she pleaded for something more, something to ease the ache that was slowly consuming her.

He began to suckle her, hungrier than he could ever remember being with a woman. She sobbed as if he was hurting her, but he knew he wasn't. His long, powerful leg inserted itself between both of hers in the slacks she was wearing and began to move sensuously, making the hunger even worse.

He rolled over onto her completely, hesitating just long enough to open the buttons of his shirt and pull it apart over the thick hair that covered his muscular chest. When he went down against her, it was bare skin against bare skin, something she'd never felt.

Her arms went under the shirt, around him, her hands digging into his bare back. Odd how it felt there, she thought dimly, because there was a definite depression, a coin-shaped one. But he was moving on her and she felt the power and heat of him, the sudden surge of his body that told her graphically how capable he was.

His mouth ground into hers. He groaned as he pushed between her long legs and right against the heart of her in that soft fork of her body. She lifted up, shivering, and he moved roughly on her, feeling the passion burn him alive.

But his mind froze the passion as he realized how innocent she was. This was wrong. He could live with it, he could love it, but it would shame her, make her feel soiled. He couldn't do that to her. He couldn't, even if it was agony to stop.

He rolled over, shivering, and pulled her hard against his side. "Don't move," he whispered unsteadily. "Just lie still. Please, honey. Help me. I hurt like hell!"

She managed that, just. She was on fire and he'd stopped. Why had he stopped? She wanted him so desperately, just as desperately as he wanted her.

But sanity slowly returned. Was this what she really wanted, to have sex with a man on a sofa in a room with an unlocked door, a man to whom she had no real ties except physical ones? She was religious. She didn't believe in sex before marriage. But she wanted Mikey. She wanted him so badly that she'd have given in right here, without a single protest. In fact, she'd done that. But he'd stopped. She could feel how difficult it had been for him to do that. His body was shaking with unfulfilled needs. Now she felt guilty that she'd let it go so far. How would she have felt afterward? She didn't even know how to protect herself. What if she'd become pregnant? How would she live with that in a small town where everybody knew her, and knew that the only man she'd kept company with in recent years was the one lying so stiffly beside her right now? It would be no secret who the father was. Mikey had a casino in Las Vegas. He was a big-city man. It was highly unlikely that he'd throw all that up to live in a little town like Jacobsville with a woman who might end up an invalid in a very few years.

Besides that, he had a past, and bad men were after him because of a man he worked with, who was hiding from assassins. This was a terrible time to start an affair. In fact, she had to admit she wasn't the sort of woman who could even have an affair. It just wasn't like her, despite her aching hunger for Mikey and the violent attachment that she felt to him.

He was breathing easier now. He stretched and laughed softly when he felt her breasts against his bare rib cage.

"Well, that was a damned near thing," he whispered as he turned over, rolled her onto her back, and looked at her pretty firm pink breasts with their hard, dusky crowns. He touched them very gently. "I didn't want to stop."

"We're on a sofa," she began, flushing.

"Honey, all I had to do was push your pants down and go into you," he whispered blatantly, smiling at her expression. "It wouldn't have taken three minutes, as hot as I was. That's how easy it would have been. You didn't realize, did you?"

She caught her breath. "Not really," she confessed. "I haven't ever…"

"I noticed." He bent and brushed his mouth over her bare breasts. "God, woman, you're so beautiful," he whispered. "I'll dream of you every night of my life after this!"

"You will?" She thought how comfortable she was with him, how easily they'd slipped into intimacy. It felt so right. She wasn't even embarrassed.

He chuckled. "Yes, I will." He lifted his head and drew in a breath. "When all this is over, you and I are going to sit down and have a very serious talk." He brushed back her damp, disheveled hair. "Very serious."

She smiled slowly, her heart lifting. "Okay."

He laughed. "Everything's so easy with you, Bernie," he said, touching her cheek gently. "You never make waves, do you?"

"Not much, no."

"I love that about you," he said. "I feel at ease with you. Safe."

"I feel that way with you, too."

His big hand brushed tenderly over her breasts. "I guess we should put our clothes back on and watch the movie," he said with a sigh.

She nodded.

He pulled her up beside him, but before she could pull her sweater and bra back down, he turned her into his lap and pulled her inside his shirt, shivering as he felt her bare skin rub gently over his. His arms contracted hungrily and he held her, rocking her, in a blistering silence of passion.

"You'd do it with me, wouldn't you?" he whispered at her ear.

"Yes," she replied in a husky, shaky little voice.

"I don't even have anything to use," he confessed gruffly. He held her even closer. "You know what? I don't think I'd mind."

"You wouldn't?"

His hand went to the base of her spine, and he rubbed her against the hardness of him, holding her there firmly. "I like babies," he whispered.

She shivered. "Oh, Mikey," she sobbed, and her arms tightened.

He shivered, too. "Oh, God, I've got to get up and lock the door," he groaned. "On the sofa, on the damned carpet, against a wall—I have to have you, right now!"

"Yes," she whimpered, pushing closer. "Yes!"

He eased her away from him, his eyes blazing as he looked at her breasts. "I'll lock the door…" he said.

Just then, footsteps sounded down the wood floor of the hall and there was a sudden knock at the door.

"How's the movie going?" Sari called.

Mikey and Bernie looked at each other in a moment of shocked embarrassment while they waited for that doorknob to turn…

Chapter 9

"Just a sec!" Mikey called in a strained, deep voice.

There was a muffled laugh from the door. "Mandy's got more coffee. Come on out when your movie finishes."

"We will. Thanks!" he called back.

The footsteps withdrew.

He let out the breath he'd been holding. Bernie sat beside him as if in a daze, her top still up around her neck, her breasts pressed hard into the thick hair on Mikey's broad chest. He looked down at her with wonder.

"I guess the jig would have been up if Sari had opened that door," he laughed.

She smiled dreamily up at him. "I guess."

He drew in a hard breath. "I suppose we'd better stop while we're ahead." He drew back and looked down at her bare breasts with fascination. "Over the years, I've seen a lot of women undressed," he murmured. "But none of them were half as beautiful as you are, honey." He stroked her soft, firm breast and leaned down, putting his lips reverently to it. "I'll live on this my whole life."

Her heart skipped. She just looked at him with everything she felt for him in her green eyes. His jaw clenched. He still wanted her, now more than ever. But he managed some control as he pulled down the bra and fastened it, then drew the sweater down over her waist.

She smiled and fastened the buttons of his shirt. He looked rumpled and his hair was mussed from her hands in it. She loved the way he looked. He was a little flushed, too, and his dark eyes danced as they met hers.

"You'd like Vegas," he said. "For visits, anyway, it's an exciting place. Plenty of music and neon lights. An oasis in the desert."

She put her hands on his chest, over the buttoned shirt. "I don't guess you'd like a little Texas town that draws the sidewalks in at dusk," she said without meeting his eyes.

"I'd like wherever you called home, Bernie," he said solemnly. "We come from different places. But that doesn't mean both of us can't adapt to something else, even if it's just for a little while." He bent and kissed her very softly. "I didn't want to stop. You go to my head like whiskey. It was like sailing on the clouds."

She laughed and pressed close. "For me, too."

His arms contracted, holding her close and rocking her. "We'd better finish watching the movie. There may be a quiz after."

She laughed with pure delight. "Okay."

He drew her gently down beside him and clasped her hand tight in his. They watched the screen until the credits came on. Mikey turned off the entertainment center and drew Bernie along with him out the door and into the kitchen.

Paul and Sari looked up as they came into the room. Both were grinning.

"Yeah, we got a little friendly," Mikey said defensively. "It was me, mostly."

"It was me, too," she said, and smiled up at him.

"You don't need to excuse anything to us," Paul chuckled. "We've only been married three years."

"He means, we're still on our honeymoon," Sari teased. "So how about that coffee?"

"Sounds lovely," Bernie said, and stars were in the eyes she turned toward Mikey, who looked like a cat who'd just eaten a canary.

That expression went along with Bernie to work the following Monday, where Jessie saw it and grew sarcastic and insulting.

"We all heard about you and Mikey going over to his cousin's place. Some mansion," Jessie drawled sarcastically, glancing at Sari as she paused by Bernie's desk. "Got your eyes on that nice rich fish, don't you? But do you think a little hick like you could land a man that sophisticated?"

Bernie's face flamed, but she didn't back down. "Backgrounds don't make much difference when people have feelings for one another," she said.

"As if he'd have feelings for you," Jessie said with a laugh. "I don't know him personally, but I know about him. He's had women who were movie stars, and debutantes and millionaires' daughters. He's not likely to take up with a woman who's looking at a wheelchair a few years down the road."

"That's enough," Sari said icily, standing up. "One more word and Mr. Kemp is going to get an earful."

Jessie knew when to quit. She shrugged. "Just stating facts, that's all."

"Ooh, somebody's so jealous she can't stand it," Olivia drawled with an amused look at Jessie. "What's the matter, sweetie, did he slap you down over at the courthouse and you're getting even?"

Jessie actually flushed. 'He did not," she spit. "I could have him if I wanted him."

"Do be my guest and try," Olivia taunted. "We heard that you made him sick."

Jessie was almost vibrating by now. She started to speak just as Mr. Kemp's door opened and he came out. She went quickly to her desk with a forced smile at the boss and pretended to work.

Kemp, no fool, looked from Bernie's flushed face to Sari's angry one and drew a conclusion. He didn't say a word, but the look he gave an oblivious Jessie wasn't one that would have encouraged her about her longevity in this office.

Glory Ramirez came in the door, a little fatigued. "Court is bound over until tomorrow," she told Mr. Kemp. Glory was an assistant DA, like Sari.

"Does it look like the jury will convict?" Sari asked.

Glory made a face. "Who knows what a jury will do?" she asked with a sigh. "I hope I'm good enough to put this guy away. He lured a fourteen-year-old girl in with promises of true love and she fell for it. He's thirty-five," she added coldly.

"What a mess," Sari said.

"It's worse than that. She's pregnant," Glory said.

"Oh, that's no problem," Jessie laughed. "She can just go to a clinic and have them take it out."

"She and her people are deeply religious," Glory replied. "Not everybody thinks of termination as birth control, Jessie."

There was a whip in her voice. The other women knew why. Glory had lost her first baby after a horrible fight with her husband when they were first married, before they really knew much about each other. It had taken her two years to get pregnant again. She and Rodrigo had one child, a boy, and Glory's precarious health made another unlikely. Her blood pressure was extremely high and she'd already had angioplasty for a blocked artery that had caused a mild heart attack.

"You people take everything so seriously," Jessie muttered.

"Babies are serious business," Mr. Kemp broke in. Everybody except Jessie knew that he'd been in love and engaged, and his fiancée had died after a local woman spiked her drink with a drug. The fiancée had been pregnant at the time, and the child died with her.

"Babies are a nuisance. They cry and keep everybody upset, and you never get your waistline back again. I'd never want one," Jessie said.

"I would," Bernie said on a long, happy sigh.

"Good luck with that, in your physical condition," Jessie said sarcastically.

"If I could have a child, with my blood pressure, there's no reason Bernie couldn't have one with her limitations."

Bernie smiled at her. "Thanks."

"Not a chance I'd take," Jessie muttered.

"Thank you for your input, Miss Tennison, and how about that call I asked you to make half an hour ago to the DA in Bexar County on the Ramsey matter?" Kemp asked shortly.

Jessie flustered. "Oh. Sorry. I forgot. I'll get him for you right now, Mr. Kemp!"

Kemp gave her an angry glance, smiled at the other women and went back into his office.

Bernie went to lunch at Barbara's Café and there was Mikey, holding down a table for them. He got up as she joined him, after she'd given her order and paid for it.

"I could have gotten the tab, honey," he said.

"I can pay for my own stuff," she teased. "But thanks for the thought."

His hand slid over hers and held it tight. "You don't look so good. Bad morning?"

"Sort of," she said. "But it's improving already," she added with a loving glance at his handsome face.

He grinned. "That's better. I like it when you're happy."

"I usually am." She didn't mention the confrontation with Jessie or the woman's harsh words. She pushed them to the back of her mind while she and Mikey had nice pieces of roast beef with perfect mashed potatoes and gravy and home-cooked green beans.

"This is so good," she sighed. "I love to cook, but it's hard for me to stand for long periods of time. Still, I used to do it when I lived at home with my parents."

"We were going to talk last night," he mused.

She flushed.

He laughed sensuously. "We didn't do a whole lot of talking, though, did we, baby," he whispered. "It's hard to think of things like that when I'm with you. I just go nuts when I touch you."

"I go nuts, too," she whispered back, and her face colored even more as she looked at his mouth and recalled the havoc it could create suckling at her breast. She caught her breath just with the memory of how it had felt.

"Oh, this won't do," Mikey said, and shifted uncomfortably. "We'd better not think too much about last night. Especially in a roomful of people."

She laughed softly.

He laughed, too.

"What sweet memories we're making, honey," he murmured as he forced himself to go back to his roast beef. "And we'll make plenty more, I promise you."

"You still have your shadow, I see," she replied under her breath, glancing out the front window at the black sedan parked there.

"They're being careful. After all, one guy almost got by them." He made a face. "It makes me wish I'd made fewer enemies along the way. This isn't the first time I've had somebody come after me over territory."

She was looking at him with open curiosity.

"What is it?" he asked.

"Nothing much. Just... Well, there's a coin-shaped depression in your back," she began. "I felt it last night."

"Noticed, did you?" He wasn't offended. He just smiled. "Yeah, I caught a bullet there when I was overseas in the Middle East. Punctured my lung and almost killed me, but I survived."

"I'm so glad you did," she said demurely, and she was unspeakably grateful that it had happened in a combat zone and not as a result of conflict with gangsters. He spoke of that world as if he knew it very well. Certainly he had to, if he was mixed up with a Mafia don whom he was protecting. It made her just a little uneasy. She didn't know much about organized crime. What she'd seen in movies and read in books was unlikely to be a mirror of the real thing. That word Mikey had used, *omertà*, she'd seen it in print somewhere. She couldn't recall where. She was going to do a search on Google when she got home that night, just to see if she could find the connection. No need to tell Mikey. She looked at him with hungry eyes that she couldn't help. He was becoming the most important thing in her life.

But what if Jessie was right? Mikey was rich and sophisticated. Yes, he liked going out with her and kissing her, but that wasn't a future. She knew some gangsters married, but most of them seemed to just live together. Or so she thought. And she couldn't do that.

It would break her heart if Mikey didn't feel the same way she did. If he was only playing with her, she was going to die.

"Hey, what's wrong?" he asked. "You look tragic."

She forced a smile. "It's been a long morning, that's all," she said brightly. "Lots of people breaking the law. Of course, that's not a bad thing for us."

"Not at all." He looked up and his dark eyes sparked.

Bernie followed his gaze and there was Jessie, just picking up a salad and coffee at the checkout. It was on a tray, which meant she wasn't leaving.

"The bubonic plague has arrived," Mikey muttered.

"Well, hi there, Bernie. I didn't know you were coming here for lunch. And Mikey, how's it going with you?" she added, almost purring.

He looked up at her with cold eyes and took a minute to answer. "We're having a private conversation, if you don't mind."

Jessie shrugged. "Well, excuse me, I'm sure," she

drawled. She went to a table nearby, at the window, and put down her food.

Bernie was crestfallen. She'd hoped to have a nice quiet lunch with Mikey, but Jessie was already staring at them. Cooking up plots. Bernie was certain that the woman was searching for ways to split her from Mikey, because Mikey was rich and Jessie wanted him.

"Don't look like that," Mikey said, smiling at her. "She's trying to upset you. Don't let her."

"She really likes you," Bernie said, almost choking on the words.

"It isn't mutual."

The way he looked at her sent all her fears flying away. She smiled slowly. So did he. The rest of the world faded away until there were just the two of them.

They didn't look in Jessie's direction at all. She glared at both of them the whole time. She didn't stop even when they were walking out of the café.

"If looks could kill," Bernie said on a heavy sigh when they were back on the street.

"Why doesn't Kemp fire her?" he asked abruptly.

"I think he'd like to, but he has to have a reason that will hold up in court."

"Lawyers," he muttered.

She laughed. "You sound like one of the men we prosecuted for theft. He was sure that lawyers were all bound for a fiery end."

His hand caught hers. "I've gone my rounds with prosecutors," he mused as they walked toward her office.

"You have?" she asked, curious.

He looked down at her solemnly. "We really are going to have to have a talk," he told her. "There are things about me that you need to know."

She drew in a long breath. "There are things about me you need to know, too."

"Come over for lunch Sunday," he invited. "Paulie said Sari was going to ask you, anyway. We can walk down through the woods and talk without people watching us all the time."

"Would you be safe if we did that?" she worried. "I mean, snipers love deserted places, don't they?"

He chuckled. "The one who's watching me surely does," he pointed out.

"Oh! I forgot."

He grinned. "I'm glad. I don't want you upset. I can take care of myself, honey. I've been in worse jams than this. I'll tell you about it, Sunday." He paused and turned toward her. "You think you can live with my past. I'm not sure you can. But I'll leave the decision up to you."

"You undervalue yourself," she said, searching his dark eyes. "I said it wouldn't matter. I meant it."

He smiled and touched her cheek gently. "You think it wouldn't," he said sadly. "That may not be the case."

"You can tell me Sunday."

"And there you both are again," Jessie said from behind them.

"Yeah," Mikey said, glaring at her.

She made a face and went past them into the office, slamming the door behind her.

"Sore loser," he muttered after her.

Bernie smiled. It made her feel good that Mikey preferred her to the beautiful woman who'd just gone past them. She felt valued.

"Idiot," he whispered. "You're worth ten of a woman like that." His head jerked toward the office. "She's anybody's. She'll play up to a man for what he's got, nothing else. Women like that are after hard cash, not love."

"I don't care about money," Bernie said.

"I know that. It's one of your best traits, and you've got a lot of them."

"Me?" she laughed. "I'm just ordinary." She drew in a breath. "You know, I have flares in the winter," she began. "I spend a lot of time in bed…"

He put his forefinger over her lips. "That won't matter, either. You nursed me through one of the worst headaches I've ever had. If you get down, I'll take care of you," he added huskily.

Tears stung her eyes. She lowered them to his broad chest.

"Don't cry," he whispered. "People will think I'm being mean to you."

She laughed. "Sorry. It's just that I've never really had anybody take care of me, not since my father died."

"I don't want to be your dad," he pointed out. He frowned. "You know, Bernie, I'm a lot older than you."

"Bosh," she mused, looking up into his face. "You'll never be old. Not to me."

His breath caught in his throat. He looked around. Cars everywhere. People on the sidewalks. Her boss, coming toward them.

"Oh, damn," he said under his breath.

Her eyebrows arched. "What?"

"Bernie, I want to kiss you so badly that it hurts and we're surrounded by people. Damned people!"

She grinned up at him. "There's Sunday," she teased.

He pursed his lips. His dark eyes twinkled. "Yeah. There's Sunday."

"Lunchtime's almost over, Bernie," Kemp teased as he came up beside them. "Back to boring routine."

"It's never boring, Mr. Kemp," she said, and meant it. "Tedious and maddening, but never boring!"

He grinned, nodded to Mikey, and went inside the building.

"I'd better go in. When?" she asked. "Sunday, I mean."

"About eleven suit you?"

She nodded. "That sounds great."

"I won't see you for a couple of days," he said. "I've got some people to see up in San Antonio. Santi and I have a room reserved for it. But I'll be here to pick you up Sunday, okay? And tell Mrs. Brown not to rent out my room while I'm gone!"

"I will, but she never would. She thinks you're terrific. So do the other boarders." She lowered her eyes to his chest. "So do I."

He bent and brushed a kiss over her forehead. "I think you're terrific, too, kid," he whispered. "Now go to work before I wrestle you down in the grass over there and do what I'm aching to do!"

Her breath caught. "It's in public view!"

"So would we be, and they'd be snapping pictures for the local paper, too," he assured her. "See you Sunday, honey. Be careful. Don't go out at night for any reason at all. You're being watched, but don't take chances. I couldn't live if anything happened to you." He touched her cheek and walked away before she could get the words out that she'd wanted to say.

No matter, she told herself. She could recite them on Sunday.

Jessie was wary of Sari and Glory, so she kept her hot words to herself. But just before quitting time, she stopped by Bernie when the other women were getting their coats and leaned close.

"You think he's hooked? You just wait," she threatened softly. "There's never been a man I couldn't get!"

And before Bernie could say a word, she was out the door and gone.

Bernie was agonizing over what she was going to have to tell Mikey on Sunday. She knew that he had a past, and she was sure she could live with whatever it was. But she wasn't so sure that he could live, not only with her disability issues, but with what had happened in her family. It was so horrible that she never spoke of it. Only a few people in Jacobsville knew. Her father was a good man, a kind man, who was wonderful to his daughter. But her grandfather had been a different story. He'd been notorious, in fact, and the story was so gruesome that it was fodder for the tabloids for the better part of a month.

None of that was Bernie's fault. She'd only been involved because he was part of her family, but it stung just the same. She felt dirty because of it. There had been survivors who were outraged. Her father had been targeted by one. Only the quick arrival of the sheriff's department had saved Bernie and her dad, because the man had been armed. She couldn't even blame him. The grief must have been horrible. But her father was no more responsible for it than Bernie was. It was just that the survivors couldn't get to the people responsible, so they went after the people who were left.

That had eventually blown over. Tempers cooled, people went back to church and remembered that part of their religious faith was the very difficult tenet of forgiveness for even the most horrible crimes. Bernie and her dad moved from Floresville back to Jacobsville, and distance helped. But that didn't mean that Bernie might not be a target in the future from some other relative who was frustrated by not having a means of vengeance.

She'd have to tell Mikey that. She'd also have to make him understand about her illness. There was no cure for rheumatoid arthritis. There were many treatments, most of which worked, but the most useful were beyond Bernie's pocket. Even with them, she would still have flares, days when she couldn't work at all. And because the drugs required worked at lowering her immune system to fight the RA, she was more disposed to illness than healthy people. She had bad lungs and often had respiratory infections. Mikey had to understand that just an occasional flare was the least of her health issues.

If he still wanted her after all that, well, it would make him a man in a million. Her family's notoriety was going to make things more complicated.

But it might work out, she told herself. They might actually be able to make it work, if they could keep Jessie at bay. She was an odd sort of person, very narcissistic and pretty horrible. She didn't feel compassion and she had an acid tongue. What in the world was she doing in a small town like Jacobsville when she was obviously more suited to big cities? It was a puzzle.

There was a cold rain on Friday afternoon just as Bernie was getting ready to go home. She hadn't worn a raincoat or brought an umbrella, and it was pouring outside. Even in south Texas, it could get pretty cold in autumn.

"Let me drop you off at your boardinghouse, Bernie," Sari offered. "You'll get soaked going home and you'll be sick."

"Yes, you have to stay well or Mikey won't be able to take you anyplace, will he, sweetie?" Jessie purred as she passed them outside, her umbrella raised.

"One day," Sari said with venom, and glared at the other woman.

Jessie made a harrumphing sound in her throat and went on down the street to where her car was parked. Strangely, it was an expensive foreign one. How could she afford that on what she made as a stenographer and receptionist for the local DA, Sari wondered.

"You should have a car," Sari chided gently as the limousine driver started off down the street with his two passengers in back.

"They break down," Bernie said with a smile. "I can't afford to run one. And I can mostly walk to work, except when I'm having flares. Then I get a cab."

"You can always ride with me," Sari said. "Anytime you need to."

"Thanks," Bernie said. "But I do okay."

Sari laughed and shook her head. "Honestly, you're the hardest person to do anything for."

"I guess so. Sorry."

"It's not a bad trait. Jessie would do anything for someone with money," she added harshly. "That woman makes my blood boil."

"Mikey can't stand her," Bernie said with a wicked little smile.

Sari laughed. "So he said. I guess he's seen that sort so much in his life that he hasn't got any interest in them anymore."

"He said that he was a bad man," Bernie mentioned.

"Some bad, some good, like all of us."

Bernie looked at her warmly. "I told him it wouldn't matter, whatever he'd done."

"That's like you," Sari replied. She studied the other woman quietly. "He'll tell you the truth. I know about it from Paul. He and Mikey both had hard lives as children. They grew up with people who weren't good role models. Mikey went the wrong way. I think he's trying to leave that behind him now. But…" She hesitated, noticing how Bernie hung on every word. "But he'll have to tell you the rest. And you'll have to make a choice." She paused. She didn't want to say it. "That choice may be harder than you think right now."

Bernie drew in a long breath. "It's too late for choices," she said softly. "He's my whole world, Sari. He's…everything."

Sari smiled. "Paul is mine. I understand. It's just… Well, Mikey will explain it to you," she finished.

Bernie studied her hands, poised on her purse in her lap. "He's mixed up somehow with organized crime, I think," she said without noting Sari's sudden alertness. "I watched *The Godfather*, so I sort of know about that stuff."

She didn't know anything, not a thing, about the harshness and the blood and the savagery with which Mikey's associates did and could act. Sari didn't want to enlighten her, though. It was going to be up to Mikey. If Bernie truly loved him, they'd find a way to make it work.

"Paul says he's never seen Mikey so happy," Sari said, instead of voicing her thoughts.

Bernie beamed. "I've never been so happy, not in all my life." She looked at Sari. "You know all about my family, about what happened. Will Mikey be able to handle it? I mean, there are people who went after Daddy, when he was alive, because of what my grandfather did."

"Nobody's ever come after you, and nobody ever will. If they even try, we'll sic Mr. Kemp on them. He'll handle it. Okay?"

Bernie let out the breath she'd been holding. "Okay."

"And Mikey's the last person who'll blame you for something someone in your family did," she added.

"I was notorious for a while," Bernie said hesitantly.

"Only for a while, and never after you moved here with your dad," Sari added.

"I suppose so." She lowered her face. "I don't want Mikey to be ashamed of me."

"As if that would ever happen! Honestly, Bernie!" she laughed. "He's crazy about you. It won't matter."

Bernie smiled. "Okay."

"And the past doesn't matter. For either one of you."

"If I stay sick all the time, it may," Bernie voiced her other fear. "I've got a weak immune system already, and the medicines I have to take for RA make it even weaker. I get sick a lot, especially in cold weather."

"It won't matter," she said firmly. "Besides, Mikey could afford those outrageously expensive medicines that they think might help you," she added with a smile.

"As if I'd let him do that," Bernie began.

"Under certain circumstances, you would," Sari drawled, and laughed at the expression on her coworker's face. "Life is sweet. You're just finding that out."

"It's never been sweeter, in fact."

"So live one day at a time," Sari counseled, "and let tomorrow take care of itself."

"That sounds easy. It's not."

"Nothing is easy. But we get by. Right?"

"Right."

"And if Jessie makes one more snide remark about how unhealthy you are, I'm going to encourage Olivia to pour coffee on her head!"

"Oh, don't suggest that—Olivia would do it on a dare," Bernie laughed uproariously.

"I heard about the coffee incident after I got back from vacation this summer," Sari said mischievously. "Nobody had made coffee. Agent Murdock came to see the boss on a case, and he made coffee just for himself and turned off the pot. Olivia went to get herself a cup. It was barely lukewarm by then, but she thought she'd drink it anyway. She took a sip, spat it out, glared at Murdock, who was flushed by then, and she poured the whole carafe right over his head and his suit. Lucky it wasn't hot!"

"Mr. Kemp came out of his office to usher Agent Murdock in," Bernie recalled, laughing so hard she almost choked. "And when he saw Olivia with the empty pot and the full cup in Agent Murdock's hand, he put his hand over his mouth and went right back into his office and closed the door. I swear, he laughed for five minutes."

"What did Agent Murdock do?"

Bernie whistled. "He got up, in the ruins of his suit, stared at Olivia for a minute, and then poured the contents of his own coffee cup over her head."

"And?" Sari prompted.

"He walked out the door in a huff and she went home to change. We're still laughing about it. Except that when Agent Murdock comes through the door, they both pretend that the other one is invisible. It makes things interesting."

Sari just grinned.

Chapter 10

Sunday morning, Mikey came by to pick up Bernie at Mrs. Brown's boardinghouse. He was preoccupied at first, frowning.

"What's wrong?" she asked gently. "Can I help?"

He turned toward her and smiled slowly, oblivious to Santi's quick and amused glance in the rearview mirror from the front seat. "There's that sweet compassion that I've hardly had in my whole life," he said. "You really are one in a million, kid."

She flushed. "So are you. But can I help?"

"You can listen, when we get to Paulie's house," he said. He glanced in the front seat. "And you can have the day off until I call you to take us home, Santi," he added with a grin. "You might go take in a movie."

"Not a bad idea, boss," Santi said with a big smile. "Thanks!"

He shrugged. "I'm not a bad guy."

Santi made a sarcastic noise, but Mikey ignored him. They got out at the front door of Paul's house, and Santi raised a hand and waved as he drove off.

Mikey held Bernie's hand tight in his and put his finger on the doorbell.

Before he could push it, the door opened. Sari and Paul welcomed them in.

"We have lunch," Sari announced. "Mandy made a macaroni and ginger and chicken salad, and sliced some fruit to go with it."

"That sounds wonderful," Bernie said.

"It does. Nobody cooks like Mandy," Mikey said.

"I heard that," Mandy called from the kitchen. "Come on in. I've almost got everything on the table."

She did. The place settings were immaculate, like the white linen napkins. Mikey pulled out a chair for Bernie and then one for himself.

Mandy came back in with a basket of blueberry muffins and put them on the table. "Who wants coffee?"

Every hand went up.

Mandy laughed. "That's what I figured," she mused. "Coming right up."

Bernie was a little self-conscious at first. She wasn't used to mansions and elaborate dining room place settings, and this was her first real meal with the Fiores. But the conversation and Mikey's attention thawed her out in no time at all.

"This is delicious," Bernie commented as she savored a bite of the chicken dish.

"We like it as a light meal," Sari said. "Neither of us likes anything heavy in the middle of the day. Or in the evening, for that matter."

"No wonder you're both so slender," Bernie teased.

"People in law enforcement have to be fast," Paul chuckled. "I had to run down a counterfeiter just last week," he added. "If I overeat, I lose my edge."

Mikey grinned at him. "Not likely," he commented. "You do okay, cousin."

"Sari says Jessie is giving you two a hard time," Paul noted.

Mikey's lip pulled down. "She's persistent, I'll give her that. But she has the appeal of a skunk on acid. Know what I mean?"

Paul laughed. "I do."

"Besides," Mikey said, his eyes on Bernie, "I have other interests."

Bernie beamed and almost spilled her coffee. Her heart was going so fast that it shook her blouse. Mikey noticed that and flashed her a wicked smile.

After lunch, Mikey took Bernie's hand and led her down the wooded path that eventually ended at the stables where the Grayling racehorses lived in luxury.

"I love it here," Bernie said, looking around at the leafless trees next to tall fir trees that were still green. "Fir trees are awesome."

"Yeah, they are," he agreed. "Out west, we've got Colorado blue spruce that go right up into the sky."

"Are they really blue, or is that just a description that stuck?"

"They're really blue," he replied. He stopped walking and turned to her. "Next time I go to Vegas, you can come with me. We'll go by way of Wyoming and have a look at Yellowstone and Old Faithful. It's a sight you'll never forget."

She hesitated.

He noticed that. "I have plans," he said softly. "First, I have to take the heat off Tony and get him out of the mess he's in. He's family, you see?" he asked, scowling. "It's loyalty. You take a solemn vow. You fulfill it. If you don't, there are terrible penalties. Nobody ever sells out anybody in his family. If he does, the penalty is unspeakable." He didn't add that he'd participated in such retribution. He had to confess as much as he could to her, but there were things he had to keep to himself.

She looked up at him with her heart in her eyes. "It won't matter," she said stubbornly.

He touched her cheek with the tips of his fingers. "Bernie, I've been involved with the mob since I was old enough to carry a piece. I've done things..." He hesitated. It had never really bothered him before. Now it was hard to reconcile what he'd done with what he wanted to do now. He drew in a breath. "You've watched *The Godfather* movies, haven't you?"

"Oh, yes. They're great movies," she said.

"You remember about the horse's head being in bed with the producer who wouldn't give the outfit's singer a job?"

She nodded.

"And the way Michael's older brother was murdered, a hit organized by a rival family?"

She felt cold chills down her spine. "Yes," she said huskily. "I remember that, too."

"Well, that was glossed-over stuff," he said flatly. "Family hits are just plain gore. You don't know what happened to Paulie, do you?"

She just shook her head.

"He had a wife and a little girl, before he came down

here to work for old man Grayling as a security expert," he said. "Paulie was the only person in our whole family who went straight. He worked with the FBI in Jersey, and he shut down one of the minor crime bosses. He felt great about it. But when he went home that night, his wife and his little girl had been done with a shotgun."

Bernie put a hand to her mouth. "Oh, the poor man!" she exclaimed, shocked.

"He took years getting over it," he said. "Eventually, he fell in love with Sari, but he got cold feet and made some excuse to quit. It was three years before he came back. In the meantime, Sari's father had beaten the girls to within an inch of their lives. Sari blamed Paul and had nothing to do with him when he worked out of the FBI office in San Antonio. But she was in a hurricane down in the Bahamas. Paul thought she was dead, but he and Mandy went to bring her home. She turned up alive and they were married the same week. Paulie never got over losing his family, though. He blamed himself for pushing the crime boss too hard and going after his whole organization."

"What happened to the man who killed his first family?" she asked.

His face grew hard. "I knew a guy who was inside," he said shortly. "I took care of it."

She felt the blood drain out of her face. "You...?"

"I took care of it," he repeated quietly. "Yes. I have that kind of power. I worked my way up through the organization for years, to get to where I am now. I own one of the biggest casinos in Vegas and I'm filthy rich. I was arrested once on a murder charge, but I had witnesses swear I was nowhere near the scene of the crime. They had no real evidence, so they dropped the case."

She moved to a big oak tree and leaned back against it. This was news she hadn't anticipated, and it was shocking. She looked up into cold dark eyes.

"I'm so sorry, honey. I didn't want to have to confess how bad a man I am. But you had to know," he said. Inside, he was churning like storm clouds. He hadn't wanted to tell her these things, but he couldn't offer her a future without making her aware of the past. "There's more," he told her. "A lot more. But this is enough for now."

Her lips parted on a long breath. She looked at him helplessly. She loved him. He was a criminal. He would probably never give up that life. He'd told her graphically what the family he belonged to would do if they were betrayed.

"Omertà," she whispered heavily.

He moved closer. "Yeah. Omertà," he replied. "It's the code we live by. Or die by, if we betray anybody in our family. They don't just kill you. They kill everybody you love. It's like erasing your whole life."

She leaned her head back against the hard bark of the tree and just looked at him. She didn't understand what he wanted from her, why he was telling her something so personal.

"So that's the secret I keep," he said. "It's bad. It's horrible. But it's a part of my life that you have to understand if we go forward together. So. What secrets are you keeping?" he added in a tender voice.

She took a deep breath. "My grandfather owned a little store over in Floresville. He and my grandmother ran it. We noticed that Granddaddy was forgetful, and sometimes he had rages, when he just went wild over something he saw on television, or something a politician said. We overlooked it because we thought it was just the product of normal aging."

He moved closer. "But it wasn't?"

"It wasn't. One day, he was listening to what a politician said about the economy and new regulations that were going to go into effect. Granddaddy started yelling that those people needed to be killed, slaughtered."

She hesitated, then plowed ahead without looking at him. "Maybe he would have calmed down, but the mayor was in his store buying some hardware, and he and Granddaddy got into an argument about politics. They were completely opposite in their views. The mayor tried to calm my grandfather down, and he thought he had. My grandmother chided him for being so violent over just stupid politics. She said he needed to lie down for a while. Granddaddy didn't argue with her. He went out from behind the counter without a word. My grandmother was relieved, she thought he was over his anger. Not five minutes later, he came back into the front of the store with an automatic pistol." She swallowed hard. "He killed my grandmother and the mayor, and then he turned the gun on three customers and killed them, too. The survivors screamed and ran out of the store. A local policeman heard the screams and went into the store with his pistol drawn. Granddaddy shot him dead the minute he walked into the store. The police called in the SWAT team from San Antonio. Granddaddy was holed up in the store, and he wouldn't come out and give up his gun." She sighed. "Long story short, the SWAT team went in and shot my grandfather. He died on the way to the hospital. My mother was so ashamed and sick at what her father had done, so grieved at the loss of her mother and the forthcoming fury of the townspeople, that she locked herself in the bathroom and slashed her own throat with a razor blade. We thought she was taking a bath." Her eyes closed. "By the time we realized something was wrong and Daddy got the door open, it was much too late. She died."

"Oh, God," he said. "You poor kid!"

She bit her lower lip. "Daddy sold the house and moved us here. It was horrible, the aftermath. We were hated by so many people who lost loved ones that day. I didn't blame them, you know, but Daddy and I had nothing to do with what happened. Nothing at all."

He moved forward and pulled her into his arms, folding her close, rocking her while she cried. "And I thought I'd had a hard life," he whispered at her ear. "Baby, I wish I'd known you then. Nobody would ever have hurt you!"

She pressed close, resting her wet cheek over his heart. "I thought you might not want anything else to do with me when you knew about what happened."

"Dopey girl," he murmured, and laughed softly. "I'm hooked. Haven't you noticed? Who do I hang around with all the time? Who do I take to movies and into rooms where we do naughty things together?"

She laughed through her tears. "Me, I guess."

"You." He drew in a long, slow breath. His arms tightened. "I pledged allegiance to Tony. I have to fulfill my vows. I can't let him die, whatever I have to do to save him."

"Family is more important than your own life, isn't it?"

"Yes." His breath was warm at her ear. "I'm mixed up in this in a bad way. I can't make commitments right now. But when it's over, when I clear Tony..."

She didn't move. Her eyes closed. "I told you," she whispered. "I meant it. It won't matter."

"God!" His mouth moved over hers and he kissed her with subdued passion, with pure hunger. He hadn't imagined that she could live with the things he'd done, that she could still want him after she knew them. She was an extraordinary woman. "Bernie," he said unsteadily, "you're the very breath in my body!"

She couldn't even find words to express what she felt, so she kissed him with her whole heart, her arms stealing up around his neck, her mouth answering his with the same hungry passion that he was showing her.

He groaned and his hands ran up and down her sides, his thumbs pressing under her breasts.

"Ahem."

Mikey lifted his head and stared at Bernie blankly. "What did you say?"

"I didn't say anything," she began.

"Ahem." It came again. Mikey frowned and felt around his lapel. There was a device that had been placed there in San Antonio. He glowered at it.

"Yes?" Mikey asked abruptly.

"I have a bead on you and quite frankly if you don't break that up, I'm going to have to leave you defenseless and go get several drinks of hard liquor."

Mikey's teeth ground together. "Damn it, Billings," he muttered.

"A lot of drinks," Billings continued. "Maybe a whole damned fifth. It's been a long dry spell and I have to watch you. Get it? Watch you."

Mikey drew a long breath and stared at Bernie with amused regret. "Okay. We'll go look at the horses."

"Good idea. Blakely's in there. You can drive him nuts!" There was a click and the device went silent.

Bernie was flushed and embarrassed.

"Hey," Mikey said, pushing back the unruly long, blond hair from her face. "Billings is right. This isn't the time or place."

"Did he hear all we said?" she worried.

"Not likely. He doesn't eavesdrop. I guess we were getting pretty heated, huh?" He laughed. "Okay. Let's behave." He caught her fingers and entangled them with his. "Let's go look at the pretty horses."

She laughed. Life was sweet. He didn't mind her past. She didn't mind his. This was a relationship with a future. She'd never been so certain of anything.

They wandered through the stables. There was a man in charge of the thoroughbreds. He explained them to Bernie.

"They're descended from three stallions imported into England in the seventeenth and eighteenth centuries, the beginning of their line. We won the Kentucky Derby with this fellow," he said, smiling as he approached the big stall where the racehorse lived. "He has his own pasture and he's at stud. We get fabulous amounts of money from his colts. He's a grand old fellow."

Bernie looked at him with awe. He was grand, elegant and handsome, and he knew it, too. "He's gorgeous," she said.

The stable manager chuckled. "We think so, too. He has a colt that was born just two months ago. It's down here."

He led them down the paved aisle to another stall,

where a handsome young thoroughbred was playing with a big ball.

"Horses play?" Bernie exclaimed.

The manager laughed. "Of course. They're like puppies or toddlers at this age. When they hit adolescence, or the horse equivalent, that's when the problems start. Right now, they're just children and it's a whole new world for them."

Bernie just watched the colt play, fascinated. "I've never been around horses much," she confessed. "We had a small ranch in Floresville where my people had a few head of beef cattle. There were a few horses for the cowboys, but I never rode one. I was afraid of them."

"Never let a horse know that," the manager told her. "They'll take advantage."

"I'm not likely to be put on a horse anytime soon," she assured him.

"If you ever did want to ride, we have a fifteen-year-old gelding, very gentle, who would be perfect for you. If you ever did," he added.

Mikey chuckled and pressed her fingers with his. "There may come a day," he said with a gentle smile at Bernie, who returned it.

"There may," she said.

They went back to the house.

"You're back soon," Sari commented.

"Yeah," Mikey said with a rueful smile. "Billings is a wet blanket."

"Chet Billings? You saw him?" she asked.

"No. We heard him. He's got this device on me," he added, indicating the electronic thing on his lapel.

"Oh. He talked to you?"

"He threatened to get drunk is what he did." Mikey looked at Bernie and sighed. "I guess there's no real privacy left on earth."

"Yes, there is. The conservatory is very nice, very quiet and it has a door. However," she added mischievously, "not being stupid, I'll call you when supper is ready and I'll probably open the door to do it."

Mikey sighed. "Speak loudly, okay?" he teased.

Sari laughed. "Very loudly." She gave them a knowing look and went back into the kitchen, where she and Mandy were sharing coffee. "Do you want coffee?" she called over her shoulder.

"Later," Mikey said. "When supper's ready. Thanks, Sari," he added.

"I wasn't always married," Sari replied, and grinned.

Mikey took off the lapel pen, put it on a table in the hall and drew Bernie into the room with him. He closed the door behind him and, as an afterthought, locked it.

"Just so you know," he said as he pulled her gently into his arms, "we're big on innocence. Some people might call us reactionary, but we respect our women and we don't dishonor them. You get what I mean?"

He was telling her that he wouldn't let it go too far. She smiled. "I guess you know all about me."

His mouth brushed hers. "I know that you're an innocent, Bernie," he whispered. "It excites me and maddens me, all at once."

"Maddens you?"

"Obstacles are frustrating," he mused. He kissed her with slow, hungry brushes of his mouth, feeling hers follow it helplessly. "But we'll muddle through. When things get too hot, and they might, all you have to do is remind me that I promised not to let things go too far."

She laughed. "Okay."

He smiled as he kissed her again. "You make me hungry for things I never wanted before," he murmured as he maneuvered her onto the cushy sofa and came down beside her. "A home, a family, roots," he whispered. He had her blouse off and her bra unsnapped in seconds. "Belonging," he murmured as his mouth opened over her taut nipple and suddenly suckled her, hard.

She came right off the sofa, a tiny, shocked cry pulsing out of her throat, a sound she'd never heard from it before.

"Shh," he whispered gruffly. "They'll hear."

She bit her lower lip and pulled his head closer, her fingers spearing through his thick, wavy black hair as his mouth made magic on her body.

"Glory!" she moaned. "Mikey, do it harder," she whispered frantically. "Harder!"

"I'll hurt you," he groaned.

"No. You won't. Please...!"

He took all of her firm breast into his mouth and his tongue worked on the nipple until she was writhing wildly under the sudden heavy press of his body.

One big hand was under her hip, grinding her against the growing hardness of him, letting her feel his need. It was desperate.

She felt guilty. She was inciting him, and they couldn't be intimate. She remembered suddenly what he'd told her about heavy petting, that he could have the clothes out of the way and be inside her in less time than it would take to react.

She thought about feeling him inside her, and she shivered with the sudden need.

Her nails bit into the back of his head as she held it closer, arching so that he could feed more easily on her breast. She shivered rhythmically as he suckled her, harder and harder. All at once she arched and sobbed and felt a shaft of pleasure pierce her that was beyond anything she'd ever dreamed. She convulsed, shuddered, flew up into the clouds and exploded.

Then she cried, embarrassed. He cuddled her close, denying his starved body the release it begged for. "It's all right," he whispered. "It's natural, baby. It's all right."

"It really is? Natural, I mean?" she whispered brokenly.

He laughed softly. "That only happens to one woman in a hundred," he said. "Maybe one in a thousand. I've never seen it happen to a woman I was with." His mouth brushed over hers. "God, what a thrill it was! You've never felt it, have you?"

"Not…until now," she managed.

He drew in a rough breath. "I'm better than I thought I was," he teased.

She laughed. "You're better than I thought you were, and that's saying something."

He lifted his head and looked down at her bare breasts. "You know that you belong to me, don't you?" he asked, and met her eyes with his. They were solemn. "You're mine, Bernie."

She melted into the sofa under the hard, sweet pressure of his body. "Yes. I know it."

He moved over her, his body pressing her down. He fought his shirt out of the way so that his muscular hair-roughened chest was rubbing against her bare breasts. He shivered.

She did, too. "If you want to," she said unsteadily, "I will."

"Right here?" he asked huskily.

"Right here."

"You don't know how much I want to," he bit off.

She moved her hips just a tiny bit. "Oh, yes, I do," she said, feeling him swell even more.

"Baby," he whispered. He moved between her legs and pushed up, so that he was intimately pressed against the heart of her.

She sobbed, because it was beyond anything she'd felt before. Her legs moved apart, inviting him.

"It would have to be quick," he said gruffly. "Very quick. And it will probably hurt."

"I don't...care," she said unsteadily.

He kissed her softly, and his hand went under the band of her slacks, under her briefs. She caught his wrist, embarrassed.

He lifted his head. "You have to let me do this," he whispered, his voice shaken. "I have to know how careful I need to be with you. Okay?"

She bit her lip. "I've never..."

"I know that. But you belong to me."

She let her body relax, let the hardness of him fit against her so that it was heaven to feel. "Yes," she said, her voice tender, her eyes wide and rapt on his taut face.

His hand smoothed over her belly and he thought of a baby who would look like her or like himself. He had something to use, but he didn't want to use it. And he didn't want to take her here in a rush, the way he'd taken women in his youth. She would need time, lots of time, and he couldn't give it to her if they went too far.

His fingers moved down. She hesitated and tightened

as he suddenly began to probe where she was most a woman. She bit her lip hard enough to draw blood as he explored her intimately. Even loving him as she did, it was hard to give up control to another person.

He whispered, almost groaning as he drew his fingers back and smoothed them over her stomach, "It will hurt like hell, and I'm not sure I could even get through the barrier, you understand?"

"Oh!" She winced.

"Sorry." He rolled over onto his side and pulled her into his arms, grinding her breasts into his chest. "No, I'm sorry. I never meant to take it this far." His arms contracted. "God, Bernie, I want to get you pregnant so badly…!"

He kissed her shocked mouth and groaned again as he pushed her hips closer to his. "I want you. I want to go inside you, so deep, so hard, that you'll shoot up like a rocket!"

She flushed under the pressure of his hard mouth, moaning as she felt him move her rhythmically against his hips. "I'm so sorry…"

He managed a husky laugh. "Think of it as a chastity belt. It will keep me in line until we can make things legal."

She hid her face against his throat. Make it legal. Could he mean that he wanted to marry her? She was so entranced that she didn't even hear footsteps in the hall.

Neither did Mikey, who was kissing her as if he couldn't manage to stop.

The hard, insistent knock on the door and the rattling of the locked doorknob broke them apart.

"Supper!" Sari called.

Mikey laughed. "Okay! We'll be right there."

"I have a master key, you know. It fits all the locks," Sari threatened.

Bernie went beet-red. Mikey just chuckled. "We're behaving, starting right now!"

There was a laugh outside the door. "Fair warning. Five minutes and I unlock the door."

"Got it!" Mikey called.

Footsteps retreated.

Mikey took one long, last look at Bernie's half-nude body and groaned. "I hate dressing you," he muttered, as he refastened her bra and pulled her blouse down.

"I hate dressing you, too," she teased as she buttoned his shirt again. "I love the way you look undressed."

"Yeah. I feel exactly the same way about you."

"You're not upset by what I told you?" she asked, worried.

He cocked his head and stared at her. "I've done things almost as bad as your grandfather," he said flatly. "I can't sit in judgment on somebody else. Not my business. But now that you know what my business is," he added quietly, "you have to decide if you can live with it. There's no way I'll give it up. I can't. It's for life."

She was beginning to realize that even though he ran an honest gaming hotel in Las Vegas, he was firmly entrenched with a group that routinely broke the law. He could go to prison in certain circumstances. She'd have to be in the company of people who thought of crime as a way of life, an occupation. She'd be the outsider. Would the women in his organization hate her? And what about the women he'd had before her? Would they be around? Would they be like Jessie and make her life miserable?

"Deep thoughts, huh?" he asked quietly.

"Very deep." She drew in a breath. "Mikey, I'm not like you. I don't even jaywalk. My great-grandfather was a United States Marshal. I have a cousin who's a Texas Ranger. Law enforcement runs through my whole family."

"I see," he said heavily. "You don't think you could handle it."

"No!" She went close to him. "I'd be the outsider. The freak. They wouldn't accept me."

"Baloney," he mused. He smiled as he tangled his fingers in her hair. "You have no idea how much they'd accept you. They'd go places with you, protect you if you needed protection. They'd sit with you when you were sick, when you have flares. It's another whole world, baby. One you've never seen. It's violent, yes. But the people are just like anybody else. The women are a close-knit group, because there's always some danger involved that the men have to handle." He winced at her expression. "I don't know any other way of life, Bernie," he concluded. "I can't change what I am, what I do." He shrugged. "I don't want to. If that's selfish, I'm selfish."

She pressed herself close to him, sliding her arms around him. "I can try," she whispered.

His heart jumped. It lifted as if a dark cloud had dissipated in the sunlight. His arms tightened around her. "That's all I ask," he said. "That's all I want."

She smiled and closed her eyes.

There was a click and the door opened. Sari looked in with pursed lips when they turned toward her. She chuckled. "I warned you," she said, lifting the key to show them. "Supper."

Mikey grinned. "We're right behind you."

"Yes," Bernie agreed.

Mikey linked her fingers with his and the two of them looked, to Sari, like two halves of a whole. She had no doubt that there would be a wedding in the future.

Bernie clung to his hand and smiled. She looked up at Mikey with wonder, with adoration.

He saw that look and it made him feel a foot taller. His fingers contracted gently around hers. She tightened her own grip. She'd never known such wonder, such joy. It spilled out around her like sunshine. She smiled. So did Mikey. They both knew where this was leading, now more than ever.

Chapter 11

Supper was as uproarious as lunch had been. Paul had a dozen stories of things that had happened to him in the course of his duties. Foremost among those stories was the one he'd heard from Sari about agent Murdock. He recited it for Mikey and chuckled at his cousin's amusement.

"I like Olivia," Mikey said. "She seems very nice."

"She is," Bernie agreed. "Mr. Kemp hired her so that there would be another paralegal in the office on the days I can't work," she added, and felt uncomfortable talking about her limitations.

"You do very well, considering your obstacles," Sari told her. "We don't think of you as handicapped, you know," she added. "You have a disability. Lots of people have them. Look at poor Glory. She had dangerously high blood pressure and a light heart attack. But she overcame that to work here, where she and her husband and little boy live."

"I'd love a little boy," Mikey said, glancing at Bernie, who flushed. "Or a little girl. I'll bet little girls are sweet."

Bernie laughed. "I was never sweet," she teased. "I got into so much trouble when I was small. The worst time was when I climbed into the corncrib and couldn't get out, and a king snake decided to come in with me. He was huge. Over six feet long. I was terrified. But he didn't strike at me or even threaten me. He just stretched out on the corn and looked at me."

"Probably hunting rodents," Sari remarked. "They love corn."

"Probably," Bernie agreed. "All in all, he was a very polite snake. He didn't even seem bothered when Daddy came to find me and lifted me out of the corncrib."

"He might also have just eaten a few rats and was feeling lazy," Paul chuckled.

"Equally possible," Bernie laughed.

"Well, I've got briefs to read," Sari said.

"And I've got cases to work," Paul added as they both got to their feet. "You two can watch movies or just sit in the conservatory and watch the plants grow. You're both always welcome. Anytime."

"Thanks, Paul," Bernie said.

Mikey echoed the sentiment.

They were left with Mandy, who started to clear away the dishes. "You two want coffee?" she asked with a warm smile.

"Not for me," Mikey said. "I don't sleep good. It keeps me awake."

"Me, too," Bernie said.

Mikey stood up and helped Bernie out of her chair. "I think we'll go watch Sari's plants grow for a while, if you don't mind."

"Help yourselves," she said with a knowing grin.

Mikey led Bernie into the conservatory and locked the door.

"Nobody's likely to try it, but who knows?" Mikey teased. He took Bernie into his arms and kissed her hungrily. "Dessert," he whispered. "Sweeter than cake."

"Sweeter than honey," she agreed on a moan.

He picked her up and sat down with her in his lap, kissing her all the while.

She didn't protest his hands under her blouse. He was so familiar to her now, so dear, that she welcomed anything he did.

He knew that, and it kept him honest. He didn't want to take advantage of an attraction she couldn't help. She was very innocent. It made his head spin, that lack of sophistication. He loved it.

He eased her blouse and bra down to her waist and unbuttoned his shirt, pulling her hungrily inside it.

"Oh, glory," she choked when she felt thick, soft hair and warm muscles against her bare breasts. Her face sank into his throat while he caressed her.

"We're good together," he whispered. "Better than I dreamed. God, I want you!"

Her arms tightened around his neck. "I want you, too," she whispered back.

His hands smoothed over her hard-tipped breasts. "We've talked around it," he said after a minute. "But not any particulars." His hands moved her away and he looked at her breasts with possession and appreciation.

"You're beautiful like this, Bernie. It makes me hungry just to hold you. But this goes to my head like whiskey."

She arched backward, her body demanding, hungry, ignoring her mind's attempt to be sensible.

"This what you want, sweetheart?" he whispered, and his mouth swallowed up one small, taut breast almost whole.

She moaned and shivered.

"I thought so." His voice was rough, but his mouth was tender as he worked at the hard nipple slowly, tenderly, with a growing suction that very soon made her go stiff and then suddenly burst with pleasure that made her whole body convulse in his arms.

"God, I love this," he groaned against her breast. "I love that I can make you go off like a rocket when I suckle you!"

Her nails dug into him. It was a little embarrassing, but she was too exhausted with pleasure, with satisfaction, to protest. She shivered and clung to him in the aftermath. "I never felt anything like it in my whole life," she said brokenly. "It embarrasses me…"

His arms contracted. "Don't you dare be ashamed of something so beautiful," he whispered at her ear. "No two people ever belonged to each other more than we do right this minute, Bernie."

She swallowed, hard. "Do you feel that, too?"

He chuckled and turned her just a little, so that her hips were pressed to that part of him that was male and very hard. "Do you feel this?"

"Mikey!" she protested.

"A man can't fake that, honey," he said at her ear. "It's as honest as the way you react when I put my mouth on you." He drew back and looked down at her with pure possession. "There's nobody in the world like you."

She reached up and touched his cheek. "Or like you," she said solemnly.

He bent his dark head and smoothed his mouth over her breast tenderly. He drew in a breath. "We need to talk."

"We are."

"We need to talk when we're both dressed," he said with a droll smile.

"Oh."

He put her clothes back on and buttoned his shirt. When they were calmer, he drew her onto the love seat and sat holding her hand.

"Bernie, I'm not proud of what I'm about to tell you. But there's more about me that you need to know." He drew in a breath. "My family has belonged to what's known to outsiders as La Cosa Nostra for three generations. My father died working for them. I've been with Tony Garza since I was sixteen. I don't know any other way of life."

"You mean, you work outside the law," she said very calmly.

"That's exactly what I mean." He studied her face. She was a little pale, but she wasn't trying to get away from him. "We're like normal people. We pay our taxes, go to church, work for charitable causes, all that stuff. We just earn our living in ways that aren't conventional."

"I told you that I watched *The Godfather* movies," she said.

He brushed her disheveled hair back from her face. "That was a sanitized version of what really goes on," he said after a minute. "I won't, I can't, tell you how brutal it can be. You don't ever quit. And you don't rat out your associates. There are deadly penalties for that. Remember what I told you about Paulie's family?"

She just nodded. Her eyes were sketching his hard face as if she were painting it.

"I could go to jail one day," he persisted. "I could die."

"A meteor could land on the boardinghouse and take us all out," she said matter-of-factly. "Nobody is ever guaranteed even one more day."

He just looked at her.

"I'm not Italian," she said. "Would that make me an outsider?"

He smiled slowly. "The wives come from all sorts of backgrounds," he said, and noticed her flush at the word. "Some are American. Some are Italian and Spanish, even Polish. But they have one thing in common and that's family. We all belong to each other. If you shared that life with me," he said, "you'd be part of it. You'd never be an outsider. And if anything happened, anything at all, you'd be taken care of as long as you live. That's how it works."

She bit her lower lip. She drew in a breath. "Mikey, I won't get any better," she began. "There's no cure for what I have. They can control it with medicine, although I can't afford the kind that might make it easier. But they can't stop it. Eventually, I'll end up with twisted hands and feet, and even if I can walk with a cane at first, there's a good chance that one day I'll be in a wheelchair." She said it without a plea for pity. She just stated it as a fact.

He tilted her chin up. "I can live with your limitations. Can you live with my profession?"

She just nodded. She didn't say a word. She didn't have to.

He wrapped her up in his arms and just rocked her

slowly, his face in her throat. They sat that way for a long time until there was a brief tap and the sound of a key in the lock.

Sari peered around the door and burst out laughing. "And I was afraid I'd have to run for my life when I opened this door..."

Mikey and Bernie both laughed.

Mikey got up and drew her up beside him. "We were talking about the future," he said, smiling. "It looks pretty sweet."

"Pretty sweet, indeed," Bernie said with a long sigh as she looked up at him.

"I'd better get her home," Mikey said. "She has to work tomorrow."

"I know. So do I," Sari wailed.

"There, there," Bernie comforted her. "But there's always next weekend!"

They all laughed.

Mikey took her back to the boardinghouse and left her at her door with a discreet kiss on her forehead because Mrs. Brown was lurking.

"It was a lovely day. Thank you," Bernie said.

"It was one of many to come," he replied. He smiled at her with his heart in his eyes. "See you in the morning, kid. Sweet dreams."

"Oh, they'll be sweet, all right," she whispered, and then flushed.

He wrinkled his nose at her and winked.

She watched him all the way down the hall before she went back into her room and closed the door.

Work was difficult. Bernie's happiness lit her up like a Christmas tree, and it showed. Olivia teased her. But

Jessie watched and smoldered. She was furious that a plain little country girl like Bernie, one who was likely to end up living on disability, had attracted a man who could buy half a county with pocket change. Mikey was sophisticated, handsome and loaded. Jessie wanted him, and she couldn't get to first base. He avoided her like the plague when he was in town.

There had to be some way she could get him out of Bernie's life so that she had a chance with him. Being rude and unpleasant didn't do any good. But if she could play one of them against the other while pretending to turn over a new leaf... Well, that was a promising idea. She began to plot ways to accomplish it.

Her first step was to stop being abrasive to the other women in the office. She toned down her bad attitude and took on her share of the work instead of avoiding it. She offered to bring coffee to Olivia and Bernie when they were swamped with paperwork, and she even brought lunch back for them once.

Everyone was surprised, even Mr. Kemp, who actually praised Jessie for her changed attitude.

Nothing had changed at all except that Jessie was playing a new game. But she smiled and did her best to look humble. She even apologized for the way she'd behaved before. It was hard being a city girl in a small Texas town, she explained to the other women. She'd always had to fight to get ahead, where she'd come from, and it was difficult to stop. But she wanted to fit in. She was going to try harder. The other women in the office, suspecting nothing, warmed to her.

And Jessie just smiled to herself. So far so good, she thought. She even lost her fear of being fired, which she couldn't afford just now. She had a job to do. So

she smiled and answered the phone and stopped flirt-
ing with rich men.

Bernie mentioned the changed attitude to Mikey on
one of their dates, and he laughed. Bernie, he commented, was rubbing off on the other woman. He was
happy to see it. So the next time he came across Jessie
in the courthouse, where he'd gone with Paul to talk to
a judge, he smiled and was pleasant to her.

Several days later, there was a complication. Bernie
was walking back to the boardinghouse from work,
after refusing a ride from Glory, and a car ran off the
road, up onto the curb, and missed her by a few feet.

It sped away while she was getting back onto her
feet. She was badly shaken. She picked up her pocket-
book and her cane, and stood shivering while she tried
to catch her breath. Had it been a car that just lost control, or was it deliberate? She worried the question all
the way home.

She'd have told Mikey, but he was out of town on
business. He'd mentioned at the boardinghouse that he
had to meet with one of the deputy marshals in San
Antonio, but he'd be back in time for a date they'd arranged for Saturday. He and Bernie had planned a sight-
seeing trip to San Antonio because they had plenty of
chaperones. Bernie had always wanted to go through
the Alamo, but there had never been time since she'd
been an adult. Now she looked forward to seeing that
part of Texas history with the love of her life.

Mikey picked her up in the limo, with Santi at the
wheel, just after she got off work at one o'clock on Sat-

urday. She was wearing a beige sweater and skirt with flats and a cane that matched her outfit.

"Color coordination, huh?" Mikey teased as he helped her into the back seat and climbed in beside her.

"I like things to match," she teased.

He indicated the beige suit he was wearing with a white shirt and a brown paisley tie. "And so we do," he laughed.

She grinned. "We do, indeed."

"I wanted to see the Alamo when I was here last time, when Merrie was in trouble. But I never had the time. You Texans are pretty proud of it, aren't you?"

She nodded. "We really are."

He sighed. "I don't know much about history, even in Jersey," he commented. "Well, maybe one sort of history, but it's not told in polite company," he chuckled.

"I won't ask," she returned, smiling up at him.

"You haven't carried the cane lately, until today," he pointed out. "Having a flare?"

"Well, not really. I had a fall the other day on my way home from work."

He scowled. "A fall?"

She nodded. She bit her lower lip. She hadn't wanted to mention it. "A driver lost control of his car and it came up on the curb where I was walking. It missed me by several feet," she added.

"What sort of car?" he asked with barely concealed anger.

She blinked. "That's the thing, I really didn't have time to notice. I fell and, while I was getting up, it sped away."

"Big car, small?"

She frowned. "Medium."

"What color?"

She tried to remember what it had looked like. "I think it was dark. Not black, but not a colored car, like blue or red or anything."

He looked troubled. He pulled out his cell phone and texted a message to someone. She couldn't tell who.

"I don't think it was deliberate, Mikey," she added softly. "I mean, it didn't come right at me."

"Warnings don't," he said curtly. He typed some more.

Her heart jumped. He was thinking it might be his enemy. But she was thinking it might be an enemy of her family, someone who'd tracked down the one surviving member and tried to avenge a loved one. It wouldn't be the first time it had happened. That worried her.

He put down the phone. "I wish you'd told me sooner," he said. His big hand reached out and touched her long hair lightly. "I couldn't bear it if anything happened to you, Bernie."

She beamed.

He caught her hand in his and held it tight. He leaned back against the seat, clearly concerned. "I sent a text to Paulie. Did you tell Sari about it?"

"No," she said. "She's been in court all week and then she had to go and depose a witness in an assault case she's prosecuting. And honestly, we've been pretty busy at work all week, too."

He was weighing it in his mind. He knew Cotillo was after him, that the man could also target Bernie. But it wasn't the way Cotillo did business. He'd already sent a cleaner after Mikey. That was how he handled threats. Aiming a car at a woman and missing her by several feet, that wasn't the way a man used to violence did business.

Bernie's hand in his tightened. "Maybe it was just an accident," she said. "People do lose control of their cars for all sorts of reasons."

"Yeah. They do. But it's suspicious."

She leaned her head on his shoulder and laughed. "That's you. Suspicious."

He kissed the top of her head. "I've spent my whole life being suspicious. It's why I'm still alive, kid," he teased.

"I suppose so." She looked up into his eyes. "It could be somebody from my own past, from my family's past, still hunting vengeance, you know. Daddy was almost killed once for it."

"How many years ago was that?" he asked.

"Well, quite a few," she recalled.

"It's more likely that it's somebody connected to me," he said. "But in any case, the feds will hash it out." He slid an arm around her shoulders. "Your coworker Jessie has changed," he commented. "Even Paulie said Sari's talking about it." He glanced down at her. "Is she pretending?"

She laughed. "You really are suspicious. She said that it was hard to come from the city and get used to a small town, that she was used to having to be on her guard with people."

"Did she say what city?"

She shook her head. "She came down here from San Antonio. But she's originally from somewhere up north, I think, like her friend Billie who works at the courthouse. They room together."

He frowned. He hadn't considered that the two of them were both from up north. "Have they been here a long time?"

"Not really. Jessie's only been here a few weeks. I

believe she and her friend moved from San Antonio together. Billie knew somebody at the courthouse who
wanted a temporary secretary after his got sick. They
know the cook at Barbara's, too—he's from New Jersey."

Mikey felt his heart stop and start again. He hadn't
been asking the right questions. Neither had Paulie.
What if the two women and the cook were part of Cotillo's bunch? If nothing else, the timing was right. He
was going to suggest to Paulie that they get somebody
to keep an eye on those three as well. It was too convenient to be a coincidence.

"You're worried," she said, breaking into his thoughts.

He smiled at her. "Nothing major," he said. "Just
thinking. We're going to see the Alamo. No worries
for today, at least. Okay?"

She grinned. "Okay!"

They walked around the old fort like tourists, holding
hands and watching leaves drift down out of the trees.

"It's going to be Halloween next week," he pointed out.

She grinned at him. "Are we going trick-or-treating,
then?"

He burst out laughing. "Oh, that would be one for
the books, wouldn't it?"

"I used to go when I was a little girl," she recalled.
"Mom and Dad would drive me up to some of the nice
neighborhoods in San Antonio door-to-door so that I
could get candy. We had only a couple of close neighbors, and they didn't celebrate it at all."

"Paulie and I went with a bunch of the guys from our
neighborhood," Mikey recalled. "This one house, a little
old lady always invited us in for hot chocolate. It was

a hoot. She'd been a Hollywood agent in her younger days. She could tell some stories!"

"I'll bet!"

"I imagine kids in Jacobsville have a great time at Halloween. And the other holidays."

"They do. Christmas is the best time, though. They stretch garlands of holly and lights all over the streets and across them. There are Christmas trees everywhere, and the local toy store has trains running in the window." She sighed. "It's just magic."

He chuckled. His hand tightened on hers. "Grandma always made Christmas special for me and Paulie," he said. "Of course, we had to go with her to midnight mass every Christmas Eve and it went on for a couple of hours. You know how kids are. We squirmed and suffered, but we didn't dare complain. She was scary for a tiny little old lady," he added.

She smiled. "I know what you mean." Her eyes were sad. "My grandmother was so sweet. She was always baking for people who had family die and sitting with sick people. She was wonderful. My grandfather was violent and dangerous. Daddy said he'd been in trouble with the law a lot when he was a young man. But I never thought he'd do something so terrible."

"Listen, kid, lots of people do terrible things they never planned. Kids get on drugs and kill people. Old people get dementia and kill people. Alcoholics get behind the wheels of cars and kill people. I don't think most of them go out with the idea that they'll do harm. It just happens."

"I've never used drugs," she said.

He laughed softly. "Why am I not surprised?"

She leaned her head against his arm. "I'm predictable."

"Very. I love it," he whispered.

She drew in a long breath. "I've never been so happy in my whole life."

"Neither have I, baby," he said gently.

She looked up at him and he looked back, and the world vanished.

It took a car horn out in the street to snap them back to reality, and they both laughed.

They walked through the dark halls of the Alamo, paused at the door to the Long Barracks, looked at the graffiti on the walls where the last stand had been held. They were solemn as they filed into the gift shop for souvenirs.

"It's a sad history," she commented.

"Most history's sad," he returned. "Life is violent."

"I suppose it is."

"What would you like?" he teased, indicating the gifts in the glass display case. "Come on. Be daring. Pick out something outrageous."

She looked up at him, searching his dark eyes. She looked down into the shelves and when the saleslady came over, she indicated a pretty inlaid turquoise ring."

Mikey's hand tightened on hers. "Yes," he said under his breath.

The saleslady handed it to her and she started to try it on her right hand, but Mikey stopped her and slid it onto her left ring finger, his eyes holding hers. It was a perfect fit.

"We'll take it," Mikey said.

The saleslady took the credit card he handed her while Bernie touched the pretty ring.

"You can think of it as an engagement ring until we can do the thing right," he whispered at her forehead.

She caught her breath and fought tears as she looked up into hungry dark eyes.

"An engagement ring?" she asked.

"I can't let you go," he said quietly. "I'd have no life left. Whatever happens."

She bit her lower lip. "Whatever happens, Mikey," she whispered huskily.

And just that simply, they were engaged.

Mrs. Brown cried when she saw the ring and heard the story. "It's a lovely ring!" she said.

"Not a diamond just yet," Mikey chuckled, "but it's standing in for one. I have to text Paulie and tell him." He bent and kissed Bernie's cheek. "I have to go up to San Antonio tomorrow, but we'll do this again next weekend, okay?"

"Okay," she said softly.

"I'll see you at breakfast in the morning, honey. You sleep well."

She reached up and kissed his own cheek. "You, too."

He laughed. "I doubt I'll sleep a wink." He grinned, smiled at Mrs. Brown, and went along to his room.

"Congratulations," Mrs. Brown said.

Bernie hugged her. "I'm so happy!" she exclaimed. And then the tears did, finally, fall.

Bernie showed her ring off at work. Olivia was over-joyed, so was Glory. And when Sari saw it, she just hugged Bernie.

"He's never been the sort of man who wanted to set-tle down and get serious about anyone," Sari told Ber-nie. "But I can see why he wants that with you."

"Me and my limitations," Bernie said with a sigh.

"He could have any woman he wanted, you know. Somebody young and beautiful and, well, whole."

"Oh, you'll be fine," Jessie said, and she even smiled. "Men don't think about obstacles, you know. They just plow right ahead when they want something. Congrats," she added.

"Thanks," Bernie replied.

Jessie noticed that nobody thought she was the least bit insincere. Which worked to her advantage.

Later in the day, Billie alerted her to the fact that Mikey was at the courthouse with his cousin Paul, talking to a man in a black suit.

"I'm going to lunch early so I'll be here when all of you leave, is that all right?" Jessie asked them.

"Sure," Glory said.

"I won't be long," she added, and smiled again. They were so gullible, she thought smugly as she left. Nobody suspected a thing.

Mikey was by himself while Paul and the man in the suit went into an office nearby. Jessie walked up to him.

"Hi," she said breezily. "How's it going? We heard about the engagement. Congratulations!"

He grinned. "Thanks."

She sighed. "I know you'll be happy with her." She made a face. "It's just, she was talking about your past, you know? I couldn't help but overhear."

He felt his face go taut. "About my past?"

"She's such a straight arrow," she continued. "It's not surprising that she'd be upset when she knew your family had ties to organized crime. She said she gave her word and she'd keep it, but she didn't know how she was going to live with a man who was accused of murder, a man who lived with other men who killed people without guilt." She smiled sadly. "I'm really sorry. I guess I shouldn't have mentioned it..."

"No, it's okay," he said. "Really."

"She'd never tell you herself," Jessie added. "She's so sweet." She grimaced. "It will be hard for her to get used to another way of life. But, hey, she's young. She'll adjust, right?"

"Right," he said, but he didn't look convinced.

She glanced at her watch. "Oops, I'll be late getting back. I dropped by to see what Billie wanted for lunch. I'm bringing it to her." She smiled at him. "I've got two uncles who worked for a local crime boss in New York," she said. She shrugged. "I don't have a problem with it. But some people, you know, they don't quite understand the life. See you."

"Yeah. See you."

She walked toward Billie's office, feeling proud. She'd just put the first stick in the spokes of his relationship with Bernie. She had him off balance. Now it was just a matter of keeping him that way for some people she and Billie knew.

The next step was to talk to Bernie and make a similar confession to her about Mikey. Funny how easy it was to make them believe things about each other. But she knew people like Mikey. He'd never ask Bernie directly if she'd said such things because he wouldn't really want to know. He'd be afraid to hurt her feelings by accusing her of it, and of course she'd deny it—because it wasn't true. But he'd have doubts. Big doubts. Jessie was going to make them even bigger.

Chapter 12

Mikey went back to San Antonio with Paulie to talk to the feds, and he was morose. Could Bernie feel that way about his lifestyle and not be willing to tell him? She'd certainly been shocked when he'd told her about the man who'd killed Paulie's family. Well, he hadn't confessed that he'd ordered the hit—although he had. What he'd told her was enough to shock her, even without that. Had he been too truthful? Maybe he should have waited until they knew each other much better before he confessed just how full of violence and turmoil his life had been.

"Sari ever have a problem with your past?" he asked his cousin, who was driving them in a Bucar, the designation of a bureau vehicle used by the FBI.

Paul frowned. "Well, she wasn't overjoyed, if that's what you mean. She's an assistant district attorney, you know. A real straight arrow. I guess it bothered her some, but she loved me enough not to let it matter. Why? Is Bernie having second thoughts? She told Sari the two of you just got engaged."

"We did. But I told her a lot of it," Mikey said quietly. "She's got violence in her own past, something tragic. But hers was the result of an unbalanced relative. I'm not unbalanced. I've been a bad boy, Paulie. I'm not sure she can make a life with me, the way she is."

"You should talk to her."

"And say what? That I'll change? That I'll go straight and sell out my family? Fat chance, and you know why. You get in this racket for life. Nobody gets out except feet first."

"Marcus Carrera did," he was reminded.

"Yeah, Carrera. Well, he was a big fish and people were scared to death of him. Sure he got out. He always made his own rules. I'm not Carrera. I'm a small fry, compared to him."

"You own a casino in Vegas," Paul reminded him drily. "You drive a Rolls back home. You've got millions in overseas banks. And people are scared of you, too, kiddo."

"No kidding?"

"No kidding."

One corner of his mouth pulled down. "Well, that won't matter much if I turn my back on the outfit."

"Sadly, no, it won't. Hey, there's always the witness protection program," Paul teased.

"I noticed how well that worked out for the guy who squealed on the big bosses. He got hit right in protective custody, now, didn't he?" Mikey chuckled.

"He did."

"You don't get out. Hell, I don't want to get out," Mikey muttered. "It's the only life I've ever known, from the time we were kids. I like being part of a big family. I like the style and the cachet."

"Will Bernie like it? She's more of a butterflies and wildflowers girl than she is a showgirl."

"Yeah. I know that. But she's so sweet, Paulie," he replied heavily. "She's the sweetest human being I've ever known. And I don't think I can give her up, unless she wants me to. Even then, I don't know how I'd go on without her. It's only been a few weeks and I'm lonely when I'm not with her."

"It was that way with me when I was mooning over Sari and thinking how hopeless it all was. She was worth two hundred million, and I worked for wages."

"You're still working for wages," Mikey pointed out.

"I'm not a sit-at-home type of guy. I love my job." He glanced at Mikey. "So what are you going to do?"

"Rock along until I'm sure she can cope. Then I'm getting her to the nearest justice of the peace before she changes her mind," he chuckled.

Bernie, meanwhile, was still basking in the glory of her first proposal and looking forward to years of happiness with Mikey.

The others were getting ready to go to lunch. Bernie got to her feet a little unsteadily and picked up her cane.

"Rough day, huh?" Jessie asked in a gentle tone.

"Just a little," Bernie confessed. "I had a bad fall on my way home the other day. A car went out of control and almost hit me."

"Gosh, here in Jacobsville? People need to learn to drive!" Jessie muttered.

"Just what I was thinking."

"Bernie, we'll wait for you outside," Glory called as they went out the door.

"Be right there," she said, reaching for her purse.

"Mikey was in the courthouse when I went to take Billie her lunch," Jessie said. She made a face. "I really shouldn't tell you what I overheard him say to his cousin."

Bernie's heart dropped in her chest. "What?" she asked, and sounded a little breathless with worry.

Jessie sighed. "He told his cousin that he was worried about what you'd be like in a few years, because his grandmother had what you've got, and she was twisted like tree roots and almost helpless. He said that it was going to be hard to live with somebody who was sick so much. But that he'd made a promise and he was going to keep it. He said he was going to marry you because he gave his word. But that it was going to be like pulling teeth. He was used to women who could keep up with the pace. He went all over the world on trips for his family, vacationed in foreign countries. He didn't know how you'd manage the travel. It was hard for a healthy woman, but you'd never keep up. He said," she added with sad eyes, "that he'd rushed in because he was infatuated with you, and then it was too late to turn back after he'd thought about the difficulties."

"I see." Bernie's heart was beating like a drum. She felt sick inside.

"I knew I shouldn't have told you," Jessie groaned. "I'm sorry. But I thought you should know. I mean, he'd never tell you himself."

"Of course, he wouldn't."

"Please don't tell him I told you," Jessie pleaded.

"I don't want to make an enemy of him. He gets even with people. You don't know how dangerous he is," she added. "I come from up north. I've heard things about him. He scares people. Even bad people." She laughed hollowly. "I don't want to end up floating down a river…"

Bernie felt sick inside. Even Mikey had hinted at something of the sort, that he had power in his organization. She remembered what he'd said about taking care of the man who'd killed Paul's first wife and his child. It chilled her. "No, of course I won't tell."

"Thanks. I'm truly sorry. I know you're crazy about him."

Bernie managed a smile. She didn't answer. She went out onto the street with her coworkers and pretended that nothing at all had happened. But she was devastated.

Jessie smiled to herself. She was going to reap rich rewards for her little acts of "kindness." Throwing Mikey off balance had been the first step. Now she had Bernie doubting. The next thing was going to happen just as they'd planned it. And soon.

They spent all too much time in the Jacobs County courthouse, Mikey was thinking as he waited for Paulie to come out of an office where he was comparing notes with a contact in the probate judge's office.

He was staring at a plaque on the wall, denoting the building of the courthouse almost sixty years ago, and the names of the men on the county commission who'd authorized the construction. Farther down the wall were portraits of judges, many long gone. He was bored out of his mind.

"Fancy seeing you here again," Jessie said with a smile. She was carrying a box with food and a cup of coffee in it. "I came to bring lunch to poor Billie. She hurt her foot and she can't walk far."

"How're you doing?" he asked, and smiled, because she really did seem to have changed in the past week or so.

She shrugged. "Can't complain. It's just hard to get used to these Texans," she laughed. "They aren't like people up north."

"Nobody's like people up north. Where you from?"

She hesitated. "Upstate New York originally. You?"

"Jersey," he said. He grinned. "Doesn't the accent give it away?"

"It does, sort of." She cocked her head and studied him. "I've heard of your family. You were an underboss to Tony Garza, weren't you? Shame about him. He was a decent guy."

"He still is," Mikey said.

"I'm truly sorry that Bernie has such a hard time with your lifestyle…" She stopped and gritted her teeth. "Didn't mean to say that," she added quickly.

He scowled. "What did you mean?"

"Well, it's just," she hesitated. "Bernie doesn't understand the world you come from and she's afraid of it."

He felt his heart sinking. "She told you that?" he asked suspiciously.

"Of course not. She'd never talk to me about you," she said. "I told you about it before, remember? I heard her talking to Olivia, the other paralegal in our office. She said she was crazy about you, but that she wasn't sure she could cope with the way you made your living. She said she'd never fit in with a bunch of, well, criminals."

He could barely get words out. The pain went all the way through him. He'd wondered about the way Bernie accepted what he was, that she said it wouldn't matter. But she was a girl who'd never cheated in anything. She had a tragic past that predisposed her to loving the police. After all, they'd saved her and her father from a potential killer after the tragedy her grandfather had caused.

Apparently he hadn't been thinking straight at all. Rather, he'd been thinking with his heart instead of his brain. Bernie wasn't like him. They had different backgrounds, and she didn't understand the forces that honed his family into a criminal element over the years. The scandals of the Kennedy era, the unmasking of the five families, the scattering of bosses had been a wholesale offensive against organized crime. And it had largely succeeded. There were still bosses like Tony, who commanded power, but there was no more real commission that met and decided on who got hit, who had which territory, which politicians to support. Now the bosses were largely autonomous until they crossed the line. Nobody liked drawing attention to the outfit that was left, and people who did it got punished. Mostly, the days of wiping out a man's relatives to make a point were over. But there were still renegades who paid insults back with blood. Cotillo was one of those. That would never really end so long as there were power-mad people in the loop.

"I'm sorry," Jessie was saying. "I shouldn't have said anything."

"It isn't anything I wasn't already thinking," he confessed.

"You live in the fast lane. Fast cars, fast women, easy money," she said. "Bernie likes band concerts in the park and watching television in her room." Her mouth twisted. "Not a good mix."

"No." He wished he could forget what she'd told him about Bernie, the other day and now. But he knew it was true. He'd seen the way Bernie had reacted when he described his life to her. She'd said she could cope, that it wouldn't matter. It would matter.

"Please don't tell Bernie I said anything to you," she said softly. "I'd hate to have her mad at me now that we're getting along so well."

"I won't mention it to her," he said absently, and he was thinking that there was no way he could discuss it with Bernie without putting her on the defensive, making her ashamed of her feelings. He couldn't blame her. His lifestyle would be hard for any woman unless she came from a similar background. He'd been living in a dream. It was a sweet dream. But it wasn't real.

"I'd better get Billie's lunch to her. Nice seeing you." She walked away with a smile. It wouldn't do to lay it on with a trowel.

Paul came out of the probate judge's office with a worried look. He fell in beside Mikey and they walked outside. "Harvey," he said, referring to his contact inside, "told me that Billie and Jessie at Sari's office came down here at the same time. It's a little too cozy for coincidence."

"You think they're Cotillo's?" Mikey asked.

"They could be. We're going to do a thorough background search on all of them. What about that car that barely missed Bernie? Did she tell you anything about it?"

He shook his head and stuck his hands in his slacks pockets. "Only that it was a dark sedan. It happened too fast." He glanced at Paul. "Do you know about Bernie's grandfather and what he did?"

Paul nodded. "Tragic thing to happen to a child. There was a serious attempt on her father's life not long after it happened, by a member of a victim's family. He's doing time."

"She said it might have been somebody like that, trying to scare her." Mikey frowned. "It's not Cotillo's style, you know? He has people hit if he has a problem with them, like he tried to hit Tony and me. He doesn't make threats."

"Neither do you," Paul mused.

"Hey, I am what I am." He strolled along beside Paul. "I've been having second thoughts about this engagement," he confessed.

"What?" Paul stopped in the middle of the sidewalk. "But you're crazy about Bernie. She's crazy about you!"

Mikey took a breath and smiled cynically. "She likes small towns and band concerts, Paulie. She's never been in trouble with the law in her life. How's she going to like jetsetting, mixing with celebrities and crooks, wearing designer clothes, traveling around the world with me when I've got people to meet? How's she going to feel if I ever get arrested for something?"

Paul took a deep breath of his own. "I don't know. I don't live in that world. I never did."

"Well, I do. I have to." He grimaced. "And there's her health to consider. I remember our grandmother. She got twisted like a tree in a hurricane. She was in bed most of the time at the end. She got upset and she had flares, remember that? Bernie would be stressed-out all the time. It would affect her health."

"You've done a lot of thinking," Paul said. He wasn't saying anything, but his tone was full of curiosity and suspicion.

"Yeah. She's the sweetest woman I've ever known. I'd like her to stay that way. Involved with me for life? It would…kill something in her."

Paul didn't speak. He knew that Mikey's lifestyle involved stress. But he'd never seen Mikey involved with any woman to the extent he was involved with Bernie. He thought that love would resolve all those issues. Mikey clearly didn't.

"What are you going to do?" Paul asked.

"Ease off. Just a little at a time, so it doesn't look like I'm shooting her out of my life." He smiled sadly. "I want her to be happy. I can't give her the sort of life she deserves."

"You, being unselfish. Call the journalists," Paul drawled.

Mikey chuckled. "Out of character, isn't it?" he agreed.

Paul threw an arm around him. "Not anymore, it isn't, cuz," he said quietly. "But I'm sorry for both of you."

"Me, too," Mikey said. His eyes were solemn. "Me, too."

Mikey and Bernie were subdued at supper at Mrs. Brown's. Neither spoke much although they went through the motions of participating in the conversation.

But afterward, when Bernie started toward her room, Mikey stopped her.

"Listen," he began quietly, "I've been thinking—"

"Me, too," she interrupted.

She looked as uncomfortable as he did.

He shoved his hands into his pockets and felt his heart breaking inside him. He wanted to say something, but what could he say? His life wasn't butterflies and roses. And, realistically, she wasn't the sort of woman who could adjust to partying and casinos and jet travel and organized crime. It was impossible, but he hadn't realized it until Jessie told him what Bernie had said.

He looked down at her tenderly. She was so unworldly. It would be like her not to want to hurt his feelings or make him feel bad about what his world was like.

She was thinking the same thing about him, that he didn't want to hurt her feelings by admitting that he couldn't live with a woman who might be an invalid one day, a woman who could barely keep up with him on a slow walk in the woods. He needed somebody vibrant and healthy, who could thrive in his company, not a woman who would limit his activities.

"It might be an idea to cool it, just for a little while," Mikey said finally. "I've got people working on that car that almost hit you. We'll find out who it was."

"Probably somebody drunk who misjudged the curb," she replied with a faint smile. "It's a small town. Odd things happen here."

His dark eyes seemed even darker as they searched her light ones. "I've never enjoyed anything more than this time with you."

"Me, either," she confessed, and tried not to show that she was dying inside.

"But we need to give each other a little space. Just for now," he added quickly so it didn't sound like he was trying to dump her. He couldn't bear to hurt her feelings.

She nodded. "It's a good idea." She fingered the ring that stood in place of an engagement ring. She started to take it off.

His big hand went over both of hers. "No," he said, and sounded choked. "You keep that. You keep it forever. Think of me when you wear it."

She looked up, fighting tears. "I'll never forget you. No matter what."

"Yeah. It's like that with me, too." He hesitated. "Santi doesn't like having me apart from him at night, the way things are going."

Her eyes widened with worry. "They haven't sent somebody else after you...?" she asked almost frantically.

He almost bit his lip through. That soft concern made him hate himself. "No," he lied quickly. Some quick thinking by Paulie and the feds had saved him, already. "It's just that he thinks a bodyguard should stay with the boss, and he can't live in the room with me here. So...well, I'm moving over to the motel, and Santi and I can have adjoining rooms."

Her heart sank. She'd gotten used to seeing him at the table when they had meals, in the hallway, everywhere. "That's probably a good idea," she said softly. She looked up. "You take care of yourself, okay?"

His big hand touched her cheek. "You do that, too. Don't go out alone after dark. Be aware of your surroundings."

"I always do that. Well, almost always," she amended. "But the car came out of nowhere. I didn't even hear it coming."

That wasn't surprising. Most newer model cars had quiet engines. It still bothered him that it didn't sound like an accident. Paul was checking. If there was anything sinister, he'd find it.

"So," Mikey said. "I'll see you around."

She forced a smile. "Yes. Well, goodbye."

She went into her room, resisting the urge to look behind her. She closed the door and let the tears fall silently. It was the biggest pain of her life, almost as bad as knowing what her grandfather had done, losing her sweet grandmother and the community where she'd grown up. It was like losing a loved one.

Outside the door, Mikey was feeling something similar. But he had to do it. If he stayed here, seeing her every day, he'd go nuts. He couldn't keep away from her, not unless he distanced himself from her. It was the hardest thing he'd ever done in his life. It was the only thing he could do. Bernie couldn't live with the man he was. He didn't blame her. It was just that she was the only woman he'd ever wanted to live with him.

He let out a weary breath and went into his room to pack.

"You moved out of the boardinghouse," Paul remarked a week later, when Mikey was having supper with him and Sari while Mandy bustled around in the kitchen making a cake.

"Yeah," Mikey said. He moved his cup around in the saucer. "Santi kept harping on it. He said he couldn't protect me if he was several blocks away. I finally listened."

Paul, remembering an earlier conversation, knew what the truth was. Mikey was distancing himself from Bernie, removing temptation.

Sari glanced at Mikey's lowered head and started to speak, but a sharp jerk of the head from Paul silenced her. Instead, she started talking about a reality show she and Paul had been watching lately.

After Mikey went back to his motel, Sari questioned Paul about his odd behavior.

"He's doing it for her own good," Paul said on a sigh. "He thinks she couldn't cope with his lifestyle. You know, Isabel, it's not the same life as this one. Not at all. He's in constant company with people who break the law. He travels in high social circles just the same, rubs elbows with movie stars and politicians and gamblers. He couldn't settle down here if his life depended on it—well, except briefly, like he's having to do now. But Bernie would never fit into that sort of world."

Sari met his eyes and nodded sadly. "But she was so happy," she said softly. "Bright as the sun. She almost radiated with it. And now she's so quiet we hardly know she's around. She never jokes and smiles anymore."

"Neither does my cousin," Paul said. He pulled her close. "You and I came from different worlds, but we worked it out, because we loved one another. You can tell how Mikey and Bernie feel about each other just by looking at them. Why couldn't they work it out, too?"

"I don't know," she said with a sigh. She laid her head against his broad chest. "What about the sudden residents? Any new intel on them?"

"Not a lot," he confessed. "Jessie and her friend Billie are both from New York originally. They do have mob ties, but not to Cotillo or Tony Garza. Their connections aren't apparent, but we're trying to run them down. There's still a family that operates in New York, even covertly, but it's fragmented and the boss is in prison."

"He can still run it from prison. It's not even hard."

"True. He has an underboss holding power for him. Jessie may have something to do with him. That wouldn't necessarily mean she or the boss favored Cotillo. He's an outsider and he does a bloody business. You know how well that goes over in mob circles. They don't like attention. Cotillo's getting them a lot of it."

"Wouldn't it be lovely if somebody in one of the old outfit families decided to take Cotillo out of the equation?" she asked on a sigh. "Shame on me. I work for the court system. I should be ashamed."

"Yes, you bad girl." He kissed her hungrily. "You need to be severely reprimanded. Come right over here and I'll do my best."

She laughed as he tugged her down onto the bed. "Oh, this is a reprimand I'm going to love," she teased.

He chuckled as he started to remove her gown. "You bet, you're going to love it!"

The driver of the car that almost hit Bernie was a local businessman who'd had three drinks too many out at Shea's Bar and misjudged the curb, just as Bernie had figured. He turned himself in to Cash Grier with many apologies and Cash got him into rehab.

Bernie listened to Cash's explanation in the office a couple of weeks after Mikey had moved out of the boardinghouse.

"I thought it was something like that," she said quietly. "I mean, if people in organized crime want to hurt you, they just kill you, don't they?"

"More or less." They were alone in the office. It was just after lunch and the other women hadn't returned.

"What about you and Mikey? I thought that was going to be permanent."

She flushed. "I'm not healthy," she said. "His grandmother had what I've got. She was an invalid, bedridden, when she was old. I'm likely to end up in that condition a lot sooner." She fought down panic at the thought that she might not even be able to work. She was far too proud to ask for government relief, even though she might one day be forced into it.

"There are new drugs," he pointed out.

She smiled sadly. "Chief Grier, the sort you're talking about costs over a thousand dollars a month. They do have programs to help people afford them, but it isn't that much of a reduction."

He grimaced.

"I get by. My rheumatologist has me on a regimen of medicines that mostly take care of the pain. I have flares, days when I can't get out of bed, and I have to use a cane from time to time. But there are lots of people worse off. Look at Glory in my office, and what she had to go through in her life. She still limps from time to time because her hip was broken long ago and it has arthritis in it, and her blood pressure is controlled but still subject to spikes. She lives with it. I live with my problems."

"But you don't think Mikey could?" he fished, his eyes piercing hers.

She toyed with a pen on her desk. "He was overheard telling his cousin that he wasn't sure that he could." She looked up. "Don't you dare repeat that, ever. It would hurt his feelings. He can't help what he thinks. He lives with glitzy people, rides in limousines, travels all over the world. I'm lucky if I can get from work to my boardinghouse without falling over my feet. How would I fit into that sort of lifestyle? I'd be a sparrow among peacocks, if you see what I mean."

He did see. But she was a sweet, kind woman. "If he loves you, it won't matter."

"That's the thing, though," she continued. "He said it would be better if we sort of let things cool off. And he's probably right. He has enough problems right now. They won't kill him, will they?" she asked, and looked agonized by the thought.

"He has powerful friends," he replied. "Marcus Carrera is one of them. Carrera runs a legitimate operation in the Bahamas, but he wasn't always a good guy, and his reputation still strikes fear in people who knew him back in the day." He chuckled. "He's got Tony Garza so surrounded by experienced mercs that only a suicidal maniac would try to get to him."

"Sari said that Mr. Garza gave her sister away at her wedding to that Wyoming rancher," Bernie said.

"He did. He's not what he seems." He cocked his head and studied her. "Neither is Mikey. His reputation is fearsome. But he's not as bad as people think he is."

"He was arrested once, though," she said.

He nodded. "And charged with attempted murder. But the charges were dropped," he reminded her. "Nobody's ever been able to bring him to trial on a major crime. For a man who operates outside the law, he's amazingly conventional."

She smiled sadly. "He's amazing, period," she said softly. "I'll never forget him." As she spoke, she twisted the turquoise-and-silver ring he'd given her. She wore it on her right hand, though, not her left. She didn't want it to get back to him that she considered herself engaged, not when he was backing away.

Cash muttered something about men being fools, smiled, and left her.

"What in the hell is wrong with you?" Cash asked Mikey when he saw him with Paul at Barbara's Café one day at lunch.

Mikey's eyebrows raised. "Excuse me?"

"You have almost as much money in foreign banks as I do," Cash said as he joined them for coffee and pie. "You could easily afford the newest treatments for rheumatoid arthritis, whatever they cost."

Mikey stared at him. "I don't have arthritis."

"Bernie does."

Mikey averted his eyes. "I know."

"She wouldn't let him, though," Paul said, and he was giving Cash expression cues that asked him to cool it. "She's too proud."

"Besides that, we're not… Well, we're not an item anymore," Mikey added. "She has her life, I have mine."

"Yes, but she…" Cash continued, ignoring Paul.

Before he could finish the sentence, Jessie came in the door, spotted Mikey and came right to the table, smiling.

"Don't forget, you're taking me to Don Alfonso's for supper, right?" she asked.

Mikey chuckled. "You bet, doll. Santi and I will pick you up about five."

"I thought maybe you could drive us both and leave Santi at home," she said with a husky laugh.

"Sorry. Santi drives, I don't."

"Well, okay. It doesn't matter. I'll be ready on time.

Hi, Chief Grier. Mr. Fiore," she added, a little unsettled when Paul just glared at her without speaking. "See you later."

She went to the counter to pick up her order. Paul glared at Mikey with much more venom than he'd shown the gorgeous, well-dressed woman waiting for her order.

"She doesn't mind riding around with a criminal," Mikey said sarcastically. "She loves casinos and fancy restaurants and she's classy enough to take to ritzy gatherings. So?"

"You're about to ruin your life," Paul said curtly. "What if Bernie finds out? Jessie works in the office with her, for God's sake!"

"I told you," Mikey said, averting his eyes. "Bernie and I are no longer an item. I can date any woman I like. Jessie's not so bad."

But Paul was thinking that Jessie was every bit as bad as she seemed. She was rubbing Bernie's nose in the fact that she had Mikey's attention. Not only that, she was pressuring Mikey to be alone with her, without Santi. That was suspicious. Very suspicious. He glanced at a taciturn Cash Grier and had the impression that the police chief was thinking the same thing.

"I need a night on the town, anyway," Mikey said as he finished his pie and washed it down with coffee. "I've been vegetating down here in cowboy town."

"You watch your step," Paul said shortly. "Don't forget that Cotillo may have people here that we don't even know about."

"Surely you don't think Jessie's one of them?" Mikey drawled. "You checked her out and found no connections to any of Cotillo's people."

"Yeah, I checked out our last limo driver, too, and

he almost got Merrie killed because the perp had con-nections I didn't ferret out," he was reminded.

"I can handle myself," Mikey reminded him curtly.

"You'd better have a concealed carry permit if you walk around with a weapon in my town," Cash told him humorously, but with a cold glint in his eyes.

"I got one the second day I was in town, for your in-formation," Mikey said smugly. "I know you, Grier. No way I'm stepping out of line around here!"

Cash just chuckled.

Paul cornered him after Grier left, while they were waiting on the sidewalk for Santi to collect Mikey.

"This is going to ruin any chance you have of get-ting back together with Bernie," he told his cousin. "You know that, right?"

Mikey's eyes were hollow with pain. "She can't live with a crook, Paulie," he said shortly. "That's what she said."

Paul's lower jaw fell. "She said that to you?"

"Of course, she didn't say it to me! She wouldn't hurt my feelings for anything. But she was overheard say-ing it," he added, and flushed, remembering who'd told him. "There's Santi. I gotta go. See you around, cuz."

"Watch your back!" Paul called after him.

Mikey waved and climbed into the limo.

Paul stood watching it pull away from the curb. Something Mikey had said piqued his curiosity. He was going to speak to Sari about it when he got home.

Chapter 13

Sari was going over a brief when Paul walked into the study and closed the door.

"What's up?" she asked, because he looked worried.

"Did Bernie say anything to you about having an issue with Mikey's background?" he asked curiously.

"No," she replied. She grimaced. "But she doesn't really discuss Mikey with me," she added. "I guess she thinks I might tell him what she said." She put down the pencil she was using to edit the document she was working on. "Why?"

"He said she told somebody that she couldn't live with a man who made his living outside the law, with a criminal," he replied. "Would she tell somebody at work something so personal?" he persisted.

She frowned. "Well, I don't really think so. Bernie's a very private person. She's not the kind to blurt out intimate details of her life to people she works with. It's not the way she is. And there's not really anybody else she might tell, either. She has no close friends."

"That's what I thought. Mikey has the impression that she can't live with his past."

"I know that's not true," Sari said gently. "She loves him."

One side of his mouth pulled down. "I tried to tell him that. He wouldn't listen. He's destroying any chance that he could get back together with Bernie."

"How?"

"He's taking your coworker Jessie out on the town in San Antonio tonight," he said through his teeth.

"Oh, no!"

"I tried to warn him. It will ruin everything. But he wouldn't listen. He's convinced that he's so bad, only a bad woman would ever want him."

"What an idiot. Even if he is your cousin."

"Hey, no argument from me. I said the same thing, to his face."

"It will kill Bernie if she finds out."

He laughed coldly. "If? Jessie will tell the world tomorrow. I don't doubt she'll embroider it into something even more than it is."

"Jessie." Sari made a rough sound. "She was our worst nightmare for weeks. Then overnight she turned into a caring, worrying coworker who did everything she could to make things easier for us."

"And all an act," Paul said. "I can see right through her. I wish Mikey could."

"I didn't. Neither did Bernie or Glory or Olivia," Sari said.

"I've spent my life with people who bend the truth. I'm good at recognizing phonies."

"Poor Bernie."

"Poor Mikey, when he finally realizes he's been had," Paul said flatly. "I'm checking out an acquaintance of Jessie's in Upstate New York. I have a suspicion that she didn't just happen down here with her friend Billie."

"What about the cook from New Jersey who's working in Barbara's Café?"

He laughed. "I'll tell you about that," he said. "It's a hoot." And he did tell her.

"Now, this is my kind of place," Jessie said as they were seated in the five-star restaurant.

"Mine, too," Mikey said, but without any real enthusiasm. He studied the gorgeous woman across from him with only vague interest. She was wearing a couture cocktail dress with diamond earrings, necklace, bracelet and several rings. All diamonds. The best quality and set in 18 karat gold. He knew, because he'd spent a fortune on them for various women over the years. He was curious about how she afforded that kind of jewelry on a receptionist's salary.

Even as he had the thought, he felt cold chills inside. He was carrying. He had a snub .38 in a pancake holster behind his back, and a hidden gun in an ankle holster. He never went anywhere without being armed. Would he need to be? Santi was at the next table, apparently oblivious, but watching.

Odd, how he suddenly remembered that if the family ordered a hit on you, they sent your best friend to do it. He was warned that if he didn't, somebody else would, and he'd end up as dead as the intended victim. His blood ran cold as he stared at Santi.

But his bodyguard just grinned at him and went to work on a huge plate of spaghetti. He was getting paranoid, Mikey considered, just like his old man.

He remembered his father with loathing. The man had been a dirty jobs soldier for the underboss in New Jersey, the one who'd preceded Tony Garza. Mikey's dad had killed men over and over again, never felt the least remorse, and spent his life at a local bar where the outfit hung out. Mikey rarely saw him, and if he ever did, his father treated him like a disease. He hated Mikey and made no secret of the fact that he thought the kid was some other man's son. Mikey's mother, long dead, had an affair, he'd told the boy one day, and Mikey was the result. It was to get even with him for something he'd done to her. So Mikey had no real family at all until his maternal grandmother, Paulie's grandmother, too, took both boys in and raised them. The old lady was Greek. She still spoke the old language. Mikey and Paulie had been schooled in Italian by the other kids and the families they associated with, but their grandmother taught them Greek, as well. Mikey could even read in it. Not a lot of people knew that. He kept his intelligence hidden; it gave him an advantage if his colleagues thought he was stupid.

"How was it you heard what Bernie said in the office?" he asked out of the blue.

Jessie's hand, which was holding her wineglass, jerked, but she recovered quickly. "Oh, she and Olivia didn't know I was there," she replied. "I'd just come out of Mr. Kemp's office and they were in the hallway."

"I see." He didn't know Bernie well, but it seemed unlike her to confide something so personal to an office worker, even one she was close to. She was, like him, a very private person.

"This place is nice," she said, changing the subject. She smiled at him alluringly. "You know, I have the use of a friend's apartment here in town," Her voice changed to a throaty purr. "We could be all alone there."

Mikey just stared at her. His dark eyes were cold, as cold as they'd ever been when he had another man at gunpoint. "Really?"

His glare disconcerted her. "You know, Bernie won't change her mind, and she'll never tell you what she really thinks of you," she said.

He cocked his head. "You're trying too hard."

"Excuse me?"

He just laughed, but it had a hollow sound. He was just beginning to believe he'd been had. And he was out with this jeweled barracuda, who would go back to the office Monday and tell Bernie all about this date, probably with some embroidering. He took a big sip of his Chianti and cursed himself silently through the rest of the meal.

"Oh, it was the most wonderful date!" Jessie enthused to the other women, including Bernie, the following Monday. "Mikey made me feel like a princess! And we went to this apartment a friend loans me..." She stopped when Bernie's face went white. "I'm so sorry, that was cruel," she added in a conciliatory tone. "But you know how he feels about you, honey."

"She knows what you told her," Olivia replied, her eyes narrow and suspicious.

"Odd, how you knew something so personal," Sari added her own comment to the discussion. "I mean,

Mikey isn't the sort to discuss personal things with Paul, even in private, and Paul's the only person he's really close to."

Jessie looked uncomfortable. "It was just a comment he made—he didn't seem to think it was very personal."

Mr. Kemp's door flew open and he looked livid. "Miss Tennison!"

Jessie actually jumped. "Yes, sir?"

"Come into my office, please," he said icily.

Jessie collected herself quickly and forced a smile. "Yes, sir, at once." She jumped up and headed toward him without looking back.

"Don't you believe her," Sari told Bernie firmly. "Mikey never told Paul anything about you, not ever, in private. He would never blurt out something like that in a public place."

Bernie wasn't comforted. She forced a smile. "I could never keep up with him, don't you see?" she asked softly. "He lives in the fast lane. Some days, I can't even get out of bed. He'd get tired of it. I don't like bars and flashy places. I've never even owned an evening gown." She cocked her head and smiled at Sari. "The people in his circle would think he'd lost his mind if they ever got a look at me, and you know it."

Sari wasn't convinced. "Bernie, if somebody loves you, things like disabilities and things they've done in the past—none of it matters at all."

Bernie's green eyes were sad. "I believed that, once. But he took her out on the town," she added, indicating the door behind which Jessie was closeted with Mr. Kemp. "And he slept with her. It's over. I'm going to get on with my life. It's obvious that he's gotten on with his."

And she went back to work.

* * *

Jessie came out of Mr. Kemp's office with an absolute snarl on her face. "I'm fired," she said icily. "Just because I told that old man on the phone that Mr. Kemp didn't want to talk to him and not to go to court because I thought it was canceled that day!"

"What old man?" Olivia asked.

"Oh, some rancher named Regan."

Olivia's eyebrows arched. "Ted Regan?"

"Yes, I think that was it," Jessie muttered. She started pulling things out of desk drawers.

"Old man Regan," Sari told her, "is worth millions. He owns the second biggest ranch in Jacobs County, and properties all over the country. He's also a prime witness in a case we're prosecuting." She pursed her lips. "Or he was. I'm assuming Mr. Kemp lost the case, if you told Ted not to show up. Judge Drew was presiding and he didn't want to try the case to begin with."

Jessie just ground her teeth. "Well, it doesn't matter now, I'm fired," she muttered. She looked up and noted the pleased expressions on all the faces except Bernie's. Bernie wouldn't even look at her. "It's just as well," she commented. "I've done what I came to do. Aren't you the gullible bunch? I put on an act and all of you bought it. You pitiful little small-town people, you'll never know what life is all about."

"It's about family," Glory Ramirez said.

"It's all about family," Sari agreed. "Something you'll never understand."

"The only family I care about is the one I take orders from," Jessie muttered absently, and then looked up and flushed as she realized what she'd said. "My dad, I mean," she corrected, "and he's not from some little Texas town!"

But Sari picked up on what she'd said at once and hid her suspicions. She went back to work, ignoring Jessie.

"Well, so long," Jessie said as she carried the cardboard box with her things in it to the door. She turned and stared at Bernie. "I'll tell Mikey you said hello, Bernie," she purred. "After all, we're going to be seeing a lot of each other. I know his world and I love it. Unlike you, I don't mind being seen with him and his criminal friends," she drawled sarcastically.

Bernie felt shocked. "What do you mean?"

Jessie had slipped again. She shrugged. "Nothing at all. Goodbye."

She went out the door and closed it behind her.

Bernie didn't say a word. She brooded, though. Mikey was already involved with that vicious woman, but perhaps he liked that sort of person. Maybe he was frustrated because he'd wanted Bernie and she wasn't the sort to sleep around. But it still hurt to think of him in bed with Jessie. It hurt terribly.

"She was lying," Sari said gently.

Bernie looked up. Her eyes were sad and wise. "No, she wasn't," she said quietly. "And like I said, it doesn't matter. We were mismatched from the start. Opposites attract, don't they say, but the divorce rate for marriages like that is pretty dismal. I'd better get back to work."

Sari didn't say any more, but she was livid.

"Mikey did what?" Paul Fiore asked at supper, his fork poised in midair.

"He slept with Jessie," Sari said angrily.

He whistled, aware of Mandy's curious stare. "Well, damn, that's the end of it all."

"I know." Sari picked at her food. "Jessie was poison. I'm glad Mr. Kemp fired her. It was all an act, that sweetness and light attitude."

"No surprise, there."

"She let something slip when we were talking about families and how they mattered," Sari continued. "She said the only family she cared about was the one she took orders from."

Paul dropped the fork. "Families. Like Cotillo's."

"Maybe," Sari replied, watching him retrieve the utensil from the floor and carry it to the sink before he got another and returned to the table. "Don't you have somebody checking her out?"

"I do. I'll call him after we finish eating. Damn the luck! If she's involved with Cotillo, then her friend Billie may be, too. It's been right under our noses."

"What about that cook at Barbara's?" Mandy asked as she refilled coffee cups. She made a face at Sari. "And you should be drinking milk, not caffeine!"

Sari flushed. "Mandy…"

Mandy was grinning.

Paul, caught unaware, looked at Mandy's twinkling eyes and his own darted to his wife, looking flushed and guilty.

"Okay, spit it out," he told Sari. "What's going on that I don't know about?"

She cleared her throat and glared at Mandy. "I was going to tell you later."

"Tell me now," he persisted.

She drew in a breath. "I'm pregnant."

Paul sat very still for just a minute, then he rose,

picked her up in his arms, and kissed her and kissed her, whooping in between at the top of his lungs.

Mandy pursed her lips. "Well," she said to nobody in particular, "I guess it's no secret that he's happy about it."

Bernie went home to a lonely apartment, her heart down in her shoes. Mikey was sleeping with that rat, Jessie. Mikey was a rat, too, she told herself. He'd taken her in, pretended to care about her, then backed off because she had an incurable disease.

If he'd been that concerned about her illness, why hadn't he stopped seeing her in the beginning? Why had he spent almost every day with her? Why had he bought her a ring and then asked her to marry him?

None of it made sense, unless he'd truly thought he could make it work and then decided he couldn't live with her limitations. She felt miserable. She couldn't help what was wrong with her. She couldn't cure it. Maybe she could have adjusted to travel, to his friends, to flashy places, if she'd been given the chance. But what did it matter now? She would never get over the fact that he'd promised to marry her and then cheated on her with another woman. She had too much pride.

"Are you out of your mind?" Paul demanded of Mikey the next day when they were having a quick lunch at the house.

Mikey blinked. "Excuse me?"

"Sleeping with Jessie. My God!"

Mikey's lips fell open. "Sleeping… Good Lord, do I look crazy to you? I wouldn't touch her with a pole!"

"You took her out on the town, didn't you?" he persisted.

Mikey grimaced. "I was feeling pretty low. I needed to feel like a man again."

"Great job."

"Bernie didn't want me!" he burst out. "She said she couldn't live with a man who'd been a criminal most of his life!"

"She told you this, huh?" Paul asked.

Mikey sighed. "No. She'd never want to hurt my feelings like that. She told somebody else and she was overheard."

"Let me guess—by Jessie."

Mikey scowled. "What?"

"Jessie told Bernie that you went with her to an apartment in San Antonio."

Mikey grimaced. He could only imagine how much that had hurt Bernie. He was hurting from her rejection, but it wounded him to think he'd caused her even more pain.

"She let something else slip. She has a 'family' that she takes orders from."

Mikey lost color. "Hell!"

"I've got a man digging hard into her past. He's hit a couple of dead ends, but he thinks he's onto something. I should have an answer today," Paul told him.

"You think she's on Cotillo's payroll."

"I think she might be," Paul replied. "Think about it. She and Billie are as out of place here as roaches in a ritzy hotel. So why are they here? Maybe to watch you and report on your movements to a third party."

"Like a cleaner," Mikey said, referring to a contract killer.

"Maybe. It depends on which family she has ties to. Cotillo's not the only man in the game. He has enemies. She's from New York. Cotillo's moving on Tony Garza in Jersey. Suppose another boss has Cotillo in his sights and wants to know if you're protected before he orders a hit."

Mikey toyed with his coffee cup. "That's a possibility."

"Cotillo's drawn a lot of attention to himself and to the outfit in general with this takeover thing. He's harking back to the mob wars in the past, which were bloody and public and ended in the congressional hearings that tore the Five Families apart. They can't really afford to make themselves too visible even today. Cotillo's a threat to them as well as to you and Tony. They might decide to act."

"If Jessie was lining up a hit, she had a perfect opportunity while we were at the restaurant," Mikey said. "Santi was at another table. Of course, I was watching the door. I know how hits go down."

"Which is why I don't think her boss is Cotillo."

Mikey drew in a long breath. "That might be." He looked into the coffee cup at the thick black liquid. "Bernie will never forgive me. I don't guess it matters. She didn't want me to begin with."

"Or so Jessie told you. She likes rich men. Kemp already called her down about it at least once. Of course, he fired her this morning."

"What?"

"She mouthed off to Ted Regan, of all people, and told him court had been canceled. Since she was calling from the DA's office, he believed her. He didn't show up and the case was thrown out of court. Kemp was livid."

"I guess so. She'll get another job, I guess."

"She and Billie left town late this afternoon," Paul replied. "I got that from Mandy. She knows everything that goes on in this town. But I'm sure Jessie will keep in touch with you," he added sarcastically. "I mean, since you're dating her and all."

"You don't understand," he burst out. "I lost everything! Bernie couldn't live with what I am, and I don't know how I'm going to live without her! Jessie kept asking if we could get a meal somewhere and I said yes. I know I shouldn't have done it. I was so damned low I didn't care about how it would look."

"Jessie is poison," Paul said. "I'd bet real money that she told Bernie some tale about you, as well, to the tune of your not being able to live with a woman who might be an invalid later on."

Mikey was very still. He just stared at his cousin.

"Think about it. She told you that Bernie hated your past. Maybe she told Bernie that you hated her disease."

"Dear God," Mikey said huskily, and buried his face in his hands. "Oh, God, what am I going to do?"

"Talk to Bernie."

Mikey removed his hands from his face and drank the coffee. "Sure. I'm going to walk into the office, and she's going to throw me out headfirst, or the verbal equivalent. She thinks I slept with damned Jessie. She'll hate me."

"Sari hated me, too, when I first came back here." Paul grinned. "Remember what I did when she wouldn't speak to me?"

"Everybody in Jacobsville remembers," Mikey chuckled. "They even talked about it at the boarding-house and it was three years ago."

"Whatever works," he commented pointedly.

Mikey drew in a breath. "I'll think about it."

"Meanwhile, I have news."

"About Cotillo?"

Paul chuckled. "Not yet. About Sari."

Mikey's eyebrows arched.

"She's pregnant," Paul said, and smiled from ear to ear.

"Damn, that's great! Absolutely great!" Mikey burst out. "I'm happy for you."

"It's the nicest surprise," Paul confessed. "We've been trying for a long time, but, well, nothing happened and I thought maybe we couldn't have kids. It wouldn't have mattered. I love her so much. I'd rather have her and no kids than the biggest family in the country with any other woman."

"I know how that feels." Mikey put his cup down. "I wanted them with Bernie. Never with anybody else. Even with her limitations, she could carry a child. I asked a doctor." He flushed. "There are medicines she can't afford that I could have bought for her, and they would have helped. She could have private duty nurses, anything she needed. I'd have…taken care of her." He stopped, choking up.

"It isn't too late."

Mikey looked up, with the saddest expression Paul had ever seen. "Yes, it is, Paulie. It's too late. And I did it to myself, by not telling her what Jessie said and giving her a chance to tell me what she felt."

"We all make mistakes."

"Even you aren't in my class, cousin," Mikey said. He leaned back in the chair. "At least you're having that happy ending people dream about," he added with an affectionate smile. "You got lucky."

"I wish you had, too."

Mikey shrugged. "Let's just hope that Cotillo doesn't."

* * *

They were prophetic words. A day later, the story broke on all the major news networks. A New Jersey mob figure named Anthony Cotillo was found dead in his apartment of apparently natural causes. A friend said that the man had no apparent health problems and that it came as a shock to his associates.

"Can they detect an air embolism?" Mikey mused. "It doesn't matter—they'll have people in the coroner's office to make sure that doesn't go into the report."

Paul sighed. "Well, it's a novel way to take care of an interloper without getting the government all stirred up," he agreed. "No mess, no blood trail, no nothing. But I wonder who hit him?"

Mikey smiled. "Marcus Carrera has many friends from the old days," he pointed out. "Some of them owe him really big favors."

Paul's eyebrows arched.

"Really big," Mikey emphasized. And he smiled.

Tony Garza came home to New Jersey amid promises from an obscure New York outfit family that the loose association of bosses, the one that had existed since the Five Families were scattered by pressure from the feds, had no problem with him. They assured him that no more problems were expected, and that they had several people making sure of it. The message was clear—Carrera might not be a mob figure any longer, since he'd gone straight, but he was still a power to contend with in the States. A lot of people were afraid of him. Tony was going to be safe.

"So I guess I'll go home now," Mikey said sadly,

when he was having supper with Paul and Sari. "I'll come back for the christening, though," he teased.

"Wrong church," Paul teased. "We're Methodist. Although, Reverend Blair does have a sort of christening ceremony, but not like the one you're thinking of."

"We can pretend. I'll come anyway." He toyed with his food. "So I guess Jessie and Billie worked for the New York boss."

"I guess so," Paul said.

"Carrera was a terror when he was younger," Mikey remarked with a smile. "You could just say his name ten years ago and people would start running for the door."

"It shocked everybody when he went legit," Paul said. "Even the feds. Now he's got a wife and two sons and he's the happiest man on earth."

"Families are nice," Mikey said absently.

"You should get married and have one," Sari said firmly.

"Chance would be a fine thing."

"You never know," she replied. "Strange things happen when you least expect them."

He smiled at her. "They do, don't they? What do you guys want, a boy or a girl?"

"Either," Paul said.

"Both," Sari said, and grinned.

"No twins on our side of the family, cousin," he told Paul.

"But there are loads on my side," Sari laughed. "Distant cousins, but at least three sets of twins among them."

"Son of a gun! You could have your whole family in one year."

Paul laughed. "Who knows?" he teased, and he

looked at his wife with eyes that absolutely ate her.
She looked back at him the same way.

Mikey felt more alone than he ever had in his whole
life. Much more, although he was happy for his cousin.
But he was leaving town. His heart would stay here,
with that sad little woman who lived in Mrs. Brown's
boardinghouse. She'd never forgive him for Jessie. He
knew it without asking. It was the worst mistake of his
life, and he couldn't fix it. Nobody could.

He packed his bags and Santi packed his. His heart
was breaking. Bernie was the light of his life and he
was leaving her behind. He hadn't felt so low since the
death of his grandmother, and the murder of Paulie's
wife and little girl. He felt the grief like a living thing.

"Where we going, boss," Santi asked. "Vegas or Jersey?"

"Vegas," Mikey said without missing a beat. "I need
a diversion. A big, bright, flashy, glitzy diversion."

"Vegas is a nice place," Santi said. He grinned. "Lots
of glitzy girls there."

"You're welcome to all you can find," his boss replied glumly. "You can have my share, too."

"That's nice," Santi replied.

They packed their things into the convertible. Mikey
went to the office and took care of the bill. Santi was
waiting just outside the door in the limousine as he
came out.

Mikey put himself into the back seat and leaned
against it wearily as Santi pulled out into traffic. It was
early morning, so they'd probably hit the work traffic on the way to the airport. He didn't care. Santi had

been a wheelman for Mikey in earlier times. He was still a great driver.

"Do me a favor," Mikey said suddenly.

"Sure, boss. What?"

"Drive through town. Past the courthouse."

Santi didn't say anything. He just smiled.

The women who worked in Kemp's office were just filing in. There was Glory Ramirez and Sari Fiore. Olivia was ahead of them all. And there, behind them, in an old tweed coat, walking slowly with a cane, was Bernie.

"Slow down, okay?" Mikey asked, sounding half out of breath as he watched Bernie's slow progress to the door. She was hurting. It was a cold, rainy day, and he imagined she was having one of her flares.

He remembered her sitting up with him when he'd had the migraine. He remembered carrying her into the boardinghouse the day they'd met, when she had fallen in front of the car and he thought she was playing him. It seemed so long ago.

She made her way into the building, not looking behind her. She'd screwed her beautiful blond hair up into a bun. She looked tired and in pain, worn-out. He grimaced as he watched her disappear into the office. The door closed behind her.

Mikey felt the loss of connection like a blow to his chest.

"We leaving now, boss?" he asked Mikey.

There was a hesitation, only a very brief one. "Yeah," Mikey said finally. He slumped a little. "Yeah, we're leaving. Let's get to the airport."

"Sure thing," Santi said, and sped up past the office building, leaving it and Bernie behind, perhaps forever.

Chapter 14

Bernie, never a late sleeper, woke very early the next morning. She couldn't get what Sari had said out of her mind. Suppose Jessie had told lies to both her and Mikey? She had been too shy to speak to him about something so intimate, and he would probably have been reluctant to say anything to Bernie about her supposed distaste for his background.

Jessie had been putting on an act. Why? The woman was patently out of place in Jacobsville, which led to a worrying conclusion. What if she was a lookout for that man who was trying to have Mikey killed? It really bothered her.

She got up and dressed, aching and barely able to walk for the pain and stiffness. After a few minutes, she felt better, but she'd still need the cane, even on level ground. Rheumatoid arthritis flares were painful and fatiguing. She took her medicines regularly, but they'd begun to be less effective, as many drugs became over the years. She recalled the wonder shot that was used to control it, but even with a large discount, she'd never be able to afford the monthly expense. It might have made a difference in her quality of life. Days like this, cold and rainy, were agony to people who lived with arthritis.

She didn't tell the other women that she'd walked to work, because they'd have fussed. Any one of them would gladly have offered her a ride, but she wanted to be independent. It wasn't good to lean on people. Her father had always said that they had to take care of their own problems and not advertise them to the world. It was a burden that honorable people shared. She smiled, remembering the wonderful man who'd raised her. She missed him.

"You're just on time," Sari Fiore teased, smiling.

"I'm always on time," Bernie replied with a small laugh. "I wouldn't want Mr. Kemp to fire me."

"No danger of that, as long as you don't tell Ted Regan that court's been dismissed," Olivia said, tongue in cheek.

They all laughed as they filed into the office.

Bernie was the last one inside. She almost stumbled going in, but she regained her footing quickly, holding on to the doorknob. The back of her neck tingled. Odd, she thought, that feeling. But it was probably nothing. She ignored it and went on inside the building.

Sari was pregnant. It was happy news, and the whole office went wild when they knew. Even Mr. Kemp congratulated her, grinning from ear to ear.

"You'll find that babies are addictive," he teased. "Which is why we have another one on the way, too."

"That's wonderful," Sari said, smiling. "I know Violet's over the moon. Are the twins coping with your toddler?"

"The twins?" Bernie asked curiously.

"He has two Siamese cats," Sari explained. "He made them mad one day and they tag-teamed biting his ankles and ran under heavy furniture afterward."

Mr. Kemp chuckled. "They've calmed down. Well, a little. Violet learned early that they like salmon, so she keeps cans of it handy."

They all laughed. Bernie was thinking about children. She'd wanted one so badly with Mikey. Just as well, she realized, that she'd never been intimate with him, considering the way things had turned out.

In his world of glitzy women and casinos, he probably had a procession of beautiful women at his beck and call. Including Jessie.

But she remembered that Sari had told her Mikey was no longer in danger; nor was his boss, Tony Garza. Apparently a group of bosses had decided that Cotillo was calling too much attention to certain underworld figures, and he'd been taken out of the equation. It was called "natural causes," but Sari said it wasn't at all, that the mob knew how to cause sudden death that looked natural.

That was Mikey's world. Death. Violence. Glitter. Of course, she was well out of it. Her health wouldn't have allowed her to endure the stresses of his profession, much less the strenuous lifestyle he enjoyed.

But she missed him terribly. It had sent her into days of depression when she knew he was gone. He'd left without even bothering to say goodbye. But what, she reasoned, could he have said? That he couldn't live with a disabled woman, that he preferred her sexy coworker, that Jessie was great in bed? All those things? It would have tormented her forever. No. It was better the way it had happened—a quick ending, as painless as possible. It was over.

Now all she had to do was adjust to her new reality. Maybe one day she could look back and remember a handsome, dashing man who'd taken her places and kissed her as if he'd have died for her mouth, who'd seemed to love her. Maybe she could recall just the joy of being with him, without remembering how it had ended. It would be a pretty memory, tied up with ribbon and tucked away in a scrapbook.

Mikey watched people come and go in the casino with hardly any interest at all. Beside him, Tony Garza, who was breaking his California trip with a stop in Las Vegas to see Mikey, was sipping a whiskey highball.

"They ever find out who hit Cotillo?" Mikey asked.

"No. And they never will. The New York family arranged it all. Cotillo was about to point the finger at one of their underbosses. It would have devastated the family. So they sent Jack the Mackerel and Billy Tenspot down to visit Cotillo. They had a guy in the coroner's office swear it was a natural death."

"What about Cotillo's family?" Mikey persisted.

"Running scared. It wasn't that big, and most of them tried to talk Cotillo out of biting off more than he could chew. The New York boss even spoke to him personally and told him how it was. He didn't listen."

"Terminal error," Mikey commented.

"Very." He sighed. "At least we're off the hook. I owe you, Mikey. Big-time. You ever need a favor, you know where to find me."

Mikey shrugged. "No sweat. You'd have done it for me, boss."

Tony chuckled. "Yeah. I would have." He paused. "What's this about some Texas girl you got involved with?"

Mikey's face closed up. "Closed chapter," he said tautly.

"I got a good look at Texas women when I gave Merrie Grayling away at her wedding," he reminded Mikey. "They're good people."

"She was. But she couldn't live with my profession."

"I heard you couldn't live with her maybe being an invalid one day."

Mikey turned. His eyes glittered. "I never said that," he replied. "Never! It wouldn't have mattered to me if she couldn't even walk. I'd have carried her—" He broke off, averting his eyes.

Tony laid a big hand on his shoulder. "Jessie Tennison belongs to the New York boss. She's his mistress," he continued. "She made trouble for you because it's what she does. Nobody likes her, and one day the wife is going to complain loudly enough that the boss will have to do something about her. Something unpleasant. She's making her own sad future and she doesn't even know it."

"I won't mourn her," Mikey said.

"Your cousin said she carried tales to both of you," he said. "She lied and you both believed her."

Mikey's face hardened. "Bernie told me herself that she was always on the right side of the law."

"And you told her that it didn't matter that she might become disabled one day, yes?"

Mikey's teeth clenched. "For all the good it did me."

"It's your life, *paisan*," he continued. "But you've been moping around here like a lost soul ever since I walked in the door, when we should both be celebrating. If I were you, I'd go back to Texas and talk to the woman. Really talk to her."

Mikey grimaced. "I took Jessie out on the town. I know, it was stupid. I was feeling low because of what I'd heard, what Jessie told me that Bernie said about my past. I wanted to feel better, so I took her up to San Antonio for supper. She told Bernie I slept with her. It's a lie, but Bernie had every reason to believe her. So even if I wanted to go back and talk it out, she'd never trust me again. She'd probably shut the door in my face."

"There are these things called roses," Tony mused. "Women go nuts over them. I know my late wife did. Chocolates. Greeting cards. I went through all those things while I was courting her." His eyes were wistful with memories. "She didn't even like me at first, but I wore her down. I was a bad man, too, Mikey, and her dad was a cop, but it didn't matter. She had leukemia," he added softly. "I took care of her when she had relapses, right up until the last one that took her out. I never minded. She knew it. We loved each other. None of the small stuff mattered. Love kept us together in spite of the difficulties we faced."

Mikey hadn't said anything. He just listened. "That's a lot like me and Bernie," he said after a minute.

"Yeah. How about that?"

Mikey took a deep breath. "I'll think about it." He glanced at the boss. "Roses, huh?"

"Might send yellow ones," Tony suggested. "Isn't there some song about yellow roses and Texas?"

Mikey actually laughed. It was the first time he had since he'd left Jacobsville.

It was the middle of the afternoon when the florist brought them in. Judy, who owned the flower shop, came herself, grinning from ear to ear as she carried them straight to a shocked Bernie at her desk and placed them on it.

"Oh!" Bernie's hand went to her throat. She couldn't believe what she was seeing. There must have been three dozen yellow roses in the arrangement, along with flowers of every single color, and greenery highlighting it all.

"I know, it's closer to Thanksgiving than spring," Judy laughed, "but the man said yellow roses, so that's what you get."

"The man?" Bernie was dumbfounded. Her coworkers were grinning from ear to ear.

"Read the card," Judy suggested, indicating it on a plastic stand inside the arrangement.

Bernie pulled it out with hands that held a faint trembling. She opened the envelope. The card only said, "Miss you terribly. Can you forgive?" And it was signed "Mikey."

Tears were rolling down her cheeks. She read the card again, just to be sure that she wasn't seeing things.

"Well?" Sari prompted. "What does it say? Who's it from? Or should we just guess?" she added with a grin.

"Mikey," Bernie said in a husky tone. "The flowers are from Mikey!"

"Doesn't he do things in a big way?" Olivia mused,

studying the huge arrangement. "Amazing that your back didn't break under the weight, Judy," she teased the florist.

"I have liniment," Judy chuckled.

"They're so beautiful," Bernie said, caressing a petal on one of the roses, most of which were in bloom.

"I guess he thinks you are, too, sweetheart, because let me tell you, I could almost retire on what this arrangement cost," Judy laughed.

Bernie struggled to her feet and hugged the florist. "You always do the most beautiful arrangements, but this one is extraordinary."

"Thanks." Judy hugged her back.

Mr. Kemp came out of his office, stopped dead, and gaped at the arrangement that took up most of Bernie's desk. "Did somebody die?" he asked.

They all burst out laughing. Kemp grinned.

"Mikey, huh?" he asked Bernie, who flushed. "I figured he'd work it out sooner or later. Okay, people, back to work."

"Yes, sir," they chorused.

Bernie and Judy moved her beautiful floral arrangement to a side table so that the desk was clear, but all day Bernie's eyes went to it, and she felt as if she could walk on clouds.

Paul and Sari Fiore drove her home so that Paul could carry the arrangement inside for her. It was very heavy.

"Right there, if you don't mind," Bernie said, indicating the cleared-off part of her chest of drawers. "It's so beautiful!"

"Good thing that Judy makes arrangements that don't

have a loud scent," Sari teased, "or you'd smother in here from the fumes."

"Oh, I wouldn't even mind." Bernie sighed. "Nobody ever sent me flowers in my whole life," she added softly.

Paul and Sari exchanged glances. It was obvious that Mikey's peace offering had struck pay dirt.

He phoned Paul that night.

"Well?" he asked. "Did she donate them to the hospital or her church?" he prompted, and sounded worried.

"No. She cried," Paul said. "Then Sari and I brought her home so I could carry them inside for her. God, Mikey, did you buy out a florist? I never knew there were that many yellow roses in the whole damned state," he added, chuckling.

"I wanted to make an impression," Mikey replied. There was a smile in his voice. "So she liked them, huh?"

"She loved them."

There was a sigh. "In that case, Santi and I might come down for a visit in a week or so. Just to get the lay of the land."

"I think that would be a very good idea," Paul replied.

Bernie was walking home late in the afternoon, wrapped in a coat against the chill, using her cane because it was rainy and her footing wasn't good.

A big, black limousine pulled up beside her and the window rolled down while her heart almost beat her to death.

"Now, don't fall under the wheels this time, okay?" said a man with a New Jersey accent.

Bernie laughed. "Hi," she said softly.

The door opened. Mikey got out, leaving Santi behind the wheel. He stuck his hands in his pockets and moved close to Bernie. His dark eyes searched her wan face in the late-afternoon dimness. They were intent, as if he was looking at something almost out of a fantasy.

"You look good," he said. "A little worn. You've lost weight, I think."

"Just a little," she confessed. Her eyes went over his lean face. "You look worn, too."

"I never slept with Jessie," he blurted out. "I like to stick to my own species."

She laughed in spite of herself.

"I did a dumb thing," he muttered. "I should have known that you wouldn't pour your heart out to somebody in a public place."

She grimaced. "I should have known the same thing about you."

He drew in a breath and smiled. "So. Suppose we start over? Hi. My name's Mikey. I sometimes break the law, but I'll try to restrict myself to jaywalking for the rest of my life if you'll take a chance on me."

Her heart leaped. "Hi. My name's Bernadette, but everybody calls me Bernie. I never break the law, but I'd take a chance on you no matter what you did for a living."

His lips parted on a husky breath. "Oh, baby," he said in a rough whisper. "God, I've missed you…!"

She would have told him the same thing, but he had her up in his arms and was kissing her as if there was no tomorrow. Her arms were around his neck, her cane was on the sidewalk somewhere getting wet. She was kissing him back.

Long minutes went by. The rain was coming down

in buckets and they were both soaked. Finally Santi got out of the car and stopped beside them, coughing loudly.

Mikey drew back, shivering a little with the overwhelming hunger he felt for Bernie. He looked at Santi blankly. "What? You got a cold?"

"Boss, it's raining. Really raining. You know?"

Mikey blinked. Santi's hair was plastered to his head and face. He scowled and looked down at Bernie. Her hair was plastered to her head and face, too. He laughed out loud. "Damn. So it is! I guess we should find a dry place, huh?"

"I guess," Santi mused. He opened the car door.

"But I'm wet," Bernie wailed.

"The seats are leather, honey, they'll dry. Santi, find her cane, would you?"

"You bet!"

Santi closed the door.

"Now," Mikey murmured, drawing her close. "Where were we…?"

They were married in the courthouse, in the office of the justice of the peace. Bernie wore a winter-white coatdress and carried a bouquet of white roses. She had on a little saucy white hat that had a veil, and Mikey lifted it as he kissed her for the first time as Mrs. Michael Fiore.

Sari and Paul were their witnesses, and Tony Garza came down with his entourage for the wedding. In fact, Marcus Carrera and his Delia, and their little boys, also came to town for the event.

"I owe you a lot," Mikey told Marcus.

The big man waved away the thanks. "No sweat,"

he chuckled. "But if you come across a bolt of antique cloth, you know where to mail it, right?" he teased.

Mikey clapped him on the back. "You bet I do."

The honeymoon was in Jamaica, in Montego Bay, where they swam and acted like tourists. Well, at least, after the first night they were together.

"You don't need to worry about a thing," Mikey whispered to her as he undressed her very slowly and eased her under the covers.

She shivered a little at the first contact with his nude body, but he kissed her and caressed her until she didn't care what he did as long as he didn't stop.

He carried her from one breathless plateau to another, from one side of the bed to the other, for what seemed hours before he finally moved over her with intent. She was so sensitized by then that she barely felt the little flash of pain that hallmarked his slow penetration of her welcoming body.

She was aching for him, so hungry that she knew nothing, saw nothing, except his face above her as the passion grew and grew and grew and finally exploded into pleasure beyond anything she'd ever dreamed.

"Oh, my goodness," she moaned as they finally moved apart. She shifted her hips and the exquisite sensations went on and on.

He chuckled, drawing her to his side. "It's addictive."

"Very!"

He pulled her onto him and looked up into her soft eyes. "I've never missed anyone the way I missed you. I was just ashamed to even call you, after what I did."

She bent and kissed him tenderly. "We both believed lies because we were insecure."

"But no more."

"Not ever," she agreed.

"There's still the matter of the little unlawful things," he said, grimacing. "But I've got a legitimate casino now, and two of the biggest mob bosses in history in my corner. So if I want to move out into the world, so long as I don't betray any secrets, I can leave the old life behind. Not that I'll give up my house in Jersey. You'll like it," he added softly. "It's old, but it's got character."

"I'll love anywhere you live," she said simply. "And I'll cope, however I have to." Her pale eyes met his dark ones. "I love you."

He hugged her close. "I love you, too, baby. And don't you dare think I mind about the cane and the days you have flares, or if you get sick. I can afford nurses, anything you need. But I'll take care of you myself," he added, lifting his head, and his eyes adored her. "Because you're the most important thing in the whole world."

"So are you to me," she whispered, and kissed him.

"Listen, I spoke to your doctor," he said. "Louise Coltrain said there are medicines you can inject, that will make your quality of life a hundred times better."

"Yes, but they're so expensive—"

"I could fund the treasury of a small country, honey," he interrupted. "It will be money well spent, especially when the kids come along. You won't need to try and keep up with me," he chuckled. "I'll carry you, if I need to. But you *will* need to keep up with our kids…"

She laughed with pure delight. "Are we having several?"

He grinned. "However many you want. And I'll learn to change diapers and give bottles, just so you know."

"We can do it together," she said softly.

"We'll do everything together," he replied quietly. "As long as we live. Yes?"

She bent and kissed him hungrily. "As long as we live."

And they did.

* * * * *

IRRESISTIBLE FORCES

Brenda Jackson

Chapter 1

A baby.

Taylor Steele's heart began beating rapidly the way it always did whenever she thought about her most ardent desire. A mixture of relief and anticipation soared through her upon realizing that she was about to embark upon a phase in her life that she had been looking forward to for a long time.

Motherhood.

She leaned back in the chair behind her desk and stared out the window while tapping her fingertips against her bottom lip. For the first time she wasn't appreciating the view of the Lincoln Memorial. Her thoughts were on something else entirely. She was inwardly counting her blessings.

During this past year she had achieved a number of her goals. First by venturing out and starting up her own wealth and asset management firm, which she named Assets of Steele, and then moving from New York to the nation's capital and purchasing a beautiful condo with a view of the Potomac River from her bedroom window. That wasn't at all bad for a twenty-five-year-old woman who'd made the decision after college not to return to her hometown of Charlotte, North Carolina, and work for her family's multimillion-dollar manufacturing company. Instead she had set her sights on New York after accepting a position with one of the major banks as a wealth and asset manager.

Now she could turn her attention to the final stage of her plan that she needed in place before making her most sought-after dream a reality. And that was the man she had chosen to father her child without the benefit of marriage. She was even open to joint custody of the child, if he wanted to go that route.

A permanent hookup with someone was not what she wanted, not even a teeny-tiny bit. Nor was she looking for a long-term lover, either. A short-term one could handle the task intended quite nicely. The last thing she wanted was a long-term romantic commitment of any kind.

But she was selective.

She had decided very early in her plans that not just any man would do. It had to be someone with all the qualities she wanted to pass on to her offspring. He had to be handsome, intelligent, caring, healthy and wealthy. Definitely wealthy; after all, wealth was her business. And with those "must-have" qualifications embedded deep in her mind, she could think of only one man who met her criteria.

Dominic Saxon.

She tried ignoring the warmth of sensations that seeped through her veins. Dominic was one of her clients and she had never met a man who radiated so much sensuality. Part African-American and part French, at thirty-four he was the epitome of every woman's fantasy and a major player in numerous women's nightly dreams. The sexiness was there in his looks, his body, when he walked, talked or just plain stared at you. He was definitely the most gorgeous man she'd ever encountered. Besides that, she knew from the many charities he was associated with that he was highly intelligent and caring. And although she wasn't privy to his health records, she had no reason to think he wasn't in the best of health and could not father a child. The man was as virile as any man could get.

From the very beginning she had been attracted to him and for the past two years it had taken everything she had to keep their relationship strictly business, although he'd never given her the impression he expected anything else. Whenever they met he was always professional and courteous. She knew that he merely saw her as one of his employees and nothing more. He was paying a hefty fee for the services she rendered and her job was to take all the wealth he'd accumulated in his thirty-four years and make him richer, which wasn't hard since he was an ace at making the most of every financial opportunity.

It was common knowledge that he was the son of a wealthy Frenchman and his beautiful African-American wife, and from the time Dominic was born he'd had the best of everything—schools, social contacts and money, and he'd used all three to his benefit. He rotated residences between the United States and France, although she heard he also owned a beautiful apartment in London, as well as a private island off the French coast of Normandy.

Taylor picked up the brochure that had been sent to her compliments of her youngest sister, Cheyenne. It was meant to be a joke after a conversation the two of them had shared a week ago when she'd told Cheyenne that she wanted a baby, but not a husband.

Cheyenne had sent her the pamphlet that she'd come across in her travels as a professional model that advertised procreation vacations. *A week on a Caribbean island, plenty of dirty talk with trained professionals, exotic food and aphrodisiac-laden drinks…and if needed, a week's supply of Viagra.* It was advertised as a dream come true and the Bahamas resort encouraged potential guests to use their facilities for a week of near-constant, mind-blowing sex just for the purpose of making a baby. The packet Cheyenne had sent included several pictures bordering the brochure that could be considered X-rated. But they did a good job of getting their point across.

Compared to the frosty March weather they were experiencing, the island seemed like a really nice place to be right now. She could spend her time resting, relaxing and, of course, making a baby. Now if she could only convince the man she'd chosen to father her child to go along with her plan…

"Ms. Steele, Mr. Saxon has arrived."

Taylor's secretary's voice coming across the intercom interrupted her thoughts, and immediately she took a deep breath when more heady sensations coursed through her. It was time to put her plan into action. "Please escort him in, Mrs. Roberts."

* * *

Dominic Saxon checked his watch. He had just about an hour to meet with Taylor Steele and then he had an unexpected meeting back at the hotel. He had received a call from his parents saying they were flying into D.C. from California and wanted to meet with him. His father's voice had sounded urgent but he had refused to say what the meeting was about.

Whenever Dominic made a pit stop in the nation's capital it was usually to check on the Saxon Hotel, just one of many his family owned in several major cities around the country. Usually Taylor would fly into New York for their meetings, so it came as a surprise when he'd gotten a call asking that he drop by her office on this trip.

She had been assigned as his financial advisor when she had worked for a bank in Manhattan. From the very beginning, the degree of her intelligence when it came to wealth management, as well as her comprehensive view of his personal portfolio, investment goals and financial objectives had amazed him. He was already a successful businessman but together they created a long-term strategy that was increasing his fortune exponentially.

Besides being very knowledgeable on financial affairs, he'd found Taylor to be an extremely beautiful woman. Even now he could recall the desire that had consumed him the first time he'd seen her and because of it, he had concluded the less he saw of his wealth and asset manager the better off he was. He had decided that first day that she was definitely a woman worth taking to his bed—he was one who didn't believe in mixing business with pleasure, no matter how entic-

ing the thought or deep the craving. Yet the thought
had remained lodged in his mind. He would be the first
to admit it had been hard as hell to control the urge to
take things further. He was used to beautiful women
but there was something about Taylor Steele that caused
him to think of hot sex every time he was in the same
room with her.

Regardless of the iron-clad control he was known
for—physically and emotionally—he was definitely
a hot-blooded man, which was something he seemed
to remember each and every time he breathed Taylor's
scent.

"Ms. Steele is ready to see you, Mr. Saxon. I'll escort
you in."

He stood and smiled at her secretary, a nice older
lady, who seemed more suited to baking cookies for
her grandkids than trying to tackle the huge computer
sitting in front of her. "Thank you, and I don't need an
escort."

"Yes, sir."

He fought for control of both his body and mind
as he headed toward the door that had Taylor Steele's
name plate on it.

Taylor inhaled a deep breath as she stared across the
room at the man who walked into her office. He was
wearing a black business suit with a white shirt that
spelled out his wealth, and at thirty-four his mixed heri-
tage made his looks striking. A sensuous shiver glided
down her spine. He was simply gorgeous. His height,
tall and imposing at six foot three, was hard to miss.
She had seen photographs of him and his mother, a re-
nowned fashion designer, earlier that year in *People*

magazine. Megan Saxon was known for her beauty as well as for her skill and talent with fabrics.

From his mother, Dominic had inherited the shape of his lips, which could only be defined as full and sultry even on a male. He had his father's startling green eyes, which were a breathtaking contrast to his maple-brown coloring. Then there was the thick, black, curly hair that flowed past his shoulders when he wasn't wearing it back in a rakish-looking ponytail…as he was now. And last but not at all least were the chiseled jaw, cleft chin and high cheekbones.

As she stared at him, her courage began wavering. Anyone would say she had a lot of nerve to proposition Dominic Saxon to father her child and then expect him to back off. But then anyone who thought she had a lot of nerve would know that in essence she really did. She was known to be gutsy enough to try anything once— as long as it was legal. And there was nothing illegal about making an offer. The only thing he could say was yes or no, and inwardly she crossed her fingers that she would get a yes.

What did she have to lose? A very profitable client was the first response that popped into her mind. Would he still want her to handle his financial affairs after she made such an outlandish request?

"Taylor?"

She let out a relaxed breath with the sound of her name from his lips. She loved his accent, a blend of English and French. More than once during the course of their business meetings he would lapse into French without realizing he'd done so, and would quickly catch himself and revert back to English. She smiled. He hadn't yet figured out the fact that she also spoke

French, not as fluently as he did but enough to get by. In fact she spoke several different languages, thanks to all those classes she'd taken while attending George-town. She had prepared herself to tap into the international markets.

"Dominic, I'm glad you were able to meet with me today." She liked the fact that they were on a first-name basis, a rule he had established the first time he had walked into her office as a new client. She also liked the fact that he had given her an appraisal from head to toe, which meant this new cobalt-blue business suit had made an impression. When she'd purchased it yesterday, she'd hoped that it would.

"No problem, but I do have an important meeting back at the hotel in a few hours, so my time with you will have to be brief," he informed her, breaking into her thoughts.

"I understand. Please have a seat," she said, coming from behind her desk.

He took the chair she offered and she sat in the one across from it, thinking it would be better not to sit behind her desk. Although she would be making what she considered a business proposition, she wanted less formality than usual.

"Thanks for seeing me on such short notice."

"No problem." What Dominic had said was true.

It hadn't been a problem although he'd been surprised by her request to meet with him. She had moved from New York a few months ago, striking out on her own and leaving the company that had given her a start. Although her former employer had tried making a fuss, it had been Dominic's decision to follow Taylor, preferring to continue to do business strictly with her.

Today, as usual, she looked good. Because his mother was considered by many to be a fashion goddess, he appreciated anyone, man or woman, who displayed good taste in clothing. He considered himself, as well as his father, a fairly stylish dresser since Megan Saxon wouldn't have it any other way. He thought Taylor had great taste when it came to selecting her clothes. She was definitely a fashion-minded person who knew not only how to dress for success but also when to dress to impress. And he'd always been impressed each and every time he'd seen her.

And on top of that, she was a very attractive woman. Young, but attractive. Her dark brown hair was cut in a short and sassy style that was perfect for the oval shape of her face and her creamy cocoa-colored complexion. She was tall, leggy, with a curvy figure that enhanced the business suits she liked wearing.

When he'd first met her he'd thought someone at the bank was trying to pull a fast one over on him. There was no way a woman her age could handle the vast extent of his wealth. She had proven him wrong.

"How was your flight into the city?" she asked, reclaiming his thoughts.

"As usual Martin was excellent at the controls," he said of his private pilot. "It was good flying weather and he made the most of it."

Taylor nodded, trying not to stare at the way he was sitting in the chair—perfect posture, immaculately groomed and sexy to a fault.

"What kind of business deal have you put together that was so important you wanted us to meet today, Taylor?"

His question pulled her back in, made her aware he

was staring at her while waiting for her response. She swallowed. She couldn't get cold feet now. She was a risk-taker and this would definitely be a risk worth taking.

"This *is* a business deal but then it's also sort of personal."

She watched the lifting of his dark brow before he asked, "Personal? In what way?"

She paused for a second before she said, "I want to make you an offer that really won't cost you anything." *Just your sperm*, she decided not to add.

He tilted his head slightly and gazed at her.

"Then what would be the investment on my part?" he asked. "And what will be the return?"

She was not surprised by his questions since the majority of their meetings always addressed investments and returns. "The return is based on something I heard you say that every man should have a right to do."

"Which is?"

"To father a child."

He frowned. "I don't recall ever saying anything like that to you."

She wouldn't expect him to remember. "It was last year, during the bank's Christmas party at Rockefeller Center. You made my boss extremely happy by making an appearance. One of the secretaries had dropped by and brought in her newborn baby for everyone to see. I believe you were speaking to yourself out loud more than making conversation with me."

His frown deepened as he continued to stare at her. "And just what did I say?"

"You were staring at the baby and said that every

man should have a right to father a child and you regretted not having done so yet."

He nodded and she felt a rush of gratitude that he didn't deny having said such a thing. She shifted in her chair and met his gaze. "Is that true, Dominic? Is that something you regret not doing? Do you want a child?"

For the first time in their business relationship, she could feel his defense mechanism go up. He had often used it with others but never with her. And a part of her understood his need to use it now. He was a private person and she *was* asking him some rather personal questions.

"Why are we discussing this, Taylor?" he asked gruffly, narrowing his gaze at her.

Her emotions flinched at the look but she knew despite that, she had to go on. She paused a moment and then said, "We are discussing this because I feel the same way. I think every woman who wants a child should have the chance to mother one. And I want one."

The glare in his eyes indicated he wasn't quite following her, was still somewhat confused. "Then why don't you have one?" he asked flatly.

"I plan to do so…and that's why I've asked you here. It seems the two of us want the same thing and then again we don't want the same thing. We both want a child, but I've read you quoted many times as saying you will never marry again." She knew his wife had been killed in a car accident four years ago.

"Yes, and I was quoted correctly."

She nodded. "And getting married is the furthest thing from my mind, as well."

He leaned forward in his chair, holding her gaze under the penetrating stare of his green eyes. "Let's cut to the chase, shall we, Taylor. I still don't follow this business proposition of yours. You've established the fact that we both would like a child, but I don't know where that is leading."

She stood and picked up the brochure off her desk. "To this," she said, handing it to him. "You and I. Together. And a week spent on a procreation island in the Caribbean for the sole purpose of making a baby."

He looked at her as if she'd lost her mind as he accepted the brochure. He moved his gaze from her to the pamphlet. It took him a few moments to read it and then he lifted his head to meet her gaze again. "Aphrodisiac-laden drinks? Constant mind-blowing sex? Are you serious?"

She nodded nervously and grimaced when she heard the incredulity in his voice. Chances were he thought she had really lost it. "Yes," she replied, knowing she had to somehow convince him that she was still sane. "And I'd like to make you an offer. I want a baby, Dominic. Yours. A baby we will get to share. And to start things off we get to spend a week on that island. Many obstetricians even recommend such trips to couples who might find it difficult to conceive…not that I think we would have any problems. But it would take the tension off some and there is a guarantee of privacy. I've considered other options, such as having the procedure done by artificial insemination, however, I chose this route because I want my child conceived the normal way, a way I consider natural, with the two of us making love."

She inhaled deeply as he continued to stare at her. "Good heavens! Do you know what you're asking me?" he queried, his voice low and husky.

"Yes, trust me I know," she said, refusing to look

away from the intensity of his stare. "But you are a man I have come to respect and admire and when I thought about a potential father for my child, I couldn't think of anyone else I would rather have. You have all the qualities that I want."

Dominic wasn't quite sure what to say to that, so instead he slowly got to his feet. The nature of this meeting was definitely a surprise to say the least. "There's no way I can decide on something such as this right this minute. We need to discuss your business proposition further and I suggest we do so tonight over dinner. Let's say around seven o'clock at the hotel. Is that time okay?"

She swallowed. At least he hadn't given her a flat-out no. "Yes, that's fine."

"Good. I'll send my driver for you around six-thirty. My secretary will contact you later today for an address."

"All right."

He walked toward the door and before reaching it, he turned back around and said, "I'll see you tonight, Taylor."

He stared at her for a moment longer and then she watched as he turned and walked out of her office. It was only after he left she realized he had taken the brochure with him.

The driver opened the door and Dominic slid onto the plush leather seats of the limo. "Where to, Nick?"

"Back to the hotel, Ryder."

When the car began moving Dominic glanced down at the brochure he still held in his hand as his mind recalled everything Taylor had said. The brochure was proof he hadn't imagined it. She wanted a baby. His baby. And she wanted them to spend a week on some island in the Caribbean to make it happen. To say he was stunned would be an understatement, but he had heard the sincerity in Taylor's voice. She was dead serious.

He began reading the piece of literature. If the words didn't hit him below the gut, the pictures most definitely did. Procreation vacations. Just when he thought he'd heard it all. Evidently not. According to the brochure, it was a growing trend for couples that wanted to conceive. And Taylor Steele wanted to conceive.

If he were totally honest with himself, he would admit that so did he. The thought had crossed his mind several times in the past year, ever since his father's bout with prostate cancer last year. Thanks to early detection, surgery hadn't been needed and there were only short-term side effects.

His father's condition had made Dominic realize two things. His parents weren't the invincible couple he'd always assumed them to be. And although they both appeared to be in great physical shape, nonetheless, they were aging with each passing day.

Another thing he had come to realize, although they'd never mentioned it, was that his parents longed for a grandchild. He saw it in their eyes each and every time any of their friends talked about their grandchildren. There was no doubt in his mind if Camry had lived they would have had a child or two by now. But she hadn't lived and for the past four years he had somehow managed to go on, with the beautiful memories they'd shared to sustain him.

His parents had understood that after Camry's death the thought of ever marrying again was as foreign to him as life on another planet. Without realizing she had done so, Taylor may have provided him with the very solution to a problem that had been bothering him for some time.

He resumed reading the brochure. The success rate of the woman returning from one of these trips pregnant was very high but what intrigued him the most was the mere thought of checking into a resort with Taylor with the sole intent of having a full week of constant sex. He was getting aroused just thinking about it, about the possibility of making all those fantasies he'd tried pushing to the back of his mind about Taylor a reality.

But still, all things considered, he and Taylor would need to discuss the issue more in detail. There were a number of questions he needed answered, such as what joint custody of a child they shared would entail, and why did she think him making her pregnant would not cost him anything? Did she expect him to walk away from any financial obligations he had toward the child?

He settled back in the cushions of the seat thinking he was very much looking forward to his dinner date with Taylor later tonight.

"Your parents are waiting for you in your suite, Mr. Saxon."

"Thanks, Harold," Dominic said to the hotel manager moments before crossing the huge lobby to the bank of elevators that would carry him up to the penthouse. The Saxon Grand was a beautiful hotel and had been the first Saxon Hotel. It was built twenty-five years ago and Dominic was almost certain Harold was hired in some position at that time, which would make him one of Saxon Hotel's oldest employees. And Harold was good at what he did, based on the customer satisfaction surveys that were periodically done. Customers visiting the area kept coming back knowing they would receive first-class service.

Moments later Dominic walked into his suite unannounced to find his parents in a loving embrace. He was not surprised nor the least embarrassed to see them standing in the middle of the floor sharing a passionate kiss. Despite having been married for thirty-six years, Marcello and Megan were still deeply in love. That was obvious to anyone around them for any length of time. As long as he could remember, his parents were openly affectionate. He'd always known how much they loved each other as well as how much they had unselfishly loved him.

He cleared his throat to let them know of his presence. "Mom and Dad, it's good seeing you," he said, and knew he didn't have to add that it was also good seeing they were still very much in love.

His parents had met when Marcello Saxon had arrived in the United States from France to attend Yale. In his senior year he met the beautiful and vivacious Megan Spectrum and they fell in love immediately. It hadn't mattered that he was French and she African-American. What had mattered was the love they had for each other. They had gone so far as to defy Marcello's father, who'd threatened to disown his son—the heir to the Saxon wealth—if a marriage took place. Choosing love over wealth, Marcello had married Megan a year later and good to his word, Franco Saxon had practically disowned his son, had barely spoken to him since and only recently had acknowledged the marriage.

Dominic saw the worried look in his father's gaze. "What's wrong, Dad?" His father had recently had his annual checkup and Dominic inwardly prayed there wasn't bad news in that regard.

Marcello read the concern in his son's gaze and said, "No, I'm fine. The doctors gave me another clean bill of health after my last checkup. But we did get some news last night that your grandfather has taken ill."

Dominic stared first at his father and then at his mother. Finally he shrugged nonchalantly as he crossed the room to give his father a bear hug. "Have you forgotten, Father, that I don't have a grandfather?"

"Nick," his father said in a frustrating tone, "how can you be so unforgiving?"

Dominic arched a brow. "And how can you be so forgiving? That man refused to accept my mother as your wife, publicly denounced your marriage and you, didn't speak to you for years, never acknowledged my birth and then out of the clear blue sky last year when he'd heard you had taken ill, he showed up and expected everyone to kiss and make up. Well, I wasn't in the kissing mood then and I'm not in it now," he said in an angry tone.

He switched his gaze from his father to smile down at his mother. "Except for this beautiful woman here," he said, before hugging her close and placing a soft kiss across her cheek. "How are you, Mama?"

Megan Saxon returned her son's smile before giving him a scolding look. "I'm fine, Nick, and your father is right, you know. You can't distance your grandfather forever."

"Would you care to bet on that?"

She frowned. "You're just like your father. Stubborn."

A smile touched Dominic's lips. "Yet you love us anyway."

Dominic then glanced at the man who'd sired him. The man he loved, admired and respected above all else. The man who had not let his father's rejection of the woman he loved destroy his determination to make her his wife and to make something out of his life—even without the Saxon wealth behind him. After college Marcello had started from the bottom and with keen intelligence, his father built his own Saxon empire, which consisted of hotels, cruise liners, restaurants, publishing companies and various auto dealerships across the country.

His mother hadn't done badly, either, he thought with a proud smile. Megan Saxon's name was known throughout the world and graced the garments of several international celebrities. She had a remarkable reputation for outstanding design and had established her own empire in the world of fashion.

The one thing his parents had taught him, Dominic concluded, was to increase his own wealth and not depend on what he might or might not inherit. And so he had. With their blessings he had carved out his personal legacy and thanks to a sharp wealth asset manager like Taylor, he was doing quite well for himself.

Taylor.

He glanced at his watch. They would be sharing dinner in less than four hours.

"Regardless of what you say or how you feel, Nick, he is still your grandfather."

Dominic decided not to justify his father's statement with a response.

"Will you at least think about going to see him, sweetheart?"

That question came from his mother. He glanced

down at her. She was five feet, eight inches tall and in a room with her son and husband she looked small and delicate. But he knew the latter was far from the truth. She had to be one of the most headstrong women that he knew, definitely no pushover.

It was on the tip of his tongue to say there was nothing to think about and that under no circumstances did he intend to go see the man, but the last thing he wanted was to upset his mother any further. It bothered her that he disliked his grandfather so much because of the old man's treatment of her.

"I'll think about it," he said, although he knew deep down that he wouldn't.

"And that's all we ask you to do, Nick," his mother said softly. "We're staying in the suite across the hall tonight and flying to France in the morning."

He nodded. If they expected him to drop everything and fly to France with them because the old man had taken ill then they were wrong. He leaned over and swept another kiss across his mother's cheek. "And I hope the two of you have a safe flight."

He saw the flash of disappointment in her eyes and chose to ignore it. "Now if the two of you will excuse me I have a few things I need to take care of before my date tonight here in my suite."

His mother's brow lifted in surprise. "You have a date?"

He smiled. His mother was well aware that he rarely entertained anyone in a place he considered his private domain. "Yes. But don't waste the excitement. I'm merely meeting with my financial advisor."

"Oh."

He chuckled. "The two of you can join us if you like," he invited, knowing they wouldn't.

"Your mother and I have other plans," his father said, smiling and gently pulling Megan out of Dominic's arms into his and kissing her lips. "We're having dinner with friends."

"Okay then. Enjoy yourselves." And then Dominic's thoughts immediately went back to Taylor and her outlandish proposition. He glanced at his watch again. He couldn't wait to see her later.

Chapter 2

"Do you really think he's going to go along with it, Taylor?"

Taylor heard the uncertainty in her sister's voice through the phone. Vanessa was the one with doubts; however, Cheyenne was the sister who was convinced Dominic would accept her offer. And it wasn't that Vanessa was a naysayer. She was just being realistic that most people thought logically. And what Taylor was posing to Dominic was highly illogical.

The three of them, she, Vanessa and Cheyenne, always had a close relationship growing up and over the years that hadn't changed. Vanessa, the oldest at twenty-seven, was the one who, after getting a grad degree at Tennessee State, had returned to Charlotte to work at the family's manufacturing business, The Steele Corporation, along with their four older male cousins—Chance, Sebastian, Morgan and Donovan. After college,

Taylor and Cheyenne had chosen to seek opportunities far away from North Carolina. Cheyenne, who was twenty-three, was a professional model and that meant a lot of traveling as well as living in some of the most exotic places in the world.

Vanessa was in the midst of planning a June wedding to a very handsome man by the name of Cameron Cody. Taylor couldn't help but smile when she thought about how Cameron had pursued her sister with a vengeance, and finally succeeded in capturing Vanessa's heart. Taylor was happy for Vanessa and looked forward to returning home for a brief stay this weekend to be fitted for her bridesmaid dress.

"Taylor?"

Vanessa didn't have to repeat the question for Taylor to respond. She knew what Vanessa wanted to know. "Um, I don't know if Dominic will go along with my offer or not. It would certainly make my day if he did. At least I'll have another chance to convince him that I haven't lost my mind at dinner tonight."

"Well, good luck."

"Thanks, Vanessa." Deciding to change the subject, she said, "So tell me how the plans are coming for the wedding."

An hour or so later, Taylor was stepping out of the shower to get dressed for her dinner meeting with Dominic. His secretary had called earlier to get her address and to let her know that a car was being sent to pick her up exactly at six-thirty. She would be taken to the Saxon Grand Hotel, where she would be dining with Mr. Saxon.

Taylor glanced at the outfit and accessories she had placed on the bed earlier. She would be wearing a mauve embroidered overlay dress with gold covair beading on the empire bodice and a hem that stopped well above the knee to show off her legs. The dress wasn't flashy, but she had to admit it was eye-catching. Deliberately so. She needed an outfit that would make Dominic take notice and quickly conclude that a week spent with her on a tropical island indulging in unlimited bedroom activities wouldn't be all bad.

With less than thirty minutes before the car was to arrive, Taylor was standing in front of the mirror in her bedroom studying the finished product. She tilted her head back, liking the way the earrings dangled from her ears and the matching necklace around her neck. Both had been Christmas gifts from her oldest cousin, Chance, and his wife, Kylie.

Taylor still found it hard to believe at times that within a three-year period her staunch bachelor cousins, Chance, Sebastian and Morgan, had fallen in love and gotten married. And then there was Vanessa, who would be marrying Cameron in June. Taylor was happy for all four of them. Her thoughts shifted to the one lone single male cousin, Donovan Steele. At thirty-two, marriage was the furthest thing from his mind. She had even heard him swear that he would be a bachelor for life.

Her sister Cheyenne was pretty much like her—too involved in a career to take the time to settle down and get involved in a serious affair. But Taylor was determined that no matter how involved she was in her career, she would take time out to become a mother. Having a child had always been her lifelong desire, but she hadn't known to what degree until a few months back when she returned home to attend Morgan's cel-

ebration party, after he won the council-at-large seat in
Charlotte, becoming the first Steele to enter politics.

Vanessa's best friend, Sienna, had just given birth
to a little boy, who in keeping with Bradford tradition
had been named Dane William Bradford IV. The moment Taylor had held Little Dane in her arms she'd
known that she didn't want to wait any longer to become a mom.

Sighing deeply, Taylor glanced at her watch. Dominic's driver would be arriving to pick her up any
moment and she wanted to be ready. When she saw
Dominic again, she definitely wanted to give him a
few things to think about. He would discover tonight
that she was a lot more than a mover and a shaker. She
was a woman who went after what she wanted and
more than anything, she wanted Dominic Saxon as her
baby's daddy.

Dominic glanced at his watch periodically as he
paced around his hotel room waiting for Taylor's arrival. He couldn't recall the last time a dinner date had
him on edge.

Earlier, during a relaxing moment, he had shared a
glass of wine with his parents, and as always, he had
enjoyed their company. They didn't always see eye to
eye on everything but he couldn't ask for better parents. They had always been there for him, supportive
in every way.

He couldn't help noticing how worried his father
was about Franco Saxon's health. It had taken Marcello
years to finally put the anger behind him and accept the
olive branch that Franco had held out after over thirty
years. Dominic hadn't been that forgiving and to this

day he had come face-to-face with the man who was his grandfather only twice. The most recent time was the day Franco had flown in from Paris and had shown up at Dominic's parents' home in Los Angeles after getting word that his only son—the one he had years ago disowned—had a life-threatening illness. Luckily, Marcello's condition hadn't been as bad as all that, but it had reunited father and son. Marcello was of the mind that too much hurt and pain had passed and as long as Franco finally accepted his marriage, all was well. Before he had left to return to France, Franco had given his blessings to the marriage.

Dominic frowned. As far as he was concerned it had come years too late and he had told the old man as much. But it seemed Dominic's words had fallen on deaf ears since Franco had refused to give up, determined to forge a bond with his only grandchild. Dominic had repeatedly turned down his grandfather's attempts. A part of him could not put aside the deep animosity he felt and move on.

Before taking a shower he had touched base with his kitchen staff. Dinner would be served here in his suite, which was a first for him. He rarely brought company to his hotel room, but given the topic of his and Taylor's conversation, it was important that whatever was discussed was done in private.

Hours later, after getting dressed, he paused to think about everything he knew about Taylor.

He knew from past conversations with her that her mother was still alive but that her father had died years back of lung cancer. He also knew she had two sisters and she was the middle child. And he was well aware that her family owned a multimillion-dollar business,

The Steele Corporation, where she had a seat on the board of directors. He knew Chance Steele, her cousin, who was the CEO of the company. They had met years ago at a business conference and Dominic found him to be a very likable person.

Dominic also was acquainted with Cameron Cody, the man her oldest sister would be marrying. They moved in the same social circles and had even been involved in a highly successful business venture a few years back. When it came to business Cody was sharp as a tack.

Dominic wondered if Taylor's family was aware of how she intended to branch into motherhood. She wanted a baby, but not a husband. All things considered, he could certainly entertain the thought of having a baby without a wife. However, before he agreed to Taylor's proposal there were a number of things he had to think about, questions he needed answered.

On the flip side, he definitely had no qualms about accepting her proposal. He was attracted to her and had been from the first. Making a baby with her would definitely give him the excuse he needed to cross over the line of business only. The thought of having Taylor in bed beneath him while making love to her had kept him aroused all day.

The phone rang and he was jerked out of his thoughts. He quickly moved across the room to pick it up. "Yes?"

"Your guest has arrived, sir. Do you want me to escort her up?"

"No, I'll be down to meet her myself."

He hung up the phone feeling, oddly, a bit nervous.

Taylor glanced around thinking that this was the first time she had been in a Saxon Hotel. It was big and spacious with an understated degree of refined elegance. It was definitely a five-star that was replete with a luxurious-looking grand interior and a uniformed staff on duty to satisfy a client's every whim. A person could definitely get swept away with such grace and style.

"Mr. Saxon will be coming down for you, Ms. Steele."

Taylor glanced at the uniformed man who had spoken. He was the same one who had picked her up from her condo and now stood solidly beside her. "He is?"

"Yes."

She figured once inside the hotel she would be on her own. Apparently not. It appeared Dominic had other ideas. When he had invited her to dinner she'd known they would be dining in his suite. He hadn't said as much but she had assumed it. He was a private person and the majority of the time when they had dinner meetings he always made it a habit to suggest a private room. It wasn't uncommon for him to cause a stir, especially among the media who enjoyed writing about the wealthy Saxon heir.

"Here is Mr. Saxon now."

Taylor glanced in the direction of the elevators and caught sight of Dominic walking toward them. She had prepared herself to see him again. Or so she thought. The man was so extraordinarily sexy, so ridiculously sensual that her entire body began responding. As he crossed the wide stretch of lobby toward her, people, mainly women, stopped to stare.

She suddenly felt her heart take a nosedive into her stomach. He was wearing a tailored suit and blue shirt that fit him with precision and even at a distance she could detect his calm restraint. She was about to look away and place her focus elsewhere, when his gaze suddenly snagged hers. His penetrating stare was doing things to her, forcing her to embark on one hell of a fantastic voyage. Heat rushed through her, zinged her with a force she hadn't felt before. The man had enough sex appeal to bottle for future generations.

Damn. Definitely not what she wanted to be up against tonight. How was she going to get through a meal with him when already she felt trapped in his gaze? *All right, I can handle this. I can handle him.* Those words flowed through her mind as he got closer. With a half smile she expelled another breath and forced back the thought that suddenly entered her mind about just how great it would be to share a hotel room with him, a bed, the same intimate space. Hot sex. Heated Sex. Never-ending Sex. And all for a full week. With her lips barely moving, she released a soft laugh. There would be little time for chitchat.

That thought put every nerve ending in her body on red alert. But she refused to give anything away. So she stood there waiting, looking more poised than she actually felt. She was here for a good reason and knowing that reason gave strength to her resolve. It would be pointless to fight off the sexual heat the man generated but she wished she wasn't so aware of him. She would have appreciated it if he didn't make such a powerful impact on her vital signs and wasn't oozing such raw physical force.

And more than anything, she wished he didn't look like all the millions he was actually worth. Boy, how she wished.

When he finally came to a stop in front of her, and she saw the beauty of his green eyes as he gazed into her dark ones, she had never wished for anything so much in her life.

* * *

The first thing that had hit Dominic, even before he'd reached Taylor, was her scent. He had to compliment whatever perfume she was wearing. It was both soft and sensuous and had a punch that could drive a man to distraction. But then he had been blown away the moment he had stepped off the elevator and had seen her standing with Ryder. She looked delicate beside the huge hulk of man. Above all, she looked stunning.

The dress she was wearing definitely brought out her sensual side. Thanks to his mother he knew enough about fashion to realize that not every woman would be able to pull off wearing an outfit such as this. You had to have the small waistline, curves and legs to make it happen, otherwise it would be a total waste of good fabric. Taylor had the small waistline, the curves and the legs. Another added bonus was that she also had the breasts, since the square-neck bodice emphasized them. Yes, altogether he would give the outfit an A-plus.

Even now as he stared at her, with her head tilted and meeting his intense gaze, he was fighting for control. He had always admired Taylor for her intelligence, her investment savvy, but now he was about to bestow on her accolades for her ability to take him on at a personal level. He was beginning to discover that she was one irresistible force.

"Dominic."

His name on her lips seemed to warm his skin. He even felt his insides beginning to melt. He figured he needed to get her up to his hotel room before his sexual response to her became too obvious. "Taylor, I hope you had a pleasant ride coming here."

She smiled as she glanced over at Ryder. "Um, it was rather interesting."

Only someone who knew Ryder Sanders as well as Dominic was aware of the man fighting the urge to smile back. Evidently his driver had broken several speed limits.

Years ago, when at the age of fourteen, a kidnapping attempt had been made on Dominic, Franco Saxon, in one of his rare but manipulative moves had sent Ryder. Marcello had been too distraught at the thought of someone trying to use his son in a ransom scheme to send Ryder back. By the time Dominic had learned of his grandfather's gesture, Ryder had become not only his bodyguard, driver and traveling companion, but the now fifty-something man had become his good friend. Dominic moved around freely knowing that Ryder had his back.

"Interesting?" Dominic said. "I'm sure it was. Are you ready to go up to my suite for dinner?"

"Yes, I'm ready."

The sound of her voice stoked the fires within him once again. There was a whole world of difference between the Taylor he met each month to discuss his financial portfolio and the one standing in front of him looking good enough to devour. All of a sudden the menu that he'd carefully selected lost its appeal and he was developing a taste for something else altogether. Something that was just as succulent.

He gestured toward the bank of elevators. "There's a private one that goes up to the floor where the owner suites are located."

She began walking beside him across the lobby floor. He saw several heads turn and knew everyone was probably thinking they made a beautiful couple. Little did they know that during the course of the next few hours they would be encased in his hotel room discussing whether or not they should make a beautiful baby together.

His heart began to thunder in his chest. He had a feeling it would be a long and tempting evening.

This had to be the longest elevator ride that she'd ever taken, Taylor thought as she tried looking at everything other than Dominic. He was standing beside her and she felt tension grip her stomach.

She didn't feel like engaging in a nice conversation just to pass the time. Although she and Dominic had spent many hours together poring over his financial portfolio, their meeting tonight would be altogether different. She was now a woman with a plan. And it was a plan that she hoped he would go along with.

"I should have asked before commissioning the cook to come up with something special for dinner tonight if you're allergic to anything."

She glanced up at him. "No, there's nothing I can think of that doesn't agree with my system."

"I'm glad to hear that."

She met his eyes. They were staring deep into hers.

"And don't be surprised if we see my parents at some point tonight."

She arched a brow. "Your parents?"

"Yes. They're here at the hotel. They flew in from California and are on their way out of the country."

She nodded. "I've seen pictures of them together in various magazines. They make a nice couple," she said, meaning every word. Marcello Saxon was an extremely handsome man with his classic French looks. And Dominic's mom was a beauty, who didn't look a day past forty. In a rare photo that Dominic and his parents had taken together that had appeared in *People* magazine earlier this year, Megan Saxon looked young enough to have passed for his sister.

"Thanks, and I agree. They do make a nice couple. I am fortunate to have them as parents."

The elevator came to a stop and the doors swooshed open. Dominic stood back for her to walk out ahead of him and then he was there again, by her side, leading the way down an elegantly carpeted hall toward a set of double doors at the end.

They came to a stop at the doors. "The kitchen staff was arriving when I was leaving so everything should be set up now," he was saying. "We can discuss things over dinner and, if need be, converse further afterward."

As she stared into his green eyes she suddenly felt a heated rush, a swamp of sensations of the strongest kind. It was nothing more than a business meeting over dinner, yet she had to get Dominic to see how useful they could be to each other, how together they could bring something or rather someone special into each of their lives.

As he opened the door to his penthouse she knew she was about to have her one shot at it and she didn't intend to blow it.

"So, Taylor, when did you come up with the idea of wanting me to father your child?"

Dominic watched as she took a deep breath before raising her eyes from her plate to look at him. He had caught her off guard. She hadn't been expecting his question, especially not now. They were in the midst of enjoying a delicious and impressive entrée the hotel's restaurant had prepared and had been discussing a recent documentary that had aired on television that focused on the plight of finback whales. He had discovered a while back that they were both lovers of sea life.

She put her fork down beside her plate. "I made the decision once I knew I wanted to move ahead with my plans to become a mother."

He lifted his hand in the briefest gesture before asking, "And? What were your other options?"

"I had several," she said, leaning back in her chair. Anyone observing would assume she was rather comfortable with their conversation, but he had a feeling she really wasn't.

"I could have contacted a sperm bank where the identity of my child's father would never be known by me or by him or her. Or I could have engaged in a one-night stand for the sole purpose of getting pregnant. Neither appealed to me."

"But I did."

"Yes, you did," she answered in what he thought was a polite tone. "You had all the characteristics I looked for in a man and those I want to pass on to my son or daughter, as well."

He didn't say anything for a moment and then, "And you were sure I wanted a child?"

"Yes, after the night of the Christmas party, I was sure. Although there was the question of whether you would be interested in doing what I was proposing. For all I know you might already have a woman selected as the mother of your child."

He took a sip of his wine, thinking that he didn't. In

fact he had pretty much dropped the thought from his mind. He figured that there were a number of women who would love the opportunity to mother his child— most of them were gold diggers and would use the child to keep a tight rein on him and his finances.

"If I decide to go along with what you're proposing I know what I'll be bringing to the table, Taylor. What will you bring?"

Again his question had caught her off guard. He knew what she would bring to the bedroom—that was a given. Sitting across from her, inhaling her scent while visions of all the things they would be doing together on that island ran through his mind was playing havoc with certain body parts. She was fully dressed now, but he could see her naked while he made love to her, day in and day out. She was temptation at its finest and the thought that he wouldn't have to resist temptation for an entire week had his body throbbing.

"I'll bring to the table the assurance that your child will be loved and well cared for. I consider myself intelligent, motivated and financially secure."

"What about custody?" he asked.

She frowned slightly. "I'm open to joint custody."

"So you won't have a problem with me being a part of my child's life?"

She shook her head. "No. I'm not one of those women who believes a child doesn't need a male presence in its life. I have four male cousins who I'm close to, but still, I'd want my child's father to be a part of its life if possible."

Dominic absorbed her words while his gaze settled impassively on his wineglass. He then lifted his gaze to her. "And just what will our relationship be? After our visit to that island?"

"If I get pregnant…" She paused then corrected the sentence by saying, "*After* I get pregnant, then our relationship will become that of expectant parents and not lovers. The job at that point would have been done. Of course, I'm hoping that I will continue to be your wealth and asset manager."

He thought she didn't have to worry about that unless the island rendezvous turned into an absolute fiasco. He was one who normally didn't mix business with pleasure, yet if he agreed to her proposal he would be doing just that. But she was right. He had on several occasions entertained the thought of having a child without having to deal with a wife. Since his wife's death he'd dated but hadn't yet met a woman he wanted to share his name again.

He and Camry had been childhood sweethearts, their parents the best of friends. It had seemed natural for them to eventually marry. In a way they had been best friends instead of two people who were deeply in love with each other. They'd shared a close relationship. He could talk to Camry about anything and she had understood him better than anyone. She had been his confidante as well as his wife. He doubted he would find such closeness with another woman. And to be honest, he wasn't interested in doing so ever again.

"You seem certain that you will get pregnant," he said, inwardly smiling to himself and thinking he was just as certain she would get pregnant. He wanted her and as far as he was concerned that said it all. Heat had been running through every part of his body since she had arrived. It wasn't easy now sharing table space with her.

"I don't have any reason to think that I won't, given the planned agenda," she said. "I've been under a doctor's supervision for the past three months. I've been tracking my basal body temperature, which will help me to pinpoint the best time to conceive and that's the week I want us on that island."

"In that case why go to the island? Why not stay here?"

"I prefer the island. It will provide a more relaxed environment."

He had to agree with that. "And you have no problem sleeping with me for no other reason than to make a baby?"

He watched her lips curve into an assured smile. "No, I don't have a problem with it." She fell silent for a moment then asked, "Do you?"

He thought about her question. He would be breaking rules he'd put in place for specific reasons, rules he'd always enforced when it came to his business relationships. When it came to women, period. Although he was not suspicious regarding her motives for what she wanted to do, he still wasn't a hundred percent certain it was what he wanted to do.

"What if we aren't compatible, Taylor?"

"Excuse me?"

His mouth formed into a smile. Apparently she found the idea absurd. "I said what if we aren't compatible? How do we know we're even attracted to each other? That we'll be able to click?"

She chuckled softly. "Trust me. We'll be able to click."

"How do you know?"

"Because I do."

"Prove it."

One of the first things he had discovered about Taylor was that she liked challenges, which was one of the reasons she was successful at what she did. However, he could tell from her present expression that proving what he'd suggested was the last thing she wanted to do. Still, not one to forgo an opportunity to prove him wrong, she released a long, slow breath as she stood. He then watched as she walked around the table until she came to a stop beside him. Reaching out, she touched his hand and the impact of that touch for some reason almost took his breath away. He then tossed his napkin aside, slid his chair back and got to his feet to face her.

"Not that I'm an expert on sexual chemistry or anything," she said in a low, sultry tone. "But I think this will eliminate any doubt in your mind on whether or not we will click."

She reached up on tiptoe, placed her arms around his neck and brought her mouth to his. His heart pounded hard in his chest the moment their lips touched. And when their tongues began mating with an intensity that shook every nerve in his body, he had to fight the urge to break the connection for fear of losing control. At that moment he wasn't aware of anything but the feel of his tongue stroking hers, the feel of hers stroking his, the rush of sensations flooding and overpowering him. He was also aware of the fire stirring in his loins and of the way his body was beginning to ache.

When she slowly pulled back, their lips reluctantly separating, he felt a tremendous sense of loss. "So," she said slowly, dragging the word out softly as she eased away from his lips. "Did we click?"

He struggled to free his mind, as well as the tight

squeeze on certain body parts as he studied her. He saw her lips that had been thoroughly kissed, lips that had to be the sweetest pair that he'd ever tasted, sampled, devoured. His response to her was as potent as any intoxicating drink he'd ever taken. And from the heated look in her eyes, she was just as affected by the kiss as he was.

"Yes," he finally said, pulling in a deep, hot breath. "I can say with all certainty that we click."

Chapter 3

Taylor stood at the window that had the Jefferson Memorial as a backdrop as she thought about the kiss she and Dominic had shared. Lucky for her a slight reprieve had come when his cell phone rang and he'd excused himself to take the call in private.

She refused to believe that she had bitten off more than she could chew. She had known from the beginning that Dominic was the epitome of a sexy male, a challenge to any woman's hormones and a mass of French-American testosterone all rolled into one. At the time she had decided she wanted him as the father of her child, there was no doubt in her mind that she could handle him. What she hadn't done was take the time to consider all of the consequences.

She traced her lips with her tongue, still tasting him there. She hadn't counted on not being in control of any situation with him, but if that kiss had lasted any longer than it had, she would have lost control. Completely. She had been kissed before, several times, but she had never considered or remembered the occasions as being the highlight of her life. One kiss was the same as another. Mouths connecting. Lips tasting. Tongues playing.

But what she had shared moments ago with Dominic was all those things and more. She hadn't counted on the rush of desire that had radiated through every part of her body at the same time that her insides began a slow meltdown under intense heat. She wished she could claim her reaction had been the result of restless energy being tapped or the release of bottled-up sexual tension. What Dominic had done was place an all-out assault on her senses, each one of them, and it would take her some time to recover from the tingling rush of desire she still felt. It was desire of a magnitude that had never invaded her body before. Even now she could imagine his hands on her, stroking her naked skin, his lips tasting every inch of her willing body and their bodies connecting in the most primitive way known to man. There was no doubt in her mind that when and if they shared a bed they would literally burn up the sheets.

"Sorry about the interruption."

She slowly turned around. He might have been sorry about it, but she had welcomed it. It had given her time to pull herself together or at least try to. "No need to apologize. You're a businessman who works 24-7." She smiled. "As your asset manager I can certainly appreciate that."

Her eyes roamed over him, liking the way his muscles filled out the suit he was wearing. There were a number of other things she could appreciate at that moment but decided it would be safer not to think about them right now.

When he stood there staring at her without saying anything, she felt a bit cornered, placed under his personal microscope, and she couldn't help wondering what he was thinking. So she decided to ask. "You seem absorbed in some intense thought, Dominic. What are you thinking?"

A smile stretched his lips as he crossed the room to her. And when he reached out and ran the back of his hand along her cheek, the throbbing between her legs intensified. "I was more envisioning than thinking," he finally said in a deep, husky tone. "I was trying to picture in my mind you pregnant with my child."

Taylor bit her lip. He should have said anything but that. She knew at that moment her fate was sealed. He had made a decision or was close to making one. And although what they would agree to do would be illogical, definitely outlandish to some people, to her it would be absolutely incredible, a dream come true.

"Does that mean you've made a decision, Dominic?" she asked in a quiet voice. Her pulse was racing a lot faster than her calm words would indicate.

"Yes. And I just hope it's what you really want. You would not only be giving me a child, but also my parents their first grandchild. I might as well warn you that it won't be easy being the mother of the Saxon heir." Dominic's mouth set in a grim line when he added, "That might be something you need to really consider."

She knew how it was when it came to first grandchildren. Her cousin Chance's son, Marcus, had been the first for her aunt and uncle and she had been around to experience the hoopla that for years seemed endless. "I would welcome your parents' involvement in our child's life, and if they get too overbearing I believe that I'd be able to handle them."

When he didn't say anything for a while and she felt the throb in her body becoming an ache, she asked, "What is your decision, Dominic?" She stared into the intensity of his green eyes, wanting to hear him say it, refusing to assume anything.

"My decision, Taylor, is to take you to that island, spend a week with you and get you pregnant."

Taylor's breath caught in her throat. His words had been straightforward. No way for any mis—understanding. He had agreed to what she'd asked for. Confident that he could. He was giving her just what she wanted and she couldn't hide her happiness. It was there in her smile. She felt overwhelmed. Touched. Totally elated. "Thank you. It's what I want."

She didn't miss the look of desire in his eyes when he said in a deep, husky tone, "Me and you both."

Dominic knew it was time for Taylor to leave or else he would be considering things that he should not have— not at this point. Deciding to be the father of her child was enough for now.

"Did you enjoy dinner?" he asked, trying to control the situation.

"Yes."

"Good. It's getting late. I'll walk you downstairs for Ryder to take you home," he said, grabbing his jacket off the back of the sofa and slipping into it.

"I'm going home for the weekend," she said casually. He knew home to her was Charlotte, North Carolina.

"If you change your mind about anything while I'm away then—"

"I won't be changing my mind," he said in an assured tone as they walked toward the door. "In fact, I'll give my attorney a call to draw up the necessary papers." At her surprised look he said, "I'm sure you know that I'll feel better about the situation if we treat it like a legitimate business deal—which it is. That means a binding contract between us that we can agree on."

"Of course."

He glanced over at her. She said the words but to his way of thinking sounded none too pleased. Had she thought he would give her a verbal agreement on anything and not follow it up in writing? Not only would doing so protect him but it would protect her, as well. All he had to do was recall what had happened to his childhood friend Matt Caulder.

Matt had fallen in love and had gotten married a few years back. The woman had been bad news from the first, but love had blinded his friend to that fact. Within months the woman had gotten pregnant and had tried using the child as bargaining power whenever she'd wanted anything. Luckily, Matt had been able to take Rhonda to court and prove he was the better parent.

He couldn't imagine ever having to take Taylor to court for anything, but still he wanted his rights regarding any child they made together protected.

"I'll arrange for my attorney to get the papers to you within a week. That will give you time to let your own attorney review them," he said as they walked toward the bank of elevators. "Do you have any idea when we'll be leaving for the island? There're a few business matters I'd want to wrap up before then."

"In two weeks. I'm contacting my travel agent to-morrow to set everything into motion. I'm looking at the first week in April. Will that work for you?" Whether it did or not, he intended to make it work. A week spent on an island with her was worth shifting anything around that needed to be changed. "Yes, it will work."

When they stepped onto the elevator she said, "Sorry I didn't get to meet your parents."

He nodded. He was sorry, as well. They would like her. "They were meeting friends but I thought that perhaps they would return early. I was wrong. However, considering the circumstances of our business arrangement, it's inevitable that you'll eventually meet them."

He had to continue to think of what they would be doing as a business arrangement and nothing more. He glanced over and caught her staring at him. Her head was tilted in a way that gave the impression she was trying to figure something out. Most likely it was him. Although she had been his asset manager for a couple of years she'd never really seen the personal side of him. Things had always been kept on a strictly business level.

"Will you tell your parents everything?"

"No. They have purely romantic minds and won't understand how we can do such a thing without being in love, so the less they know the better."

He sighed knowing in a few moments the elevator would be back down in the lobby. He turned to her. "Are you sure this is what you want, Taylor?"

Now he was giving her the chance to reconsider all they had agreed to this evening.

"Yes, I'm sure. I want a baby."

"In that case," he said slowly, "I'm going to try my best to give you one. To give *us* one," he clarified.

Unable to resist, he leaned forward and placed a gentle kiss on her lips. It was a lot tamer than the lip-locker, tongue-thrasher of earlier, but he still managed to feel blood sizzle through his veins. Kissing her was definitely increasing his sex drive, arousing everything male within. Considering the number of beautiful women who routinely crossed his path, he found it strange that he would want her so intensely.

The elevator door opened and he saw Ryder across the lobby, standing and talking with one of the hotel workers. The older man caught his gaze and nodded. Dominic returned his eyes to Taylor. "This is where I must bid you good-night," he said, trying to sound normal when he felt anything but. "Have a safe trip to Charlotte and I'll see you in a couple of weeks."

He tried not focusing on her lips. They were lips he wanted to kiss again and was grateful when Ryder appeared. "Make sure she gets home safely," he said.

"Sure thing."

Not able to fight temptation and not caring that they weren't alone—besides Ryder there were a number of people mingling around in the lobby—he leaned over and kissed her lips once more. The moment he did so, tingles of awareness shot through him. The thought that suddenly jackknifed through his mind was how was he going to spend a week with her on some exotic island and maintain his control? The answer came to him just as quickly.

He wouldn't have to.

Elated beyond belief, Taylor bid the driver good-night and walked toward her front door. She glanced over her shoulder. Ryder had not moved and was still stationed by the car. Dominic had instructed the man not to leave until he saw that she was safely inside her home and Ryder was definitely following orders.

After unlocking her door she opened it and went inside. After scanning the room, she quickly moved to the windows and flipped the blinds, letting him know she was okay. It was only then that he got inside the sedan and drove off.

She checked her watch. It was almost ten. To Taylor it was still fairly early, but someone like Vanessa, who was known to retire early, would normally have been in bed by now. But Taylor knew she'd want to hear this—she had news worth sharing. She picked up the phone to begin dialing. After she talked to Vanessa she would call Cheyenne, who was doing a photo shoot somewhere in China. The three of them would be together this coming weekend in Charlotte when they got fitted for their bridesmaids' dresses.

"Hello."

Taylor raised a brow. It was a man's voice. Cameron's.

"Yes, Cameron, how are you? Is Vanessa asleep?"

She heard his smooth chuckle. "No, she's awake. Hold on a second."

Taylor really liked Cameron and, unlike Vanessa, she had from the first. It hadn't bothered her in the least that at one time he'd tried taking over her family company. She hadn't taken it personally as Vanessa had. Increasing a person's wealth was Taylor's business and she couldn't help but admire anyone who wanted to increase their riches.

"Taylor, what happened?"

Taylor rolled her eyes. "What makes you think something happened?"

"Ha! Cut the act, Taylor. We both know what was supposed to go down tonight. So give up the details!"

"Details? Why did Cameron answer your phone? Isn't it kind of late for him to be visiting?" Taylor asked, grinning.

"Nope. In fact he's staying the night. And unless I change the locks he'll stay the week. He likes keeping me in his sights and I like having him around."

Taylor could hear the smile in Vanessa's voice. Her sister was happy and she was happy for her. In fact she was happy for herself, as well, which was the reason she had called.

"So don't change the subject. Tell me everything."

"Can we talk now or am I taking you away from something?"

"I can talk. Cameron just got in the shower," Vanessa said.

"He's agreed to do it."

"Dominic Saxon agreed to get you pregnant?"

She could hear the excitement in Vanessa's voice. "Yes."

"So I'm going to be an aunt?"

Taylor smiled. "More than likely. There's no reason to think we won't click." Especially after tonight, she thought, remembering how Dominic had to be assured that they would.

"When you come home this weekend, we're going to have to celebrate."

Biting down on her lip, Taylor fought to control her happiness and discovered that she couldn't. Both of her sisters knew how much she wanted a child.

"Can I tell Sienna?"

Taylor smiled. Sienna Bradford was Vanessa's best

friend and had been since grade school. "Yes, tell her but don't tell the cousins anything. You know how over-protective they can be at times."

"Okay. So there's a chance you'll be pregnant at my wedding."

Taylor sighed. She certainly hoped so. If everything worked out as planned, she and Dominic would be going to the Caribbean the beginning of next month and Vanessa was having a June wedding. Taylor wouldn't be so far along that she needed to worry about an adjustment to her bridesmaid's dress, but she hoped to be very, merry pregnant.

"I'll let you get back to Cameron and I prefer that you not tell him. He and Morgan have a friendship," she said, thinking of her cousin, "and he might let something slip."

"I hate to say it, but you're probably right. You've taken a big step, Taylor. Are you sure you're ready for the next one?"

Taylor felt a nervous flutter in her belly, the same belly that would be her child's home for nine months. "Yes, I'm ready for the next one."

"Tell me you're joking about this, Nick."

The look on Matt Caulder's face indicated that he was expecting Dominic to say the diabolic plan he'd just laid out to him was a joke. But the more Matt studied his best friend's expression the more he could tell Dominic was dead serious.

Accepting that when Dominic made his mind up about something, then that was it, he looked back down at the brochure he'd been given before meeting Dominic's eyes again. Although he doubted it would do any good, he said, "The Caribbean is a nice place to be this time of year, but as your attorney I'm advising you not to go for what you have in mind."

Dominic had expected as much. He leaned back in his chair. He had arrived at Matt's office knowing Matt would try to talk him out of what he saw as disaster waiting to happen. Dominic saw something else waiting to happen when he arrived in the Caribbean.

"Your advice is duly noted although it won't be accepted," he said smoothly. "As my attorney, what I want is for you to draw up a document that will protect me in the event Taylor has a change of heart and doesn't want me to be a part of my child's life once she becomes pregnant."

"That can easily be done but what makes you think you're going to get her pregnant?"

Dominic smiled and stretched out his legs in front of him. "After looking at that brochure and knowing what you know about me, is there a reason I won't?"

Matt shook his head, chuckling. "No, but why this way?"

"You, the king of one-night stands, have the nerve to ask me that?"

"Mainly because I feel differently about life and love than you do."

Dominic knew that to be true. His and Matt's friendship spanned years. They seemed destined to be friends, the way he had been destined to marry Camry. Matt's mother, Deena, had been Megan's best friend in high school, and although the two had attended difference colleges, their close friendship remained intact over the years.

When Deena got pregnant from a short-term affair

it was Dominic's mom she called on. Megan who had invited her to move to D.C. to stay with her until she was able to get on her feet to take on her role as a single mother. Matt was just a few months older than Dominic, but the two had been raised so close they considered each other as brothers. When Deena had died a few years ago from breast cancer it was Megan, Marcello and Dominic who had stood beside him as the only other family he had.

Dominic came to his feet. "Well, draw up something that Taylor and I can both live with and make sure it's airtight," he said, recalling what Matt had gone through with his wife, Rhonda.

"I can't wait to meet her."

Dominic shot Matt a surprised look. "Why?"

"Evidently Taylor Steele has caught your attention."

"No, her proposal has. There's nothing going on between me and Taylor other than a business arrangement."

"And you're certain that's all there is to it?"

"I want her," Dominic said honestly.

"And beyond that?"

"There's nothing beyond that."

"And again I'm going to ask if you're sure."

Dominic met Matt's unconvinced stare. "Yes, I'm absolutely and positively sure."

Chapter 4

"Welcome to the island of Latois, Mrs. Jones."

"Thank you," Taylor said as she smiled at the perky receptionist. She and Dominic had made a decision to register under a false name as a way to avoid unwanted publicity. Although the resort's management prided themselves on providing absolute privacy, the media had a way of finding out anything they wanted.

Another thing they had decided to do was to let the management and staff assume they were married. She figured most of the couples at the resort were and felt there was no reason for her and Dominic to be the oddballs.

Taylor checked her watch. She had flown in straight from D.C. and Dominic would be arriving a little later that day from New York. That would give her time to get settled and relaxed in their suite before he got there. The past two weeks had been extremely busy. After visiting with her family in Charlotte, she had attended a financial conference in Texas that had lasted an entire week.

She had spoken to Dominic only once and that was when he had called to ask if she'd found his attorney's contract satisfactory. She had. In fact her attorney had been surprised at just how fair Dominic was being. She would have full custody of the child and he would be entitled to a certain number of visits during the year. They were to rotate holidays, which she felt was reasonable. The financial package he would provide for his child was very generous; actually more than she had expected.

"An attendant will escort you to your room, Mrs. Jones."

The woman's words pulled in Taylor's thoughts. "Thank you." She took the passkey and the gift bag she was handed.

She had been given a schedule of activities for the week that included body massages for the both of them. Later that day they were to share a romantic candlelight dinner in their room.

The first thing Taylor thought when she entered her room was that the accommodations were absolutely wonderful. The suite was divided into a spacious sitting area, a wet bar and a massive bedroom. The huge windows in the bedroom provided a panoramic view of the ocean. It was beautiful. Inviting. Breathtaking. She could imagine her and Dominic walking barefoot on the beach later in the near-perfect spring weather.

She then took a look at the larger-than-king-size bed that was swathed in snow-white bedcoverings and huge fluffy pillows. It gave the room a serene and tranquil look, totally out of sync with the hot, passionate love-making that would take place between the sheets over the next seven days. She then thought of the lingerie she had bought, a different color and style for each and every night. Each piece carefully chosen for its sexiness and the ability to entice, seduce and persuade.

Taylor knew that a lot of the couples she would meet over the next few days were fertility challenged and thought a change of climate, the removal of stress would help the problem. She honestly didn't think she and Dominic would have a problem conceiving. Her main purpose in wanting to make a baby here on the island versus back in D.C. was wanting to conceive in style. This would be her only child and she wanted the special moment of conception to happen in a way that would be memorable.

Something else memorable, something she couldn't erase from her mind was the kiss she and Dominic had shared that night in his hotel suite. She had been kissed before, many times, but nothing had sent sensations firing through her the way Dominic's lips and tongue had. She had liked it. A lot. And even now she couldn't help but anticipate it happening again. Here in this room. Plenty of times over the next week.

A visit to her doctor indicated this was her hot week, the best days to conceive, and she was more than eager to get started in making a baby. She knew it was ridiculous but she felt her body was ready, overanxious to begin. The thought of exotic foods and aphrodisiac-laden drinks were nice but she really didn't need either to want to tumble all day and night with Dominic between the sheets. She suddenly began to feel hot and

on edge. Maybe the nature of this place had something
to do with it.

And as she headed for the bedroom to start unpack-
ing, she thought it was more than that. It was the anticipated arrival of one particular man.

Dominic's limo pulled in front of the Capri Resort
on the private island of Latois. Just as the brochure
had depicted, the place was grand, simply exquisite.
Someone who was entrenched in the hotel business, as
he was, could appreciate such a place from the beautifully landscaped property to the stunning ocean setting.

He checked his watch. By his calculations Taylor
should have arrived on the island hours ago. Was she in
the suite waiting for him? He knew a lot of their activities for the next seven days were prearranged, but then
a lot of them weren't. One thing the resort encouraged
was couples spending a lot of private time together,
preferably in their suite in bed procreating. He definitely didn't have a problem with that. In fact he was
looking forward to it.

A few minutes later upon checking in, he was told
his wife had arrived and was in their suite. He was
given his own passkey and a bottle of their house champagne, which, he'd been informed, contained a special
potent ingredient intended to boost their sexual drive.
The clerk hadn't batted an eye when she'd said it.

After stepping onto the elevator that would take him
up to the tenth floor, in no time at all it seemed, he had
reached his floor and was walking down the long hallway toward his room. The bellman would be bringing
up his bags later.

When he stood in front of the suite's door he swallowed hard, knowing what the week entailed. He had tried not to notice the couples he'd passed and just how openly amorous they were with each other. Another thing he noticed was that unlike a lot of resorts, there weren't a lot of people out and about. Most were probably busy behind closed doors trying to accomplish what they had come here to do.

He opened the door and stepped inside the exact moment Taylor was walking out of the bedroom area. Immediately their gazes locked. He was rendered momentarily speechless by how quickly blood shot from his head straight to his groin. His mouth suddenly felt dry and every muscle in his body—some more so than others—felt hard as a rock.

She was wearing a light blue sundress with spaghetti straps that revealed just what beautiful shoulders she had. An ample amount of cleavage was showing, enough to make him appreciate the firm shape of her breasts, as well. Then there was her face and well-defined features. He decided at that moment that Taylor wasn't just beautiful; she was what fantasies were made of. There was an inborn sensuality about her that had been hidden behind her business suits. The business suits represented her profession. The outfit she had on now showed her perfection, especially her curvy figure.

"Dominic."

His name was spoken in a soft tone and he watched her hands come to rest at her sides. For some reason he'd always enjoyed looking at her hands whenever she met with him and flipped through papers she would have for him to sign. Her nails were always neat with a French manicure displaying a non-flashy look. The same extended to her fingers. Some women liked showing off their diamonds practically on every finger. But Taylor didn't even wear a ring, Her hands were long and graceful. Elegant. Sturdy. And he could just imagine those hands touching him, caressing the length of his hardened...

He sucked in a deep breath when he saw where his thoughts were headed. He closed the door behind him as he tried to maintain his control, but found himself losing it and quickly recalled how long it had been since he'd had a woman for a bed partner and decided it had been way too long.

"Aren't we on speaking terms?" she said as a teasing smile touched her lips.

Instead of answering her, he placed the bottle of champagne on a nearby table and crossed the room to her. There was no need for formality. They both knew why they were there and as far as he was concerned, now was just as good a time as any to get the ball rolling. And speaking of balls...he felt his thicken. His testosterone level was so high that he wouldn't be surprised if he were to impregnate her with twins.

The thought of such a thing actually happening made him that much more aroused. It actually made his body ache. Seeing her again was doing a job on him, a real exclusive number. He couldn't recall ever wanting a woman so badly. When he stood directly in front of her, he reached out and cupped the back of her neck to guide her mouth to meet his.

The moment their lips touched he felt it. Passion so thick you could lap it up. Spread it about. Get smothered by it. And when he went past her moist lips and inserted his tongue inside her mouth, he knew he had been anticipating this very moment ever since the night they had dined together over two weeks ago.

Her response was immediate, absolute and totally delectable. The reason they were here might be staged, predestined so to speak, but the sexual chemistry between them was as instant and spontaneous as it could get. The depth of her sensuality was enough to make him want to jump in the ocean to cool off. A cold shower just wouldn't work off the heat. He had discovered over the past two weeks, ever since she had placed her proposal into his lap and he had accepted, that he desired her to the point of madness. And this was the result. He was getting a pretty good taste of her and she was getting a good taste of him, as well.

He heard her groan low in her throat and knew if he pushed hard enough they would be making love right here, possibly on the floor, which wasn't where he wanted his son or daughter conceived. He knew she could feel how aroused he was from the way his body was pressed against hers. He wanted her to feel it. Get used to it.

He really did need to slow down, he thought, as he continued to lap her up. He would take things slow the next time around. But now this seemed appropriate. This is what he wanted. And he was struck by the enormity of just how much passion was in one single kiss. Of how much tongue action was required. He was enjoying sharing both with her. There was nothing gentle about the kiss. Far from it. There was hunger, greed and a desperation he hadn't been used to before, but was getting familiar with now. For some reason she felt right in his arms. Right in his mouth. Right with her body pressed intimately against his.

It wasn't easy, but he finally gained control and pulled back. She gasped for breath the moment their mouths separated. After pulling air into his own lungs he leaned back close to her, lowered his head close to her ear and whispered in a deep, husky tone, "Hmm, so much for us not being on speaking terms."

For a full minute Taylor was speechless, too awed to form any kind of coherent words. It was hard to believe that this was the man with whom, until three weeks ago, she'd shared a strictly professional relationship. And now what they were about to share was anything but that. And considering the reason they were there, she could hardly suggest to him to slow down.

Her heart was racing as she stood rooted in place. Dominic, however, seemed rather at ease, unerringly calm, as he walked over to the sofa to remove his jacket.

"I take it you had a nice flight here?"

She blinked upon realizing he had spoken. She glanced across the room at him and felt a sweet craving invade her body. The man was simply gorgeous and exuded a degree of sensuality that should be outlawed. He was wearing an expensive tailored shirt with a pair of dark slacks. He was tall and lean. His shoulders were broad and his hips narrow. What a body! She didn't want to think about that same body, naked and in bed with her, flesh to flesh.

"Taylor?"

It was then she realized she hadn't answered his question. She pulled in a rather shaky sigh. "Yes, it was nice. What about yours?"

He stood beside the sofa. His hair was loose and flowing around his shoulders and his feet were braced apart, again making her conscious of what a good-looking man he was and what a fine physique he had. He was in great shape and she would undoubtedly find out just how great later that night.

"The same. I took a nap so now I'm pretty well rested."

Taylor swallowed. Was he giving her fair warning? His expression was inscrutable and she couldn't tell by his eyes what he was thinking.

"What's this?" he asked, picking up the gift bag off the sofa.

She looked at the bag he had in his hand. "That's something I was given at check-in. I haven't had a chance to see what's in it."

"We may as well take a look together," he said. The first thing he pulled out was a book. His chuckle made her wonder what type of book it was. He glanced over at her, evidently saw her curious expression and said, "I guess you can call it a selfhelp manual. It's titled *Best Sexual Positions for Baby-Making.*" He flipped through the pages and looked back up at her. "There are even pictures. Umm, interesting."

She could just imagine, but even if curiosity killed her, she would not cross the room to take a peep. He placed the book on the table next to the sofa as though he intended to take time to delve between the pages more later. He then pulled out several jars of what looked like creams and other items. He proved her right when he said, "An assortment of flavored creams, a bottle of lickable lotion and several gels. This feminine arousal gel I would assume is for you and the erection gel is for me."

Taylor's gaze automatically shifted to his crotch. She

was staring at it, but at the moment she couldn't help herself, imagining...

"There's also a notice about a free movie they're showing tonight on the television. It's guaranteed to put us in the mood if we're not already there," he was saying.

The thought that crossed Taylor's mind at that exact moment was that literally, she couldn't speak for him but she was already there. In fact her body didn't rightly seem connected to her brain. It wanted to do one thing while her brain was trying to drill some sense into her. She really wasn't paying attention.

"There's also a notice that dinner will be served in our room around six." He checked his watch. "That's a couple of hours away. Is there anything you'd like to do until then?"

Taylor took a deep breath while thinking that, yes, there was something she would like to do until then. Jumping his bones seemed like an activity worth trying. But she knew she couldn't do that. She had put too much work into her seduction scene tonight to get carried away by a few errant hormones. Well, maybe more than a few.

"What about a walk on the beach?" she decided to ask.

From the look on his face she could tell her suggestion surprised him. "A walk on the beach?"

"Yes, and then we can return to the room and shower for dinner," she said.

"Ok, then let's take a walk on the beach."

She glanced at his clothes. Not the typical attire for walking on the beach. "Do you want to change first?"

He smiled. "No, I'm fine."

He most certainly was.

He moved toward the door. Paused and glanced over his shoulder. "Are you coming?"

Not yet, she thought, but she had a feeling that's all she would be doing later tonight underneath his hard, muscular body. "Yes," she said, crossing the room to where he was standing. He smiled again and she felt all kinds of flutters fill her stomach. She couldn't wait until tonight.

Dominic thought the same thing as he walked beside Taylor on the long stretch of beach. He couldn't remember ever taking the time to do something so relaxing. He definitely hadn't ever done so with Camry. Their lives had been fast paced—jetsetters—with no thought of settling down and taking things slow or making a family. They'd figured that would come later. And they had been so wrong.

Not wanting to think of his life with Camry—and what he'd lost with her death—he wanted to concentrate on what he would gain with Taylor. Since he had no intentions of every marrying again, at least he would have a son or daughter who would inherit what he was working so hard to acquire. His own Saxon dynasty.

He had removed his shoes and socks and actually liked the feel of the sand beneath his feet. He also liked having this woman beside him. They continued walking down the long stretch of beach. The sugar-white sand gave way to a clear blue-green sea and the scent of the ocean filled his nostrils. Taylor wasn't saying much but then neither was he. He was too busy thinking of what he would love to be doing with all those jars of flavored creams this week. What he *intended* to do with them.

"The beach is simply gorgeous, isn't it?"

He turned his head and caught her gaze. His eyes moved to her lips, remembering how they'd tasted and a sensation passed through his body. "Yes, it is," he responded, thinking so was she. "I can't recall the last time I've done something like this."

"Really?" she said, looking at him. "But you own an entire island on the ocean."

He wasn't surprised she knew that. Other than his parents, Matt and the IRS, she was the only other person who knew the vast extent of his wealth. The media thought they knew but in essence they really didn't have a clue. His grandfather was determined to make sure Dominic took his place as the rightful Saxon heir and had set up various accounts for him in all parts of the world. Dominic wanted no part of it and to this day refused to acknowledge the old man's generosity. Dominic was determined not to accept his grandfather's money, which he saw as a device Franco Saxon was using to alleviate his guilt and buy his way into his grandson's affections. As far as Dominic was concerned, it would not happen.

"Yes, I own that island but I rarely have time to enjoy it. You of all people should know how busy I am."

It seemed he was driven to accumulate even more wealth and was beginning to believe the accusations his father had once made were true. As long as he maintained a degree of his own wealth, he would not be tempted to accept what his grandfather was offering.

"In that case I'm glad at least you have this week to relax and unwind."

He chuckled. "Um, is that what I'll be doing?"

Her grin was almost contagious when she said,

"Somewhat. But I promise it will be a week you'll remember."

She sounded confident. Certain. But then he was also convinced it would be a week he would remember. Deciding he needed to talk about something, anything that would take his mind off bedding her, he said, "I understand your sister is getting married in June to Cameron Cody."

She glanced at him. "Yes. You know Cameron?"

"Yes. We've met. We've even been partners in a few business ventures. He's an astute businessman."

"So are you. It doesn't surprise me that you know Cameron. We met when he tried to take over my family's business."

Dominic lifted a brow. "You're kidding, right?"

She smiled. "No, I'm not kidding. It was supposed to be a hostile takeover, but he never got all the voting shares he needed."

"So your family became friends with him instead?" he asked, amazed. He'd been involved in a few takeover attempts himself. The last thing the parties involved felt toward each other afterward, regardless of whether the attempt had been successful or not, was friendliness.

"Yes, at least, my four male cousins did," she was saying. "It was a male thing. I think they admired Cameron's tenacity and respected his drive to succeed. They never saw him as a threat because the Steele family is so close, so we weren't worried about anyone defecting. But Cameron had to learn a valuable lesson."

"Which was?"

"No matter what, blood is thicker than money. And trust me, he was offering a lot. But for us it wasn't about the money. It was about the legacy that my father and uncle passed on to us. They started the company many years ago and had always intended for it to be family owned and operated."

Dominic nodded. "And now Cameron will become a part of your family."

"Yes, he will be. He loves my sister very much and she loves him."

Love. He was familiar with that word because of his parents but had yet to experience the emotion himself. He had loved Camry but not in the same way that he knew his father loved his mother. What he'd felt for his wife had been more fondness than love. They respected each other and were good friends during their brief marriage.

"Ready to head back?"

Taylor had stopped walking and was smiling politely at him. "Yes, I can certainly use that shower," he said.

And he could also use something else. Something he was looking forward to getting later.

"Are you going to take a shower with me?"

Dominic's question made Taylor's stomach lurch in heated lust. An ache started at the juncture of her legs. They had returned from their walk on the beach and were standing in the bedroom. He had wasted no time removing his shirt and stood with his hands in his pockets, which caused the material of his pants to stretch tight against his thighs. And they were such muscular thighs.

She cleared her throat to swallow the lump that had formed there. "I'd rather wait until later, after we make love."

He looked amused at her statement. "And may I ask why?"

Yes, *why?* She shrugged. "Although we won't know the exact moment it happens, I know that I will get pregnant from you this week and I'd rather not let the first time we come together be in a shower."

He gave her a smile that intensified that ache in her body. "You don't think we can share a shower without making love?"

"What do you think?" she countered.

He stared at her for a moment, in that way that always got to her, making her hot all over, as his gaze traveled up and down her body. Finally, he said, "I think that you're probably right."

Oh, yeah, I am right, trust me, she thought. "I'll wait in the other room for you to finish and then I'll take my shower," she said, heading for the door.

"Taylor?"

She turned back around. "Yes?"

"I think you should know that I want you."

She saw the heat in his eyes, felt the lust and desire in them from across the room. She was no novice at being wanted by a man, but this was the first time she could actually feel the intensity. And what was so amazing was that she craved him just as much.

"Thanks for telling me," she said softly. "And I want you, too." She decided to lay her cards on the table since he was laying down his.

"Come here. I want to give you something to think about while I'm in the shower alone," was his comeback in a husky tone.

She started to tell him that it wasn't necessary. She had enough to think about already. But she figured he was going to kiss her again, which she didn't have any qualms with. She was looking forward to it. Her lips were still tingling from their last encounter.

She retraced her steps and crossed the room to him, trying not to focus on his naked chest and finding it hard not to do so. Especially downward, where the sprinkle of hair seemed to take a low path toward his waist, even lower toward his...

"Taylor?"

She shifted her gaze from his chest to his eyes. "Yes?" She'd been caught staring.

He didn't say anything for a moment; he just continued to look at her, especially her mouth. And the more he stared the more her lips itched for him to taste them. "I'm going to enjoy being here with you for the next seven days," he said, as he reached out and untied the straps at her shoulders, and then gave each a quick tug.

She hadn't been expecting it and before she could blink, the top of her sundress dropped and she was naked to the waist. She opened her mouth to say something and that's when he inserted his tongue inside. At that moment she forgot about everything else except what his mouth was doing to hers. He was part French and she wondered if it was an inborn part of a Frenchman's nature to master the art of French-kissing, because he certainly had. She would even go so far as to say he was an expert. She'd been French-kissed before but never like this. His tongue was definitely a weapon of mass seduction.

Automatically, she angled her head to get more of the pleasure. If this was what he wanted to give her to think about then he was succeeding. He had her thinking. He also had her panties getting wet.

He released her mouth. They were standing so close, their lips mere inches apart, as if ready to go at it again, devour each other senseless, when she discovered the kiss wasn't all he wanted to give her to think about. She sucked in a deep breath when she felt his fingers touch her breasts. At that moment her brain seemed to turn to mush. He cupped her breasts in his hands and began ardently caressing them, letting the tips of his fingers rub gently across her hardened nipples.

He met her gaze and the heat she saw in the depths of his green eyes made her a lost cause. At that moment she wanted to make love to him and she didn't care if they conceived their child right there, while standing up. She wondered if that particular position was in that little book.

He lowered his mouth to her breasts and like a vacuum he sucked a hardened tip into his mouth. Then his tongue went to work like a man famished for the taste of her. She responded with a soft moan and reached out and sank her fingers in his hair to hold his head to her, experiencing a heated breakdown of all her senses. Her stomach began quivering with a need that was as intense as anything she'd ever encountered.

She let out a deep, startled moan when he suddenly slipped a warm hand under her dress and immediately went to the area between her legs. Slipping underneath her panties, he planted his fingers in her sensitive flesh. Blood pounded in her ears when he began stroking her intimately. She wasn't sure what was sending her over the edge the fastest, his mouth or his fingers. She released a soft sigh when he intensified the kiss at the same time he increased the tempo of the stroke of his fingers.

He was showing no mercy. She tightened her grip on his head and called out his name when a shudder of immense proportions rammed through her, shaking her to the core. She squeezed her eyes shut when everything in the room seemed to come rushing together, bearing down on them. She could barely stand and her mind was void of any conscious thought except the intense pleasure ripping through her.

When he finally released her it took a few moments to get her mind back in check. She opened her eyes and nearly lost it again when he took his finger, the same one that had intimately stroked her, and brought it to his lips and tasted it.

The corners of his mouth distended into a serious smile when he said in a huskily erotic voice. "Take my word for it. The last thing you need tonight is arousing gel."

Chapter 5

At the sound of the shower going Taylor expelled a sigh. She then began pacing the room, needing to do something. Otherwise, she would be tempted to strip off her clothes and join Dominic.

The man had given her one hell of an orgasm just from foreplay. She didn't want to think just how explosive the real thing would be. If his aim had been to prep her for tonight then he had succeeded—she was set on go. In fact, she'd been ready for Dominic ever since he had agreed to this week.

The ache returned to her body just picturing him standing naked in the shower under a spray of water. She'd gotten a glimpse of his chest, more than a glimpse actually. Before she had left the bedroom, he had pulled her in his arms, letting her taste the essence of herself off his lips. Her naked breasts had pressed against his bare chest, and the contact had nearly given her another orgasm. She had a history of being someone not prone to climax easily. In fact, usually it would take a while for any man to light her fire to the degree where she would want to make love more than once in one night.

Deciding she needed to sit down and relax she dropped down on the sofa and then out of curiosity, she picked up the book Dominic had pulled out of the gift bag earlier. Her eyes widened at each page. She hadn't known there were so many positions a couple could use. Not surprisingly, it said the best position to conceive was man on top. It didn't take much to fantasize about Dominic on top of her in bed, inside her body and...

She stood up and tossed the book on the table, deciding she'd imagined enough for now. She needed to take her mind off things, namely sex and Dominic. After he finished his shower, she would take hers, and then they would get ready for dinner, which would be delivered to their room at exactly six o'clock. Once dinner arrived their night of initiating conception would begin. Lord, she hoped they made it through dinner because they would need all their strength for later.

One way to get her mind off Dominic, she decided, would be to call Vanessa and talk to her for a short minute. She had spent time with her sisters while home getting fitted for the bridesmaids' dresses. It didn't go unnoticed by her that Cheyenne wasn't as talkative as she usually was and looked a little on the thin side. Not that her sister's perfect model figure still didn't look to die for. Vanessa had picked up on it, too, and had pulled her to the side and asked her if she knew what was wrong with their baby sister. She didn't have a clue then and didn't have one now. As far as they knew it couldn't be man trouble since Cheyenne didn't have a steady beau.

Crossing the room, Taylor pulled her mobile phone from her purse and clicked on Vanessa's number. She smiled when Cameron answered. That, she noticed, was becoming a norm. "Hi, Cameron, is Vanessa around?"

"Yes. Hold on."

Moments later her sister came on the line. "Taylor, are you okay?"

Taylor lifted a brow. Vanessa sounded breathless, like someone who had run a marathon. Or someone who had just finished making love.

"Yes, I'm okay. Sounds like you're okay, as well," she couldn't help but say. She knew if she was there she would see a huge blush on her sister's face.

Vanessa gave a shaky laugh and said, "Well, yeah, I'm okay. Cameron is here."

"So I notice. Am I interrupting anything?"

There was a pause and then. "No, I'm fine. Cameron just went into the kitchen. He's going to do the cooking tonight. I was hoping you would call. How are things going?"

"Fine. I arrived here around eleven o'clock today and Dominic got here around two. We've taken a walk on the beach."

"That's all?"

She shook her head. Her sister had turned into a regular little miss hot pants since hooking up with Cameron. Vanessa figured just because she spent most of her free time in bed that everyone else should do the same. "Yes, that's all. We don't want to rush anything. We have all week."

"Nothing like getting a head start. The more you do it, the better your chances of getting pregnant, right?"

"Right, but it only takes one good time and according to the doctor I'm all set. I took my temperature early and now's the time. He said it's important for me to make love a day or two before I ovulate and then the day of."

"That sounds so technical. Just roll with the flow."

Taylor smiled. "Have you heard from Cheyenne?"

"No. Have you?"

"No."

"Really, Taylor, I'm worried about her. She looked somewhat under the weather when she was here a few weeks ago. I called last night but got her machine. I told her to call me back but so far she hasn't."

"Is she out on a photo shoot?"

"No. She talked to Mom last week and told her she had come down with the flu. She was canceling her trip to Ethiopia and remaining at her Jamaican home to get some rest. She probably hasn't been eating right and her resistance is down. I'm going to try calling her again tonight. I'm really going to give her a good looking-over when she flies in for Marcus's graduation in a few weeks."

Taylor nodded. Their cousin Marcus, Chance's oldest son, would be graduating from high school. The family was excited about his acceptance into Yale University. "Okay. Let me know if you get Cheyenne and she tells you anything. Like you, I think she hasn't been eating properly."

"Do you plan on leaving your phone turned on during the time you're on that island?"

"No, but I will make it a point to check my messages."

Vanessa laughed. "Do you think Dominic is going to give you the time to do that?"

She knew what Vanessa was insinuating. "I'm going to take the time regardless."

"If Dominic Saxon is the man I think he is, the man I read about in all those magazines, you won't have time to do much all week but stay on your back."

"Vanessa!"

"Just being honest, so get prepared."

At that moment Taylor heard a sound behind her and turned around. Dominic was standing in the doorway that separated the sitting room from the bedroom, still wet from his shower with only a towel wrapped around his waist. The heat in his eyes, the ones staring at her, were scorching. She swallowed the lump in her throat.

"Vanessa, I've got to go." Taylor clicked off the phone without waiting for her sister's response. She was suddenly filled with the thought that even if she tried, there was no way to get prepared for Dominic.

"The shower is yours, Taylor. But let me go on record as saying this is the last time I plan on taking a shower alone while we're here."

Dominic didn't even attempt to understand why he was so adamant about that. Probably because all the time he had spent in the shower, standing under the jets of the water, he'd been thinking of how it would be to have Taylor in there with him, all the things they could do. *Would* do.

"And if I protest?" she asked with a teasing smile on her face.

Of course, she could protest, but he figured she wouldn't. He would make sure of it. Besides, any woman who got as hot as she did just from a man kissing her, stroking her intimately, wouldn't be hard to persuade. Not only had he felt her heat, he had tasted it. "Go ahead, if you think that you can."

The look that suddenly appeared in her eyes let him know he had been right—she would be wasting time to try to deny him. They clicked. They would probably burn up the sheets. And in the end, they would make a baby. For some reason he felt very confident about that.

His gaze roamed up and down her. She had fixed what he'd done to her sundress, but he much preferred seeing it down to her waist. He liked her breasts. The feel of them in his hand. The taste of them in his mouth.

He saw she hadn't moved from the spot. "Aren't you going to take your shower now…or do you prefer we get into something else?"

She crossed her arms over her breasts. "You're blocking the doorway."

"Oh. You don't think I'd let you get by?"

She chuckled. "Not without trying something."

He smiled. "I thought one of the perks for this week is for me to try just about anything."

"Yes, but the key is perfect timing."

His smile widened. "Trust me, every time we come together will be perfect" He stepped away from the doorway. "Go ahead. I'll behave."

She gave him an *I don't believe you* look, before heading toward the bathroom. When she got close by him she slowed her steps and looked at him up and down. "Something wrong?" he asked.

"No, nothing's wrong."

"Then I can only assume that you like what you see, Taylor Steele."

She met his gaze and his heart began thudding hard with the look in her eyes. "Yeah, I like what I see."

"Do you want it?" he asked, feeling a sizzle low in his belly.

She tilted her head at an angle that got his attention because it made him see just what a beautiful neckline she had. "Not only do I want it, Dominic, I plan on getting plenty of it. Later."

When she slipped by him and went into the bedroom and closed the door, a heated rush flooded his insides at her bold statement. As far as he was concerned, later couldn't get here quick enough to suit him.

Taylor leaned back against the door the moment she shut it behind her and breathed in a deep, shaky breath. How on earth was she supposed to get through dinner when Dominic exuded so much temptation? And he knew exactly what he was doing to her. She didn't have to be convinced that he was a man who knew how to please a woman in bed. There was no doubt in her mind that he would please her. And just thinking about the degree of pleasure she would receive made her weak in the knees.

When she thought her wobbly legs could support her, she moved away from the door toward the drawers where she had placed her undergarments earlier after she'd unpacked. She would get everything she needed now before coming out of the bathroom after her shower. Chances were Dominic would use the room to dress for dinner and she wasn't ready to walk in on him while she was half-naked. Grabbing a bra and a pair of panties out of the drawer, she headed for the bathroom, taking time to grab one of the courtesy bathrobes out of the closet.

After a walk on the beach she needed the shower, but more than anything, she needed to take a shower to cool off.

Except for the sound of the shower, the suite seemed quiet, Dominic thought as he finished dressing. Never before had he wanted a woman the way he wanted Taylor. He was beginning to feel restless, on edge, horny. He couldn't help thinking of just how sexy she was, and how much she seemed to enjoy his kisses. He took pleasure in the art of seduction and kissing was just one of the elements he used. There were numerous others and he planned to put each one into practice before leaving the island.

It didn't take much to see that Taylor was a very passionate woman and she wasn't trying to be coy about it. He could tell she was someone who was confident with the degree of her own sensuality. But not to the point where it swelled her head. And she had to be one of the most positive people he knew. He had discovered that fact the first time they had met. She wasn't all somber and serious like most financial advisors tended to be. He recalled her saying once that she believed that one of the biggest secrets to achieving what you wanted in life was believing that you could. Just the way she believed that the two of them would make a baby this week. And because she believed it, he was convinced, as well.

There was no doubt in his mind that she would be a good mother. In his opinion his mother had been a stellar mom, and, although Taylor was fairly young, she possessed his mom's strong characteristics, as well. It amazed him at times how she had the ability to feel him out before he could utter a single word. And he liked the way she always kept her cool. She wasn't one to freak out or get frazzled easily—like the time he had invested a large sum of money without consulting her and had come close to losing it all.

Then there was her playful side. Once when she had detected him getting tense about a risky business venture, she had encouraged him to take time off and go with her to Coney Island for an afternoon of fun. Officially that had been their first date, although at the time he hadn't thought of it as such. But still, she had shown him how important it was to occasionally get in touch with your carefree side, something he failed to do often enough.

Deciding that since he had finished dressing there was no reason to linger around in the bedroom, he walked into the sitting room. For his peace of mind he felt the best thing to do was to remove himself from temptation's way. Put his mind on something else. So he thought about his parents. He had spoken to them yesterday. After spending two weeks in France they were back in the U.S. According to them, Franco Saxon's health had greatly improved. Conversely, they had known that Dominic really didn't give a royal damn but his mother had mentioned it anyway. There had been so many times when he'd been younger, when after hearing his classmates talk about their grandparents and what a blessing they were in their lives, that he had longed for grandparents of his own. His father had told him his mother—Dominic's grandmother—had died when he was a little boy, but his grandfather was in France. As a young boy, Dominic could not understand if he had a grandfather that existed, why he never came to visit to spend time with him like his friends' grandparents had.

Much to his parents' credit, they had never spoken ill of Franco Saxon. Over the years they had accepted the older man's decision not to be a part of their lives. It was only when Dominic was grown that he discovered why his grandfather was not a part of his life. And it was a reason Dominic had found unacceptable.

His ears suddenly perked up. The shower was no longer going, which meant Taylor was finished with that particular segment of her toiletry. Dominic could imagine her damp body wrapped in one of those huge fluffy towels. He wished he was there to dry her off and thought of just how he would complete the task. He would go slow, taking time to pamper every inch of her body, starting with those luscious breasts he had tasted earlier, then moving lower to her flat stomach and small waist and then to that gorgeous pair of legs.

He sighed deeply. It was self-torture just thinking about all the things he would do after that. There was no denying that he wanted Taylor and he'd told her as much. But she wasn't fully aware of the intensity of that want. It had literally turned into a deep, throbbing need. A need that wouldn't go away.

Taylor looked at the outfit she had chosen to wear to dinner tonight, a black clingy halter dress. But nothing, she thought, would raise Dominic's temperature quicker than the sexy red lace, sheer mesh baby-doll nightie with a matching G-string that she would put on later. It was seductive. It was daring.

Why wait till later?

She licked her lips at the thought of the sweet torment Dominic would endure if she appeared at dinner wearing it. No doubt she would become the main entrée. She liked the thought of that.

Taylor stared at the outfit that hung in the closet a few seconds longer before deciding what she would do. Crossing the room, she pulled the red piece of lingerie out of the drawer and tossed it on the bed. It was time to turn the heat up a notch.

Dominic straightened in the chair, feeling his body get hard. The last thing he should be doing was sitting here looking through a book showing various sexual positions while waiting for Taylor. But he couldn't help himself. The pictures were definitely sexually arousing. There was not one position he couldn't picture him and Taylor trying. And if he played his cards right, before the week was out, they would try every one of them.

A faint smile touched his lips. He could just imagine the joy he would see on his parents' faces the day he told them they would be expecting a grandchild. There was no doubt in his mind that they would make wonderful grandparents. Taylor would have to be resigned to the fact that his parents would set out to make sure their grandchild was thoroughly spoiled.

"Dominic."

He turned his head to the whispered sound of his name. *Holy hell!* he thought, coming to his feet.

His mouth dropped. Blood rushed through his veins, his heart was pounding in his chest and his pulse was beating erratically. His already hot body suddenly burst into flames. Desire. Intense chemistry. Sexual need. All three hung in the air like a sensuous mist and seeped through the material of his shirt to tantalize his skin and shoot his testosterone level through the roof.

And when she moved away from the door, slowly crossing the room toward him, his mouth was suddenly dry and his body flared into an erection he couldn't hide even if he wanted to. He could only stare and come to grips with the enormity of his desire for her. She had to be wearing one of the sexiest scraps of lingerie he'd ever seen on a woman. And if Taylor thought she could sit at a table across from him wearing something like that, she definitely had another think coming.

She came to a stop in front of him and he stared into her eyes, fully understanding the message in her gaze. "Would you be terribly upset if I asked that we postpone dinner for a while?" she asked in a deep, sultry tone.

He gave her what had to be a heated smile before taking a step closer to her with his total concentration on her mouth. "Only on one condition."

"And what condition is that?"

He was still looking at her mouth. Inched his lips down closer to it. "That you let me devour *you* instead."

He watched her lips form into a sultry smile. "Only on one condition," she countered.

Now it was his turn to ask, "And what condition is that?"

She moved her lips closer to his and murmured in a soft, sexy tone, "That I get to devour you, as well."

His body immediately responded to her words, but before he could fully react, she wrapped her hands around his neck and connected their mouths. When his lips parted on a low groan, she took full advantage of the opening and darted her tongue inside. Consumed by desire so intense that it shook him to the core, he began mating his tongue with hers in a French kiss intended to rattle her the same way she was rattling him, and destined to build a need within her to the degree he was experiencing.

Their kiss was hot. It was passionate. It was possessive. At that moment they claimed the right to belong to each other for the next seven days. To fulfill each other's fantasies, give in to each other's desires. And most important, to create a life. Tongues mingled hotly, explored greedily and devoured incessantly.

He broke off the kiss just long enough to sweep her into his arms. "We're about to burn up the sheets, Taylor," he said on a low growl, and he began walking toward the bedroom. And that, he thought, would just be the beginning.

Taylor gazed up at Dominic, drawn to the intensity of his green eyes. They were eyes that underscored what he'd said earlier. They would burn up the sheets. He wanted her. She wanted him. She was his for the taking. He was hers. Simply stated, they were two passionate individuals who were answering the mating call in the most primitive way.

When he laid her down on the bed, their gazes locked and she felt the heat of his desire all the way to her toes. It was affecting her the most at the center of her legs, an ache that was about to get satisfied.

She watched as he took a step back away from the bed and leaned over and began removing his shoes and socks. Straightening, he took off his shirt to expose his muscular chest. Tossing it aside, he then went for the zipper of his trousers. Her breath held as he slowly eased it down and while doing so he kept his gaze fastened on hers.

When he lowered his pants, along with his briefs, to the floor, her gaze shifted and went directly to his midsection, then lower. There it lingered while taking in the glory of his manhood, the enormity of his erection that accentuated the degree of his arousal. He was big, thick and hard. And there was no doubt in her mind to the degree of his need.

Or hers.

She wanted to reach out and touch him, hold his hard, warm flesh in her hands. Slide her fingers all over it and feel its texture, its strength and its heat. Her gaze shifted to his face. As if he had read her thoughts, he gave her a slow smile before moving his completely naked body toward the bed.

Taylor inhaled a deep breath and whispered his name the moment he placed one knee on the bed and reached for her. She rose up and went into his arms willingly, without haste, and the moment he leaned over and captured her mouth, she knew she was a goner. His mouth was hotter than before. It ignited every cell in her body, causing low groans to circulate in her throat, get caught in her lungs.

Then his mouth became demanding, excruciatingly dominant in a way that made her stomach clench. And when he suddenly pulled back, she inhaled deeply before lifting her gaze to his.

He didn't say anything. He simply reached out and with a flick of his wrist, in one smooth move he took off her gown and tossed it aside.

"Red is my favorite color and I liked it." He murmured the words against her throat, seconds before she felt the gentle nip of his teeth, the lap of his tongue and the sucking on the soft skin of her neck. She knew what he had just done. He had put a passion mark there, branding her as his. If there ever was a man designed to make her a mother by giving her a baby, he was.

"You're beautiful."

His words, spoken as a deep growl from his throat, had her lifting her face up to his. The heated desire in the gaze looking back at her made her heart beat that much faster in her chest. And when he reached out and trailed his fingers from the top of her shoulders down to the twin peaks of her breasts, she swallowed deeply, trying not to detonate from his touch alone. His touch was smooth and slow, as if he would not be rushed, and when he reached her nipples, he took his fingertips and gently caressed each hardened bud with a skill and a purpose that shot intense hunger through her. Then he leaned down and his tongue outlined each tip, before taking them in his mouth one at a time and gently sucking on them the way their child would. And with each tug she felt the intensity of her need for him in the center of her legs.

"Dominic!"

He reached down and his hands found their mark between her legs. She was hot, wet and ready. And there was that annoying ache that she needed him to take away. Intense emotions were tearing into her and creating a raw need she had never felt before.

"And now I give you my baby," he rasped near her ear.

Dominic's words, both confident and arrogant, nearly took her breath away. But she didn't have time to think about that when she suddenly found herself flat on her back beneath him. His masculine physique towered over her, every perfectly formed muscle.

She looked up into his eyes, locked in his gaze the moment he gripped her hips and raised them to him. Then he entered her. It was a joining so grand, so absolute that it almost brought tears to her eyes. Her body automatically gave in to him, stretched for him. And when he began moving, it had her trembling inside. Heat flared within her, taking over her mind and body with an intensity that shook her to the core. But Dominic didn't let up. He painstakingly increased the tempo, amplified the pace. Holding her body immobile beneath his, he began pumping into her nonstop with possessive deliberation, timeless precision.

Taylor's body was suddenly hit with something akin to an electrical shock and she felt her muscles clenching, tightening. She pulled him deeper inside of her when waves of pleasure consumed her body. The exact moment she came, he did, as well, and she heard Dominic's deep, guttural growl and felt his hot release shoot to her womb.

He bucked inside her again at the same time she felt the warmth of his breath on her lips mere seconds before he took her mouth with a hunger that sent her over the edge yet again. Sensations rippled through her body when she was hurled into yet another orgasm and felt intense pleasure consume every part of her.

Dominic had been right. They were burning up the sheets.

Chapter 6

Dominic felt himself floating back down to earth after having soared to the stars and beyond. He felt as if he'd had an out-of-body experience and had been blasted right out of this hemisphere. There had never been a time when he'd made love to a woman and had been left feeling that way. He lay there transfixed, drained and completely satisfied.

But still, that didn't keep him from wondering what the hell had happened. Why even now, when Taylor was trying hard to catch her own breath, he wanted to make love to her again, detonate into another explosion. How had it come to this?

Maybe it had been that sexy red much-of-nothing nightie she'd been wearing. Or it could have been the fact that the last time he'd made love to a woman had been months ago. And just possibly, it could have been

that damn book he'd been flipping through earlier, seeing all those different lovemaking positions in vivid
color. He knew any number of things could have raised
his testosterone to a degree that even after two orgasms
still had him hard and refusing to disconnect his body
from hers. That was the strangest thing of all. Never had
he made love to a woman and not wanted to come out
of her afterward. But with Taylor, he liked the thought
they were still intimately joined.

"You haven't gone down."

He moved to let his gaze rest on her eyes. An incred-
ulous look glazed their depths with that observation.
"No, I haven't," he admitted, feeling his erection harden
even more as he spoke. "I like being inside you." And
that wasn't a lie, not even close to a mild exaggeration.

He then ran his eyes over the rest of her. She was
lying on her side facing him, her naked skin a dark
hue against the sharp whiteness of the bedspread. Her
breasts were full and firm, her stomach taut and flat
with a small tattoo of a panther near her hip bone. That
was the most of what he saw, since his leg was thrown
over her, locking her body in place to his. He had her
in one hell of a pose.

Even now what was so vividly clear in his mind was
the exact moment he'd reached his first climax with her
while thrusting into her repeatedly, liking the way her
inner muscles had clamped tight around him, holding
him in their grip, milking everything out of him and—

"Now you're getting bigger."

Her voice sliced through his thoughts. Then with
full awareness of what was taking place, he tightened
his legs, keeping her in a fixed position beside him. "I

know," he said huskily, unable to stop what was about to happen yet again.

He heard her suck in a trembling breath, watched as her eyes darkened to the point where he could barely see the long lashes covering them. But he was able to make out the expression on her face. There was something about seeing the look of an aroused woman, especially a totally naked one.

He reached out and rubbed the tip of his finger around her belly button. His caress didn't alter when he heard the sharp change in her breathing pattern or when he felt the slight quivering of her thighs beneath his.

"What are you doing to me?" she asked softly, barely able to enunciate any of the words.

Hearing the lack of comprehension in her voice endeared her to him even more. He figured that he could show her better than tell her. Leaning forward, he came within inches of her lips. "Um, what do you think I'm doing?" he asked, as he softly stroked the flat planes of her stomach with his fingertips.

"I—I can't think," she whispered, closing her eyes on a throaty sigh.

"Then don't. Just feel."

And then he began moving, excruciatingly slow, deep inside her, gradually withdrawing, then filling her again, deeper still in a leisurely measured thrusting motion. He felt sensations sear through the both of them from such a long, drawn-out and unhurried mating process.

"Open your eyes, Taylor," he whispered in a raspy voice, as he continued to thrust slowly in and out of her, savoring each and every time he did so.

He watched as she did what he asked, met her gaze

mere seconds before he leaned closer and took her mouth. The stroke of his tongue with hers was as slow and deliberate as the mating of their bodies—surging forward, retreating and then surging forward again.

Then something inside him snapped and without disconnecting from her, he shifted his body astride her, crossed her leg over his in a scissors position, allowing deeper penetration with her being the one in control using her thighs. It was different from the more common lovemaking positions because all four of their legs were intercrossed. He had seen this particular position in the book but was well familiar with "cuissade," which derived from the French. It was a position he had first used with a woman the year he'd turned eighteen when his parents had sent him to spend the summer in Paris with his father's childhood friend Jacques Gaston and his family. The Gastons' young, sexually active housekeeper had been more than happy to visit his room every night when her employers were asleep. He had received quite an education that summer.

Not wanting to think of anything other than the woman in his arms, Dominic lowered his head and kissed Taylor at the same time he slowly began moving in and out of her again. He could feel his erection expanding inside her with each gentle thrust he took.

She suddenly pulled her mouth away from him. "Dominic!"

He felt her muscles tighten around him and clench him in an unwavering grip. Her thighs began to quiver uncontrollably and due to the deliberate pressure of her thighs on his legs, the motion had the ability to shake him to the core. Sensations began spurting through him, eliciting his own torrid release. He felt the full impact of their orgasm in every part of his body.

"Taylor," he said in a guttural groan before leaning over and kissing her while simultaneously releasing inside her the life-creating substance that would produce a baby.

His baby.

Their baby.

Never before had he wanted such a thing to happen more than he did now. He released her mouth and reached out and placed a gentle hand on her stomach as if willing it so. She gazed up at him, as if understanding the meaning of what he was doing. The possibility that she was perceptive enough to interpret his thoughts had a nervetingling effect on him.

For a fraction of a second, he just stared at her, feeling the heated flush of their connected bodies. It was nothing short of pure, raw sexual pleasure. And as he eased his body to lie beside her, still not ready to pull out of her, he looked forward to the next time they would make love.

"Thank you for calling room service and asking that they deliver our dinner at a more convenient time," Taylor said after taking a sip of her iced tea. It was harder than she thought it would be to sit across from Dominic and attempt to eat a fullcourse meal. Each and every time his gaze touched her, she would feel the potent, invisible caress all over her body, making her remember what the two of them had shared in the bedroom.

"I think they understood, since we weren't the only couple who postponed dinner to later," Dominic said, pushing his plate back.

Taylor watched the gesture and swallowed deeply. It had been but a couple of hours since they'd last made love yet he wanted her again. The realization sent a shiver down her spine, because she wanted him, too. She picked up the tea glass and looked at it. The server had blatantly told them that it was plum tea, known as the ultimate erotic energizer. She believed him. After taking only a few sips she had felt a surge in her pulse, a pull in her belly and a throb between her legs. She'd thought a full stomach would rectify the problem but it hadn't.

Still, she took another sip of the tea, knowing it was coursing through her bloodstream, releasing something she really didn't need, considering her and Dominic's actions of earlier. All he had to do was look at her and she felt the need to jump his bones. After making love that last time they had fallen asleep, only to wake up and make love again. Four times in one evening was definitely setting a record for her.

"Did you want to watch that movie later?"

She glanced over at him. "What movie?"

"The one the resort suggested that all the couples watch."

Oh, that movie. Her heart began thumping at what the movie was probably about. "Do you think we need to watch it?"

He chuckled. "No, but we might find it interesting."

She was pretty certain they would. "I'll do whatever you want to do," she decided.

He met her gaze. "What if I told you I wanted to clear this table and take you right on top of it?"

A vision of such a thing happening immediately

speared through her mind and had hot blood rushing through her veins. "Would you really want to do that?"

"Yes." He didn't miss a beat in responding. "You would be my dessert, Taylor."

He was giving her a wicked smile but she knew he was dead serious. She could feel her muscles weaken, her insides tremble. She also knew he was getting her hot and bothered on purpose. They were sitting across from each other wearing the resort's complimentary bathrobes without a stitch of clothing underneath. It wouldn't be hard to do what he'd suggested. In fact it would be downright easy with the way she was feeling.

She leaned forward knowing she was exposing a little of her cleavage in the process since her robe wasn't pulled tightly together. "I've never been taken on a table before but I don't want my first time to be planned. I want it to be spontaneous. I want it to just happen."

"Okay."

He had agreed as if such a thing happening wouldn't pose a problem. "I like surprises," she decided to add.

"You also enjoy giving surprises," he said, taking a sip of his own tea. "I wasn't expecting that sexy red number you put on earlier."

She smiled, pleased she had caught him off guard. "Yes, I know."

"I owe you one."

She wanted to tell him he had already delivered four times tonight, but decided she shouldn't be counting, although she was. "I'm looking forward to payback time."

Another smile touched his lips. "So, do we do the movie?"

She met his gaze. It was either do the movie or do

each other and she figured their bodies needed a time-out period. "Yes, we do the movie."

Dominic glanced at the clock on the wall. The movie titled *A Hot Winter's Night* was to start in about fifteen minutes. He was sitting at one end of the sofa with Taylor at the other. He inwardly chuckled at the thought that they had unconsciously placed distance between them and he knew why. If they got any closer they would end up not watching the movie.

He couldn't release from his mind the thought of the time he had made love to her using the cuissade position with slow, elicit detail. He had been able to stare into her face, see each and every passionate response. He had held back from taking her fast and hard, much preferring to savor each and every thrust. There was another particular position he wanted to try with her before the week was out and he felt his erection throb at the thought.

"Tell me some more about your family," he said, to pass the time and to get making love to her again off his mind...for now.

She glanced over at him. "What do you want to know?"

He shrugged. "Anything you want to tell me."

So she began talking, and he listened...at least he tried to. But it was hard while observing the movement of her breasts when she used her hands when talking. Whenever she moved her hands her breasts would stick out, press against the fabric of the robe. Watching it made him want to ease over her and remove the robe from her and then take his mouth and have his way with not only her breasts, but every inch of her. That was something he hadn't done yet. Taste her. His tongue was more than anxious for that to happen.

"Dominic?"

Her saying his name got his attention. "Yes?"

"I've finished telling you about my family and was asking you to tell me about yours." She smiled. "You obviously weren't paying attention."

He laughed. "Obviously." He leaned back against the sofa. "So what do you want to know?"

"Anything you want to tell me since my baby will be a Saxon. Any aunts and uncles? Grandparents?"

He shook his head. "No, neither of my parents have siblings." And because he didn't consider himself as having a grandparent, he said, "And no grandparents, either. I do have godparents, though."

He then told her about the Gastons. In the middle of the conversation the movie started and all talking between them ceased as their attention was drawn to the big television screen in front of them.

Taylor bit the insides of her lip as she stared at the television screen. The movie was as erotic as it could get. It definitely had to be X-rated or possibly double X-rated. The first time a love scene had flashed on she'd actually blushed watching it with Dominic. He, on the other hand, seemed pretty relaxed and at some point had stretched his legs out into a more comfortable position. But he had remained on his end of the sofa and she on hers. However, even with distance between them, seeing the naked actors and actresses hadn't stopped heat from traveling up her spine or her imagining her and Dominic in the starring roles.

"Do you know why the resort wanted us to watch this tonight?" he broke into the silence between them to ask.

She figured he knew the answer but wanted to hear her opinion. "Because it's sexually explicit imagery, designed to stimulate."

He glanced over at her. "Is it?"

Her eyebrows pressed together. "Is it what?"

"Stimulating you?"

She shrugged. "Somewhat. I guess seeing two sexy people on a screen making out would stimulate most since it shows variety, new ideas and different positions."

She glanced over at him. "Is it stimulating you?"

"Yes."

Suddenly the television screen went black and it was then that she noted he held the remote in his hand. She wanted to think "typical male" but she knew there wasn't anything typical about Dominic.

"Slide over here for a minute, Taylor."

She swallowed deeply as she met his gaze. Emotions swirled within her at the desire he wasn't trying to hide in his eyes. "Why?" she asked, barely able to get the single word out.

"Because I want you over here with me right now."

She heard the tenseness in his voice and for a long, endless moment, she didn't say anything, and then, "Is it necessary?"

"Trust me on this, Taylor. It is."

She had been watching the television as he'd been doing and recalled what had been playing before it had gone black. The couple had been making out on the sofa, performing oral sex on each other.

He was still staring at her when she finally slid over

toward him, coming to sit directly next to him. With a throaty chuckle and not knowing what to expect, she said, "Well, here I am."

He leaned his face closer to hers. "I want you even closer."

She felt sizzling heat flow through her veins. "If I get any closer, Dominic, I'll be in your lap."

He gave her a sexy smile. "Yeah, I know." And then he reached out and lifted her into his lap. She quickly realized the enormous size of his erection. It was protruding hard against her bottom. She placed her arm around his neck, which made her bathrobe gape open. Before she had a chance to pull it back together, Dominic's hands were there. "No, let it stay open," he said in a deep, husky voice.

The warmth of his touch on her skin sent shivers down her spine. He then leaned closer and gently dropped his head in the center of her chest and brushed a kiss there. Then she felt a flick of his tongue and a lick in that very spot. She could feel the area between her legs getting wet. So easily and just that quickly.

He suddenly shifted positions and she felt herself gently being pushed back against the sofa's cushions with him looming over her. He had stretched her out on the sofa and had gotten on his knees beside it. "I think reality is much better than sitting here watching a movie," he said, reaching out and completely opening her robe.

Taylor couldn't restrain the heat from suffusing her body when Dominic's gaze roamed over her nakedness. And as she stared at him she saw his eyes darken even more and detected the exact moment his breathing changed.

He lifted his gaze and looked at her. "I think I'm becoming addicted."

She paused mentally as she took in what he'd said. Would his addiction extend beyond the week they would share here together? They really hadn't made any ground rules. She'd just assumed he understood that anything beyond this week was not a possibility. She had to start planning her life around a baby and she was sure his schedule was just as demanding. He traveled a lot. He had a lot on his plate. From what she'd read in the magazines, his affairs were more misses than hits, intentionally so on his part. He liked affairs. She didn't have time for even that much of a relationship. The only reason she had carved out this week was because more than anything she wanted a baby. Not a fulltime or part-time lover.

Any thoughts were suddenly snatched from Taylor's mind when she felt Dominic's fingers settle between her legs. She recalled what had happened the last time he had touched her there. With the skill of his fingers, it wasn't long before he had her entire body trembling. There was no doubt in her mind that his intimate touch was being branded on her brain. Sensations were drumming through her and she dug her teeth into her lower lip to stop from screaming out.

She met his gaze and saw the heated lust that darkened his eyes and knew they had to be a mirror of hers. He was deliberately taunting her feminine core, making her want him to the point where she was almost ready to beg.

"You're extremely wet, Taylor," he said in a low, throaty voice as he continued to stroke her with expert precision.

"Your heated scent is powerful, intoxicating and arousing. Do you know what I want to do?"

Make love to her, she hoped. *Now.* He was looking at her expectantly since he had asked her a question. Was he really expecting an answer? She doubted her mind could form coherent words to give him one. Instead she pushed herself to say, "No, what do you want to do?"

"Taste you."

When he lowered his head between her legs it hit her that he hadn't been asking permission. He was taking what he wanted. And when his tongue flicked out and gave her that first intimate touch, she felt boneless; pleasure of the most intense kind seeped through her pores.

"Dominic." She closed her eyes on a blissful sigh as he continued to kiss her in the most intimate way a man could. Even while part of her mind was telling her to resist him—to reach out and jerk his head up—the only thing she could do was reach out and grab hold of his head to hold it in place.

But the reality of it was that it didn't look as though he planned to go anywhere anytime soon. He was assaulting her with thorough, leisurely strokes of his tongue, relentless in his actions. And she was unashamedly enjoying it.

She became aware of the shiver that raced through her body, and his tongue probed deeper, becoming more demanding, greedier. She let out an intense moan from deep within her throat. Her hands holding his head tightened as if to draw him closer and he continued going at her as if her taste was something he just had to have.

Her body exploded, seemingly into a thousand pieces, and she let out a high-pitched scream as deep

gratification seared through her with the impact of con-
crete hitting steel. She realized his hold on her was just
as immobilizing as her hold on him. He had a firm grip
on her thighs, not intending to let her go anyplace until
he'd gotten his fill, and that thought sent her over the
edge again.

Never in her life had anything happened to her like
this before. Not only this time, but all those other times
tonight with Dominic. This just wasn't normal for her
and she wondered if it would have been normal for any
woman. She suddenly had a fleeting thought that continuing beyond this week wouldn't be bad if she got to
experience something like this. Her job could be stress-
ful and making love to Dominic could certainly take
the edge off things.

She finally felt her body floating back to Earth when
Dominic lifted his mouth from her. He raised his head
to stare down at her while licking his lips in the process, and the gesture was so erotic she reached out and
pulled his mouth to hers. She tasted herself on his lips,
his tongue, leaving her with no doubt of how intense
his intimate kiss had been.

And then she felt her body being lifted into his strong
arms and knew they would finish what they had started
in the bedroom.

Dominic stood at the window and looked out at the
ocean. It was dark outside yet he could see the waves
hitting the shore. He turned slightly to glance at the
clock on the nightstand. It was almost two in the morning. Taylor was still sleeping. He, however, had gotten
out of bed after finding it impossible to sleep. So here he

was, standing at the window gazing out into the night. It was either that or wake up Taylor to make love again.

Sheesh. He had made love to her more times in one night than he had to any woman in such a short span of time. He tried convincing himself not to be bothered by that statistic since to make love was the reason they were here, and the more times they did it the better the chances of her getting pregnant. He could accept that. But what he didn't want to accept was just how much he was enjoying it. Not that he thought he wouldn't. He just hadn't figured on doing so to this extreme—especially not to the point where his erection hadn't gone down any over the past twelve hours or so. That was simply remarkable.

He shook his head thinking that no, *that* was Taylor.

The woman had the ability to excite him by doing the smallest things. Hell, just looking at any part of her body made him want her, and to think they had six more days to go. If they kept going at it the rate they were doing now, by the end of the seventh day the hotel staff would have to come in with a crowbar to pry their bodies apart.

He rubbed his hand down his face thinking that come morning they needed to get out of the hotel room for a while and take a tour of the island or something. Anything that would get them out of their suite. Taylor was becoming one hell of a temptation.

None of the brochures had mentioned any outside activities since the sole purpose of the procreation vacation was focused on a single activity that was mainly done indoors. But still, if necessary, he was ready to take drastic measures since what he'd told Taylor earlier was true. He was becoming addicted to her and that thought didn't sit well with him. In fact, it was beginning to annoy the hell out of him. It wasn't his intent to become obsessed with any woman to the point that he couldn't walk away when he was good and ready, and without any lingering thoughts. Taylor was making it hard as hell to consider doing so.

Deciding he needed a definite plan before she woke up, he moved away from the window and grabbed his shirt and pants off a nearby chair. Within minutes he was heading out the door to talk to the person at the front desk.

The moment he stepped into the elevator he wished he hadn't. There was no doubt in his mind what he'd come within mere seconds of catching the couple doing. The woman was quickly getting off her knees and the man was turning his back to him to rezip his pants. Dominic wasn't sure who was the more embarrassed, so he stared at the elevator door as though he was oblivious to everything and was glad when the elevator came to the lobby. Since the couple made no move to get off, he could only assume they intended to continue what they were doing before his interruption and this time he hoped they had the good sense to stop the elevators between floors.

Glad at the moment that he no longer had a boner, he walked briskly over to the check-in desk. An older man looked up, seemingly surprised to see him or anyone up and about at that time of morning. "Yes, sir, may I help you?"

"I hope you can. Is there anything else around here to do?"

The man, who appeared to be in his late fifties, gave him a strange look as if to say, *the main thing around here takes place in the bedroom and you obviously aren't there.* However, he merely said, "It depends on what you want do."

"What I want to do," Dominic heard himself say, "is something that will take me and my wife away from the resort for a few hours."

The man looked appalled. "You want to leave your suite?"

Dominic couldn't help but smile. This man evidently took the resort's ability to produce results—specifically those that came nine months from now—pretty seriously. "Yes, just for a few hours but don't worry, this place is definitely living up to our expectations."

A relieved expression appeared on the man's face when he said, "Thank you, sir, and we do have a couple of activities outside the resort that some of our visitors seem to enjoy on occasion. We can arrange for you to rent a sailboat, and then there's horseback riding along the beach, a private picnic at one of the remote cottages and—"

"I like the idea of going sailing," he quickly said, deciding he didn't need him and Taylor going anywhere slightly remote. "Make the necessary arrangements, and since we'll probably be gone past lunch, I think a picnic lunch would be nice."

"Certainly, sir. I'll take care of everything for you."

Chapter 7

Taylor slowly opened her eyes and saw Dominic sitting in one of the chairs across from the bed. He appeared bigger than life and was definitely impossible to miss. The sunlight shining through the window was beaming on him at an angle that made her insides flutter. He was an incredibly attractive man.

She shifted in bed and the ache she felt in certain muscles quickly reminded her that he was also a skillful lover—and she hoped a very potent one. After their passionate encounters last night she was pretty convinced she was probably pregnant already. But they had six days and nights to go.

"Good morning."

At the sound of his voice she forcibly put those thoughts to the back of her mind. She was still having delicious aftershocks of last night and seeing him sitting lazily in the chair with his legs stretched out in front of him wasn't helping matters. At least he was fully dressed.

"Good morning," she said, pulling herself up in bed, making sure she kept a tight grip on the bedspread covering her. He might be dressed but she was still completely naked. So much for all those nightgowns she had brought along. At the rate they were going she wouldn't be using them. At least she'd had on the red one for a split second before he'd taken it off her.

"How would you like to go sailing today?"

The low, sexy tone of his voice had tiny little shivers moving down her spine. "Sailing?"

"Yes."

It would get them out of the suite for a while, she thought, and couldn't help wondering if that was the reason he'd come up with the idea. Was he getting tired of her already?

"Trust me, that's not it."

She blinked. "Excuse me?"

He eased his tall frame from the chair and came to stand beside the bed. She thought he looked simply gorgeous in a pair of jeans and a blue polo shirt. "I saw something flash in your eyes just now that I've never seen before. Not in all the time I've known you," he said softly.

She bit her lip nervously. "What?"

"Doubt. And you're one of the most confident people I know, male or female. The only reason I think it's best that we remove ourselves from this suite for a while is because if we don't, we're liable to try every damn position in that book and there're close to sixty of them."

She couldn't help the smile that touched her lips. "Sixty-five to be exact."

There was an electric silence in the room as if they were both remembering the ones they had tried so far. "I'll leave so you can get dressed," Dominic finally said, as he turned toward the door.

"I thought you said you wouldn't be taking any more showers alone," she couldn't help but say.

He stopped walking and turned back around. The look he gave her was filled with desire, as if it wouldn't take much for him to cross the room and strip her naked. "Trust me. It took all I had not to wake you when I took mine, but the next time I won't spare any mercy. I plan to have you in there with me."

His eyes challenged her to deny what he'd said as a fact and she couldn't. Doing so would be pointless. In just one night she had discovered she enjoyed making love with him way too much. The man was too down-right irresistible for his own good…and hers. She had never responded to another man the way she was responding to him.

The moment he closed the door behind him, she eased out of bed, hoping he wouldn't change his mind and decide to join her in the shower anyway. She moved around the bedroom gathering up everything she would need for her bath and trying to decide which of the outfits she'd brought along would be appropriate for sailing. She placed her underthings on the bed and before going into the bathroom she strolled to the window and looked out. She was again in awe at the beauty of the island. The ocean looked inviting and she would enjoy being out on it in a sailboat.

Moments later she stepped under a jet of warm water thinking a shower was what she needed for her sore muscles because they had definitely been put to the test. The last time when they'd made love before finally drifting off to sleep, they had used another position from that book. A smile formed on her lips. The leapfrog position definitely had had its merits.

Deciding she needed to get dressed quickly before Dominic was tempted to come find out what was taking her so long, she turned off the water and stepped out of the shower and began toweling dry with one of the huge fluffy towels. Once she was dry she wrapped the towel around her before making her way back to the bedroom to select something out of her closet.

She found an outfit she thought would be perfect, a pair of crochet-trim gauchos with a matching tunic top that tied at the back of the neck. It was an outfit she had purchased last summer while visiting Cheyenne in Jamaica.

Moments later she stood, completely dressed in front of the mirror, viewing the results and finding them acceptable. She hoped when Dominic saw her he would like the results, as well. One thing she noticed was that with the style of the outfit, several passion marks were blatantly visible. A shiver passed through her. She could recall the exact moment each and every single one was made. Dominic had made sure of it.

She took a deep breath as she glanced at the unmade bed and could actually feel her body beginning to throb with the memories of last night. The thought that she could even now be pregnant filled her with intense pleasure as she walked to the door.

"If I didn't know better, Dominic, I'd think you were a born seaman."

Dominic glanced over at Taylor, his gaze roaming

over her from behind dark aviator sunglasses. He liked the outfit she had chosen to wear and thought that she looked sexy in it. She was leaning against the ship's railing with the sun in the background, seemingly shining directly on her. It was a perfect day to be out on the water and he was glad she was out here with him.

His mind shifted back to her comment and he decided not to tell her that in essence he really was a born seaman. The Saxons of France had made their fortune in the shipping industry for centuries and his father had been taught to navigate a watercraft before learning to walk. If you bothered to dig up the family history, the Saxons had been and always would be men of the sea. Marcello Saxon had passed his love for the ocean on to him and Dominic intended to pass that love on to his son or daughter. Some of his fondest memories were of the times when his father had routinely taken Dominic and his mother with him on his father's first luxury cruise liners.

"How are you feeling?" he asked her, more out of genuine concern than a way to change the subject. He hadn't missed the fact that her steps were a lot slower today and he knew why. She knew why, too, which he figured was the reason a blush appeared in her face.

"I'm fine," she answered and turned to look back over the ocean.

He smiled. After all they'd shared last night, every single thing they'd done, how on earth could she get embarrassed by his question? He was discovering a lot about his wealth and asset manger turned temporary lover. He knew she was allergic to certain types of nuts, had a tendency to overindulge in chocolate and loved watching scary movies. And in the past hour, with his encouragement, she had shared more about her family with him. There was no doubt in his mind the Steeles were close. She admired her male cousins and thought the world of her two sisters.

It had always been his parents' wish to have another child but miscarriages before and after his birth made them change their minds and decide he would be the one and only. Listening to Taylor made him realize that, other than Matt, he hadn't had a lot of friends or family while growing up. He had been sent to private schools most of his life, some outside the United Sates. And after that kidnapping attempt, it was a long time before his parents or Ryder would let him out of their sight.

"Hungry yet?" he decided to ask her.

She turned, lifted a brow and smiled. "What if I am? It's not like we're going to find a restaurant out here."

He gave a soft laugh. "No, but we do have that," he said, nodding to the huge picnic basket she hadn't yet seen near the bow.

She followed his gaze and smiled. "Who brought that on?"

"The management of the resort," he said. "I ordered lunch for us when I requested the boat. I'm ready to eat when you are."

She smiled. "Okay then, I'm ready."

"Wow, the resort really did it up, didn't they?" Taylor said while watching Dominic unload the picnic basket. There were numerous sandwiches, a platter of cheeses, bags of chips, a container of fruit, a Thermos filled with coffee and a bottle of chilled nonalcoholic wine.

"Um, I specifically told them about the nonalcoholic wine just in case you're in a delicate condition already.

And since I'm the captain of this vessel, I can't drink on the job," he said, putting the empty basket aside to pour wine into their glasses. "I have to make sure we get back to land safely before nightfall."

Taylor grinned. "And I appreciate that." She placed the plate filled with food in her lap. Dominic had done the serving and had given her a little bit of everything.

She glanced over at him. "So, what kind of kid were you while growing up, so I can know what to expect?"

He threw his head back and laughed. "It might be too late to determine that, isn't it? It wouldn't surprise me any if you're pregnant already."

She had thought the same thing but to hear him say it out loud made goose bumps appear on her arms. "Too bad there's no way we can find out."

"I don't want to know," he said, taking a sip of his wine.

She lifted a brow. "Why?"

He met her gaze over the glass. "If you knew you were pregnant already then you wouldn't need for us to stay the remainder of the week. Just think of all the fun we'd miss out on."

She was thinking. But then she knew that eventually all good things came to an end. "So tell me," she encouraged. "What kind of child were you? Spoiled I bet."

A small smile touched his lips. "I guess there was a little of that since I was the only child, but I knew just how far to go in riling my parents. I didn't have any siblings or a bunch of cousins like you have, but I had Matt."

"Matt?"

"Yes, Matt Caulder. He's my attorney and best friend. Our mothers were childhood friends, and in a way Matt and I were raised together. Then his mother died of breast cancer. It was our final year of high school. That was a difficult time for him."

"I can imagine," she said, thinking of the time she had lost her father while in high school, as well. "I know how he felt. I lost Dad while in high school, too. He died of lung cancer."

"Was he a smoker?"

"Yes, of the worst kind. We tried to get him to quit and never could." She was silent for a few minutes. "So tell me about Matt. Is he married?" she asked curiously.

Dominic shook his head. "Divorced. Unfortunately things didn't work out. But he'll be quick to tell you the best thing to come from his marriage was Dee— short for Deena. She's his two-year-old daughter and was named after his mother. I'm her godfather. I've got pictures. You want to see?"

"Sure."

Taylor watched as Dominic put aside his plate to pull out his wallet. He would make a wonderful father, she thought, and a sense of pride touched her in knowing his child would be hers.

She took the photograph he handed to her. Dee was definitely a pretty little girl. "She's blessed to have both you and her father in her life," Taylor said as she continued looking at the picture. "It's important for little girls, as well as little boys, to have strong male role models."

"Yes, it is," he agreed.

Taylor handed him back the photograph and their hands touched. The sensation that hit the both of them, simultaneously, made their breaths catch. Her eyes flew to his face. "Sorry about that," she said apologetically.

"It's not your fault," he said, intentionally not looking at her while placing Dee's picture back in his wallet.

No, and neither was it his, she thought. It seemed they were two irresistible forces that attracted, even when they weren't trying to. They couldn't help it. Weren't strong enough to stop it. Even now there was a sexually charged awareness between the two of them. The very air they were breathing seemed electrified, sensually combustible.

For the next few moments they ate in silence. That gave her a chance to look around and check out the sailboat. It was a beauty with nice accommodations. While he had been busy getting ready to sail, she had gone below to check out things. There were a number of screened ports as well as multiple overhead hatches intended to circulate fresh air. What had caught her eye was the queen-size berth in the aft stateroom, as well as the built-in lounge seat and hanging lockers. The bathroom was small but contained a shower with hot and cold water, a sink and vanity. Also below was a highly styled gourmet galley with a beautifully detailed teak interior.

When they had boarded, Dominic had said something about it being large enough to sleep six people and that the size of the boat eliminated a lot of rocking. She had to agree since so far it had been smooth sailing. He was the captain and she smiled, remembering that he had made her his mate. After bringing the boat into the wind, he had asked her to hold the wheel while he lowered the sail. She had enjoyed doing that. It had made her feel useful and a part of what he was doing.

She tilted her face up toward the sun, thinking there was a nice breeze in the air and all she could see for miles around was ocean. They had left any semblance of land behind hours ago. It seemed they were the only two people at that moment under a glorious blue sky.

Out of the corner of her eye she saw Dominic move and she turned her head and watched him. He was standing up and looking out at the sea. Before leaving the resort, he had swapped his jeans for a pair of denim shorts, and as he stood there with his legs braced apart, his shoulders bracketed against the wind and his hands jammed into the pockets of his shorts it was obvious that he was definitely a gorgeous specimen of a man. And with the sun and ocean in the background surrounding him, he looked totally at ease. Even from where she sat she could feel the sexual tension within him and it was having an effect on her. It was stirring things within her. The need she felt for him was poignant, keen and cutting sharp. It was weakening her with desire.

He suddenly turned and met her gaze. The atmosphere seemed even more stimulated. Her breath caught when she felt it. It was like fire seeping through her veins. It prickled her skin, sharpened her senses and created a relentless throb between her legs.

"I tried," he finally spoke and said grimly. But at the same time she heard an edge in his voice.

"And what have you tried?" she asked, thinking maybe it was better if she didn't know but desperately wanting to.

"I tried not to want you as much today."

She nodded then gave him a curious look. "And why not today?" she queried softly.

He gave her a tense look. "Because I had you too much yesterday."

He said it as if that should explain things. It didn't.

"Considering the reason we're here, Dominic, there are no limitations. It's all you can get."

He smiled. "If that were true then I'd keep you on your back with only bathroom breaks."

The image of that flowed through her mind, made the throb between her legs intensify. "But it is true. We came to make a baby. Don't worry about wearing me out. I can handle it. This is one case where the means will justify the results."

She didn't say anything for a second and then she couldn't help but ask, "Why are you fighting it?"

Taylor's words hung in the air, refusing to float away, Dominic thought. She had just asked him a loaded question. How could he explain that the reason he was fighting it was because he felt himself getting too emotionally attached? And that when he was making love to her, he felt things he hadn't felt with any woman. She was right. He was furiously trying to fight it and the sad part was that he couldn't. She had the ability to stir up things inside him. It was beginning to irritate the hell out of him that she was becoming his weakness, something he didn't have time for. Weak men became vulnerable men. They became men who couldn't think straight. Men who let their guard down.

"Dominic?"

She was waiting on his response but there was no answer he could truthfully give her. Instead he said, "I'm not fighting it. I thought I was being a gentleman and trying not to give the impression that I'm a greedy ass who enjoys being inside you 24-7."

"But I love having you inside me. Because I know the reason why you're there."

To make a baby, he contemplated roughly, wondering why he was getting upset at the thought that, as she said, he was just a means to an end. "Do you know what you're asking for?"

"Yes. I knew it the moment I arrived on the island. Even before that. I also knew that because I hadn't been sexually active in quite some time that the first couple of days wouldn't be easy for me, they would probably be uncomfortable. But my body is adjusting. I'm fine."

Dominic heard her words. He also saw how the sun was playing across the beauty of her features. His glance then moved slowly over her entire body and suddenly, he didn't want to talk anymore. He wanted to do what he'd been fighting all day.

There were no other boats around. It was as if they were in their own private world. There was no shoreline in sight. It was just the two of them and the wide-open span of the Atlantic Ocean. More than anything he wanted to make love to her here, on the deck, under the sun. Right this minute. But then he thought of her comfort.

"Will you go down below with me?" he asked silkily, more than sure she knew the reason he was asking.

She didn't hesitate when she responded. "Yes."

Taylor's breath quickened at the way Dominic was looking at her. She knew why he wanted to take her below and the thought of making love with him on the open seas made hot blood rush through her veins.

Determined not to give him a chance or a reason to change his mind, she walked over to him. When she came to stand in front of him, she said, "I've never made love on a boat before."

The look he was giving her made her skin tingle.

"Then your first time will be special. I'll make sure of that." He swung her up into his arms.

Somehow he managed to get the both of them below and placed her on the bed. Once her body touched the mattress, she didn't want them to waste any more time and began removing her clothes, beginning with her top.

"No, please let me."

She glanced up when Dominic moved closer to the bed and reached out his hand to pull her to him. Then his arms folded around her and he simply stood there for a second holding her in his warm embrace. His manly aroma teased her nostrils and her stomach began to quiver. Moments later, he leaned back and met her gaze and the look she saw in his eyes let her know there wouldn't be time for any small talk. The idea of that made her pulse leap, her heart beat fast and furious in her chest. Then he began removing the rest of her clothes, taking his time as a cooling breeze came through the screened porthole and touched her naked skin.

When she was completely naked, his gaze moved over her, taking its time and lingering on those marks of passion that were still there. "I've branded you," he whispered as a satisfied smile curved his lips.

Taylor swallowed, thinking he had done a lot more than that. There was no way she would tell him how she felt at this very moment. What was between them was an agreement, one as personal as it could get; however, things were to have remained unemotional. But it seemed whenever they came together like this, things were as emotional as they could get.

"Now I want to undress you," she said softly, reaching out and lifting up Dominic's shirt over his head. When she had removed it, she tossed it aside and went to the snaps of his shorts. He was aroused, she noted when she eased down his zipper. His manhood was huge, she saw when he stepped away from the bed to remove his shoes. And when he eased his shorts and briefs together down his thighs, she saw that he was also extremely ready. The size of him no longer bothered her as it had that first night. Her body had been able to take him right in.

He came back to the bed. "I want to try something different," he stated huskily.

She tilted her head back and met his gaze. "What?"

"I want you to ride me."

He had thumbed through that book as many times as she had, and he knew that the "woman on top" position was the least effective to use to get her pregnant, due to the law of gravity. But it was a position that she knew gave the woman the most pleasure because it placed her in a dominating role. She understood what Dominic was doing. He wanted them to make love for the sheer enjoyment of doing so, not for the sole purpose of making a baby.

A part of her wasn't sure she was ready for what he was asking. It would add a piece to the equation that she hadn't counted on. Even doing what he asked only one time would still throw a monkey wrench into their week here. She had a tendency to let herself go when they made love and had convinced herself she was only doing so because each time they came together, there was a chance they were creating a life—a life they both wanted. What if she let herself go anyway? What if he still had the ability to rock her world although he was placing her in control?

She had to fight hard to retain her composure. Just

being here with him, sitting naked in the middle of the bed, staring into the deep green of his eyes was rocking her world, slinging her into an arena of emotions and feelings she hadn't counted on, nor was prepared for. He was unshaven and the mass of hair on his head was tousled around his shoulders. Her gaze raked over his face and her breathing quickened when her eyes lowered to move across his manly chest and then down past his waist to his huge manhood that was fully erect in a bed of dark curly hair.

And she knew at that moment that yes, she would ride him. The need to do so had become an ache in her belly. There was no other position that could remove it and an abundance of rising excitement filled her entire being.

"Taylor?"

She moved her gaze back up to his face. She saw the intensity in the dark pupils staring straight at her. She felt the heat and the potent force of his sexuality. It was dominant, overbearing and lethal, and it was reaching out to her, touching her in some of the most private places. Instead of giving him an answer, she eased toward him and reached up and wrapped her arms around his neck. She studied his lips and thought his mouth was temptation at its finest, and with a gentle pull he was tumbling down on the bed with her.

Their mouths connected immediately and she began drowning in his heat the moment their tongues connected. And knowing just where their kiss would lead kicked a response in her that went beyond anything she'd ever encountered before.

And then he was shifting their bodies to place her on top and she pulled back and stared down at him.

She wanted him.

Her arms grabbed hold of his shoulders and she felt his muscles tighten beneath her fingertips. She felt his manhood in the center of her legs and it was a struggle not to lower her body onto it. However, temptation made her lean down and take a swipe of his lips with her tongue. His sharp intake of breath made her smile.

"I think I'd better warn you that I took horseback riding as a child," she informed him softly.

He continued to look at her and lifted a brow. "And?"

She chuckled. "And I'm no novice. I like riding."

She saw the way his eyes darkened. She felt the way his hard length seemed to thicken beneath her. Then suddenly he gripped her hips and lifted them enough to position his shaft at the opening of her womanly core. She felt the tip of its head right there. "I like riding, too," he said in a strained voice, lowering her hips downward to inch inside her.

She felt the heat of him, big and thick, as it entered her, stretching her body again to accommodate its presence. He continued to lower her onto him and she could barely breathe at the feeling of him filling her so completely.

She felt the exact moment he lifted the lower part of his body off the bed to drive into her to the hilt. "Let's ride," he growled from deep in his throat.

He had told her to ride him, not to kill him, Dominic thought as Taylor's body slammed down on his once more, pressing her knees into his sides, holding firm to his shoulders. Her head was thrown back and she was giving the bed one hell of a workout while at the same time driving his body over the edge, time and time again.

He'd come twice already and so had she, but she wouldn't let up and he couldn't seem to go down. She was doing more than just rocking the bed. She was also rocking his senses, tilting his world, filling him with more pleasure than he could have imagined possible. He'd heard of women who were experts when it came to riding, but until now he'd never encountered one. The sheer impact of how she was making him feel simply overwhelmed him. And the scent of sex along with the fragrance of her perfume wasn't helping matters when he inhaled it into his nostrils. It only made him that much more aware of what they were doing and how they were doing it. And the knowledge that they were out in the middle of the ocean only added to the allure, the deep throb in his veins and the degree of his arousal that wouldn't go away.

She kept going and going and going, as if working up to that one big explosion that would be the granddaddy of them all. So each time she came down on him, he was there to thrust up into her, grind his body, going as deep inside her as he could, and the more he did so, the more vigorously she bucked and pumped into him, going at it wild and untamed.

He felt another climax ready to hit him at the same moment he felt her inner body clench his muscles and felt this release would be too good to waste, so he quickly shifted positions and brought her beneath him the moment her body jerked. She let out one hair-raising scream when she exploded. He followed her and flooded her insides with the very essence of him, and held her, refusing to let her move, wanting her to feel what he'd done. Take it all in. Keep it.

Her response didn't help and when she wrapped her legs around him, locking him in, he continued to kiss her—harder—while slipping his hands into her hair to grip the silkiness of it and to hold her mouth in place. She was being held hostage, under his intense desire.

He knew that he was being held hostage under hers, as well.

Chapter 8

Taylor felt Dominic's touch when he slid his hand between her legs, gently stroking her there. He was lying beside her, facing her, and when her lips parted with a soft purr he leaned forward and took advantage, letting his tongue begin an intimate dance inside her mouth that only he had the skill to perform. Feeling like putty in his hands, under his lips, she clung to his mouth in a kiss of possession that she felt all the way to her toes.

Moments later, he released her mouth and whispered softly against her moist lips. "You okay?"

She was also too absorbed in the sensual spell he had placed her in to speak. She felt totally drained in a way that still had parts of her body quivering. Even now there was a heated pulse between her legs in the area where he was stroking.

"Yes, I'm fine," she whispered back, filled with an

emotional need she didn't want, but was too weak to resist. Each time she made love with him she felt herself being pulled in toward something she wasn't sure had a name, but was certain didn't have a place in her life. She didn't like things getting complicated. The only thing she wanted from Dominic was the one thing she believed he would give her this week—a baby.

"It's getting late. We need to head back," he said softly.

She heard his words. "I'm ready when you are," she said quietly, hoping she sounded more excited that she actually felt. In truth, she could stay here like this with him forever.

Forever.

She suddenly felt a shiver of apprehension slide down her spine. Why in the world would she think something like that? She'd never thought of forever when it came to any man and didn't intend to start now.

"You have beautiful breasts."

She watched his hand stroke her nipples as he spoke, using the same fingers he'd used to stroke between her legs earlier. His fingers were moist as he spread her very wetness over the hardened peaks of both breasts. Another shiver, this one of pleasure, ran up her spine. What on earth was he doing to her?

"Dominic…"

"Just close your eyes and feel, Taylor."

She did what he asked and the moment her eyelids fused shut she felt his tongue snaking out and capturing a bud, flickering over it, tasting her before closing in and taking it fully into his mouth. Desire, the kind she only knew with him, consumed her insides as she felt his mouth on her breasts, tasting, taunting and tampering with her in a way that was simply his. He feasted on one and then the other, almost sapping her of her senses, her sanity and her self-control.

And when his mouth found the indention of her belly and begin placing kisses all around it, she became lost within a maelstrom of sensations that had her surrendering to pleasure of the most erotic kind.

"You also have a beautiful stomach," he whispered with a warm breath before placing another kiss there. And then he whispered a few more French words and phrases and she wondered if he knew she understood what he was saying. She doubted it. Not that he was expressing his love or anything of the sort, but he was telling her in explicit French terms how much he loved making love to her body and just what being inside her did to him each and every time he was there. His words were making her succumb to emotions she was trying to control and didn't want to feel. They were also causing another deep hunger to take place inside her.

Then she felt the warmth of his breath move lower, and she held still, knowing what he was about to do. By now she should have grown accustomed to him kissing and caressing her there, but she wasn't. It couldn't be helped. He had a skill with his tongue whenever he went down on her that she just couldn't control, deny or resist. After all the lovemaking they'd shared that day she wondered how she would be able to handle this. She didn't know if she could take her body shattering in a million pieces again.

She opened her eyes to tell him but all she saw was his head, down between her legs and she could only close her eyes the moment his tongue flicked over her sensitive flesh.

Instinctively, her body came up off the bed and he

grabbed her hips, holding her to his mouth as he devoured her with a sense of hunger that left her gasping for breath. She closed her eyes as sensations tore into her body once again.

She reached out for him, held his head in place, inviting him to go deeper, and he did, as his sinfully skilled and seductive tongue continued nonstop, increasing the pace, redefining the urgency. Her senses were being driven wild and her fingers threaded through his hair as he continued to ply long, deep, drugging kisses into her.

"Don't stop. Please don't stop," she cried out over and over as a powerful throb overtook her. And then she felt it, some part of her that his tongue touched, that sent her over the edge, splintering her in two and making her scream yet again at the top of her lungs.

Slowly, deliberately, he continued to bestow the intimate kiss on her as she felt waves of heated pleasures float all through her, and she continued to writhe beneath his mouth.

She felt herself losing consciousness, and the last thing she remembered after moaning out his name was him pulling up and taking her mouth and she tasted herself on his tongue.

"What did you do to me?" Taylor asked moments after her lids fluttered back open. Dominic was leaning over her and wiping her brow with a warm, damp cloth.

He smiled down at her. "Do I truly need to answer that in full details, *chérie?*"

"No, but you did do something. I passed out for heaven's sake."

Yes, she had, he acknowledged silently. And just to think when they had left the resort earlier that day he had fully intended not to touch her. But whether he liked it or not, the woman made dreams a reality. She was the only woman he knew who could do something like that—and with very little effort.

"Tell me what you did, Dominic."

He heard the urgency in her voice. He'd known her long enough to realize she was someone who thrived on being in the know, especially when it concerned her personally.

"La petite mort," he said, using a French accent. "It's the French translation for *the little death* and a popular reference for a sexual orgasm. When pleasure gets so overwhelming it's considered a short period of transcendence one encounters."

"By passing out?"

"Yes."

He watched as she bit her bottom lip nervously before saying, "Nothing like that has ever happened to me before."

He was tempted to tell her nothing like that had ever happened to him, either. Although he hadn't passed out, he had felt pleasure so intense, even now parts of his body felt as if they were on fire. "It might happen again. But don't worry. You will be in good hands if it does," he assured her. He could tell from her expression that she intended to worry. Anxiety lines were forming around her lips. Her very beautiful, kissable lips. Lips that he was tempted to devour again.

Thinking he couldn't let that happen, he glanced at his watch. "Come on, it's time to get back."

He pushed the covers aside and stood and then reached a hand to help her up. He couldn't help staring at her naked body. The woman was so sinfully gorgeous, it was a shame.

"We'll take a shower when we get back," he said so she wouldn't be surprised when he pulled her into the shower with him later.

She only nodded as she got dressed. He finished before she did and glanced over at her to see her standing across from the mirror fussing with her hair. As he continued to watch her, he was amazed by the influx of emotions that consumed him, emotions he wasn't used to dealing with. Desire was something he understood. Lust was something he was used to, something he often craved. But he wasn't used to what he felt whenever he touched Taylor. And making love to her was another issue altogether.

She must have felt his eyes on her because she shifted her glance and met his gaze in the mirror. She smiled before twirling around for his inspection. "How do I look?"

He had to bite down to keep from saying, *"Like you belong to me."* Instead he said, "Beautiful as usual." He meant every word.

And then he crossed the room to her, needing to taste her one long, last time before he went up top to take his place at the wheel. Once they set sail he would have to concentrate on what he was doing and not on her. As if she knew his intent, exactly what was on his mind, she took the steps and met him halfway. And when he came to a stop in front of her, she reached up and placed her arms around his neck. He leaned down and connected his mouth to hers, angling his head for deeper penetration and releasing a satisfied groan when he got it.

Yes, this was the desire he understood, the lust he

craved. But yet he couldn't discount that somewhere in the shadows lurked emotions he didn't want to cope with.

He didn't want to think about that now. He would find a way to deal with those unwanted emotions later.

"I had a nice time, Dominic," Taylor said as they entered their suite. The first thing she intended to do was take a shower and she couldn't help wondering if he would join her. She had never been a person who constantly had sex on her mind but around Dominic such a thing seemed as natural as breathing.

"I had a nice time, too," he said, tossing the room key on the table. "It's almost dinnertime. Do you have a particular taste for anything?"

She was glad his back was to her and he couldn't see her lick her lips. If only he knew what cravings had begun controlling her appetite recently. She shook her head, thinking that something was definitely wrong with her. She'd never been this hard up to get laid in her life and suddenly became suspicious of something. The resort had been the one to prepare the lunch they'd taken on board the ship, and she couldn't help wondering if perhaps some of the foods had contained some sort of the aphrodisiac-laced ingredients that the brochure had bragged about using in a lot of their foods. After making love most of the afternoon, the idea of doing so again should be the furthest thing from her mind, but it wasn't.

"One of us got a call while we were out," Dominic said, claiming her attention as she watched him cross the room to the phone and its red blinking light.

She couldn't help wondering who could be calling.

Her secretary knew not to bother her unless it was an extreme emergency and—

"It was for you," Dominic said, hanging the phone up. "A call from your sister Vanessa."

"Vanessa?" she said in surprise as she pulled her cell phone out of her pocket. She had turned it off earlier since she knew the reception on the ocean wouldn't be good. As she punched in Vanessa's number, she hoped everything was okay. Vanessa knew why she was there and would not have called unless it was important.

"Hello."

"Vanessa? It's Taylor. What's going on?"

"Taylor, I didn't want to bother you but Roz called."

Taylor lifted a brow. Roz Henry was Cheyenne's agent and good friend. "And?"

"And Cheyenne passed out during a photo shoot and was taken to the hospital."

Taylor frowned. Wanting to make sure she had heard her sister correctly, she asked, "Cheyenne actually fainted?"

"Yes. Roz said she's okay but they are having a doctor check her out anyway."

Taylor knew how much her sister disliked doctors. "Where is Cheyenne?" she asked, knowing a photo shoot could take Cheyenne anywhere.

"She happens to be on one of those islands not far from where you are."

"Which one?"

A few minutes later Taylor was ending the call with her sister. She turned to find Dominic standing in the same spot he'd been standing when she had placed the call.

"Is there a problem?"

She glanced over at him and tried not to notice how sexy he looked standing there with his hands inside the pockets of his shorts. He had nice legs for a man. Muscular and bowed. "I don't know. Cheyenne passed out while doing a photo shoot. I need to make sure she's okay."

Dominic nodded and moved to stand in front of her. "Where is she?"

"On an island not far from here called Bimini Bay."

He appeared to consider her response for a mere second before saying, "Okay, then, let's go."

Taylor was amazed how quickly Dominic had made things happen. A half hour later a private plane had been chartered to take them to Bimini Bay. At twenty-three, Cheyenne was the youngest in the family and after a brief stint as a television reporter she'd tried her hand at modeling, saying it would give her the chance to travel and live in some of the most beautiful and exotic places. A few years ago she had purchased a home in Jamaica, but traveled back home for important family events, and like Taylor, she was on the board of the Steele Corporation.

Taylor couldn't help but smile when she thought of her sister, the rebel. She had taken being the baby in the Steele family to all-new heights. Her male cousins had thought Vanessa was a handful while growing up, but nothing had prepared them for Cheyenne. Whereas Vanessa and Taylor favored their father, Cheyenne had inherited their mother's strong Native American features, bestowing upon her an exotic look, which is why she was given the name of her mother's ancestry. She had beautiful brown skin, high cheekbones and dark eyes. Even as a child Cheyenne had gotten her share of admiring looks. It hadn't come as a surprise to anyone that while working as a news reporter a few years back, the president of a top modeling agency, who had seen her on television, had made Cheyenne an offer she couldn't refuse to come work for him.

"Here, drink this. It will calm your nerves."

She looked up as Dominic placed a cup of warm tea in her hand. From the moment she had told him of her concern for Cheyenne, he had seen to her every need. "Thank you," she said, taking the tea cup from him. She took a sip and liked the taste.

"We should be landing soon."

"Okay," she managed to say, not sure what Dominic was thinking. This was probably not the way he had envisioned their day ending. "Dominic, I know you must think it's silly that I'd want to see my sister just because she fainted and that—"

He placed a finger to her lips. "No, *chérie,* I don't think that at all. In fact I think it's rather sweet that you care for your sibling so much. But then I find that you are a very caring person."

He had given her the tea to calm her but she wondered if he knew the turbulence going through her at that moment being so close to him. In a way she felt she was out near the ocean, steadily getting pulled in by the tide. The man had that sort of effect. Even after what they had been doing that afternoon, she still wanted more of him. His heat was reaching out to her, warming her in one instant and sending shivers through her body in another.

"We'll make sure she's okay," he was saying. "And then we'll return to the resort later tonight."

"All right," she said, taking a sip.

His eyes seemed to have turned another shade of green, almost emerald. And there was a deep meaning in their dark depths. It was one she understood. He still wanted more of her, too. That thought sent more shivers through her and stirred her all the way down to her toes.

"Come here for a second," he said in a ragged breath. "Lean closer."

Placing the teacup aside, she leaned closer to him. When Dominic connected his mouth to hers, she thought that his kiss was like a drug. Highly potent. Very effective. It was electrifying every nerve in her body, uncoiling sensations she only felt when they were together.

"Buckle up, folks. We're about to land."

The pilot's voice intruded and she pulled away, reluctantly, from his hot and hungry mouth. "We will finish this later, right?" she couldn't help but ask, breathing the question against his moist lips.

"You can count on it, Taylor," was his quick response and she had no reason not to believe him.

Cheyenne Steele placed a faint smile on her face when she met Taylor's intense gaze. "I can't believe you came to check on me just because I fainted."

Taylor had found Cheyenne at the hotel where Roz had told her she was staying. After getting checked out by a doctor, Cheyenne had returned to her room to rest for the remainder of the day and had been surprised to open the door later that evening to find Taylor and a man she knew to be Dominic Saxon. After Taylor had officially introduced them, he had left to wait downstairs in the lobby.

"Believe it," Taylor said, frowning. "You just better be glad Vanessa and I decided not to mention anything about it to Mama. I noticed you didn't look well when we were home a few weeks ago and have been concerned about it ever since. I figured you're working crazy hours and not taking proper care of yourself. So tell me what the doctor said. Am I right? Are you not eating enough for that vigorous schedule you're keeping? Starving yourself to keep your weight down?"

Cheyenne waved off her words. "I'm fine. Just got a little overheated. Now enough about me. Tell me how things are going with you and Dominic."

Taylor knew Cheyenne was trying to shift the focus off her and onto Dominic, but she refused to let her. For some reason Taylor didn't believe Cheyenne's story about heat exhaustion, although with the island's hot temperature, getting overheated was a possibility. Taylor had a feeling that there was something else, something Cheyenne wasn't telling her. She could feel it. And for one thing, Cheyenne was looking everywhere but at her.

"Forget about me and Dominic. What's going on, Chey?" she asked softly "You're lying to me and I don't like it. Are you on an anorexia kick or something? I know how crazy you get sometimes about keeping your model figure and how you—"

"No, that's not it," Cheyenne said quickly.

Taylor breathed in deeply. "Then what is it? What aren't you telling me?"

The silence that suddenly descended upon the room was unnerving. And just when she thought Cheyenne would not say anything, her sister opened her mouth and spoke. "Okay, I'll tell you, but you must promise not to tell anyone. Not Van or the cousins and especially not Mama. I'll tell everyone when I come home for Marcus's high school graduation in a few weeks."

Taylor's brows drew together in a frown. "Tell them what?"

"You have to promise."

Taylor rolled her eyes. "Okay, okay, I promise. So what are you going to tell them?"

Cheyenne's eyes, a color so dark they looked black, stared straight into hers when she said, "That I'm pregnant."

"Are you all right, Taylor?"

Taylor glanced up at Dominic. "Yes, I'm okay."

The plane had landed and they had returned to the resort. After getting over the initial shock of what Cheyenne had told her, she had talked her sister into going out to dinner with her and Dominic at one of the restaurants near the hotel. The three of them had had a nice time and she could tell that Cheyenne liked Dominic. When it came to men Cheyenne could be downright nitpicky, which made Taylor wonder about the identity of the man who had fathered Cheyenne's baby. He'd certainly had to have been someone Cheyenne had been quite taken with. When she'd asked Cheyenne about the man, she had refused to talk about him, only saying that he was someone she had met once and would probably never see again.

"Are you still worried about your sister? She seems to be doing okay now," Dominic said, breaking into her thoughts.

If only you knew, she thought. Of course she hadn't mentioned anything to Dominic about her sister's condition, and didn't want to think what the family would have to say when Cheyenne dropped her little bombshell. Although Taylor had made plans to do the baby thing solo, her family wouldn't have been surprised if she was to pop up pregnant without the benefit of a husband because they all knew how much Taylor loved children, and with her methodical mind, having a child without a husband would seem like something Taylor would do.

But Cheyenne was another matter altogether. Besides being the baby in the family who got all the attention, Cheyenne was never a person to fawn over babies and had never mentioned that she wanted any of her own. Her modeling career was the only thing she really cared about and the thought of gaining weight was simply a no-no.

But when Taylor had inquired if she was contemplating getting an abortion, Cheyenne had surprised her by saying under no circumstances would she consider such a thing. That made Taylor proud of her baby sister's desire to accept full responsibility for her actions and accept whatever sacrifices that had to be made.

Once again, Taylor's thoughts shifted to the man who had gotten Cheyenne to lower her guard. Cheyenne was one to get annoyed with men easily, especially those who got stuck on her features. She said she would never know if the man loved her for herself or her looks. Since she had been oohed and aahed over most of her life, to Cheyenne a man loving her for herself and not her beauty was important. Although Taylor wasn't sure about the mystery man's feelings, she knew her sister well enough to know that during their brief encounter, Cheyenne must have fallen in love with him.

"Taylor?"

She then realized she hadn't answered Dominic's question. "I worry about Cheyenne out of habit," she said. "Vanessa and I both do, although Cheyenne has shown us time and time again that she's quite capable of taking care of herself. She's traveled more places than I ever have or probably ever will, and lives in Jamaica, a long way from home. I'm also her wealth and asset manager so I know that she's doing very well financially."

"But?"

Taylor chuckled. "How do you know there's a *but* in there?"

He smiled down at her as they stepped onto the elevator that would take them up to their suite. "Because I'm beginning to know you, Taylor. With you, some things are easy to figure out."

She wondered at that. Had he figured out how much she wanted him? Or even worse, had he figured out that she had fallen head over heels in love with him? She had been bordering on the edge since the first time they had made love, but had gotten a pretty big shove when he had seen how much she'd been worried about Cheyenne and had chartered a plane and whisked her to the island where her sister was, to calm her fears. She didn't know too many men who would have done that. Most would have been annoyed that she was letting worrying about her sister infringe upon their time with her.

"You're right, there is a *but*. However, the last thing I plan on doing is getting into Cheyenne's business. I let my sisters deal with their own issues, but they know I'm there if they need me."

Dominic nodded. "You must be exhausted. When we

get up to the room, I'll run bathwater for you. A good hot soak will do you good."

She turned toward him and placed her arms around his neck, glad they were the only people in the elevator. "Um, that sounds nice, but what about you?"

He smiled and that full smile on such a pair of sensual lips that showed beautiful white teeth started a slow, aching throb in her center. "I'll take a shower later."

She shook her head. "We agreed that the next time you got in the shower I would be there with you."

He chuckled. "Yes, but you're too tired tonight and I understand."

She knew he did understand, and that's what made him so beautiful in her eyes. He had such an understanding spirit when it came to her. "But I'm not too tired for that, Dominic," she said softly.

What she didn't add was that she needed him tonight in a way she had never needed him before. Now that she knew that she loved him, she wanted not only his seed to get her pregnant, nor just his body that always gave her pleasure. What she wanted more than anything was everything that was him. They had only five days left and she wanted to spend each and every moment intimately with him.

"Are you sure?" he asked, staring down at her. His eyes had changed to a soft green and were looking straight into hers.

"I'm positive." When it came to him, there was no way she could or ever would be not sure of anything. He was the first man she could admit to loving and probably would be the only man she would ever love. It was just her luck that the one man who had finally captured her heart would be someone who was dead set against ever marrying again, a man intent on not allowing his heart to ever belong to another woman. A man who was still in love with his dead wife.

"Why are you frowning, *chérie?*"

His gaze burned into hers with an intensity that seared her skin, made her want him just that much more. "No reason, other than I need to make sure it's what you want, too," she decided to say. "After all we've done today, are you sure you're not too tired? If you are, then I can certainly understand." She suddenly found herself whisked off her feet into strong arms and when he leaned down and kissed her, he practically drew the breath from her lungs. The scent of him surrounded her, practically oozed from wall to wall, panel to panel, in the elevator. It was warm, musky with a whiff of the sea that still clung to him, as well.

Only when he withdrew his mouth from hers, leaving the taste of him on her tongue, did she allow herself to breathe. And only when the elevator door swooshed open to their floor, and he stepped out, still carrying her in his arms, did she speak, barely breathing his name against his neck.

"Dominic…"

When they stopped in front of their door and he shifted her in his arms to pull out his passkey she realized that something hot, heavy and passionate was taking place between them, had been taking place since they had arrived on the island. Shivers of anticipation raced down her spine, sensitized every nerve and sent an uncontrollable urge to her brain, making awareness flow rapidly through her body.

When he opened the door, placed her on her feet before closing and locking it behind them, she released a long, ragged breath. It was past midnight already, but time was not a factor here; it could never be a factor between them. The only thing that mattered was that she was about to make love yet again to the man she loved.

He leaned back against the door and stared at her and she felt it like an intimate caress. She may not have his love but she definitely had his desire. And it was a potent thing, like a stimulating drug that actually had hot blood flowing through her veins, making her head spin, logical thoughts disintegrating and making the throb between her legs become an ache that he needed to take care of.

Only him.

Without thinking about what she was doing and knowing that he was watching her every move, she began undressing as she slowly walked backward toward the bedroom. First came her top and she tossed it aside. She paused long enough to kick away her sandals before continuing her trek backward. By the time she reached the bedroom door her clothes laid a trail on the floor and only her panties remained.

He stood there, still leaning against the door, not having moved an inch. But something on him had definitely grown…not that it hadn't been big before. She had felt it when he had picked her up in his arms and again when he had slid her body down his when he had placed her on her feet. But now as her gaze zeroed in on the crotch of his shorts, she saw him enlarging before her eyes just the way she wanted. And just the way she needed.

"Dominic…" She breathed out his name on a sigh, and that's when he moved, slowly walking toward her, pausing to undress, as well. By the time he reached her in the bedroom doorway, he was totally and completely naked.

It was then that she watched as he got down on his knees to remove the final piece of clothing from her body—for the second time that day—a pair of skimpy black lace panties. But he didn't stop there once he had removed them and had tossed them aside.

Dominic felt the need for Taylor all the way to the bone. He knew her scent, and after spending an afternoon making love to her on the boat, his tongue was practically drenched with her taste. He leaned forward and rested his face against the warm skin of her thigh and inhaled the essence of her femininity, so close to his face.

He felt the hands she had placed on his shoulders as if she was depending on his strength to hold her up. In his position, kneeling on the floor in front of her, he was just where he wanted to be, up close and as personal as he could get.

Not really.

There was this one thing that immediately demanded his attention, something his tongue was throbbing to do, something he hadn't gotten enough of doing earlier that day. He shifted his head and found the spot he wanted, gripped her hips and letting his tongue go to work, tasting her with a hunger that he knew she had to feel. He pushed her legs apart even farther so he could delve deeper, his tongue could penetrate farther, taking on a life of its own inside her.

He heard her moans, gloried in her groans. Felt the way her fingers were digging hard into his shoulders, the way she was arching the lower part of her body to lock in on his mouth. His heart rate began racing. His thirst for her taste was unquenchable. The more he got, the more he wanted, and he was letting her know it, feel it. There was just something about kissing her this way that made everything inside him react, summoned all his inner resources.

Moments later he felt her body jerk beneath his mouth and heard her scream, but he ignored the sound and kept doing what he was doing. He had the ability to climax just from tasting her, and was fighting like hell not to do so. He wanted to take her in the shower, while the force of the water beat down on them. At that point when it happened, he wanted something else other than his tongue inside her. He wanted to explode inside her, to give her the very thing that would give her his baby, if he hadn't already done so.

Dominic pulled back, quickly stood and scooped her up into his arms. He felt her go limp and knew if the water didn't revive her, something else definitely would. He stepped into the shower and quickly turned on the water. A soon as the water was warm he stepped under it and eased Taylor out of his arms to stand in front of him and then brought her close to him as he lifted her off her feet.

"Wrap your legs around me, *chérie*," he said in a deep, husky voice.

She did what he asked and before her mind could register what he was about to do, he swiftly entered her. Water poured down on them, blurring their vision, soaking their hair, but nothing could stop him from backing her up against the tile wall and pumping in and out of her like a man pushed over the edge. A man who wanted to die remembering how it was to be inside her this way.

And just in case those other times they had made love didn't quite do the trick, he grabbed hold of the hips that cradled his pelvis, drove deeper into her the exact moment he felt his entire body explode, forcing himself to hold still while feeling her muscles clench everything out of him, and he still kept coming, filling her to capacity in a way he had never done any other woman.

He showed no sign of even thinking about releasing her after becoming fully spent, totally drained. Like before, he wanted his body to remain connected to hers so he adjusted his stance, braced his legs apart and kept her pinned to the wall.

While the water was still cascading down on them, he lifted his head and met her gaze. The look in her eyes did something to him. There had been a sudden flash of something that had passed through the dark gaze holding his. He was certain of it. But what?

Dominic refused to take time to figure anything out. Not now and not here. He felt his body getting hard inside her all over again. He reached up and turned off the water before opening the shower door. And with her still in his arms, her body intimately joined to his, he stepped out of the shower.

With warm water still soaking their skin he managed to grab a big, thick towel off the rack and wrap it around them before leaving the bathroom. He reached the bed and then tumbled onto the snowwhite bedcovers with her in his arms. And then he straddled her body and stared down at her, not understanding the sudden obsession and possession he felt. It was more than the fact that she could even now be carrying his child, a

Saxon heir. Nor was it about the way his body was able to respond to hers, and kept responding in ways it had never done to other women. But it did have something to do with the warm prickling sensation that was running over his damp skin and the fire that was flowing in his blood. And for one pulse-stopping moment he felt as if he was going through an addiction. One part of his mind was telling him that the one thing he needed to do before getting in deeper was to pull back and take the stance that if she hadn't gotten pregnant by now, then too bad. He couldn't run the risk of letting her get under his skin, wiggle her way anywhere near his heart.

But he couldn't summon the strength to do that or think that way. At the moment he was just where he wanted to be: inside her while her muscles clenched him tight, milked him for all she could get. She had a strong hold on him as he had a strong hold on her and it seemed neither of them was going anywhere or wanted to handle whatever was happening right now any differently.

So he began doing what he enjoyed doing—moving inside her, thrusting in and out of her with long, leisurely, slow strokes, while watching her facial expression with each stimulating massage. Just as she was watching his. He was certain that his need, this unexplainable, overwhelming desire, was there, clearly visible on his face for her to see, as hers was fully exposed to him. Like all the other times before, he was putting everything into this mating, all of himself, everything that was in him he was giving to her. Freely and unselfishly. For her it seemed he could do nothing less.

And then he leaned closer to her mouth, needing the taste of her. And when his tongue began mating with hers in that same tempo their bodies were mating, something hot and urgent flared through him, uncoiled within his stomach and he increased the rhythm and began pumping madly, with a raw, primal need that had him locked in its grip. In the deep recesses of his mind he heard her scream out his name, automatically triggering something inside him and his body bucked hard at the same time that he screamed out hers.

And then it happened again, as it always did with her. He felt a scorching sensation throughout his body, shivers passing through every nerve, as he shot an abundance of life-creating fluid inside her while breathing in her scent, their scent. And he knew that if he lived to be over a hundred, he would never get tired of making love to Taylor Steele.

And as he leaned forward and cradled his face in the crook of her neck, he decided that to think such a thing was simply too disturbing to dissect at the moment.

Chapter 9

Taylor stood at the window and looked out at the beauty of the island and the way the ocean seemed to come to peace when the waves hit the shoreline. For the rest of her life she would always remember this place. It held so many memories. Memories she would cherish forever.

It seemed so unfair that the week had come and gone so quickly and it was time for her and Dominic to leave with hope that together they had created a life, a life they would ultimately share over the years. In the beginning the thought of them doing so wasn't a problem. That was when she was only interested in a baby and not a relationship...and certainly not love.

Love.

There was no doubt in her mind that she loved Dominic with every sense of her being. It was love not lust. She hadn't gotten the two confused as she had tried

convincing herself a number of times over the past few
days. She loved him in bed or out, although she had to
admit they had spent more time during the past week
in bed.

Because they were so sure she had conceived, they
had talked about names for their child and had decided
if it was a boy they would name him Amaury and for
a girl, she wanted Dominique. From the look that had
appeared on his face when she had made her request,
she could tell he had been touched that she wanted to
name their daughter after him. And then he had asked
something of her that was unexpected. He wanted to
be there when she found out if she had gotten pregnant
and asked if she would let him. She had agreed that he
could and was touched that he even wanted to be.

Suddenly, her senses went on full alert. He hadn't
made a sound but she knew the exact moment he had
entered the room. She could actually feel his body heat
getting closer as he crossed the room toward her. And
then he was standing directly behind her. She could feel
the warmth of his breath coming into contact with her
neck. Instinctively, she leaned back at the same moment he wrapped strong arms around her waist, holding her tight. Her bottom was cradled snug against his
center and she immediately felt the huge bulge she had
gotten used to.

"See what you do to me every time," he whispered in
her ear. "It's totally insane for me to want you so much."

"Mmm" was the only thing she could manage to
murmur as she closed her eyes, knowing memories like
this would have to sustain her forever. In a short while
they would be leaving to return to America—and their
lives apart. She would return to her world and he would

return to his. Their week-long visit to the island, their procreation vacation, would be something of the past, something they hoped, they truly believed would show results.

She refused to open her eyes when she felt his lips at the base of neck, then moving slightly to taste the area beneath her ear in one warm lick. Shivers ran through her body. He was making her want him and he knew it. "How much time do we have?" she asked, without opening her eyes. Instead she leaned back farther and angled her head in such a way that his lips could explore her more. Now he was kissing her cheek, the fine line of her jaw.

"As much time as we want. Martin has arrived with the plane but we fly out when I say we do."

She opened her eyes knowing just what that meant. They wanted each other again. Hadn't gotten enough. And before leaving they would make time.

She slowly turned in his arms and their gazes met. No further words were needed. There was nothing left to be said. After today there would be no reason for them to come together like this.

But today. For now. There was a reason. One that was old as time and as primal as mankind. And they would share it…one last time.

He began taking slow steps backward and she followed, not that she had a choice, with his arms still around her waist. She thought of all the things they had shared, all those different positions they had tried and those others he had thrown in—had introduced her to—for good measure. Over the past seven days she had definitely become sexually educated. Had graduated a star pupil.

Now she intended to put that education to work.

"I want to taste you all over, Dominic," she whispered, just inches from his lips. "And then I plan to ride you until you say you've had enough."

"I'll never say it's enough," he murmured back hotly, taking his tongue and flicking it out to moisten her lips.

"We'll see." And then she pushed him back on the bed and began going after him with a hunger and urgency that surprised even her. She pulled off his clothes, actually sent buttons flying in her haste and then she shifted to remove her own clothing. When they were both naked she went after his mouth, pressing hers to his, sinking her fingers into his scalp.

Three hours later when exhaustion finally claimed the two of them, he admitted it was all he could handle in one day, but had been quick to say it still wasn't enough.

"So, do you think you're pregnant?"

Taylor pondered Vanessa's question before opening her mouth to speak. Then without saying anything she closed it. Vanessa, who was sitting across the table from her, lifted a brow. "Well?"

The two had made plans to meet for lunch when Vanessa had called earlier in the week to say she would be flying to D.C. to attend a three-day seminar hosted by the Public Relations Society of America.

Taylor smiled. Vanessa had a way of getting any information out of you by doing something called "digging in." It was better to go ahead and give her an answer without subjecting yourself to such torture. "Yes, I know I'm pregnant."

Vanessa blinked. She knew that Taylor hadn't been

back from her island rendezvous a full week yet. "You skipped a period already?"

"No, not yet, but I don't need that to confirm what I already know." She didn't add that Dominic had been too thorough for her not to be pregnant.

Dominic.

Had it been only five days since she had seen him last? Five days since he had kissed her when he had dropped her off at the Reagan National Airport before continuing his flight to Los Angeles to visit his parents? Five long miserable days where her body seemed to be going through some form of sexual withdrawal when she would wake up during the night to reach for him and he wasn't there?

Vanessa slanted her a look. "For you to be so sure of something like that means Dominic Saxon is one hell of a potent individual or that he was pretty good at what you wanted him to do."

Taylor could only smile again. "Both. Enough about me and Dominic. How are things going with the wedding?"

For the next thirty or so minutes over lunch she listened while her sister told her how the wedding plans were coming and how Vanessa's best friend, Sienna, had been hired to remodel Cameron's home in Charlotte, the house where the couple would be living. Because Cameron's business took him just about anywhere in the world, he had homes in other places, as well, including a beautiful one next door to Cheyenne's in Jamaica.

"And you are coming home to Marcus's high school graduation in a couple of weeks, aren't you?" Vanessa interrupted her thoughts by asking.

"I wouldn't miss it." What she wouldn't say, because of the promise she had made to Cheyenne, was that Vanessa would find out in two weeks that she would be an aunt twice over. It was a definite that Cheyenne was pregnant, and by that time Taylor would know if she was pregnant, as well.

A week later Dominic still found that he was in that same melancholy mood. He walked through his home thinking how he had turned down several dinner invitations from friends. A woman who was someone he would often sleep with when he got the urge had called—several times—blatantly inviting him to spend the night with her and he had turned her down, as well. He knew Ivy was pretty pissed at the thought that he had ignored her not once but twice, but he hadn't cared enough to even send her flowers to smooth things over.

The only woman he could think about, the only woman he wanted was Taylor. He was convinced that during the week they had spent together, he had gotten bewitched by her beauty or her ability to please him in bed. He was totally taken by the entire package, which included those things and a lot more. Without even trying, she had left a mark on him that no other woman could wipe away.

And he didn't like the thought of that one damn bit.

He was a single man, and one with a strong sexual appetite. So why was he denying himself the company of beautiful women, women who would want more from him than just a baby? But he knew the answer to that one.

There was no woman who had the ability to literally charge the air between them the moment she walked into a room other than Taylor Steele. No other woman who could bring him almost to his knees with just one kiss—a kiss he had taught her how to perfect. And then there were the times he would be inside her...

Just thinking about it made his entire body ache for something he couldn't have but desperately wanted. When he reached the kitchen he pulled open the refrigerator and decided he needed a cold glass of water. He'd been dreaming again about Taylor, about them making love. The dream had seemed so real he had awakened in a heated sweat.

"Hey, are you okay?"

Dominic glanced over his shoulder at Ryder. "Yeah, I'm fine. Why aren't you in bed?"

"I just got in from the gym."

Dominic glanced at the clock on the kitchen wall. "This late?"

"Yes. This late."

He watched the huge hulk of a man slide into a chair at the kitchen table. Not for the first time he wondered about Ryder, the man who had been his bodyguard, his confidant and friend for close to twenty years now. Ryder never mentioned a family, although Dominic knew there was some special woman back in France and he left to return there every chance he got. At least Dominic figured it was a woman since whenever Ryder came back he had a better disposition. More than once over the years he'd tried inquiring about Ryder's other life and if it included a family, but the man had effectively and intentionally changed the subject, letting Dominic know any discussion about him was off-limits.

"So, how did you enjoy your week on Latois?"

Dominic glanced over at Ryder. He hadn't told anyone where he would be that week other than Matt and he was certain Matt hadn't mentioned anything to anyone. His secretary had been informed that if an emergency came up to contact Matt. So where had Ryder gotten his information?

"Don't bother figuring things out, Nick. I know where you are 24-7. It's my business to protect you. It's what your grandfather sent me here to do."

Dominic closed the refrigerator and leaned back against it. He felt irritated that his grandfather intended to be a part of his life even when he didn't want him to. "It's been close to twenty years now, Ryder?" he asked angrily. "You can't be my bodyguard forever. Besides, I don't need one anymore." Even though he said the words he knew over the years Ryder had become more than just his bodyguard.

"You are who you are. You will always need someone to watch your back."

"My grandfather's orders?" Dominic asked angrily.

"When are you going to stop hating him?"

Dominic sighed. He and Ryder had had this conversation several times. For some reason Ryder was very loyal to Franco Saxon.

"I don't hate him actually," Dominic said calmly. "I just don't want him to be a part of my life just like he chose not to be a part of my father's life when he married my mother."

"He made a mistake, Nick. Your father has forgiven him. So has your mother."

"I'm glad to hear it. Now I'm going back to bed." Dominic turned to leave but Ryder's next question stopped him.

"And what of the new Saxon heir?"

Dominic slowly turned around and stared at Ryder. Did he have no secrets from this man? He wouldn't waste his time trying to figure out how Ryder had known he was on Latois for the sole purpose of making a baby. It would have been simple enough since the island advertised heavily their procreation vacations.

"You tell me. What about the new Saxon heir?"

"Your parents and your grandfather would be pleased that you're carrying the family line forward."

Dominic was glad his parents would be overjoyed with the news, but as for his grandfather, he really didn't give a royal damn. "Nothing is definite yet."

Ryder chuckled at that. "But I'm sure it will be. You're a Saxon."

Dominic arched a brow. "Meaning?"

"You'll make it happen."

Dominic walked out of the room thinking he certainly hoped so. But he would continue to be on pins and needles while he waited for Taylor's call.

It was time to call Dominic.

Taylor placed the package she has purchased at the drugstore on the table. There was no reason why she couldn't just march into the bathroom and find out now and just call and give Dominic the results. Yes, there was a reason. He had asked to be present when she found out and she had promised him that he could. She would keep her promise.

It had been twelve days and five hours since she had seen Dominic last, but there had not been one single day that she had not gone to bed thinking of him or awakened with him in her thoughts, as well. And then there were those moments during the day when out of nowhere she would remember something—a look he'd given her, a touch. And heaven help her when she would recall all the times they made love, all those different positions...

Shivers of awareness ran down her spine. She didn't need a pregnancy test to tell her what she knew in her heart was already true. She was pregnant with Dominic's child. There was no way that she couldn't be.

Now she needed to place that call.

She walked over to the sofa and sat down then reached for the telephone and punched his private number.

"Hello, Taylor."

Immediately, upon hearing his strong, husky voice, an electric current seemed to have run right through her. She swallowed and then asked, "How did you know it was me?"

"Caller ID."

She nodded. That made sense. "You wanted me to call you when it was time."

"And is it time to find out?" he asked.

"Yes."

"I'm on my way over."

He'd said it as though he was right up the street. "Will you be arriving tomorrow?"

"No, I'm on my way to your place now. I've been in D.C. staying at the Saxon Hotel for the last two days. I wanted to be close by when you called and figured it would be soon," he informed her.

"Oh."

"I'll see you in less than an hour, Taylor."

"Okay."

And then he ended the call.

Chapter 10

Taylor glanced at herself in the mirror one final time after hearing the sound of the doorbell. A surge of anxiety swept through her. How was she supposed to act when she saw Dominic again? He wasn't just any man, but was someone she had spent an entire week making love with more than eighty percent of the time. The last four days on Latois had been the most intense. It was as if they were counting down the hours, minutes and seconds and wanted to make each one count.

She glanced down at her outfit, a pair of shorts and a tank top. She had wanted to appear casual, right at home and had taken a shower and put on a little makeup and sprayed on her favorite cologne.

She crossed the room and inhaled deeply, hoping and praying she would be able to keep things together when she saw him. She opened the door and whatever words of greeting she planned to say died on her lips. All she could do was stand there and stare at him.

For a few split seconds it seemed neither of them was capable of speaking, since he was staring back at her. Then, he finally spoke in a deep, raspy voice that sent shivers all through Taylor's body.

"It's good seeing you again, Taylor."

She inhaled deeply once more. "It's good seeing you again, as well, Dominic." She had to admit that she sounded slightly hoarse to her own ears. "Won't you come in?"

She took a step back and he entered, closing the door behind him. He glanced around a second before returning his gaze to her. "You look good."

"Thanks, and so do you." And she meant it. He was wearing a dark gray suit and white shirt and looked gorgeous as ever. "Would you like something to drink?"

"What do you have?"

"Whatever you want." Too late she realized how that may have sounded.

He chuckled softly. "In that case, a glass of wine would be nice."

"No problem. Make yourself comfortable and I'll be right back." She headed toward the kitchen but couldn't help glancing over her shoulder and saw that he was removing his jacket, exposing those broad shoulders she remembered so well.

A tingling sensation flowed through her as she recalled a number of other things, and they were things she wished she wouldn't remember right now. Her body was heated enough already.

Once she got to the kitchen she let out a deep breath. The sexual chemistry they'd shared hadn't been just confined to the island. It was here in her apartment. She'd felt it the moment she opened the door and saw him standing there. There was no way he hadn't felt it, too.

With nervous hands she poured him a glass of wine and poured a glass of apple juice for herself. "I can do this," she murmured softly before leaving her kitchen.

He was standing by the window, looking at the beautiful view of the Potomac and turned when he heard her enter the room. His gaze met hers and she actually saw the heated lust in his eyes. Suddenly, she felt hotter than before and could actually feel dampness form on her forehead. With all the strength she could muster, she made it across the room to him without dropping the glasses out of her hand.

"Here you are. I hope I wasn't too long."

He smiled before taking the glass from her trembling hand. "No, you weren't."

Their fingers touched and she felt a sizzling sensation all the way to her toes. All she had to do was reconnect with his gaze to know he'd felt it, as well. Thinking the cold apple juice would certainly cool her off, she quickly took a sip. It didn't do any good. Heat was still trickling through her.

"So how have you been feeling?" he asked, breaking into the silence that had surrounded them.

"I've been fine. Busy as usual. I had a lot to catch up on when I got back."

"So did I."

"The stock market has looked good for the past couple of weeks," she said, leading him over to the sofa to sit down. He sat on one end and she on the other.

"Yes, I saw that."

The room plunged back into silence and she began racking her brain for something else to say. She thought about a recent news article and brought it up. He made a comment or two and that was it. Deciding she was dragging things out for no reason at all she said, "I'm sure you have a lot to do this evening, so if you want we can find out if I'm pregnant or not right now."

"I don't have anything to do this evening," he said smoothly. "Do you feel pregnant?"

A smile touched her lips. "If you're asking if I've had morning sickness or anything like that, then the answer is no. I feel wonderful. But I have missed my period by a few days."

"Oh."

Too late she wondered if she had said too much, then decided no, she hadn't. While on the island they had talked about a number of things, personal things regarding changes that would take place to her body once she became pregnant. She had felt comfortable discussing them with him then and there was no reason she shouldn't feel at ease talking about them with him now. Although most of the time they had held the discussions while both of them had been wrapped in each other's arms, naked and satiated after having just made love.

"What about your breasts?"

Desire sparked in the center of her, right below the waist, between the legs. "What about them?" she asked softly.

He took a sip of wine before leaning forward. "Are they tender? You said that would be one sure-tell sign."

Yes, she had said that. "Ah, yes. They are somewhat tender."

"I see."

He was staring at her, more specifically her breasts. They had definitely become the subject of his intense assessment. A part of her wanted to take her hands and cover them, not that he could see anything through her blouse. But then she felt her nipples harden and didn't have to glance down at herself to know that he probably saw how the tips were pressed against her blouse.

She quickly got to her feet, feeling somewhat shaky and still feeling hot. "I—I'll go in and do the test now."

He got to his feet, as well. "There's no hurry, Taylor. I'm enjoying your company. Come on, let's sit back down."

He reached out and touched her arm and they both discovered within seconds it had been a mistake. Suddenly, it was as if the two weeks' separation hadn't happened and they were back on the island, in their suite, where getting naked and making love had become as normal to them as breathing.

Her heart began racing when she saw him lower his head toward hers and she knew what she was in for. However, she also knew what she couldn't have. She loved him but he didn't love her and she refused to be one of those women who pined away for a love that would never be.

With all the strength she could muster, she pulled her hand from within his grasp and took a step back. "I—I think I need to go and do that test now," she said with a quiver in her voice as she steadily backed away from him.

His eyes bored into hers. She could still feel the sensuous heat. "Need help?" he asked in a voice that sent more shivers up her spine.

"No, thanks. I can handle things." And then she turned and quickly rushed off toward the bathroom.

Dominic placed his hands in the pockets of his slacks as he walked back over to the window. He hadn't meant to make Taylor feel uncomfortable, but seeing her again had done something to him. The moment she had opened the door he had wanted to reach out and sweep her off her feet and kiss her with all the intensity that he felt. He had firsthand knowledge of just how wonderful she would feel in his arms and just how delicious her taste was. He had missed both over the past two weeks.

He'd had to constantly force himself to accept that he couldn't call her and she wouldn't be calling him. What had been between them was nothing more than a business agreement. He wasn't supposed to start having these intense emotions. Nor was he supposed to think of her during every waking moment, remembering what they had shared on that island.

But the fact of the matter was that he couldn't forget. Neither his mind nor his body would let him. He would wake up during the middle of the night actually inhaling her scent. It was during those times when his senses would get stirred to a degree that he thought he was losing his mind. Never in his life had any woman affected him so deeply, made him want her so badly.

The sound of footsteps had him turning around and his gaze immediately latched onto her face when she came back into the room. His heartbeat kicked hard in his chest when he saw the tears that glistened in her eyes. Were they tears of joy or of disappointment? What if she hadn't gotten pregnant as he had so arrogantly assumed?

Somehow he made his body move and crossed the room to her. Automatically he reached out and wiped one of her tears away with the tip of his finger. When she didn't say anything for the longest time, just stood gazing at him, he asked in a near-quiet tone, "Are you or aren't you?"

As he watched her face, he saw a smile touch the corners of her lips. Then she nodded. "Yes, I am. Oh, Dominic, we're having a baby," she said in such an awed voice that to him it was like a match thrown in a box of bone-dry tinder. The blaze within him had flared into a full flame.

He was going to be a father.

The realization of that hit him and he hadn't known just how much he'd wanted that until now. He could no more stop himself from kissing her at that moment than he could stop the day from turning into night. He reached out and pulled her into his arms and in one smooth sweep, captured her lips as if doing so was the most natural thing.

There was something in knowing the man whose hot and hungry mouth was insistently eating away at hers, was the man whose child she carried in her womb. Coupled with the fact that she loved him with all her heart she forgot that the last thing they should be doing was sharing a kiss.

Neither should they be tearing away at each other's clothes, but they were doing that, too. She hadn't forgotten what this was like. An intense desire to mate. Nor had she forgotten the feel of wanting him with such a raw, primitive need like what she was feeling now.

One part of her mind was saying this was crazy, totally insane. They weren't thinking rationally. All she had to say to that was, yes, probably not. But at that precise moment she was happier than any one woman had a right to be. She was having a baby. A baby that she had created with the man she loved. She would have plenty of time tomorrow to be reminded that he didn't love her. Right now he desired her and that was enough.

He broke off the kiss, mainly to give them a chance to breathe. And then he pulled her back into his arms to finish removing her clothes. But in her opinion that wasn't going fast enough. "Hurry, Dominic."

Once he had her completely naked, he began removing his own clothes at a fast pace. She wasn't helping matters when each time he exposed a portion of naked skin, her mouth and lips were there, wanting to taste him all over, practically everywhere.

It seemed at that moment he made the correct assumption they would never make it to the bedroom and pulled her down with him to the carpeted floor. He then shifted his body for her to straddle his.

She stared down at him. "You know since I'm already pregnant there's no earthly reason for us to be doing this," she said in a rushed and fevered voice.

"Is there an unearthly one?" he asked in a voice so hoarse she could barely hear him.

"None that I can think of."

"Good. Do you want me to stop?" he asked and then leaned up his head to give the hardened tip of her breast one tantalizing lick.

"Ah, no. Don't stop. Whatever you do, *please* don't stop."

"I won't," he muttered against her other breast and

flicked a lick to it before pulling and giving it a tug with his lips.

She threw her head back and let out a deep moan. It was shameless. It brought to life every sensual part of her. And when she felt the hard, moist tip of his erection, right there at the entrance of her feminine core, she only knew but one way to go. Down.

She pressed her weight down on him and the hands he'd used earlier to wipe away her tears held her hips in a tight grip. And when she felt him inside her, all the way to the hilt, she knew what she had to do. What she wanted to do.

Ride him.

And since he seemed amenable to letting her be in control, she took it. She slowly eased up, just an inch or so short of their bodies disconnecting and then she eased back down, then up again, repeating the process as she slid up and down on him, over and over again, hearing his sharp indrawn breath every time her hips shifted back and forth over him.

"Taylor…"

She didn't want to focus on the tortured way he was saying her name. Instead she stared down at the expressions on his face. The look was intoxicating her senses, practically blowing her mind. The slow, steady heat between her legs where their bodies connected suddenly seemed filled with an electrical charge that sent shock waves frolicking through her body.

She arched her back and released an intense scream. Dominic quickly pulled her mouth down to his and kissed her with a hunger that splintered her body in a million pieces. And then she felt him explode inside her while his hands kept a tight grip on her hips.

She became lost in sensations she had been certain she would never feel again. But she was feeling them now, thanks to Dominic. What they were sharing was perfect, so unerringly flawless, it was as if they were the only two living souls in the entire universe. It was as if she couldn't get enough of him and he couldn't get enough of her.

And as she clung to his shoulders as yet another orgasm struck her, she couldn't help but wonder just where would they go from here?

"You've bewitched me, Taylor."

They had moved from the living room floor to the bedroom an hour or so ago. Taylor lay beside Dominic but didn't turn her head to look at him. The truth of the matter was that she didn't have the strength to move even if she wanted to. Instead she reached out and touched his erection that hadn't gone down. "And I could give you a list of all the things you've done to me, Dominic."

She then reached out and brought his hand to her stomach. "But putting your baby in here, I think, is the most precious of them all."

Her words must have touched him because he shifted his body and lowered his lips to hers. Like all the others, this kiss was hot, sexual and sent a flaming sensation all through her. Moments later, to her disappointment he pulled back and met her gaze.

"I want to take you out to dinner to celebrate."

"Tonight?"

He gave a low chuckle and leaned down and brushed a kiss across her lips. "Yes, tonight."

"I'm not sure I can move."

"Um, you were doing quite nicely a while ago," he

pointed out as he placed his arm around her and drew her into the curve of his body.

"Yeah, well, that's why I can't move now, thank you very much."

His expression turned serious. "No, thank *you* very much, Taylor. I owe you a wealth of thanks. I'd be the first to admit when you suggested that I father your child, I had a number of misgivings. But now since it's official that you're pregnant, I can only feel elation."

He paused for a moment and then said, "I can't wait to tell my parents."

Taylor forced her head to move to look at him. "How are you going to tell them? How will you explain the situation between us?"

"Not sure yet, but they are fully aware that I'll never marry again. They're hoping that I'll change my mind although I've told them on countless occasions that I won't."

Well, that was that, Taylor thought. What he'd said had effectively removed any hope she'd been harboring that he saw what they'd shared as something other than lust. "You could just tell them the truth, that you and I both wanted a child and so we entered into this business agreement to share one."

"Yes, I could do that but they wouldn't buy it. They would try their hand at getting us together. Unfortunately, they are die-hard romantics. They are in France now and won't be returning for a week or so. I will have thought of something by then."

Taylor was curious as to what he would come up with but decided they were his parents and he would have to deal with them. She, on the other hand, would be busy dealing with her own family. Now it seemed Cheyenne wouldn't be the only one announcing plans of motherhood next weekend when the family got together for Marcus's graduation.

"But one thing is for certain, *chérie,*" he said in a raspy tone.

Tiny flutters went off in her stomach. It always did something to her when he called her in French what was the equivalency of the word *sweetheart* in English. Although she knew it was a term of endearment that probably had no special meaning to him, she still felt something when he said it.

"And what is for certain, Dominic?"

"No matter how or why the child was conceived, they will look upon its existence like I will, as that of a special gift we've been given."

Taylor had read in a pregnancy book that emotional changes were one of the side effects. Maybe that was the reason she suddenly wanted to cry at what Dominic said. His words had touched her deeply.

"Thank you," she whispered, fighting back the tears in her eyes.

He reached out and ran the tip of his finger along the side of her jaw. "And what are you thanking me for?" he asked in a husky tone.

"For wanting this baby. For wanting it to be a part of your life, your parents' life."

"Did you think I would not, Taylor? Did you honestly assume that I would settle for anything less?"

No, she hadn't assumed that. He was living up to her expectations. Instead of answering him, she leaned forward and touched her lips to his. He then gently gathered her into his arms, took over the kiss and devoured her mouth with a hunger she was used to.

As he proceeded to kiss her senseless, she fell deeper and deeper in love with him.

Chapter 11

Vanessa Steele stared at her two younger sisters. Pregnant and unmarried—the *both* of them—they seemed happy, so she was happy for them. She knew who had fathered Taylor's child, but Cheyenne was keeping a tight lip as to who had fathered hers. The only thing Cheyenne would say was that he was someone she had met one night while doing a photo shoot in Egypt but wouldn't be seeing again. Vanessa couldn't help wondering if Cheyenne's one-night lover had been an Egyptian native or an American she'd met who, like her, had been visiting the country.

"I hope the two of you know we're going to have to celebrate, don't you?" she finally asked. Taylor and Cheyenne were doing a sleepover at Vanessa's house. They had just watched a Tyler Perry movie that had finally come out on DVD—for the fourth time—while munching on popcorn.

Marcus's graduation had been beautiful and had brought out a lot of tears from those who recalled how it seemed just yesterday he was taking his first steps and now he was heading off to college—an Ivy League college at that, something Chance had always wanted for his son. Chance was proud of Marcus and everyone knew that if Cyndi had lived she would be proud of Marcus, as well, and more than satisfied at the fine job Chance had done in raising their son. Now Chance was married to Kylie, and had a seventeen-year-old stepdaughter named Tiffany and a baby son named Alden, who would be celebrating his first birthday soon.

Although surprised, the members of the family took both Taylor's and Cheyenne's pregnancy announcements well, and for once the cousins hadn't bothered asking a lot of questions. After all, Taylor and Cheyenne were grown women, financially secure and able to take care of themselves. But Vanessa knew everyone had to be mildly curious about the men in their lives since no one had ever met either of them.

Vanessa was more than mildly curious but knew there was no need wasting her time on Cheyenne. Trying to get anything out of her would be like getting blood from a turnip, so she turned her concentration on Taylor.

"So, will you and Dominic Saxon have joint custody of your baby?" she asked Taylor, since she wanted to know.

Taylor shook her head. "No, I'll have full custody, but he'll get visitation rights."

Deciding to play devil's advocate, she asked, "And what if he changes his mind later and wants full custody? What will you do then?"

"It won't happen."

Vanessa raised a brow. "You seem certain of that."

Taylor shrugged. "I am. I trust Dominic to do what he said he would do."

Vanessa decided to make an observation. "You also love him, don't you?"

At first Taylor didn't say anything and then after taking a sip of her lemonade, she said, "Yes, I love him. But it doesn't matter."

"And why doesn't it matter?" Cheyenne wanted to know.

Taylor smiled at her two sisters. "Because falling in love with him wasn't part of the deal. I may never have his love but I will have his baby."

"And will that be enough for you?" Vanessa asked softly, hearing the pain in her sister's voice.

Taylor toyed with her glass a second or so before saying, "It has to be enough, Van, because that's all I'll ever have."

Later that night Taylor couldn't get to sleep so she lay in bed and stared up at the ceiling. She couldn't help but recall the night when Dominic had dropped by her condo so he could be there when she found out whether or not she was pregnant. They had made love several times, and he had taken her to dinner later and ended up spending the night.

The following morning had been like all the others on the island when she had awakened in his arms... and to his lovemaking. He left the next morning for a business meeting in Australia. He hadn't made any promises about when he would see her again, but had promised to call to check on her and he had, practically every day. She enjoyed receiving her daily phone calls from him, although she knew he was calling more for the baby's sake than for hers.

When she had spoken to him earlier today he had mentioned that he had told his parents about the baby and they wanted to meet her. He hadn't said how he had explained their relationship and she didn't ask.

She heard her cell phone ring and glanced over at the clock. It was almost eleven. Wondering who would be calling her at this hour she got out of bed to grab the phone off the dresser. Caller ID indicated it was Dominic. Her heart jumped at the thought that he was calling her and wondered if anything was wrong, since they'd talked already that day.

"Dominic?"

"Yes, *chérie?*"

"Is anything wrong?"

She heard his soft chuckle. "No, nothing is wrong. It was only after dialing your number that I remembered there's a three-hour time difference between us. I'm back in L.A. visiting my parents."

"Oh." Earlier that day when she had spoken with him he had been in Italy. He was definitely a jetsetter, but she knew that Dominic had investment interests all over the world.

"And how are your parents?" she asked.

He gave another soft chuckle. "They're doing fine and are still walking on cloud nine at the thought of becoming grandparents. You have made them happy, Taylor. And they like the names we've picked out."

Taylor smiled. "I'm glad."

There was a slight pause and then he said, "I miss you, Taylor."

She closed her eyes at the sexiness in his voice. "I miss you, too, Dominic."

And she did, although she knew the reason she was missing him was vastly different from the reason he was missing her. She was smart enough to know that the sex between them was good, practically off the charts. Men got used to something like that. They began craving it. The reason she missed him was because she loved him and because she loved him, she enjoyed being with him whether sexual or not.

"When are you returning to D.C.?" he broke into her thoughts and asked.

"In a few days. In fact, I fly out Sunday morning."

"Call my secretary and give her your flight information. I will be at the airport to pick you up."

"You don't have to do that."

"I know, but I want to," he said smoothly in a soft voice.

"Okay then. I'll call and let her know."

Moments later after hanging up the phone she got back into bed. Her fleeting happiness was somewhat fractured by the fact that the only thing between them was sex. Good, hot, passionate sex.

And yes, of course, there was the baby.

"You're kind of antsy, aren't you, Nick? Ms. Steele's flight doesn't arrive for a full hour."

Dominic was roused from his thoughts by Ryder's observation. He glanced toward the front seat where Ryder was expertly driving the sedan toward the airport. "I didn't want to take a chance on traffic this morning," he said.

"On a Sunday morning? Who are you trying to kid? Just admit you're anxious to see the woman."

Dominic frowned. "I will admit no such thing."

"Fine, then suit yourself."

Instead of giving Ryder a response, Dominic decided to look over the papers he needed to review for a business meeting he was having in England later this week. His father was relinquishing more and more of the hotel duties to him. He didn't mind combining his father's entities with his, especially now since there would be someone they would eventually leave all their wealth, too—the Saxon heir.

It didn't take long for him to admit he was finding it hard to concentrate and tossed the papers aside. Ryder was right. He was antsy but he would never admit it. Ryder seemed to know too much as it was. But then, even as a teenager he hadn't been able to pull anything over on the man.

"So, Nick, when is the wedding?"

Now, Dominic thought, Ryder was trying to be a smart-ass. "There won't be a wedding and you know it. I've been married once."

"Yes, but Camry is gone. Besides, the two of you lacked passion."

Dominic glared at the back of the man's head. "And how would you know?"

"I have eyes. You and Camry were best friends more than anything else. You understood her whereas her parents never did."

That much was true, Dominic thought. The reason he had decided to marry her was to protect her from them. They had expected perfection and she had tried telling them time and time again that she was only human but they wouldn't listen. "Camry meant everything to me, Ryder."

"Yes, like I said, she was your best friend."

Dominic's eyes went cold. "She was my wife."

Ryder didn't say anything and Dominic was grateful for the man's silence.

It was short-lived.

"That baby is going to need a father, Nick."

Dominic didn't have to ask what baby he was talking about. "He or she is going to have a father."

"Yes, a part-time one. Marcello was a full-time father to you. How can you cheat your own child out of having what you had?"

Before Dominic could give Ryder a blazing retort, Ryder quickly said, "We're here. I'm going to let you out at the curb so you can be there when Ms. Steele walks off the plane since I believe that's what you want."

Dominic wouldn't argue with him about that, because that was what he wanted.

Taylor saw Dominic the minute she walked through the gate. He was standing there, tall and as handsome as any man had a right to be.

And he was waiting for her.

A shiver went up her spine when at that moment she realized the sexual chemistry between them was still there, even in the crowded airport. She continued walking toward him and he moved toward her. The moment they were standing in front of each other, as if it had been months since he had seen her last instead of mere weeks, he pulled her into his arms and kissed her, deeply, soundly.

Moments later, knowing they were probably causing

a scene, he pulled back and took her hand in his. "Come on, let's get out of here," he said gruffly.

It didn't take long for them to claim her luggage. Ryder was there with the car waiting for them the moment they stepped outside the terminal. Once Dominic had her settled in the backseat with him, ignoring Ryder, he pulled her into his arms and kissed her again, long and leisurely.

When he finally released her mouth he whispered against her moist lips, "Come to the hotel with me and let me fix you breakfast."

She took a deep breath. "You're cooking?"

He smiled. "Yes."

"Then there's no way I'll turn you down."

He gave her a soft chuckle. "I was hoping you would say that."

It was late afternoon before Taylor finally entered her apartment. After Dominic had prepared breakfast—and he'd done a good job of it, she would have to admit—they took a walk around the grounds of the hotel, which eventually led to Rock Creek Park. It was a beautiful day for a walk and she couldn't get over just how attentive Dominic had been to her. His parents called and when he mentioned she was there, they wanted to talk to her. They were overjoyed at the thought of having a grandchild and couldn't wait to meet her. Dominic promised to fly her out to L.A. when she was free to do so.

When they returned to his suite at the hotel, they had showered together and made love. Instead of staying in bed the rest of the day as she'd figured they would do, they had dressed and gone downstairs for brunch. Then he had taken her to the recreation room for a game of pool. He was surprised she knew how to play, and she had explained that she thanked her four cousins for acquiring such a skill. She had truly had fun, although he had beaten her each and every time.

They had returned to his suite and had made love again before he had brought her home. He had walked her to the door, promised to call once he arrived in London tomorrow, kissed her and then had left after seeing that she was safely inside.

Too tired to unpack her clothes, Taylor cuddled on the sofa and thought about her day with Dominic. Although neither had officially declared it to be so, they were lovers. They were doing all the things that lovers did.

She shook her head. This part of their relationship had not been planned. It just happened. Their week together on the island had done more than create a baby, it had created an unquenchable hunger for each other. She couldn't help wondering—when would the intense craving come to an end? When would he decide that he wanted another flavor of the month and move on?

She knew that because of the baby her life would always be connected to his in some way. But she also knew that she needed to prepare herself for the time when he would tell her he was no longer interested in her. In her job she was a risk taker, and one thing a risk taker knew was those risks to walk away from. She could not let Dominic break her heart, and unless she did something that was just where she was headed.

She had never been a needy person and she wasn't going to start being one now. She'd known when she had proposed the idea to Dominic that she would be sailing solo and nothing had changed. Time away from Dominic was what she needed. It was better if she got out of the situation now, on her own, before he forced her out.

With a heavy heart and a made-up mind, she pulled herself off the sofa and headed toward the bedroom to get ready for bed.

"Ms. Steele, Mr. Saxon is here to see you."

Taylor frowned. That couldn't be. Dominic had called her that morning from England and said he would be in business meetings all day. There was no way he could be back in the States.

"Mr. Saxon?" she asked, making sure she'd heard her secretary correctly.

"Yes. Mr. Franco Saxon."

Franco Saxon? Taylor pondered the name around in her mind. The only Franco Saxon she knew—or rather had heard of—was the wealthy Frenchman who'd made his millions through his shipping company. Could he be one and the same and why was he coming to see her?

"Ms. Steele?"

"Oh, yes. Please send him in."

Never in a thousand years would Taylor be prepared for the sharply dressed, gray-haired older man who walked into her office. He had such charisma and style that she immediately recognized him as someone who had to be related to Dominic. But then there were the features, so like Dominic's it was amazing. It was as if she was staring into the face of a much older Dominic. The man was tall and very handsome. It was evident the man was related to Dominic but in what capacity? Although she had yet to meet Dominic's father, she had seen pictures of him in magazines and he wasn't as old as this guy. Was this an uncle perhaps?

"Madam Steele, thank you for seeing me," he said with a deep French accent as he crossed the room to her. He leaned over and placed a kiss on the back of her hand.

"You're welcome," she said, thinking whoever he was, he was a true Frenchman.

When he straightened, a smile touched the corners of his lips. "You seem in a quandary as to who I am."

"Yes," Taylor said, studying the man's features. She would put his age in his early seventies. "It's obvious you're related to Dominic."

She saw a sudden shadow that crossed the man's green eyes, eyes that were so much like Dominic's it was uncanny. "Yes, I am related to Dominic," he said in a somewhat soft voice that dampened the smile he wore. "I am Franco Marcello Saxon, the grandfather Dominic refuses to acknowledge that he has."

Chapter 12

At first Taylor could have sworn she had heard the older man wrong, but a part of her knew deep down she'd heard him right. There was no doubt in her mind that the man standing before her was Dominic's grandfather, and since Dominic had denied having any living grandparents, she could only wonder why he refused to acknowledge the man's very existence.

"B-but why would Dominic do such a thing?" she asked, knowing the man would be able to provide her with an answer.

"It's a long story, one you have a right to know."

She wondered how he figured that. He evidently saw the question in her eyes and said, "Because you are the woman who will give birth to my great-grandchild and more than anything, I want to be a part of its life."

Taylor wondered how he knew about the baby. Again, as if he'd known what she was thinking, he said, "My son and daughter-in-law were excited about the news and were happy to share it with me."

Taylor nodded. If that was the case, that meant he and Dominic's parents were on speaking terms.

If they were then why not Dominic? "I know you have a lot of questions, Madam Steele, and I would be honored if you joined me for dinner so I can explain things to you."

"Dinner?"

"Yes."

Taylor thought about the invitation. Regardless of whether or not he was on good terms with his grandfather, Dominic should have mentioned the man's existence to her. No matter what degree of discord subsisted between the two men, the one standing before was her baby's great-grandfather. So, she made a decision. "Yes, I would love to join you for dinner."

As soon as they entered the Marcinelli Restaurant, Taylor could tell the man by her side was used to dining in elegance. She glanced up at the vaulted ceilings with intricate carvings and bordered by rich-looking marble that seemed to blend into the stone walls. The spacious interior provided an air of sophistication and style, and the floor-to-ceiling windows and handmade pottery that sat on each table promised ambience as classy as the food the restaurant served.

They were led to a private room in the back of the restaurant and she was just as impressed with the furnishings and decor. The window looked out into a massive garden. Taylor was never one to appreciate a lot of greenery but she did so now.

Once they had been seated and their choice of wine

ordered, Franco Saxon glanced over at her and smiled. "I'm glad you are joining me, Taylor. It means a lot."

She believed him, just as she believed him earlier, during the drive over, when he'd said that no matter how Dominic felt about him, he loved his grandson.

"And I appreciate the invitation to join you."

They began talking about everything but Dominic for the first half hour while waiting for their food to arrive. He told her that his health hadn't been the best lately, but he was getting better and that his travels to the United States were infrequent. She discovered his love of classical music as well as his opposition to anything that restricted world trade. That was understandable considering he had made his millions in the import and export business.

"I can see why my grandson has fallen in love with you, Taylor."

Taylor froze with the glass of apple juice halfway to her lips. She wasn't sure what to say, since she didn't have a clue just what Dominic had told his parents about her. So to play it safe, she said something she knew wasn't a lie. "And I love Dominic just as deeply."

She leaned back in her chair. "So, please, share with me why there is animosity between you and Dominic."

Over dinner she listened while he told her with deep regret and sorrow in his voice how he tried to control his son's life by choosing the woman for him to marry—a woman who would increase the Saxons' wealth when the two families joined. Instead, while attending school here in the States, Marcello met and fell in love with Megan. Franco had opposed the marriage, threatened to disown his son if he didn't do what he wanted. In the end, Marcello chose love.

For the next twenty years Marcello and his father had very little contact. Franco explained that they were both stubborn men, but that within the last three years he and Marcello had put the past behind them. However, Dominic refused to do so. He just couldn't get over the fact that Franco had turned his back on Marcello for marrying his mother.

Franco admitted he had been wrong and that he had made a grave mistake, especially upon seeing how happy Marcello was. And he totally liked Megan and couldn't imagine any woman more right for his son. If he had it to do all over again, he would give his blessings to the couple in a heartbeat: But he hadn't and not doing so had eventually lost him his grandson's love.

"Have you tried talking to Dominic?" Taylor couldn't help but ask.

"Yes, but he refuses to discuss anything with me. Dominic refuses to acknowledge my very existence. And that's why I wanted to talk to you. I hope that you will find it in your heart to allow me to be a part of my great-grandchild's life. I hope you won't deny me that."

Taylor shook her head. "Of course I won't, and I can't see Dominic denying it, either."

"Forgive me for saying so, but I can see him denying it. Like I said, I am not one of my grandson's favorite people, but I love him and will do anything I can for him."

"And now that Dominic sees how his parents have forgiven you, that doesn't change his feelings about you?"

"No. It seems he has more stubbornness than me and his father put together. And he is fiercely loyal to those he loves and he loves his parents deeply. He knows how much I've hurt them and won't forgive me for doing so."

The older man paused for a second and then he said, "Dominic refuses to acknowledge his place as my rightful heir, but I'm naming him in my business papers anyway. However, I want to meet with my attorney and make provisions for my great-grandchild to be included, as well, but wanted to meet with you to make sure you are fine with that."

Taylor stared at him. Being a wealth and asset manager, she had a pretty good idea just how wealthy Franco Saxon was, and he was sitting there letting her know that he was thinking of her child and his place in its life. "Yes, I'm fine with it. In fact, your generosity overwhelms me and I don't know what to say."

"Say that as long as I have breath in my body that I will be a part of my great-grandchild's life. I messed up with my grandson but I don't want to mess up with my great-grandchild."

Taylor heard the trembling in the man's voice. He truly did love Dominic and was sorry for what he'd done all those years ago. Why couldn't Dominic see that? She reached across the table and took the man's hand into hers. "I make you that promise. You are the only great-grandparent my child will have and I am honored that you will be—want to be—a part of his or her life."

She could tell her words had touched Franco, and he quickly glanced away so she wouldn't see the tears in his eyes. Moments later, he looked back at her and said in a soft, appreciative voice, "Thank you, Taylor. You have brought joy to an old man's heart."

Later that night as Taylor slid under her bedcovers she couldn't help but recall her dinner conversations with Franco. He was a proud man, yet he had humbled himself and admitted to the mistakes he'd made years ago by alienating his son and grandson. She had made Franco a promise tonight, one she intended to keep. Besides, she liked him. He indicated he would be leaving D.C. in the morning but had given her his business card and had invited her to come visit him in France. Before they had parted ways she had made another promise to him that she would.

She almost jumped when her phone rang. She hadn't been sure Dominic would call and hoped it was him. She wouldn't mention anything about her dinner meeting with his grandfather until she saw him. She wanted to be face-to-face with him when she did so. For now, she just wanted to hear his voice.

She leaned up and reached over and picked up her cell phone off the nightstand. "Hello."

"Did I wake you?"

She smiled. "No, I'm in bed but I hadn't gone to sleep yet. Are you still in London?"

"No, I'm on a plane returning to the States."

She felt a gentle tug of joy in her stomach. He was on his way home. "You're going to Los Angeles?"

"No, I'm headed straight for where you are," he said softly. "By the time you awake in the morning I should have landed. I miss you."

She felt another pull in her stomach. "And I miss you, too."

"Will it be okay for me to come straight there from the airport?" he asked.

A grin touched her lips. "Yes, most certainly."

She heard his soft chuckle. "In that case, I'm going to let you go so you can get your rest. Trust me when I say that you're going to need it."

She clearly understood his underlying hint and countered, "I encourage you to take a few catnaps on the plane as you're going to need your rest, as well."

After Dominic ended his conversation with Taylor he leaned back in the leather seat and closed his eyes. God, he missed her. For the past week he could barely concentrate on business without thinking about her. The meetings with his business associates had been intense, and with a heaping amount of sexual frustration thrown into the mix, negotiations at times had gotten downright heated. In the end, he had closed the deal he had wanted and his mission had been accomplished. Now he could set his mind and sights to other things.

Like finally acknowledging he had fallen in love with Taylor.

It had been bound to happen at some point, he thought. The week on that island had been no joke. Since then he had been trying to convince himself his attraction to her was only sexual, and that since Camry he had enjoyed a number of women's company. But he'd known this thing with Taylor went deeper.

He would never forget the exact moment he'd realized just how he felt. It was the last time they had made love. After experiencing what he considered as the best orgasm of his life, he had lain beside her, held her in his arms when suddenly, his mind and body had begun reeling before experiencing a feeling of having been punched in the gut by one of those wrestlers Ryder liked watching on television. Dominic had been tempted to tell her then, but had decided to wait, to think more about his feelings and to give himself time to contemplate hers, as well as to set up a plan of action if he discovered she wasn't feeling the same way he was. He knew one of the things that made his parents' marriage special was their love for each other. Theirs was not a one-sided love match.

And he wanted the same thing for him and Taylor. If she didn't love him now, by the time he was through with her, she would. He loved her and she was going to have his baby. He was a very lucky man, a man very much in love with the mother of his child. Now his goal was to do whatever it took to make sure Taylor loved him, as well. His mission was to win her heart.

Taylor had gotten a good night's rest, grateful it was Saturday and that she wouldn't have to go into the office. She glanced at the clock. It wasn't quite seven but she'd hoped Dominic would have arrived by now. She had gotten up at the crack of dawn and although she hadn't bothered changing out of her nightclothes, she had washed her face, brushed her teeth and tried making her hair look decent.

If it wasn't so early in the morning she would call Cheyenne to check on her. They had talked a few nights ago and her sister was doing better with her pregnancy. The morning sickness was easing up somewhat with Cheyenne whereas so far Taylor hadn't experienced one day of her stomach feeling queasy.

Taylor's heart leaped in her chest when she heard the sound of the doorbell. She inhaled deeply as she crossed the room to answer it. The moment she opened the door to find Dominic standing there, immaculate as ever, simply breathtaking, whatever emotions she had been feeling before were nothing compared to what she was feeling now. Whether he loved her or not didn't matter. She truly loved him.

"Taylor…"

And then she realized that he had taken a step into the room, closed and locked the door behind him and had whispered her name just seconds before pulling her into his arms. The moment their mouths touched she felt it all the way to the bone, and she put her heart, body and soul into their kiss. And when she felt herself being swept up into his arms, her body began aching with need, as he headed for the bedroom. She was so consumed with wanting and desire she barely realized the moment he had placed her on the bed, joined her there and began removing their clothes.

But she was fully aware of when he moved his body over hers and began kissing her again with a hunger that sent blood gushing through her veins. And when she felt the thickness of his erection, poised against her feminine core, she wanted him with a degree that she never wanted him before. And knowing that he wanted her, as well, that he was barely holding back and that possibly the moment he entered her he would explode, had her tense on the verge of reaching an orgasm just that quick. They would savor the next one. Now what the two of them needed, what they wanted was immediate satisfaction.

He glanced down at her, opened his mouth to say something, but whatever he was about to say was lost when she lifted her hips and forced him to enter her. He threw his head back and growled out her name the exact moment he thrust forward, going deep, spilling inside her with an orgasm of gigantic magnitude. She came the moment she felt his hot release and wrapped her legs around him, locking him to her.

Bringing his head down, she pressed her mouth to his as all the passion and love she felt flowed through her, began overtaking her. Her moans of pleasure mingled with his and their bodies began shuddering and this was one magical moment that she didn't ever want to end.

"Who gave you this, Taylor?"

Upon hearing Dominic's voice it took her a moment to muster up enough strength to open her eyes. Their lovemaking sessions always left her weak as water from nearly drowning in passion.

She brought him into focus. He was sitting on the edge of the bed holding something in his hand. She blinked to bring him into focus again and saw it was the business card his grandfather had given her. She inhaled sharply, much preferring to have waited before having this conversation with him, but it seemed that that wouldn't be the case.

"Taylor?"

He had turned and was looking at her intensely. In other words, he was frowning. She slowly pulled up in bed, mindful of the fact that like him, she was stark naked.

"Your grandfather gave it to me."

The look he gave her was one as if he'd been slapped and then he said harshly, "That's impossible because I don't have a grandfather."

She rolled her eyes. "At least not one you want to claim. You should have told me about him, Dominic. I had a right to know."

He stood and stared down at her. "The only rights

you have regarding me are the ones I give you, Taylor, and an association with Franco Saxon isn't one of them. The man means nothing to me."

She glared at Dominic. "He might not mean anything to you, but he is my child's great-grandfather."

"No, he is not!"

"Yes, he is," she said, struggling to keep her voice calm. "Don't you think it's time for you to forgive him and move on?"

Dominic looked livid. He reached out and gripped her wrist and brought her closer to him. "No. And I don't want him to be a part of my child's life."

"And I intend for him to be a part of it, Dominic. I made him a promise."

He let go of her hand. "How much did he offer, Taylor?"

"What are you talking about?"

"I know the man. For years he's been trying to win me over with his money, with offers of business deals, the naming of me as his heir, ownership of his shipping company…so I'm sure he offered you something. What was it?" he demanded.

Taylor didn't like the sound of Dominic's raised voice, nor of his insinuations. "Are you saying that you believe I made a promise to your grandfather because of some money deal?"

"Didn't you? Are you saying he didn't agree to acknowledge our unborn child as his heir if you went along with him?"

His words made Taylor furious. "It wasn't like that at all, Dominic. Franco is a man who loves you and who already loves his great-grandchild. He merely wants to be a part of our baby's life and I can see no reason why he should not."

"Well, I do and I won't have it."

She leaned forward and placed her hands on her naked hips. "I don't care what you won't have so get over it. I will not break my promise to him."

"And what about your loyalty to me?"

Taylor figured that now was not the time to tell Dominic that not only did he have her loyalty but that he also had her love, but that this was one issue she could not, would not agree with him on. "I am loyal to you, Dominic, however, I will not deny my child the right to know its great-grandparent."

The room got quiet, and the tension surrounding them was almost unbearable. Then Dominic spoke as he began picking up his clothes off the floor. "Then it seems we have nothing more to discuss, Taylor."

He turned his back on her and went into the bathroom and closed the door. He reappeared in the room a short while later fully dressed. He came over to the bed, stood over her and glared down at her. His face was tight, his features still intense. "I'm leaving."

"Fine, and once you realize just how unfair you're being, please call me."

He face darkened. "I will call occasionally for no other reason than to check on my child. Otherwise, Taylor, our association is over."

Taylor fought back the tears in her eyes. "If that's the way you want things, Dominic, then that's the way they will be."

He stared down at her for a few more minutes and then without saying anything else, he turned and walked out of her condo.

It was later that day before Taylor was able to get out of bed, and only then because she knew she needed to eat something. She had to take care of the life growing inside her—the life Dominic had placed there.

As she began moving around her apartment, she couldn't put out of her mind the words Dominic had spoken. Did he hate his grandfather that much? Okay, she could imagine how he must have felt as a child growing up to discover the rift that existed between his parents and his grandfather, but if his parents could forgive the man, then why couldn't he?

"Because he is so damn stubborn," Taylor muttered as she sat down to eat a bowl of cereal and milk. "Okay, so I won't be at his beck and call anymore," she said to the walls, sneering. "It will be his loss. I should not have been at his beck and call anyway. The only thing between us was lust…at least on his end." She knew for her it was more. It was love.

After breakfast she decided to go for a walk. She had to leave the apartment for a while. And later she would take in a movie. She needed to keep her mind occupied so Dominic wouldn't consume so much of it. He'd made his feelings clear and there was nothing left for her to do but accept it and move on.

And she would. He'd given her no choice.

Chapter 13

Two weeks later, Dominic was standing at the window in his New York office, staring down at the people below. They were moving rather quickly along the sidewalk, and he thought about just how fast their lives seemed to be moving. But for him it appeared that his had come to a complete standstill.

And all because of Taylor.

He inhaled deeply. He hadn't realized just how much he loved her until he'd had to do without her. He had called her twice and their conversations had been brief. He had asked how she was doing, she had said fine, and then she had ended the call. He had said some harsh words to her that day, words he now wished he could take back.

Taylor was who she was and he couldn't expect her to have a beef with his grandfather just because he had one. She was not that type of woman. She had a mind of her own, she thought for herself. He would not have wanted her any other way.

And he did want her. Damn, he also loved her but he had been willing to turn his back on that love and let his intense stubbornness rule his mind and common sense. But it hadn't been able to eradicate what was in his heart.

"Mr. Saxon, your mother is here to see you."

He turned at the sound of his secretary's voice on the intercom. As much as he loved his mother she was the last person he wanted to see right now. She had gotten upset with him when he had told her about the argument he'd had with Taylor. His mother had called him, among other things, pigheaded.

"Mr. Saxon?"

"Yes, Liza, please send her in."

The door opened and his mother walked in, beautiful as ever, but she was frowning. She retained that frown as she crossed the room and came to a stop in front of him.

"Okay, Nicky, you have sulked long enough. By now I had hoped you would have come to your senses. I want to know just what you're going to do to get the mother of my grandchild back?"

Her question, Dominic thought, was simple enough, but to be completely honest, he didn't have a clue. For all he knew, Taylor might not want to be gotten back. The last two times they had talked she didn't seem inclined to have anything more to do with him.

"It's not going to be easy," he said quietly.

Megan placed a hand on his arm and he couldn't help noticing her eyes had softened somewhat and her frown was gone. "Do you want her back?"

"Yes, I want her back," he didn't hesitate to say. "Besides you, she is the most remarkable woman I know."

A smile touched Megan Saxon's lips. "You love her, don't you?"

Dominic met his mother's inquisitive but gentle stare and said, "Yes, I love her."

"Then you're going to have to do whatever it takes to win her heart and convince her that you were wrong and that you love her," Megan said in a soft voice. "Let love guide you to do the right thing. And when you get things straightened out, let me and your father know. We still want to meet her. Regardless of your relationship, she is the mother of our grandchild." She glanced at her watch. "I have to go, our private plane is waiting."

He lifted a brow. "And where are you and Dad off to now?"

"Paris. It's your grandfather's seventieth birthday and we're flying in for the birthday celebration planned for tomorrow night. I'll talk to you when I get back."

After his mother had left, Dominic sat at his desk while he planned his strategy to win back Taylor. Moments later after taking a deep breath he picked up the phone and punched in the phone number to her cell phone. He leaned back in the chair, waiting for her to answer.

Instead, another voice came on the line that said, *"I am sorry, but at the customer's request, this number has been changed to a nonpublished number."* Then there was a sharp click in his ear.

He slowly hung up the phone. Taylor had changed her number? Not to be denied the right to speak with her, he then pulled her business card from his desk to try reaching her at the office. Her secretary's cheery voice came on the line. "Good afternoon, Assets of Steele. May I help you?"

"Yes, this is Dominic Saxon and I would like to speak with Ms. Steele, please."

"I'm sorry, Mr. Saxon, but Ms. Steele is out of town."

"I see," he said, somewhat disappointed. "Is she visiting her family in North Carolina?"

"No, sir, she is out of the country."

Dominic frowned as he stood from his seat. "Out of the country? Where did she go?" he asked, as if he had a right to know.

There was a pause, and then as if the secretary decided that maybe he did, she said, "She's in France."

He lifted a brow. "France?"

"Yes, sir, Paris, France. If this is an emergency, she has asked that I refer those calls to…"

Whatever the woman was saying was lost on Dominic. Taylor had gone to France and he had an idea as to why and who she had gone to see. "Well, thanks for the information," he said, interrupting whatever it was Taylor's secretary was saying. He quickly hung up and then pressed a button.

"Yes, Mr. Saxon?"

"Liza, I'd like you to contact Martin and tell him to have the plane ready to fly me out in a few hours."

"Yes sir, and the destination?"

"Paris, France."

"Are you feeling better today, dear?"

Taylor smiled at Franco Saxon as she came down the steps to join him on the terrace for a midmorning meal. "Yes, a lot better."

She had arrived at the Saxon Estates yesterday after

having endured the lengthy plane flight across the Atlantic. Evidently something she had eaten had not agreed with her and in addition to jet lag, she had endured an upset stomach. After a good night's sleep she was now feeling fine.

She glanced around as she took her seat across from Dominic's grandfather. The Saxon family home was simply beautiful. According to Franco, it had been in the Saxon family since the late eighteen hundreds and was the place where all the Saxons, including Marcello, were born. The palace-style structure was composed of several reception rooms. Numerous bedroom suites with private baths and dressing rooms, game rooms, spa, gym, two swimming pools and a beautiful kitchen and dining room. It was a beautiful day and the sun was shining bright in the sky.

"I received a call this morning from Marcello and Megan. They are on their way and should be arriving later today," Franco said, intruding into Taylor's thoughts.

She nodded as butterflies went off in her stomach at the thought of meeting Dominic's parents. She couldn't help wondering what he'd told them about their now-defunct relationship.

She had been surprised when she had received a call from Franco inviting her to his birthday gala. Since she hadn't been sure if Dominic was still in the D.C. area or had returned to New York, she hadn't wanted to run the risk of a chance meeting with him—especially while her heart was still hurting—and had jumped at the opportunity to leave the city for a few days. The last thing she had to worry about was running into Dominic here.

The one thing she was certain about was that she

truly liked Dominic's grandfather. She believed that deep in Franco's heart he knew that he had made a mistake in the way he had handled his son's love for an American woman, a mistake that had cost him the love of his grandson. And from their argument the last time she and Dominic were together, she wasn't sure if he would ever forgive his grandfather. Dominic took being stubborn to all-new heights.

After their meal, she and Franco went into one of the game rooms to play checkers, something the older man seemed to enjoy. She was glad that her cousin Sebastian had taught her how to play years ago.

They had just ended one game and had started on another when one of Franco's servants approached to let him know that Marcello and Megan had arrived.

"Why, you're simply beautiful, just as Dominic said," his mother exclaimed, smiling at her.

Taylor wondered if Dominic had actually said that, or whether his mother was just being kind. Either way she decided to take the compliment. "Thank you."

They were standing together in the receiving line, greeting the guests arriving at Franco's party. Franco had asked her to be there and as far as she knew, no one seemed to question it. When introducing her, he merely said that she was a close friend of his grandson. Considering how things were between her and Dominic, Taylor thought that was really stretching it a bit.

"We certainly have a crowd here tonight."

Megan's words broke into Taylor's thoughts.

"Yes, there are a number of people here, but everything is beautiful. And speaking of beautiful…"

The first thing Taylor had thought when she'd seen

Megan Saxon was that any picture she'd seen of her in a magazine hadn't done her justice. She was a beautiful woman and it only took a few seconds in the Saxons' company to know that Marcello simply adored his wife. Dominic had once commented on what a loving relationship his mother and father had. Now she saw firsthand just how true that statement had been.

"And your outfit is divine. That color looks good on you," the older woman added.

Suddenly a deep appreciation for Megan Saxon blossomed to life inside her. That compliment meant a lot coming from a person who was considered an expert on fashion. But that wasn't the only reason she liked Dominic's mother so much. From the moment Franco had introduced them earlier that day, she had felt a connection. Maybe it had something to do with the fact that Megan was the woman who had given birth to the man who had captured Taylor's heart, or possibly the fact that Taylor was carrying inside her this woman's grandchild. Whatever the reason, she felt an accord with Megan, a closeness to her that she couldn't explain and wouldn't bother dissecting. It was enough that knowing how Dominic felt about his grandfather, they didn't have a problem with her being here or feel she was being disloyal to Dominic for doing so.

"Yes, I can see why Nicky loves you so much."

A flicker of panic went off inside Taylor. She knew Megan's statement was based on assumption rather than fact. Would it be the proper thing to do to correct her, let her know she was not the object of Dominic's affections?

At that moment it seemed the entire room got quiet and as Taylor glanced around to see what had everyone's attention, she heard Marcello Saxon, who was standing beside Megan, say, "Look who's here, Megan. I never thought I would live to see the day." Deep emotion was in the man's voice.

Taylor turned her head to see what the Saxons were talking about and sharpened her gaze to look at the single guest who had just entered and the curious on-lookers surrounding him.

She heard Franco's sharp intake of breath at the same moment the crowd dispersed somewhat and Dominic stood there, a younger version of both Franco and Marcello, but definitely more of Franco. There was no doubt in anyone's mind who he was and his relationship to the honoree.

Unease flickered inside her the moment her and Dominic's gazes connected and he began walking in her direction. "My prayers have been answered," she heard Franco say in a voice so low she barely heard him.

She continued to hold Dominic's gaze as she studied his face. How did he feel about her being there, espe-cially after their last conversation? Was he questioning what right she had to be standing with his family? But more important, was his presence an indication that he was willing to make peace with his grandfather at last?

She knew only Dominic held the answer to both of those questions and as she studied his features, she found nothing that would give her a clue as to what he was thinking.

Deciding she was making herself a nervous wreck, she just stood there as he came closer, as his gazed pinned her to the spot. She didn't have to force herself to hold his gaze. He was a man who deserved attention and he was definitely getting it.

The room was still quiet. It seemed that someone had even ordered the band to stop playing. Then she recalled all the people she had been introduced to that night. They were all friends and acquaintances of Franco, people who probably knew of the longstanding dissent between him and his grandson. Like her, they were waiting to see why Dominic was there, and hoping and praying that since it was Franco's birthday, Dominic's presence was a positive and not a negative.

He finally reached them and respectfully, he gave his grandfather his full attention. Speaking in fluent French, he said, "Happy birthday, Grandfather. And I hope my presence here tonight is taken as an indication that I want to put the past behind me and move forward."

He then glanced at Taylor and the look she saw in his eyes made her heart beat faster. He hadn't touched her, had yet to acknowledge her presence, but the look in his eyes was the look he always had in them for her. Dominic then turned back to his grandfather, and, still speaking in fluent French, said, "And thanks for the safekeeping of the woman who has my heart."

His words would have meant everything to her if she hadn't known he was merely saying them for show, she thought miserably. He couldn't very well have said, *"Thanks for the safekeeping of the woman who's having my baby,"* could he? At least not in front of an audience of about three hundred individuals.

She heard Franco's emotional response. "Thank you for coming, grandson of my heart. We must talk later."

Dominic nodded. And then he came to stand in front of her and she forced her heart rate to slow down. Instead of saying anything, he took her hand and lifted it up to his lips and gazed deep into her eyes. "You look beautiful tonight," he said in English and it was then she remembered that he didn't know she spoke French and decided to answer him in his grandfather's native tongue to make him aware that she had understood what he had said to Franco.

"And you're looking rather handsome yourself," she responded. She saw the surprised lifting of his brow and then the smile that touched the corners of his lips.

Instead of saying anything else, he moved on to his parents. She saw what amounted to tears in his parents' eyes and she knew for Marcello and Megan, Dominic's presence here tonight was the beginning to putting an end to the discord that had begun when they had been bold enough to fall in love.

Then Dominic was back in front of her, reaching for her hand. "Will you dance with me Taylor?"

She was about to tell him that there was no music, when suddenly as if on cue, the orchestra started up again. "Yes, I'll dance with you," she responded, and she then found herself led out onto the dance floor.

He's only being kind to me because of the baby, she reminded herself when he took her into his arms. But still, she couldn't stop the gratitude she felt in knowing that he had taken the first steps in putting animosity behind him and making up with his grandfather.

The moment Dominic pulled her into his arms, her body seemed to recognize him and melted against him. And she couldn't help but take note that although he was holding her decently, he was doing so with such familiarity that made anyone who was watching aware that they were either past or present lovers.

"I miss you," he whispered in her ear.

Those three words lifted her spirit, revived her hope.

She was about to respond by telling him that she had missed him, as well, but stopped herself from doing so. She and Dominic needed to reach an understanding. It would be better if they stuck with their original plan. Once she got pregnant, they were to go back to executing business as usual.

So she didn't say anything, didn't bother acknowledging his words. Instead she kept her head resting on his chest with her eyes closed as she remembered better times between them: the seven days they had been on the island and how she had felt a connection to him in a way that even now heated her blood just thinking about it.

"Come on, let's go for a walk outside," he leaned down and whispered against her ear. It was then she noted the music had stopped playing. She pulled back and nodded. And then she allowed him to lead her out of the doors that led to the terrace.

For a few moments they didn't say anything as they walked side by side along the stone walkway. It was a beautiful night in May. Stars were dotting the sky and a half moon sat in their wake.

"Why did you change your phone number, Taylor?"

His question intruded into her thoughts. "I thought, considering everything, it was best. You had my business number if you needed to contact me."

He nodded. "And how have you been doing?" he asked in a tone that let her know he truly wanted to know.

"Fine."

"And the baby?"

"Fine, as well. I went to the doctor last week and she said everything appears as it should be."

"Good." Then he stopped walking and turned to her.

"I want to apologize for all those things I said that night to you. I had no right."

No, he hadn't. She shrugged. "It doesn't matter."

"Yes, it does. In order for us to move forward I think it does matter. I've been doing a lot of thinking over the past two weeks, and you were right. I can't hold a grudge against my grandfather forever. He's done more than enough over the years to let me know that he regretted the position he'd taken with my parents. I guess it was so easy just to dislike him rather than admit how much I actually wanted him in my life."

He didn't say anything for a moment and then, "I can vividly recall a kidnapping attempt when I was fourteen."

Ignoring her flinch of surprise, he continued. "Luckily it wasn't successful but soon after that Ryder appeared on the scene as my bodyguard and he's been with me ever since, nearly twenty years now. It wasn't until I was in college that I learned that Ryder had been sent by my grandfather to protect me, keep me out of harm's way. Even then, I was too stubborn to admit that my grandfather had to have cared about me to do such a thing. I've suddenly come to realize that life is too short and that we should cherish each day that comes, along with the people who are there. My grandfather is seventy today, so many years have been wasted already and I don't want to waste others. You were right. I shouldn't deny him the chance to know his great-grandchild…or the woman whom his grandson has fallen in love with."

Taylor went completely still with his words. "What did you say?" she whispered softly, absolutely sure she hadn't heard him correctly.

"I said," he muttered, leaning down closer to her lips,

"that I don't want to deny my grandfather the chance of getting to know his great-grandchild, or you, the woman I've fallen in love with. And I do love you, *chérie.* I've known it for some time now. I just realized how much over the past two weeks."

Taylor inhaled sharply, held the air in her lungs and then released it to ask, "Are you sure?"

He smiled. "That's the one thing I am sure about. What I'm not sure about is how you feel about me."

She took a step closer to him. Reached up and cupped his face in her hands while tears glittered in her eyes. "I love you, too, Dominic. I thought I only wanted your baby, but then I discovered I wanted your love, as well."

"Now you have both. But there is one more thing I want you to have. My name."

Reaching into the back pocket of his pants, he pulled out a white velvet box. Her eyes widened and she stared in amazement at the huge diamond ring.

"Pretty soon your stomach will grow, declaring to all the degree of my passion for you. I want them to know the depth of my love for you, as well."

He took the ring out the box and slid it onto her finger. "Will you marry me, Taylor?" he asked softly.

More tears came into her eyes and complete happiness filled her entire being. "Oh, yes, I will marry you," she said, smiling through her tears.

"Tomorrow."

She blinked. "Tomorrow?"

"Yes, I want us to marry tomorrow. We can arrange a reception later in the States with our families, but I don't want to leave Paris without binding you to me. I love you so much I can't imagine my life not joined with yours. Will you let me marry you tomorrow?"

"Yes."

He smiled before lowering his mouth to hers. The moment their lips touched she knew in her heart that this would be the start of the rest of their lives.

Epilogue

June

Tears formed in Taylor's eyes as she stood as a bridesmaid and watched her sister join in marriage with the
man she loved. She could recall when Cameron had
begun showing an interest in Vanessa and how Vanessa
had refused to even consider him as a man she wanted
to love.

But today she was pledging her life to him and Vanessa's eyes were filled with so much love that Taylor could
actually feel it. Her gaze left Vanessa and Cameron momentarily to search out a man sitting in the audience.

Her husband.

Her and Dominic's eyes connected and she knew
like her, he was remembering that day in Paris when
they had done what Vanessa and Cameron were doing

now. Franco had been more than happy to make the arrangements and Dominic's parents had stood in as witnesses, and Dominic's best friend, Matt, had flown in to be his best man.

That night he had whisked her away to his island off the Normandy coast where they had spent the next three nights more in bed than out. They had returned to Paris and spent a few more days with Dominic's parents and grandfather. Dominic and Franco talked, spent a lot of time together as they tried to accept what happened years ago as history and move on. A wedding reception was planned for them here in Charlotte in August and she was very happy about it. They had also made plans to return to Latois again in a couple of years. They wanted at least two more children and thought the island had proven to be the perfect place for future Saxons to be conceived.

Taylor then glanced sideways at Cheyenne, who at the last minute had to have her bridesmaid dress altered due to her already protruding stomach. According to Cheyenne the doctor suspected she was having twins, possibly triplets, which was the reason at three months she looked like she was actually six. A sonogram was scheduled for next week. As far as they knew, there was no record of twins ever being born in the Steele family, so everyone was wondering about the man who had fathered Cheyenne's child. Was there a history of multiple births in his? Cheyenne still refused to even give the man's name.

"I now pronounce you man and wife."

Her gaze returned to Cameron and Vanessa just as Cameron kissed his bride, finally claiming her as his. Vanessa Steele was now Vanessa Steele Cody.

* * *

"It was a beautiful wedding, wasn't it?" she asked Dominic later as she lay curled up in his arms in bed. One of the wedding gifts Dominic had bought for her was this beautiful home not far from where Morgan and Lena lived. It would be available for them to use whenever she wanted to visit home.

"Yes, but nothing is more beautiful than a Paris wedding," he said, leaning down and kissing her lips. "You looked simply stunning that day."

Taylor had to agree. Thanks to the Megan Saxon original she'd been wearing. His mother was simply incredible. Megan had made a few phone calls and the dress had been delivered to the Saxon Estate just hours before the wedding. Franco had hired a photographer and numerous photos were taken. Every time she glanced through the wedding album she was reminded of the day that she married the man who now meant the world to her.

"And you looked handsome yourself," she added. And he had. "I love you," she whispered, doubting she would ever tire of telling him that.

"And I love you and I plan on spending the rest of my life showing you how much."

And then he spoke those same words to her in French as she stared into the depths of his green eyes. And she knew that she would spend the rest of her life showing him how much she loved him, as well.

* * * * *

HARLEQUIN
PLUS

Try the best multimedia subscription service for romance readers like you!

Read, Watch and Play.

Experience the easiest way to get the romance content you crave.

Start your **FREE TRIAL** at
<u>www.harlequinplus.com/freetrial</u>.